Caroline Shaw

BANTAM BOOKS
SYDNEY • AUCKLAND • TORONTO • NEW YORK • LONDON

Author's Note

The staff at Australian film funding bodies and the staff and students at Australian film schools are diligent, creative and mutually supportive people. Only the dark mind of a crime writer could suggest that any members of our film industry might like to kill each other. It follows therefore that all characters and situations in this novel are imaginary and any similarity to real people or events is purely coincidental.

EYE TO EYE
A BANTAM BOOK

First published in Australia and New Zealand in 2000
by Bantam

National Library of Australia
Cataloguing-in-Publication Entry

Shaw, Caroline.
Eye to Eye.

ISBN 1 86325 257 6

I. Title.

A823.4

Transworld Publishers,
a division of Random House Australia Pty Ltd
20 Alfred Street, Milsons Point, NSW 2061

Random House New Zealand Limited
18 Poland Road, Glenfield, Auckland

Transworld Publishers,
61–63 Uxbridge Road, Ealing, London W5 5SA
a division of The Random House Group Ltd

Random House Inc
1540 Broadway, New York, New York 10036

Edited by Jo Jarrah
Cover photograph by IPL PRO-FILE
Typeset in 11/14 Sabon by Midland Typesetters, Maryborough, Victoria
Printed and bound by Griffin Press, Netley, South Australia

10 9 8 7 6 5 4 3 2 1

Caroline Shaw was born in Yorkshire, England, in 1964 and migrated to Australia with her family, aged ten. She lives in Melbourne. Her first novel, *Cat Catcher*, which introduced the misfit PI Lenny Aaron, received international acclaim. It was selected by *The Australian*'s Graeme Blundell as one of his top three books of 1999.

For Andrew

CHAPTER 1

Unhappy Birthday, Dear Emily

If she had known this would be the last journey of her life, Emily Cunningham might not have hurried over the short distance from the car park to the gate at the school's back entrance. The eucalypts rustled, silver and eerie in the cool night breeze as she passed between them, oblivious. Happy.

It was Emily's thirtieth birthday and there was much to celebrate in her life. She was wealthy for a start. Then she had won the prize for best video in her first year and best film in her second. Soon she would get Kenneth Drage's nod for the Silver Shutter and after that there would be no looking back. Everything was perfect. She was even glad she had done her MBA before film school, though it had been dull. She could see what a clever move it had been in hindsight, how her life so far seemed to point like a beacon to exactly where she was right now; for Emily was ready now to claim her future, a future that promised a series of triumphs that came more easily to hand with each passing year. Yes, everything was just fine with Emily. Except for the thumb.

The mutant thumb. She could never forget her body's practical joke. People had often told her she could have it amputated, leaving her with four good fingers. Like a cartoon, Emily thought. But she had chosen to live with

1

her ... not handicap, they didn't call it that any more. Challenge? No. Physical disability, that was it. She was lucky to have been born into a time when people were so careful with language; although it made no difference to the hard red nodules nestling where her thumbnail and knuckles should have been.

Under her arm Emily held the cans containing her third-year production, *The Builder*. The school's official editing period was October and November after all the students had completed their films, but Emily had shot her film first this year and couldn't wait to see how it came together. Her days for the next six weeks would be taken up crewing for her fellow students but at night she intended to get in as much extra editing time as she could.

Emily was conscious that out of the six students in her year she was the least talented film maker. She didn't think or feel in images and knew she lacked the ability to make pictures tell stories. Emily's films always had a lot of dialogue, a lot of music in the background. People said they were fine, but she could tell most of them didn't really think so.

Whatever her shortcomings as a film maker, Emily's career was secure, she knew that for certain now. And as far as *The Builder* was concerned, if she had learned nothing else from her father, she had learned that money more than compensated for a lack of ability. There were plenty of out-of-work professionals who could be hired to improve student productions.

She checked her watch at the back gate and waited. There was no danger of discovery. The security guard patrolled the school once every couple of hours and always entered by the main gate on the other side of campus. He never came into the buildings unless there was some major disturbance.

The gate opened from the inside, and, punctual as usual, Pluckrose emerged from the darkness. Straight away he told her he wanted more money. Emily said no. She had grown weary of their clandestine arrangement and for some time had thought it tacky that someone in her position should have to sneak around at night handing over cash. It wasn't appropriate any more. She wanted her own key and she would give him a hundred dollars to get one for her. He said no. Two hundred dollars? He would think about it.

On the way up to the first floor edit suites, Emily stopped and took out a bottle of pink pills she had bought – at considerable expense – from Gabrielle. Amphetamines mostly. She tipped two into her palm and popped them between her lips. Later, when the drugs kicked in, they would lift her out of the ordinary, heighten her awareness; perhaps even show her what was wrong with her film.

Emily went into edit suite one and laced her film and two of her soundtracks onto the Steenbeck. At the twist of a lever, the images scrolled across the small screen, marked with scratches, bad edits and chinagraph rubbings. She lit a cigarette, cued the opening scene and began to work.

Forty minutes later she stopped, weary and exasperated. She had done little more than tape a few more scenes together in a rough sequence but as ever experienced a sense of panic, a lack of control. How to make the images flow? How to make them say something? Tomorrow she would look up the industry directory and hire an editor.

There was a noise outside. Emily flipped her cigarette into the wastebasket, swivelled round and stuck her head into the corridor. It was empty, dissolving into shadows at either end. She listened. Pluckrose would be in his workshop on the same floor and he must have dropped something. She sighed and wished she hadn't come at all tonight. Her out-of-hours visits had been risky and stupid.

Emily Cunningham must not be caught flaunting school regulations.

Then she thought: Lucy. Could it really be Lucy? No, that was over, surely. Her father had taken care of it.

She sat quite still for a moment, listening to the wind scrape clumps of leaves over the high corridor windows. There was no one there. It was childish to be afraid of the dark and she was too old to be childish. Thirty years old today. A grown-up in control of her life. She began to close the door, then pulled it open at the last moment. There was that sound again, a dry shuffle.

'Lucy?' she said into the darkness. Her voice was lost in the corridor, deadened by the carpet. The leaves rustled at the windowpanes and the natural world seemed filled with a curious, watchful dread. It seemed to Emily that something was gathering itself in the darkness.

It seemed such an obvious thing, locking the door, that she frowned at her own thoughtlessness. Why hadn't she done it automatically? After all, she was a single woman, alone at night. She placed her hand on the door and slid it until the deadlock met the clasp. She reached out to turn the silver knob. Turning that knob seemed suddenly to be the most important thing in the world. All her concentration was focused on the small, silver oval. But just as the tips of her fingers touched its cool surface, it skated sideways out of reach, and Emily looked up.

What she saw puzzled her. The face that looked down into hers was one she knew well enough, but it was trembling with a hatred she had never seen before. Strange. Relieved to know the source of her fear, Emily turned back to the Steenbeck and switched it off. Whatever the problem was, she would deal with it. Preparing a smile, she swivelled round.

Her body was only half twisted back when something

tugged at her throat, just under her chin. She hiccuped. Her neck was stinging and instinctively her hands sought the place where it hurt and found wetness there, terrible wetness. She was bleeding, the blood spurting out with a sickly rhythm; glassfuls of blood everywhere, all at once. She held out a hand in front of her eyes to see, to check, because this could not be real. This could not be happening to her, not on her birthday. But it was real. The thumb waggled before her, grotesque in a crimson gloss. The length of her arm was already traced with rivulets. Droplets quivered on her elbows and pitter-pattered to the floor, while from her torn throat the blood poured hot and thick, matting her chest with gore. She couldn't stop it. She gurgled in its richness, trying to speak to the one who had done this awful thing to her. Why, she wanted to know. Why are you doing this?

She staggered to her feet. When the knife came towards her again, she extended her hand to fend it off, felt the tip cut into the centre of her palm, saw it poke out through the back of her hand. Emily knew the time had come to beg for her life, and she wanted to. But when she tried to speak, she heard only some clotted, liquid sound. Tears ran down her cheeks. She couldn't fight any more. She felt dizzy. One of her hands fell away from her throat. Please, she wanted to say, my father will give you anything. Her eyes stayed on the tip of the knife as it moved slowly up her face. Now it was resting on her cheek, not hurting. Waiting. Letting her have a rest. Giving her time to think. Out in the corridor, Emily heard the leaves whip one last time against the glass. Then the knife slid into her left eyeball.

CHAPTER 2

Mozart and Plumbers

Film production is unique in that it is controlled, broadly speaking, by two types of character: the arty, film school-trained directors and designers, and the truck-owning, plier-wielding gaffers and grips. Imagine, if you will, Mozart having to liaise with a plumber in order to have his music performed. Film is a collaboration of opposites.

Tonight Lenny Aaron was the gaffer. Cold, damp and ready to commit murder, she had spent the evening lugging an arsenal of heavy lighting equipment up and down a hill for a bossy and indecisive Director of Photography – or DOP, for those in the know. She had taken the wrong piece of equipment down twice already and now listened, lips curling, as David O. Lincoln tore into her: 'If you'd read the handouts I gave you on day one, you'd know which lights we need right now and you wouldn't be holding up the bloody shoot.'

David O. Lincoln checked his watch and looked down to where the crew were waiting around a generator. When Lenny had found his crash-course film school listed in the Yellow Pages, she had smiled at the name: David O. Lincoln.

'Film crewing is sixty percent boredom and forty percent

6

lugging,' O told her. 'This is the lugging bit. You're a big girl, Lenny. You'll cope – if you want to pass.'

She wanted to pass all right. Three-quarters of the way through the ten-day course, Lenny couldn't wait to pass. All twelve students at the David O. Lincoln Academy were working on the same short film. It would be edited by O and they would each receive a copy. Lenny had already made private plans to have the credits removed and a new set amended awarding her the title of writer/director.

Unlike the rest of the students, Lenny had no interest in film making as a hobby or prospective career. She was a private detective about to begin an investigation into theft and vandalism at a Melbourne film school, a job that required her to masquerade as a student. To complete her disguise she needed a 16 mm film. Hence her enrolment at the David O. Lincoln Academy.

She glanced at her G-Shock. 3 am. She looked at the lighting equipment stacked in the back of the battered truck. Which one did they want then? There were so many to choose from: blondies, redheads, Sun Guns and HMIs. Barn doors and flags, blue gels for changing the hue, scrims to diffuse intensity, reflector boards, cutters, gobos and cookies. All this to make light appear natural on the screen, to make it dance and cast shadows.

Down on the set there were boom poles, shotguns and Nagras (these for sound). A DOP, a 1st AD, a grip and continuity (these being people). There were circles of confusion and depths of field, dollies, tracks, high hats and rails on which the camera – the black metal God at the centre of everything – could glide or rest while it pursued its prey.

If, as a crew member, you didn't know what all this paraphernalia was, where to find it or how to use it, you risked becoming the shoot patsy. Lenny had discovered that a good day's shoot had a cool jazz artistry to it. You went around doing your thing, minding your own business, riffing now and then, picking up on unspoken cues: when to lay down cables, when to back up, wait and keep your fucking mouth shut. Make a false move and you became the patsy.

She transported a couple of blondies down to the set and dumped them beside their stands.

There was a shrill whistle behind her. 'Hey! Lenny! Not those – the HMI!' The 1st AD's voice was sour with disgust. 'What's the point of setting up fill if you don't know your key?'

What indeed? Lenny resolved to look up 'fill' and 'key' later. As for now, the HMI – the monster light – was half a kilometre straight back up the hill and she had just caused another delay in a delay-filled night. The crew were tired and looking for a scapegoat. All eyes turned to Lenny. Patsy time.

She set off, legs aching, exhausted, trying to focus on the one thing that had kept her going through the last week – the tent with the portable heater and the doughnuts.

She reached the truck, dragged out the metre-wide HMI and strapped it to a trolley. The HMI's light was so intense that it had an ultraviolet interlock built into it to shut it down if the access doors leaked energy. There were horror burn stories, and God forbid you were standing next to one when the element blew. Lenny gazed back down the hill and set her teeth.

It began to rain.

CHAPTER 3

Most of the Necessary
Exposition Is Covered

It had been almost four years since Lenny Aaron quit Victoria Police after being brutally assaulted by Michael Dorling, a heroin dealer who got his jollies with a Stanley knife and a mallet. Her left arm still bore the scars outside and a metallic pin inside. After Dorling had finished with her she had given up on human crime and stayed home, a snivelling, cowardly wretch. On emerging from this self-imposed exile, she had drifted into the world of lost pet retrieval and found a niche in the specialised area of the missing cat.

A year and a half ago Australia's richest media family – the Talbotts – had retained H. Aaron Investigations to find their cat. She had found it – dead – and along the way had solved a murder. The Talbott job had helped her to rediscover her human investigative skills. Consequently, in the last year and a half she had spied on several cheating partners, found a missing junkie teenager for desperate parents and most recently helped in the identification of three students stealing computer equipment from Melbourne University. The university's insurance company, Galaxy, had been very happy indeed and were recommending her all over town.

The Talbott investigation, however, was still her biggest achievement. For starters, it had left her forty thousand dollars richer – serious money for a lifetime pauper. Ten thousand of it had gone straight into the car she was now driving, a '92 black Toyota Celica in good condition.

She had scored something else from that investigation. From wrist to elbow on her left arm the skin was raised and purple. Inside the damage was much worse. Vivian Talbott's knife had peeled through nerves, muscles and blood vessels. It had given her delight to cut open Michael Dorling's original scar. Lenny touched her fingertips together. A faint tingling. She would have to live with the nerve damage for the rest of her life. She couldn't make a fist any more. And if you can't make a fist, who are you?

Today was Monday. The David O. Lincoln Academy of Film graduation ceremony had been held yesterday. Lenny hadn't gone. She would receive her gold-embossed certificate in the mail. There had been some debate about whether or not she deserved it, but her knuckles gently pressed against O's weak jaw settled the matter in her favour.

It was September 1 and as she had on the first of each month for the last eighteen months, Lenny was driving to a graveyard on the outskirts of Box Hill. Given the choice she would never come here again as long as she lived, putting the whole family thing behind her. What was the point of it? The one person she had ever cared about was dead and no amount of standing in front of a piece of stone and a grass mound was going to change that.

She had been here for his funeral of course, the main event. Her father's coffin slowly lowered into the ground, dirt tossed on top. Flowers piled around. Religious words spoken. Lots of hysterical tears, none of them hers.

She needed to stop coming. If she could just persuade her mother that they had kept up appearances way past the time when other people – *normal* people – would have stopped.

She was thirty minutes late and pumped coins into the parking meter, a bunch of drooping lilies squashed into her armpit. In life her father had been unable to tolerate flowers of any kind. They had irritated his inflamed sinuses and triggered asthma attacks.

Ted Aaron was buried at the top of a hill. Lenny raised a hand to shield her eyes from the sun and saw two silhouettes clear against the sky before a row of gravestones. Her mother and grandmother, the twin banes of her life.

Don't be aggressive, she told herself. Be nice to your mother, tolerate your grandmother. At least make it look like you're a family. She had promised her father that while he lay dying, and at the time convinced herself it was achievable. In hindsight she recognised that she had told him a big fat whopper.

Veronica Aaron turned as her daughter approached and her lips described a moue of disappointment. She was still wearing her version of mourning: a black and navy woollen cardigan stretched across full breasts, with a black and red plaid skirt above fat knees. Her softly jowled face was damp with tears and something else.

'What's that slimy shit under your nose?' Lenny demanded.

'Vicks Vapor Rub. I've got an awful head cold,' Veronica Aaron said. 'You know how I am when the seasons change.'

'Wipe it off.'

'I need it.' A stifled snort confirmed the blocked passage. 'I'm closed off completely in the left nostril.'

'I'm not staying unless you wipe it off.'

'What's wrong with it?'

'It's disgusting.'

'Oh, Lenny, really!'

They glared at each other.

'Very well. But only because I don't think we should be standing around your father's grave arguing.' Her mother reached into her bag and pulled out a tissue, removed the medicinal ooze from above her lip and blew her nose dramatically.

It was unfair, Lenny thought. Viciously unfair, the way fate had chosen her to be one of the *pure*, one of those unable to tolerate germs and then forced to exist in a world of filth. It seemed everyone else on the planet chewed their fingernails, sucked their thumbs, shared food, even *kissed* without giving it a second thought. Lenny did not. Her mouth, her body, was sterile.

She placed her lilies against the headstone.

'Those are terrible, Lenny! Where did you buy them? They're dead!'

'So's he.'

'You're getting too skinny.' Veronica Aaron stared at her. 'Your granny's enjoying the fresh air, although it's still too cold for her, isn't it, Mum?'

Lenny glanced across at the creature sitting in the wheelchair. Granny Sanderman was a foul-mouthed, scratching, biting bitch who had punched her way through two generations of children. Both Veronica and Lenny had fended off her blows. Mercifully, she had been restricted to the chair since her second stroke and now had only partial movement of her right arm and none in her left. Physical power depleted, she was reduced to heckling from the sidelines. The onset of Alzheimer's had brought with it increased agitation and strange voices, but it had not softened her heart. Lenny wanted her to die. And horribly.

Her grandmother wore slippers, track pants with a food stain at the crotch and an orange sweatshirt that said

SYDNEY OLYMPICS 2000. Her Dachau-cropped grey hair stood up in odd clumps. Lenny's nose wrinkled: that diaper was full.

'He'll be rotten by now. The maggots'll be at him,' Granny Sanderman grunted.

'And a top of the morning to you too,' Lenny replied.

But the old hag was right. Lenny had wanted to cremate her father and then sprinkle the ashes somewhere beautiful, but her mother had refused. Every member of the Aaron family got a *proper* burial. Cremation was for people who couldn't afford to do the right thing. Lenny felt the speed of the purifying flame was surely better than being trapped underground in a rayon-lined box.

'Mum!' Veronica Aaron rammed the handles of the wheelchair so its prisoner lurched like a puppet. 'If you've got nothing nice to say, don't say anything.'

Granny Sanderman spat across the grave.

'That's it!' Lenny grabbed the handles and wheeled the chair away to the edge of the steep path leading down the hill. She bent and whispered in her grandmother's ear. 'The brake's off. One move and you're on the highway. Roadkill.'

They both stared down the hill at the cars whizzing by beyond a thin row of shrubs at the bottom. Granny Sanderman tried to make a fist. 'You wouldn't dare.'

'Try me.' Lenny shook the handles. 'Now remember, the brake is *off*.'

She wiped her hands on her pants and walked back to her mother. Veronica Aaron glanced towards the wheel-chair. 'Is she all right? I'm supposed to have her back at the hospice soon. They said they'd send the van.'

'I'm not coming back out here for a while.' Lenny made her big announcement.

'What are you talking about? We have to visit Daddy every month. He needs us.'

'I'm starting a new investigation. I'll be busy.'

'Too busy for your father!' Her mother bent down and began rearranging her miniature roses. 'Too busy to come to pay your respects once a month.'

Oh, for God's sake.

Lenny tried to suppress her thoughts and looked beyond the gravestone out to the sky. Concentrate. Resist the external world. Bring everything to a centre. Escape the moment. She was almost there. She . . .

'Lenny!'

'What?'

'You're not listening to me!'

'I am.'

'What did I just say?'

'Look, I'm going to be working for a few weeks. That's why I won't be coming. I may not even be able to visit you.' It would not stop her mother from making contact, though. Since the death of Ted Aaron she had become a telephonic limpet.

Her statement had the expected devastating effect. 'Did you stop to consider how I'm suffering?' Veronica Aaron, barnacle of misery, rummaged for a handkerchief in her handbag.

OK, her mother *was* suffering. Lenny had considered it many times, but she was quite sure she couldn't do anything to help. Suffering, according to Buddha, was an accepted fact of life. *By oneself evil is done; by oneself one suffers.* So, Lenny Aaron, Buddhist, comforted herself. Veronica Aaron would just have to suffer alone.

Her mother blew her nose again. 'I'm going to go to Dr Morton. I think it's gone to my chest.'

'I've got Sudafed in the car.' And aspirin and Codral and six or seven other over-the-counter medications. Not to mention the drugs stamped with the names of the Melbourne pharmacies Lenny had formed a relationship with. It was all above board. Legal. All available over the counter or on prescription. She wasn't doing anything wrong. She was coping. She brushed aside the fact that she had been *coping* solidly now for the last three and a half years and that from time to time she coped a little too much and woke up after two days asleep with her eyes glued shut and thick yellow fur growing all over her tongue. Too much cope.

'No thank you. You don't care what happens to me. Don't pretend you do.'

As Lenny struggled for the lie that politeness required, a horn sounded. It was the van come to collect her grandmother. Her mother waved down the hill to the driver, misery temporarily forgotten. At least she would have a captive audience for the trip back to the hospice.

'That's Greg,' she said, indicating the driver, the back of her hand over her mouth as though he might eavesdrop from thirty metres. 'He's just broken up with his girlfriend and he's reflooring his own house. Quite handsome, too. What do you think?'

'I think you should wait a bit longer out of respect.'

'I meant for you,' her mother snarled, stalking towards Granny Sanderman. 'Lenny! You left the brake off! Are you coming? You could follow us back to the hospice and give me a lift home.' She reached out a hand. Lenny stepped back. Touching just as a general rule was to be avoided – and she certainly couldn't let anyone with a head cold make any kind of physical contact. The whole time she had been here at the graveyard today she had carefully monitored her breathing pattern, holding her breath completely if her mother came too close. Blinking her eyes as much as possible to wipe the germs away. And as soon as she got the chance she would scrub her hands with disinfectant and then gargle.

'I have things to do.'

'I don't believe you.'

'Bye.'

When they were gone Lenny sat down next to her father's plot. The gravestone read 'In loving memory of Edward James Aaron, beloved husband of Veronica Aaron and father of Helena Aaron.' There for the world to see was her only connection with her mother – their name.

Another young woman came up the hill and placed flowers at a gravestone. Despite the chilly day, she lay full length on top of the plot and began to cry. Lenny watched until she was noticed, then turned away.

She stared down at her father's resting place. If only she could sprawl full length on top and bawl her guts out.

After her father died, she had considered going interstate, away from the obligations of her mother and grandmother. Dr Sakuno, her psychologist for the last three years, had vetoed the plan. She wasn't going to get any better changing her location when all the problems in her life were a result of her weak character. If she was miserable it was because she needed misery, he said.

Dr Sakuno had seen her through all the recent crises of her life. He had become her psychologist after the Michael Dorling assault, advising her to 'get on with it'. Translation: stop wasting my time with your cowardly complaints and get back to work. He had told her to 'stop being a big crybaby' after Vivian Talbott reopened the same wound. And when she went to him saying that her father was dead and no one else would ever mean anything to her, he had said simply 'true'. He understood her. He disliked her. And, perhaps because of this, he was the only one who could ever help her.

On the way back to the office she stopped off at a new pharmacy on Victoria Parade. A fresh source. She had been to this place three or four times in the past month, evaluating the situation carefully, examining bottles of cheap perfume, getting a feel for the place, its rhythms. So far it showed promise. There were two sales assistants. The one in her mid-fifties liked to wear a piece of silk with a black and white hound's-tooth check across her chest, tied with a golden orchid at the left shoulder. Burnt blonde hair swept back from a narrow forehead like a wave of creme caramel. She filled Lenny's prescriptions with a thin, professional smile. She was OK, but would eventually draw the pharmacist's attention to Lenny's superabundant scripts – too worried about her job. No, the other one – the one behind the counter right now – was much better. Lenny had been grooming this one for some time.

She was an innocent named Margie, sixteen. Lenny knew Margie had dropped out of high school although her parents were hoping she'd go back; that she had a boyfriend, but not a steady one; that she had once had a dog called Scoffy, but it ran away; that she would kiss on a first date if the boy were the son of a doctor or a lawyer, but not a CPA. Margie worked alone behind the counter on the blonde woman's days off. Although her father was the pharmacist, he hated dealing with customers, she said, and Lenny had only seen bits of him through the hatchway. Margie assured her that he never came out into the shop – a fact that Lenny had shown a great deal of interest in. The two had become firm friends.

'Hi, Margie. Busy day?'

'Oh! Hi, Helena! No, basically it's been really quiet.'

'What are you reading?' Lenny gazed at the open magazine on the counter. There were no other customers in the shop.

'*Cosmo.*'

'I'll take these.' Lenny dropped an Elastoplast box on the counter and frowned. 'And I think my medicine cabinet's a bit low. You'd better give me some Panadol. The big box.' Thinking again, she said: 'Better make it two. My sister's boyfriend practically lives with us. He's a professional footy player. Always getting headaches – it's all the tackling, you know.'

'A footy player?' Margie reached for the Panadol. 'AFL? Who does he play for?'

'Union, Margie, he plays union. You wouldn't know him, he's a reserve, mostly. Gammy leg. You'd better give me two packs of Dispirin and two of Tylenol as well. They're playing France next week.'

Margie hesitated, frowned. 'That's a lot, isn't it? As well as the Panadol. I mean, basically it's just one guy.'

'Heavens! I don't need all that for Gus. What a suggestion! It would kill him.'

They both giggled over this.

'No, I'm Tawny Owl for our local troop. We're having a camp-out tonight and I'm in charge of the first-aid kit. I'd better take a roll of this gauze too – skinned knees.'

'I used to be a Brownie.' Margie piled up the boxes on the counter and began to total. 'I got twenty badges.'

'Well done, Margie! Only two less than me. Oh, and I'll need this.' She slid a prescription across the counter. It was her last one. She was going to have to visit her doctor again and get some more.

Margie chatted on about Guides while they waited. Lenny nodded and smiled. After a minute a bottle of pills appeared in the hatchway behind Margie's head. Mission accomplished.

Lenny handed over her money and swept the mini mound of drugs into her shoulder bag. 'Have a nice day.'

18

'You too, Helena. Happy camping!'

And she was off, shuffling down the street with her stash.

Lenny's office was in the back of a Footscray shopping mall, although it was more mall than shops these days as more businesses shut down. Footscray had an unemployment rate almost twice that of the rest of the country. A lot of people with time on their hands. Lenny was lucky; some things are always in demand, and pets are one of them.

Sex is another, and the porn shop beside her office was open for business. The owner, Mike Bullock, was outside levering the lid off a can of hot pink paint. Someone – he suspected the youth group from the local Baptist Church – had written DEVIATE across his shop wall.

'Can't trust anyone these days.' He shook his head at Lenny. 'Turning on a man who's no different to anyone else, just trying to make a living out of what's natural and healthy as a muesli bar.' He picked at his ear, examined the large orange object that appeared on the tip of his finger, wiped it on his pants and scratched a nipple through his spandex body shirt. His hair was a large square of orange fuzz around his face and his left thumb and hand were strapped in a stretch bandage. 'Dislocated it at footy.' He displayed it proudly. 'Doctor had to snap it back in.' Mike, the British immigrant, was determined to be the best Aussie on the block – even to the extent of submitting his pudgy body to the rigours of amateur Aussie Rules.

'You're looking particularly lovely today,' he leered. Lenny's mouth twisted and he laughed. 'Now, now. No need to get all funny just because a bloke's being chival-rous. Can I interest you in a drinkie tonight?' He had asked her out once a week since she had moved into this office. Neither aloof disinterest nor outright rudeness on her part discouraged him.

She ignored the invitation, unlocked her office and hurried inside, pausing automatically to admire. It was spotless. Every inch of wall and floor space scrubbed back to its nub. She breathed deeply and experienced the full splendour of the Australian bush. Pine O Cleen Eucalyptus really lingered when you splashed it around neat every day, that handy, anti-bacterial hospital-grade disinfectant that killed Staphylococcus and E. coli. Damn it if that shapely plastic bottle wasn't her best friend!

She had spent some of the Talbott forty thousand on creature comforts: a fax machine, a Compaq computer and a trendy desk made in Sweden – all smooth and pale with pieces of steel moulded into it. She had thought about a Mont Blanc pen. She could tap it on the desk in front of clients, make herself seem classy and sophisticated. But Lenny was strictly a Bic chick.

Dr Sakuno's influence was everywhere in her little domain. It was he who had provided the *butsudan*, the little wooden hutch that was her Buddhist shrine. Today it looked particularly nice. She had placed a well-polished Granny Smith, a mandarin and a bowl of *koshikari*, Japan's prized short-grain rice, at the front. She lit an incense stick and breathed it in. A bit smoky, if she was honest, but it looked religious and that was what mattered.

There was a framed poster of Byakko-Sha, a Butoh dance troupe, on one wall and a large ceramic Japanese cat stood in the corner, paw raised in welcome. On an antique wooden table was a bonsai fig, above it a fluorescent tube and Alfoil reflectors to ensure it received enough light. This was the only bonsai she kept in the office. The rest were in her flat. The fig was eighteen centimetres tall. A tiny gnarled tree. Lenny felt the soil. It was a little dry and she added some water. This was the first tree she had controlled by pruning and pinching alone instead of using guiding wires. She was not pleased with the result. She picked up her eight-inch concave branch cutters and removed a branch with a sharp, flush cut. It was important not to tear the branch. White sap oozed from the cut. It looked better, she thought, but she wanted it to look like the specimen from last month's cover of *Bonsai International*.

Along one wall of the office was an eight-cage stack of aluminium prisons, empty save one. Her cat cages.

After she solved the Talbott case she had promised herself she would stop with the cats. Well, that wasn't strictly true. Dr Sakuno told her she must stop with the cats. He said that it was degrading and futile employment for anyone with self respect.

He didn't understand about Lenny and cats, and how could she explain it to him? Obsession? Compulsion? A simple need to hunt? It was something she was good at. At any rate, she had not stopped.

She glanced at the front page of the *Footscray Leader*. It featured the continuing story of the footballer who had changed his name to Whiskas for a week in a publicity deal with that pet food company. A cricketer was contemplating becoming Snappy Tom for a month in summer.

Lenny had seen this as a tremendous opportunity to make cash for very mild indignity and was prepared to sell herself cheaply. But after three hours of relentless phone calling, her best offer was fifty bucks for three months if she changed her name to Trill. As this wouldn't even cover the cost of printing up a t-shirt, she had been forced to withdraw from the world of corporate sponsorship.

The *Leader* also contained a series highlighting the chances of local politicians for mayoral office. Lawyer and local councillor, Thomas Walstab, was keen to strip Footscray of what he termed 'parasites masquerading as legitimate business people'. To Lenny's surprise, he particularly mentioned the pet support industry. Although perhaps it was not so surprising considering the enormous number of Australians who owned pets. Even those who didn't have a pet were reported as saying they wished they had one. Australians loved animals and anyone who could set himself up as a saviour of the small and fluffy had a sure-fire political winner on his hands.

Lenny read on.

Walstab had been inspired on this course of investigation by a recent visit to a vet, where he had been disgracefully overcharged. He had sent his 'people' out to discover if the pet industry had any other 'areas of gross exploitation'. The reports he received had 'shocked him deeply'. Home delivery pet food companies that bullied elderly pet owners into taking food they didn't need, pet shops that 'rescued' pedigree lookalikes from the pound and sold them as the real thing. And the prices at catteries! A friend of Councillor Walstab's – a dentist with a Sphynx – had paid *thirty dollars a day* to a certain cattery in Doncaster to accommodate the cat while he was on holiday in Sorrento. That would be Colin Kael up at Sparrow Haven, Lenny thought. Well, good on him! A bloke has to eat.

Then a woman on Walstab's team had heard about a friend of a friend in Sydney whose lost cat had been found by a 'cat investigator'. For this service, the friend of a friend had paid *two hundred dollars*. Walstab didn't want to believe this level of corrupt business practice could operate in Melbourne, but to his dismay he discovered it did. Apparently the most well-known of the Melbourne pet finding agencies belonged to a young woman, who operated next to a pornographer right in his own constituency! H. Aaron Investigations, he assured *Leader* readers, had been placed onto a whiteboard in his office (along with single mothers and a gay bar in Highbury Street) under the slugline: Things That Revolt Me.

Lenny reflected on the impact of this scurrilous piece of journalism on her business. It had not been good recently anyway. At present only one cage was occupied. It contained a kitty litter tray, a cloth fish on a string, a striped, well-chewed rubber ball and a baby-blue blanket. Special treatment for the special cat. For special cat it was. A year and a half ago Lenny had recovered a missing Siamese Lilac Point only to find the owners didn't want it back after all. Lenny had dumped it in the car park and hoped it would run off. It did – straight into the traffic. It had lost an eye but managed to survive. Guilt had made her pay the veterinary bills. Something else had made her keep the wretched creature. Cleo Aaron, the meanest cat on the planet, now spent her days between the office and Lenny's St Kilda flat.

'You haven't eaten your biscuits.' She unlocked the cage and took the cat into her arms. It gave a low purr then squirmed free and jumped to the ground. It didn't like to be petted. Cats were the least appropriate animal for anyone looking for affection.

'You're not getting any more tuna until you eat the biscuits.'

Cleo ignored her and jumped onto the ergonomic chair – a forbidden zone and therefore a Cleo magnet.

'Off!' Lenny swatted the sleek butt. Cleo yowled but retreated to a spot in the corner and began grooming herself. Lenny pulled a tissue out of her desk, balled it and tossed it across the room. Cleo, never failing to be intrigued by this game, raced to capture it and shredded ecstatically.

Lenny triggered the rapid-boil water jug and made herself a pot of green tea then logged on to the computer and moved quickly into Mine Sweeper at expert level. Ninety-nine bombs. She had a fastest score of one hundred and seventy-three seconds and never tired of trying to top that.

There was something sublime about the clicking, the hand–eye coordination, the red flags on the identified bombs. Time ceased to exist. It was a crude game by modern standards, but she didn't like the newer role-playing games with their layers of sophisticated images and virtual reality options masking the raw machine underneath. She still believed ping pong was the best computer game ever invented, because of its pure mindlessness.

Anastasia Cherbakov, the barber from next-door, knocked and entered at the same time. Twenty-five years old, she was white-blonde these days, with pale blue contact lenses overlaying brown eyes. In her baby-blue cardigan and matching short tunic with lemon acrylic fingernails, push-up bra and thick make-up, she was pretty in a hard, flinty kind of way.

She was an immigrant, like Mike Bullock, and like him she worked hard at fitting in, getting the right look. In his case it meant sports and the beach, though he had no aptitude for either. In her case it was the constant struggle to overcome her swarthy exterior and Russian accent. Her family were following her out from Russia as fast as they could get the visas, and Anastasia had taken to working seven days a week in an attempt to keep up.

'That one's too boring,' Anastasia looked over her shoulder at the computer screen. 'Play the one with the cards. What a fun!' Her conversation class was studying the exclamatory, 'What a – !'. What a nice day! What a good idea!

Lenny hit a bomb and glowered. 'What a pain you are. Can't you see I'm working?'

'You are not working. You don't have a cat here except that one of yours. Did you visit the grave garden?'

'Yard. Grave yard.'

'Since your Dad died you're more than usual.'

'More than usual what?'

'A misery guts. That's the correct expression, yes? I'm thinking you should be over it by now.'

'I am over it.' She opened a cat file and pretended to read.

'Then what is this?' Anastasia reached out and pinched at the inside of Lenny's fat-free upper arm. 'It's a chicken wing. I'm feeling sick touching it.'

'I need you to do something for me,' Lenny said, pulling away. 'I want you to dye my hair. Black.'

Perhaps it had not been a good choice, she thought, as they both stared into the barber shop mirror two hours later. The inch-long hair was now jet black. With her white face and recent weight loss, it was grim. Anastasia had dyed her eyelashes and eyebrows black too. It made the eyes look bigger. She wriggled the brows, pulled them into a frown.

'There. Dracula.' Anastasia unclipped the stained grey towel and tossed it into a sink full of hair cuts. The barber shop was chronically dirty. Lenny had spoken to her about it, of course.

'Why do you want to be dark anyway?' Anastasia demanded. 'Australian girls are blonde. Like me.'

'Give me a couple of earrings,' Lenny said. She pointed to a place high up on her ear. No one bothered about the lobes any more. Even the upper ears were becoming passé. Trendy now to ram metal through the eyebrow, lip, nipple or scrotum. Or press hot metal into your willing skin. Scar fashion. Surely only grafting could follow? A finger pointing out of your forehead for fifty bucks.

Anastasia went to her bar fridge and took out two pieces of ice which she made Lenny hold on either side of her left ear.

'To dull the pain,' she said. 'Do you want diamante studs or silver sleepers?'

'Sleepers. I want – aaaaahhhhhhsshhhiiiitttt!' The punch went through the hard part of her ear. A sleeper was rammed in and then the machine jabbed higher for the second hole. 'Hurry up!'

'You have too much blood.' Anastasia pressed the second sleeper in then held the ice against the ear again. 'It's not supposed to rush out like that. You must turn the sleepers and put this on.' She handed over a bottle. 'If not, warts will come on the back of your ears.'

Lenny stood up and stared into the mirror. 'Does it suit me?'

'No, to be honest. Twenty bucks for the hair and ten for the ears and product. This is my new boyfriend, Matt.' Anastasia tapped a finger on a framed photo sitting amidst a fluff of hair clippings on the counter. It was her usual type – blond, blue eyes, tanned. Except this one was wearing a suit.

'He's a lawyer.' Anastasia said it like she had won the lottery, leaving Lenny only one possible response:

'Congratulations.'

'Thank you. I usually don't go for the brainy ones. Too much talking, not enough action – if you take my meaning. But with Matt we never stop –'

'That's more than enough detail, thanks.' Lenny held up a hand.

Anastasia put the photo down. 'We're going to dinner for Young Labor. What a boring, but it's free. It's only a smorgasbord. Labor is too cheap to pay for a proper meal. He has a nice friend, if you're interested,' she added slyly. 'We all went out together to the multiplex in Chadstone last week. What a place! There were two restaurants, a games room – I beat Matt in the Star Wars race – and two shopping arcades. Then there was this booth where you get your picture made into cute stickers and a bowling alley –'

'What film did you see?'

'We didn't have time to see a film, but what a fun we had! You should come out with us next time.'

'No, thank you.'

'Well, let me know if you need anything else.' There was sympathy in the barber's voice. Lenny hurried away from it.

It was still an hour before she was expected at the film school so she reimmersed herself in Minesweeper. Pow. Pow. Pow. Bomb. Restart. Pow. Pow. Pow. Endless circling and tagging. Her back began to ache even in the ergonomic chair, but she resisted the twinge. Concentration. Control. No thought. These were the things that led to oblivion. An aroused mind that rested on nothing. This was contemplation at its purest; this was *prajna*. In time, if she was lucky, the combination of concentration, meditation and contemplation would lead to *satori* – seeing 'it' in a flash – and she would be one with the universe.

CHAPTER 4

Cate Ray's First Scene

It was getting dark when she drove down Smith Street, one of the triumvirate, the great streets of inner city Melbourne: Lygon, Brunswick and Smith. Each fed its quota of cars into the CBD in the morning and sucked them out again at night; parallel lines offering three Melbourne lifestyles.

Lygon Street – Melbourne's Little Italy – was influenced by the adjacent Melbourne University, an institution that encroached a little more on surrounding Carlton each year. The intellectual life of the university was reflected in Lygon Street's numerous bookshops and cafés. Seated in the thick of authentic Italian conversation, jaded PhDs daydreamed of tenure while their own students served them bitter coffee. Restaurateurs lolled in front of successful businesses handed to them on a plate by their fathers. 'Never mind if you don't speak Italian,' winked one window, 'we speak a good broken English.' The self-assured dig of the bilingual entrepreneur.

If Lygon Street looked to Milan for its mocha and coffee cream decor, Brunswick Street was lemons and limes and strawberry milk: the colours of permanent childhood. Bookshop, café, bookshop, café; Brunswick Street was birthday layer-cake culture. There was a cosiness to it; you were never more than a metre from a Duralex of Mocopan or Germaine Greer's latest advertisement for herself.

Smith Street, where Lenny now drove with one eye on wandering pedestrians, was turning into heroin alley. In the four minutes it took her to drive from Victoria Parade to Moor Street, she spotted three junkies. One boy was shooting up in the passenger seat of a black van outside a chemist. Further down, a girl was sprawled out, arms extended. She could have been sunbathing, except that it was almost dark and she was lying outside the post office. Some café owners, tired of losing business to the street's seedy reputation, had offered to contribute towards a centre where addicts could shoot up, just to stop them hassling their customers for spare change.

A woman in her seventies tried to manoeuvre her walking frame around the post office girl, but there was no room. The girl's legs scissored out on either side. In the old woman's youth Smith Street had been a tightly run community, supplying the city with machinists and labourers, laughing at its luck to be so close to the centre of things. What would it have made of this girl on the pavement, Lenny wondered.

She turned left up Moor towards Brunswick Street and found a parking spot. The Aquinas College of the Arts was on the Fitzroy/Collingwood border. From the front the building was a large brick square with no windows and a heavy gate guarding its entrance.

Lenny glanced at her new, student face in the rear view mirror. She wanted to look young and eager, a returnee thrilled to be back in the world of film. In fact, pasty, gaunt and shifty-eyed, she looked like a junkie herself.

She was here to meet the film school's principal, Cate Ray. Galaxy Insurance Corporation, the school's insurer, was considering terminating Aquinas's policy due to the number of claims the school had made over the last eight

29

months as a result of theft and vandalism. As the Aquinas board of directors could not afford an end to their current arrangement with Galaxy, it had agreed to allow that company to engage a private investigator and, because of her recent success at Melbourne University, Galaxy had chosen H. Aaron Investigations. With Cate Ray's grudging cooperation, they had constructed a cover story: Lenny was returning to complete a film and television degree after a five-year absence.

Theft and vandalism. Well, it was a nice little money earner, she supposed. And it was unlikely to present any danger, which was always a plus in her line of work. But it didn't promise much excitement either. She wished she could be part of the police investigation and wondered how it was progressing. It was old news now, no longer page one in any of the newspapers. But last month it had been Melbourne's hottest story. Thirty-year-old Emily Cunningham, third year Aquinas film and television student, had been murdered in an edit suite. Throat cut and – this had been the juicy gem for the media – both eyeballs gouged out and removed from the scene.

Lenny walked through the entrance. It was wide enough to allow cars to pass through, tall enough for trucks even, but she could see that when closed, the heavy, wrought iron gate would fill the entrance completely. There would be no space at the top, bottom or sides to squeeze through. A tunnel about eight metres in length was cut through the building and as Lenny walked through it, she saw trees ahead of her.

Coming out of the tunnel, she found herself in a small quadrangle of grass peppered with native shrubs, oaks and eucalypts, and skirted by a narrow lane just wide enough for a single vehicle. The brick building formed a continuous, three-storeyed structure surrounding the quadrangle on all sides. Directly opposite her another tunnel led to the back of the campus. She wondered if there was another gate.

The building was dotted with doors at ground level and while she watched, a handful of students came out of one, bags slung over their shoulders. They headed for the two exit tunnels and disappeared.

Lenny examined her campus map and then looked around again.

Above one corner of the quadrangle there rose a tower made of rough-hewn bluestone and crowned with a crenellated turret. It poked up awkwardly from the sober brick beneath it.

According to the map, the film school office was on the first floor of the section beneath the tower, at the top of a flight of wooden stairs. Lenny entered the building, went up the stairs, down the corridor and into a room marked 'Principal's Office & Reception'.

To the right of the door as she walked in was a desk of blonde wood. This was occupied by a large woman in a turquoise and purple caftan. She had a pleasant face with greying hair done up in a loose bun, a faint smell of incense, and eyes heavily lined with kohl. Lenny could imagine her singing opera. Zebra-striped bangles clanked together as the woman stood up in greeting, hands reaching in front of her as if they were pulling the rest of the ample body through space.

'I've been expecting you. I'm Alana Zappone, Cate's assistant.' Lenny admired her teeth. They had the sort of shininess that only five hundred dollars worth of professional whitening treatment could bring. 'And you must be Lenny.'

'Yes,' Lenny tried to match La Zappone's enthusiasm. 'Lenny Lypchik.'

'The returnee! I hope you'll have no trouble fitting back in after all this time.'

'Can't wait to get started.'

'That's the way.' It dawned on Lenny that Alana Zappone would make an excellent Tawny Owl. She seemed to be one of those people who can get through life taking every utterance at face value, thus deflecting the barbs of sarcasm that register deeply with the other ninety percent of the population. Lucky bitch.

The glass window of the door to the next room was marked PRINCIPAL. 'Is Cate in?' Lenny asked.

'We've had a few minor renovations since you were here last, Lenny. Cate's asked me to show you around before you see her. To reacquaint you.'

First stop on the tour was the school library on the second floor. It was a long room filled with stainless steel, glass and modular partitions, and it was well equipped with photocopiers and video players. The adjacent bluestone tower was accessed through a door in the library wall.

Inside the tower was a small, circular room ringed with shelves crammed with film cans and books on film. Zappone called it the 'old' library and said that it was a private collection which had belonged to the film school's deceased co-founder, Robert Heywood. Everything in the Robert Heywood Memorial Library was covered with dust, apparently abandoned for the hi-tech alternatives in its modern counterpart.

Above the old library was the office of the surviving co-founder, Kenneth Drage. This was reached via a spiral staircase lodged between a poster for *Les Enfants Du Paradis* and a rusty projector on a stand.

Back on the first floor, Lenny had a quick look at the video and film edit suites – poky rooms, each containing a four- or six-plate Steenbeck editing machine for film, or a smaller Sony video editor and TV monitors. The Steenbecks were layered with strips of clear editing tape and marked with numbers scrawled in chinagraph. A sign on the wall, obviously ignored, read 'Clean Machines After Use'.

The common room was a graffitied cube with grey carpet squares, a black vinyl sofa and a filthy rapid-boil jug. There were instant coffee encrusted spoons everywhere. Lenny wondered if there was any chance of getting stuck into this place with a bucket of scalding water, elbow length rubber gloves, a good quality scouring sponge and some disinfectant. Students didn't think about things like that, she reminded herself. Students were smelly. It was, she thought, the one factor likely to unmask her.

They continued the tour, looking into the screening room on the ground floor. It was small, with about thirty black velour seats, low and squashy like mini sofas, facing the small screen. Heavy black curtains covered the windows.

Next to the screening room was the television studio, its door opening onto the quadrangle. It was about twenty metres square and there were three boxy television camera dollies pointing at two battered chairs arranged as though for an interview. Off the studio was a shabby little dressing room with a make-up table and tea urn. Zappone called it the green room. A door led into the car park, which was outside the protective walls of the building. That was the end of the tour.

Back in the reception office, Zappone returned to her word processor which had a NO MINING KAKADU sticker on the side. She began logging off.

'Knock-off time for me, thank goodness.' She smiled. 'Go straight in. She's expecting you.' Lenny looked through the window into the principal's office.

Cate Ray was working alone. Her hair was jet black, a

razor sharp bob on either side of a face hardened with make-up and authority. She was writing out cheques, concentrating as though afraid of making the slightest error. Her movements were precise and her darkly lipsticked mouth was a grim straight line.

She didn't look up as Lenny knocked and entered.

'I'll be with you in a moment.'

Lenny took a seat and found herself four inches below the other woman's eye line. She looked around.

The principal's office was small and admirably tidy; files and videos packed in military rows inside spotless glass cabinets, books with titles like *Breaking Into The Movies*, *The Deal On The Table* and *Writing Screenplays That Sell*. On the wall behind Ray's head were photographs of herself with important people. Film posters covered the other walls. Lenny recognised three: an outback film in which the men were thick and the women long-suffering, a pouting drag-queen adventure on the Barrier Reef, and a ballroom love story. All the posters were signed.

'You'll recognise a few names there,' said Ray, still without glancing up from the chequebook. She had long incisors that glinted between the thin red lips. 'Graduates of ours who've made an impact in the industry.'

'I don't go to Australian films,' Lenny replied from her inferior seating position. 'I mean, I catch them on late-night TV sometimes, and I've seen a few on video. They're OK, some of them. There's a lot of shit, though.'

Ray's eyes flicked up. 'The Australian film industry is recognised for making films that attract international critical attention. There's a fresh quality about them that appeals to non-Australians.'

'Sold!' Lenny said. 'Where do I sign up?'

There was an icy pause and then:

'Very droll, Ms Aaron.' Ray adjusted the position of the

Rolex on her left wrist. There was a platinum bracelet next to it and a square-cut diamond on her finger.

Lenny pulled a film can out of her bag. 'This is the film I made. It's ...' She thought about the jumble of shots crammed into the ten minute opus. '... not very good.'

'I can imagine. I'll have it placed in the library.' Ray tapped the pile of files on the desk in front of her. 'Galaxy's report and my own files. I trust you'll be discreet.' Her tone indicated she thought otherwise.

'Where did that woman die?' Lenny needled indiscreetly.

Ray slapped her pen on the desk top and closed the chequebook. 'In an edit suite. But it has nothing to do with why you are here, Ms Aaron. That is entirely a matter for the police. Stick to the parameters of your investigation.'

'It must have been a shock though, finding the body.'

They locked eyes. There was another pause and then:

'Our technician, Graeme Pluckrose, found her. He was in his workshop and heard a noise.'

'Why was he here at night? Isn't the campus closed?'

'As well as being our technician and equipment storeman he also works as something of a general handyman about the school. He's a single man who is happy to work long hours.'

'What kind of access to the campus do the students have?'

'School hours are from nine am until six pm. After-hours work may be done until nine pm. Students must sign a logbook for after-hours access. The facilities are not available to students after nine pm.' Ray was providing answers all right, but she wasn't enjoying it. She was, Lenny thought, the sort of woman who didn't like to be questioned. Didn't like it one little bit.

'Who locks up at night?'

'The security patrol is here at quarter to nine. Entrance

doors to all the buildings and the front and back gates are checked and/or locked by them at nine.'

'Who else has the keys to the entrance gates and the buildings?'

'A master key covers them all. I have one. So does Kenneth Drage, the school's co-founder, Sue Hyslock, the head of Animation, Ben Austin, the head of Design, and Graeme Pluckrose.'

'I'll need one myself.'

'Taped inside the file. I remind you that the student lockers, storeroom and classroom locks were broken into, not opened with a key.'

Lenny nodded. 'But the front and back gate locks were undamaged, so how does the thief get in?'

'I believe that is what Galaxy is paying you to find out.'

'It also begs the question of how the murdered student got in.'

Ray's smoothly clasped hands tightened. When she spoke it was in the slow, deliberate manner of teacher to moron: 'I repeat, Ms Aaron, Emily Cunningham's death is not relevant to your investigation. She entered the grounds out of hours. She was killed. The police are endeavouring to discover by whom. Galaxy Insurance – your investigation – is concerned with *theft*; film missing from trim bins, a few bits and pieces taken from lockers and rooms.'

The principal was underplaying this. A Nagra Mark IV tape recorder and a Sennheiser microphone had been the last to vanish. Combined replacement value: $7000. This brought the total of missing equipment over the last four months to $18 000. Then there was the vandalism; equipment destroyed rather than removed, windows shattered, acid poured onto strips of film hanging in trim bins.

Although she agreed that there was probably no connection between the thefts and the death of the student, Lenny disliked the way Ray was warning her off the subject. She didn't like anyone telling her how to set the parameters for her investigations.

'What do you suppose happened to the eyeballs?' she asked.

Ray was pissed off now. She betrayed herself in the fractional narrowing of her left eye and the way her thumbs rubbed gently together. 'I have no idea, Ms Aaron.'

They stared at each other across the desk. Lenny opened the top file of the bundle before her.

'Are these all the third year students?'

'The remaining five.'

Galaxy was targeting the third year students because the Nagra recorder and the Sennheiser mic had gone missing at a time when the second years were away on a two-month location shoot at Horsham and the first years at Daylesford on a week-long film camp. A hundred percent attendance had been confirmed by the respective supervisors. Of course, the thief could be anyone from the other schools – Animation or Design – or a total outsider. But Lenny had to start somewhere.

'What about staff?' she asked.

'We have guest lecturers for specifics, of course. Casting, rehearsing actors, editing, etcetera. Kenneth does History of Cinema and Script Development himself with occasional outside assistance. For some lectures and film screenings it's possible for all three years to sit in together. We get a nice cross-pollination of ideas that way. On a day to day basis, however, one supervisor stays with the students throughout the course and assists them with everything from directing skills to use of the camera. We've found the one supervisor system builds a rapport. The current third years are with Lucy Peel.'

Lenny opened the staff folder and examined the photo

of the third year supervisor. Lucy Peel was a forty-year-old, long-faced woman with enormous lavender eyes, freckles across her nose, a pale brown ponytail and a warm smile. She was, according to her CV, a VCA graduate with a masters in media studies from Melbourne University.

'The second years are still on location in Horsham,' Ray continued. 'The first years are working on script development. You won't have much to do with them although they do a bit of minor crewing for the third years if they wish to.'

'Is Kenneth Drage the only other staff member who knows who I am?' Lenny had been told that, with the exception of Ray and Kenneth Drage, all the other staff had joined Aquinas within the last five years and could not be expected to recognise her.

'Yes, along with the security guards. And of course the police are aware of your presence.'

The police. The Homicide Squad. That would mean Detective Senior Sergeant Danny Hoyle. Her ex-partner on the force. She had read his name in the media reports of the investigation into Emily Cunningham's death. It would be strange to see him and MacAvoy again. Her old colleagues.

Lenny's eyes focused on the wall behind Ray's head. A series of small frames held portraits of students whose changing fashions represented the history of the school. All were holding the same square, silver trophy. Ray followed her glance.

'The Silver Shutter,' she explained. 'Kenneth awards it annually to the person he perceives as the best graduating student. A prize for artistic vision, you might say. He provides a cheque for ten thousand dollars. I choose the first and second year winners and present a certificate, no money. My criterion for excellence is the student's likely impact on the industry, rather than some subjective notion of –' She stopped, suddenly aware that she was criticising a colleague in front of a stranger – an investigator, no less. A professional snoop.

Lenny flipped through the staff folder again and found a news cutting of Ray, the state premier, an older man whose grey hair and beard were liberally flecked with white and whom she guessed was Kenneth Drage, and a middle-aged woman with over-painted lipstick, all holding glasses of champagne.

'Who's the other woman?' She looked closer.

'Hermione Arnfeldt.' Ray's shark gaze faltered. 'She worked at the National Film Commission and was on our board. It was a tragedy to lose her.'

Lenny remembered now. A couple of months ago Hermione Arnfeldt, National Film Commission director, pregnant with her third child, had been unable to resist a Saturday night craving for a chocolate Paddle Pop, and was run over at a zebra crossing by a drunk driver who didn't realise it until he was two suburbs away. The *Age* had done a special feature.

'Kenneth's not full-time any more,' Ray continued. 'He still does quite a bit though. This year he's focusing on an aesthetics lecture series as part of the History of Cinema program.' She paused, lips forming a steely smile: 'He's achieved great things for Aquinas, apart from co-founding it, of course.'

Lenny's stomach growled. She had eaten a small bowl of white rice for breakfast a long time ago, but she would not eat again until dinner. The challenge would be good for her. A test of will, pain transmuted into an energy of oneness, a *joriki*. It was the sort of thing a misery guts did. Anastasia was right, she thought. Since her father's death she had let herself become obsessed with the morbid. It was one of her prime reasons for taking this case. Investigative work would be a distraction.

'I'll begin tomorrow,' she said.

'Very well.' Ray paused. 'I expect you to complete your investigation in the absolute minimum of time. And as you investigate, I'd like you to keep the issue of funding firmly in mind. Aquinas needs to attract private donations and bequests. We cannot do that if we continue to have adverse publicity.'

'Isn't this a public institution?'

'Film is an expensive business. The government funding is generous, of course, but inadequate for all our needs.'

Lenny had already done a little background research in preparation for the job. Newspaper reports in the State Library archives showed that the current state government, keen to make budget cuts, was pushing Aquinas to amalgamate with the Victorian College of the Arts Film School. The minister had stated that he didn't see the point of funding two film schools.

'How much is Galaxy paying you?' Ray asked.

'Eight hundred a week plus expenses,' Lenny shot back.

'I trust you'll be worth it.' Ray returned to her cheques. The meeting was over.

Lenny studied the graffiti on the toilet walls: a few not very funny poems, feminist fury on various topics and some cartoons done in thick black texta, including a remarkably good one of Cate Ray as an evil, black manta-ray with fangs. Elsewhere, a face with red splotches where the eyes should have been had the caption: 'Here's looking at you, kid!'.

Lenny wanted to wash her hands. No soap. What a surprise.

She used hot water to scald her hands clean, then

examined her face in the chipped mirror. Smiling at herself, she thought she saw something stuck in her bottom teeth. They were horribly crooked so even when she was sure she'd got it all, there was always a remnant of food if she looked *really* close. She took out a packet of floss and pulled a strand through: better, but something still felt wrong. She took a small bottle of Listerine out of her bag and gargled. The mint-green liquid burned on her tongue. When she spat it down the sink, she thought with satisfaction of all the germs dying somewhere down there in the S bend, alone. It served them right.

Her reflection leered back from the mirror, brown eyes goggling from the gaunt, egg-shaped skull. In the sixteen months since Ted Aaron's death, Lenny had lost ten kilograms. Not so much for a chubby on a diet, but she had been a stick insect to begin with.

Outside in the quadrangle again she surveyed the building around her, mentally running through her mini tour, trying to get her bearings. The ground floor, she recalled, also housed the Aquinas School of Design, and the School of Animation faced the library across the quadrangle on the second floor.

She walked down the tunnel that led to the back gate. Like the front gate, it was wrought iron and filled the entrance completely, with no space between gate, floor, wall or the tunnel's ceiling for an intruder to enter. Lenny opened her bag and removed the master key Ray had taped inside her file. The gate opened easily, and she walked outside into the car park and looked back up at the building. There were two fire escapes on both the first and second floors. She went up to the first floor to examine one of the doors. It had no handle, being the sort that opened from the inside.

Back in the quadrangle and about to leave, Lenny noticed

that one of the doors was open. The sign attached said *Film Equipment Storeroom – Secured Area – No Unsupervised Access*. It was as good a time as any to begin her snooping and she stepped inside. It was a small, stuffy room ringed with metal cabinets and tall, wide shelves. Every surface was covered with equipment: boom poles, sandbags, tripods, cameras, Nagras and slates. Against one wall were stacked reflector boards and tracks. Two dollies stood in the corner. Everything was labelled and neat.

'I'm going to need a good explanation for your stepping over that line.' The voice came from behind her and she turned. A man filled the door space for a moment then stepped inside. He was as tall as Lenny, with pale blue eyes, grey-brown hair parted neatly to the left and a milky skin marred by a large mole in the centre of his right cheek. Late thirties, Lenny thought. He wore a white shirt buttoned up at the collar and over it a spotless white lab coat. The crease in his pants was razor sharp and his shoes were polished to a military gloss. The moist blue eyes observed her, head slightly to one side, lips compressed.

'Hi, I'm –'

A finger to his compressed lips. Another sniff. 'We don't communicate further until you're back over the line.' He pointed at the door where there was indeed a bright yellow line painted across the stone step.

'Listen –' Lenny began. His head shook and, silent as the grave, he pointed to the line again. She stepped back outside and he followed her, tilted his head back to the vertical and sniffed.

'That is a secured area. What were you doing in there?'

'I'm Lenny, Lenny Lypchik. I'm back here to finish off my third year. Just had a meeting with Ray.'

Another sniff. 'My name is Pluckrose. I'm the technician and I control the storeroom. Nothing goes out and nothing and no one comes in without my knowledge. Equipment is signed in and out here and I make it an absolute rule that no one goes through that door and over that line without my permission. If you break something, which I hope you will not be in the habit of doing, you will bring it upstairs to the first floor workshop.' He pursed his lips.

'I certainly will,' Lenny ingratiated, and then: 'Ray told me you found that dead body.'

Pluckrose looked down at his shiny shoes and sniffed. 'Not pleasant to see. There was blood all over her face and body and over the carpet too. I didn't know who it was for a moment. And the eyes ... I didn't touch anything, of course. But I had a good look around for him.'

'Him?'

'The murderer. Or her, I suppose.'

'Why do you think the eyes were cut out?'

He looked straight into Lenny's: 'I couldn't tell you. But I wonder if it's not the start of something, all this.'

'What kind of something?'

'That's how things are in this life. You've heard of chaos theory, I suppose?'

'You mean those spiral patterns on t-shirts?'

'Those "patterns" are three-dimensional representations of Mandelbrot sets. They are proof of the deterministic nature of non-linear equations, which means that they mark out for us the limits of randomness. Non-linear, unsolvable equations govern most of the physical world: the turbulence inside a river, the shapes of clouds or the discharge of electricity – sparks and what have you. Chaos theory explains that the pattern of this randomness can be predicted.'

'So there is no randomness?'

'Yes, but it's not random. That girl's death, for example, would have been the outcome of a number of causes. Think of the events that had to occur to put her in that situation. Now imagine that you could make up a calculation, an equation that was complicated enough to describe those events in purely mathematical terms. That equation would obey certain laws of chaos, the same sort of mathematics that describes apparently random events like radio static. It may not be isolated. It may be the start of a chain.'

'Chain?' Lenny prompted.

'Heard of the butterfly effect?'

'Er ... the flapping of a butterfly's wings in Beijing –'

'– causes a snowstorm in the Andes. Sensitive dependence on initial conditions. It was one of the first triumphs of chaos. Edward Lorenz saw it back in the early sixties. He was a meteorologist, wanted to predict the weather, ha, ha.'

Ha, ha, Lenny echoed. How long could this go on?

'So, a death in an edit suite could lead to ... a shattered redhead lamp or you winning the lottery, or –'

'Another dead body?' She cut him off.

Pluckrose looked thoughtful. 'Yes, perhaps.'

'Gee – hope it's not me, then!' Lenny quipped, but Pluckrose's enthusiasm for chaos seemed to have temporarily escaped him. She added: 'Listen, if I need to get into the school at night, if I'm behind with a project or something, could you get me in? I mean, if you're working late yourself. When I was here before, the other guy used to do it.'

Pluckrose didn't miss a beat. 'Nice to meet you, Lenny,' he said. 'And I'm sure I'll see you around.' He strolled back into the storeroom.

CHAPTER 5

Drugs, Data and Dwarf Trees

Monday evening and she pulled into the car park outside
the Dandenong clinic: open for business four till nine pm,
as a community service.

Cleo whined from her cat box on the back seat. She was
used to being ferried between Lenny's office and her flat,
but she was hungry for her dinner.

'Be patient,' Lenny said, poking a turkey-flavoured snack
into the box. 'My need is greater than yours.'

Dr Henderson's wife of forty years, Millicent, was water-
ing the weary plants in reception. She was a sprightly,
sixty-year-old beauty.

'Oh! You've changed your hair.'

'Too much?' Lenny asked.

Millicent patted her arm. 'Better deformity than conformity, I always say.'

'That's sweet. Thank you for that. Can I go in?'

'Henry's always pleased to see you.'

Henry Henderson GP, sixty-nine, had practised medicine
for over forty years. Lenny had met him seven months ago
through a mutual acquaintance, his ancient Siamese,
Freddy. Invited in for afternoon tea, she had immediately
seen his potential.

Dr Henderson showed her all his dentures when she came in. His hair was spider-grey, wiped sideways across his shiny skull. He was wearing a thick, cream-coloured cardigan and slippers. 'Lenny! What can I do for you today then?'

'How's Freddy?' Lenny asked, keeping it nice and friendly.

'He's in his basket pretty much all the time now.' Dr Henderson took Lenny's pulse. 'The vet says we should think about euthanasia, but Millicent won't. My, you're slow today.'

'I'm always slow. I think I just need a tonic ... or just to talk.' She fumbled in her bag for the gift she always brought. 'I got you some soft caramel.'

'Oh, you are kind!' He examined the packet.

Lenny scanned his desk for prescription pads, samples, the odd bottle of something interesting. 'Was that Millicent?' she said, turning to the door.

'Millicent?'

'I think she's calling you.'

'Oh? Well, you get undressed and up onto the table.' He went out of the room. Lenny had timed his arthritic shuffle and knew she had thirty seconds before he'd be back. She went through his drawers looking for promotional product and pills, but Millicent was a meticulous housekeeper. Down the corridor, Dr Henderson and Millicent were having a more than usually confused conversation. She heard him start back, ripped off the top few sheets from his prescription pad and stuffed them into her bag. She could do his signature perfectly.

'You must have been mistaken,' the old doctor said, coming in. 'Now, what was it today?'

'Just a headache,' Lenny said.

'Oh. Well, I think aspirin will do the trick.' Dr Henderson used a small key to open a cabinet and removed that cornerstone of analgesic therapy. 'You are an easy patient! There never seems to be anything wrong with you.' He laughed. 'Just the two, mind, or you'll upset your stomach.'

Lenny nodded vigorously and took the pills with the paper cup of water he offered. She was impatient now, his kindness holding her up. She searched for something pleasantly final to say. 'Listen, when Freddy – when the time comes with Freddy, I can let you have a new kitten. Just let me know.'

'What a very nice offer.' He beamed. Lenny stretched her lips to imitate him.

In the car she wrote herself a generous script and stopped at a twenty-four hour pharmacy on the way home. Haldol – Haloperidol – was her favourite controller of erratic emotions and bringer of peace; pale lavender tablets that made you feel warm and together instead of angry and alone. Dr Sakuno might well say she could overcome emotional crises unmedicated if she wanted to, but Lenny suspected that there were some things – in her case twenty-four hour a day crabby tension – that were ingrained and unassailable.

The lesbian couple who lived downstairs in Lenny's St Kilda flats waved to her from their kitchen window as she squeezed her car into the only remaining space. She waved back. Mel and Sally were literature students in their early twenties who were planning to marry. They figured the way things were going, it would be legal by Christmas. Another gay high court judge had come out and listed his partner in *Who's Who*, advocating the same legal rights for same-sex partners as heterosexuals. If the law was out of the closet, the young couple reasoned, who could stop them?

Lenny gazed at her face in her bathroom mirror. Anastasia was right – she *was* Dracula. She tried relaxing her

47

facial muscles, aimed for the half smile, a bare movement of the lips, no teeth. Was that endearing, friendly? She thought not. Hers was a naturally belligerent face.

She went to the long mirror inside her wardrobe door and examined her overall look. She had bought one of those short skirts stylish people were wearing over the top of their trousers. And she had covered her hands with cheap plastic jewellery. In Dangerfield the same look on the mannequin had been very sexy, very now. Remodelled on Lenny, it was a broomstick's attempt at fashion. She took off the rings and the skirt and stuffed them in the back of the wardrobe. The hair and the earrings would have to be enough.

She fixed herself a double Lemsip, no ice, and went back into her bedroom. On a long low shelf above the bed sat Pikachu and his acrylic friends. 'Gotta Catch 'Em All!' screamed the savvy Japanese marketers, and she had.

Next to the bed was a single tatami mat where once a day she sat cross-legged and allowed herself to drift into a blank state. *Zazen* – Japanese meditation – was another of Dr Sakuno's suggestions. According to him, one of Lenny's biggest problems was thinking too much. There are five *skandhas* that obscure our true nature, he explained. Form, feeling, thought, will and consciousness. Through meditation it was possible to overcome these and reach a state of intellectual nothingness. It vexed Lenny to think of all the time and energy she would have to devote to achieve what came naturally to most air stewards.

She flicked on the TV next to her futon and reached for her notebook and the stack of Aquinas files. First she turned to Galaxy's background report.

There was a brief history of the school. Television had been introduced to Australia in 1956 and it had quickly become obvious that education bodies would be needed to fuel the new industry. Aquinas had been founded on the Fitzroy site by Kenneth Drage and Robert Heywood in 1968 to 'promote the art of film and television in Victoria'. Heywood had a PhD in Australian literature from Melbourne University and a passion for film theory. Drage's PhD was in art history and he had been a sound recordist for the ABC. The two friends had kick-started Aquinas's Film and Television School with bank loans, begging and youthful drive. The schools of Animation and Design were added three years later.

Although Aquinas was initially a private institution, Heywood and Drage quickly realised the school could not hope to survive without government backing. The file contained a photo dated 1974 of Prime Minister Gough Whitlam shaking hands with Heywood as Aquinas officially became a public institution. Funding had increased gradually over the last twenty-six years, as had government attempts to control access and content.

Aquinas's film school was the smallest of the three schools, taking only eight students each year. Animation took twenty, while Design – which specialised in the design of sets, lighting and costume for theatre, television and film – took twenty-five. Each of the schools had its own head: Sue Hyslock at Animation, Ben Austin at Design and Cate Ray. All of the principals were governed by the school board.

The board was comprised of Kenneth Drage and four others. Lenny noted the names of a well-known actor, a magazine editor, a Toorak socialite and Hermione Arnfeldt, the drink-driving statistic who had been the National Film Commission's director.

Lenny flipped through the file to the information about the film school. First years worked in video, second years in film. Third years could choose either, but as a general rule preferred film. There was some talk of introducing a masters course. A newspaper clipping reported that a large percentage of graduates found positions in the industry. Lenny scanned the list of graduates and identified quite a few culprits from her research into Australian film at the video store.

She examined the course structure for the third years. In first semester, which ran April to July, students concentrated on writing scripts and then began pre-production for their films. In second semester they spent August and September shooting their films (this included compulsory crewing for each other). October and November were given over to editing and the school broke up for the year in the first week of December.

She turned to the student files. Following the theft of the Nagra IV and the microphone, a representative from Galaxy had visited Aquinas and, with Ray's consent, taped interviews with the third year students. Lenny had the full transcript of these Q & As attached to each student's file. Photographs of the students, their grades to date and comments on their work by the staff were also included.

Of the eight students who would have made up the third year group, only five remained. Doug McVie had withdrawn from the course midway through first year and gone to live in Noosa with his girlfriend. Brad Glenn had transferred to the Australian School of Film and Television in Sydney at the start of second year. Emily Cunningham was dead.

The five remaining students were Harry Tuyen, Annabel Lear, Janus Onyszkiewicz, Moira Middlemiss and Gabrielle Danaher. Cate Ray had included an up-to-date third year schedule for Lenny's benefit. Apparently Danaher had already completed shooting her film and Onyszkiewicz was currently shooting his. Middlemiss, Lear and Tuyen would shoot their films throughout September. Where to begin? Lenny picked up a file at random and an A4 sized photo dropped out.

Moira Middlemiss had no hair apart from a long purple strand originating from the top of her scalp. She had a plump, moon-cream face with traces of acne on both cheeks. Her smile was large-toothed, though not unattractive, and she wore rectangular, blue-lensed sunglasses. Both her ears glistened with piercings, and there was a ring through her left eyebrow and a stud in her nostril. Around her neck a silver and turquoise pendant hung from a thong necklace. She was the type of woman Lenny's mother crossed the street to avoid.

Moira was twenty-seven. She had worked in Safeway and completed a two-year part-time photography course before getting into Aquinas. According to the transcript, she had no idea who the thief was. She had talked and cried a lot about Emily Cunningham's recent death, insisting she had been close to Emily and was destroyed by her loss. Lenny found the supervisors' assessments of her work. Her films were described by Ray as 'documentaries that show a tendency towards the art house' and by Kenneth Drage as 'adequate despite possessing a sebaceous level of political correctness'.

The second student – Annabel Lear, nineteen – was one of the most beautiful girls Lenny had ever seen. Her face glowed, the pores of her skin were indiscernible, the light blue eyes were wide and twinkling and her pink lips were invitingly soft and smoochie. A sky-blue t-shirt hugged tight against Annabel's small breasts. It had sunflowers printed on it and underneath, the words 'Cutie Little Angel' written phonetically in Japanese *katakana*.

On her application to enter Aquinas, Annabel described herself as '. . . a woman determend to find herself a place in a show run by the boys'. She had misspelt determined, writing in a large, looped scrawl. Fresh from high school, she was an exception to Aquinas's policy of not choosing applicants until they had had adult life experience. The average age of successful applicants was twenty-five. Ray described Annabel's work as 'absolutely brilliant, a real women's director … a fantastic eye for the commercial'. Kenneth Drage recorded no comment.

When the Galaxy rep asked her about the theft of equipment, Annabel said it would be ridiculous to consider her as a suspect: she had friends in the industry who could loan her whatever she wanted.

Cleo Aaron poked a head around the door, mewed, dived at the bed and landed next to Lenny's arm. She nuzzled up, rolling with purrs. It was dinner time. Lenny took a break to drag the tin out of the fridge and fill the bowl. She cleaned the water dish with boiling water, poured some Evian into it and went back to the Galaxy file.

Harry Tuyen, aged twenty-eight, had glossy black hair and large almond-shaped eyes. His sleeves were rolled up to show muscular arms and his lips were full and curled, as though the photographer had just said something he found stupid. Tuyen? Chinese? Vietnamese maybe.

Galaxy thought he was a likely candidate for theft. This was based on his expressing admiration for the thief, speculating how he could have got in and out of the school at night. Harry's theories involved ladders, camouflage suits and a lot of dramatic crawling on the stomach through flood drains.

Ray noted: 'Action movies are always commercially successful. Harry should be encouraged in this area.' Kenneth had jotted 'Male fantasy action dross competently produced.'

Student number four was Gabrielle Danaher, twenty-eight, attractive rather than beautiful, with a face that was a little too narrow and a nose a little too long. She wore a pale green t-shirt with the sleeves ripped off and her dark red hair hung to her shoulders. Her green eyes were slits under dark eyebrows. Cate Ray's assessment of her second year film was lukewarm. 'Gabrielle's work shows promise, despite having a tendency to be morbid. She needs to focus on more commercial topics for her films.' Kenneth Drage held the opposite view: 'Her subject matter often appears dark, but soon grows into something wonderful and unexpected. Gabrielle is a satirist of great promise, showing us the world through fresh, intelligent eyes. She will have enormous influence on the future of Australian film and I believe she is a genius.'

The final student was Janus Onyszkiewicz (a pencilled note on the back of his file read 'O-NISH-KIEV-ITCH'). He was twenty-six, with a triangular nose on an oblong head, a baseball cap on backwards and a flannel shirt. He was interested in the details of the thefts and asked the insurance rep a lot of questions about how much you'd get for second-hand film equipment and where you'd be able to fence the goods. Ray had made a note on his file: 'A brilliant editor and a world class DOP in the making.' Kenneth offered: 'A very talented young man.'

Lenny glanced at his address, then flipped back to Gabrielle Danaher's file. They were the same.

The phone rang, as it did every night.

'Lenny, I'm so lonely.' The usual self-pitying sniffle was amplified by her mother's cold.

Lenny sighed. 'The doctor told you it was natural to feel like this for a long time. Have you got the TV on? That's good company. What about those pills I gave you? They're like having a little friend.'

'You are good to me,' Veronica Aaron mumbled through

53

her tears. 'Oh, Lenny ... tonight I went into the kitchen to make a cuppa and I had two cups out and two tea bags and I was pouring the water in and humming to myself before I remembered.'

Lenny slumped back into her pillow.

'Maybe you should put all the extra crockery away in a box somewhere and just keep one of everything?'

There was a pause while her mother took this in. 'What sort of advice is that? I can't put Daddy's things away like they're rubbish. He might be watching. He might think I don't want him any more.'

'Have you got channel nine on? It's *Pretty Woman*. They're up to the bit where she's driving the car for him.' Julia Roberts' teeth filled the screen.

She heard the phone drop as her mother ran to turn the TV on. 'Oh, isn't she lovely!'

'Mmm hmm.' Lenny picked up her research.

'It's a Cinderella story, isn't it?'

'Sure. Shall we watch it together for a bit?' Lenny settled her pillow more comfortably behind her, hooked the phone under her chin and began to read Emily Cunningham's file. Galaxy had asked for it to be included. Despite Ray's insistence to the contrary, the insurance company also wondered if there was a connection between the thefts and the Cunningham murder.

Emily was exactly thirty years old when she died in edit suite one. It had been her birthday, Lenny noted. Aquinas had been her second degree course as she had already completed an MBA at Melbourne University and worked for her father's company before being accepted into Aquinas. Her father's company was no small deal either, but Lenny already knew that. Emily was the only child of The Cunninghams of Cunningham's Hardware, the mega-chain, a fact which had attracted national media interest on her death. There were Cunningham's Hardware stores in every state, two hundred in all, and the Cunninghams were listed amongst the top twenty wealthiest families in Australia. This was noted in Ray's fine hand at the top of Emily's student history. Emily had received the certificate for best video in first year and best film in second year, both, Lenny recalled, conferred by Ray.

Emily had long, golden-brown hair and her face combined leftover puppy fat with the faint crow's feet that appear from nowhere in the late twenties. She was smiling straight into the lens. It was a hard smile, Lenny thought, from a cold and distant woman. It was possible the photographer had caught Emily in one of those eerie, transitional expressions that make a person look unlike themselves, but Lenny had looked through a lot of police mug shots over the years and was accustomed to making rapid assessments. The blue eyes were neither large nor small, and not particularly beautiful, quite ordinary, in fact. Why anyone would want to stick a knife in and gouge them out was a mystery – and Lenny loved a mystery. She wondered if she could get a look at the police files.

She took the six photographs and laid them out on the futon in front of her. Cleo Aaron sniffed them.

'Get off, stupid.'

'What?' said Veronica.

'Nothing. Are you feeling better?'

'Yes. Yes, I am. Daddy used to love this film, you know. He and I always said we'd buy the video one day. We always hoped you'd have a life like this.'

'You wanted me to become a prostitute?'

'We hoped you'd find a nice man and settle down.'

'I have settled down.'

'We're just two lonely old things, aren't we, Lenny? We have to take care of each other.' Lenny was saved from challenging her mother's ridiculous statement of similarity by the *Pretty Woman* tooth-flossing sequence. Having eaten a couple of strawberries, and despite being a girl who gave blow jobs in the backs of cars for a living, Julia couldn't live with a stray strawberry seed. Critics had commented that this was a ridiculous, unrealistic scene. Lenny disagreed. In fact it was the only scene in the whole film she could relate to.

She opened the file on the Aquinas Film, Animation and Design staff. Glossy A4 photographs but the notes here were less detailed.

She scanned the information on the first and second year film supervisors. Phillip 'Flip' Withers, the first year supervisor, had worked as a newspaper reporter and as a producer at SBS, joining Aquinas's staff three years ago. The second year supervisor, Greg Waterman, had a background in children's television and had joined the school four years ago.

Ray had written a note stating that her staff were beyond any suspicion when it came to the thefts. She couldn't hope for a finer, more dedicated group. Lenny looked through the folder for details on Ray herself. Nothing. There was, however, a January newspaper clipping about Kenneth Drage, the school's co-founder. Celebrating his seventieth birthday surrounded by friends and colleagues, he was reported to be looking forward to the year ahead. He was currently writing a film review column for the *Age*, doing a little work at the school as a script adviser and 'keeping very busy' with his oil painting. He also did consultancy work for the National Film Commission and Cinemedia, and occasionally wrote program notes for National Gallery exhibitions. In 1971 he had directed his own film, *Hard Skies*. Ray had included a newspaper review of it: 'Certainly well shot and wearing its heart unashamedly on its sleeve.

But will it get the great Australian unwashed into our cinemas? Sadly, this reviewer thinks not.'

Lenny had never heard of *Hard Skies*.

The last page in the file was a list of names and contact numbers for the security patrol company, the cleaning company and, more helpfully, Graeme Pluckrose, the technician. But there was little to go on: Pluckrose was forty years old, single, and lived at an address in North Brunswick.

There were gentle snores coming through the phone. The Valium had finally kicked in. Lenny hung up, went into her living room and sat in a big armchair in front of her *kotatsu*, a low, square coffee table with a heater underneath. Cleo, stomach happily bulging with Ocean Fish Platter, lay on a cushion beside her, four paws in the air, as Lenny flipped through her mail. Gas bill. Phone bill. But wait – what was that?

An advertisement for a Kinky Girls Night at the local dyke bar. She perused the handbill. The photo showed a dyno-breasted person – possibly female – in a leather one-piece swimsuit, breasts exposed, nipples covered with crossed black electrical tape. She was holding a pair of handcuffs. The promotional blurb promised dominatrix demos and a spa party. Fetish/erotic dress essential. BYO towel.

In a purely theoretical sense it was tempting. But why kid herself: she had never had a relationship and never would. She didn't like to be touched. She didn't even like it if someone accidentally brushed past her arm in a crowd. She knew why. Dr Sakuno had gone over it with her: her grandmother had been abusive to her as a child. Consequently she rejected any form of physical contact. It didn't take a genius to figure that one out. As it happened, Dr Sakuno didn't much like physical contact himself, so it wasn't high on his list of Things to Cure Lenny Aaron Of. At any rate, there was no point thinking a fun night with the girls was a viable option. She'd end up standing in the corner with a sour look on her face, like an old pervert, until one of the sporty dykes told her to piss off.

She pulled out her bonsai tools and surveyed her trees: eight of them, all under ten inches high, branches wired tightly into impressions of their natural counterparts. To supply them with light, the walls and ceiling around the trees were covered in fluorescent tubes and reflectors, a sort of *Barbarella* look. Lenny decided that the Blue Moss Cypress was too dry. She laid a plastic cloth on the floor and tipped the bonsai gently onto its side. Cleo Aaron hurried over. Meeowl? Meeowl!

Lenny slipped the terracotta pot off and examined the tree roots. As suspected, there were several clear patches of roots that had spread to the edge of the soil. She took out her rake and tweezers and began to gently remove the moss and loose soil. This was the best part of the day. There was nothing more relaxing than being in absolute control of another living thing's life.

She switched on the living room TV. She had had all she could stand of the sloe-eyed hooker and turned instead to an ABC interview with the leader of the United Australia Party. Mrs Virginia Dobbs, a wide-hipped brunette in a trademark soft pink powersuit, was being asked about her views on Asian immigration and Aboriginal rights. Born and raised in Dirranbandi, Queensland, and having spent most of her adult life as an assembly line worker in a Darwin pie factory, Mrs Dobbs had emerged as the new focus of political life in the north of the country. She was spectacularly efficient at the sound bite:

'I have a dream and it's white.'

Mrs Dobbs just wanted Australians to look like

Australians. It was important that we weren't perceived throughout the rest of the world as a race of mixed breeds. We had an image (blonde) to uphold and we needed to keep our gene pool pure. She – and she knew many people like her – would do anything she had to do to protect her vision for the future of this fine country.

'I'm only saying what real Australians think,' the Dirranbandi demagogue wound up with a certainty-centred smile.

Lenny placed a new screen in the bottom of the pot and put the drainage stones on top, then added a light pad of new soil, slid the tree back in and held it up to check.

The ABC interviewer and Mrs Dobbs were beginning to raise their voices. They had been joined by an associate professor of sociology from Monash University: a red rag to Dobbs's brunette bull.

Lenny flicked channels.

CHAPTER 6

Thrown in at the Deep End

The next morning Lenny went to Aquinas. It was still early and the security patrol had not yet arrived to open the gates. She used her master key to get in and went up to the second floor library.

She made two neat piles of videos on the shiny desk top next to the monitor: the current third year students' first and second year projects. The 16 mm films had been trans-ferred to video for ease of viewing.

Harry Tuyen's first year video went into the machine. Twenty-two minutes of not much story but a great deal of muscle, expletive and blood, with an adrenaline-fuelled soundtrack. Highlights included a quick shot of an arm being severed and a pretty good motorbike chase. Lots of characters shouted straight into the lens for no apparent reason, but it was exciting stuff and Lenny could see that it would have its fans. She popped in his second year tape. Fifteen minutes this time. Better quality visuals, loads more action, a bit with a pig and a hammer, a topless girl and an improvement in storytelling. Some interesting shots and nice editing, but surely this was not the future of Australian film.

Although she was younger, Annabel Lear's work was

more authoritative than Harry's. She was interested in the modern woman and drew her with a broad, glossy brushstroke. In both examples of her work Annabel was clearly going for style over substance – many sequences were covered with funky dance music while the camera lingered lovingly over Dolce and Gabbana and perfect dentistry. Annabel's films were filled with bright young things living bright young lives: they were a publicist's dream.

In contrast, the two videos of Janus Onyszkiewicz were dour. Both were shot in black and white and told by a series of depressingly real characters; the working classes as seen through the artist's lens. There was an irritating waif in one of them who sold home-made postcards in the streets and always had a wistful smile on her old soul's face. After a number of gut-wrenching hardships, she ended up running a machinists' union and was clearly supposed to be a model of right living. Lenny wanted to hit her with a brick.

What saved Janus's films was the beauty of his framing and the precision of his editing. Each shot had been timed so that the cut was almost subliminal, never drawing attention to itself. It was the work of someone who saw the world as a series of logical progressions.

Both of Moira Middlemiss's films were documentaries, the first about a shelter for old women who, according to the voiceover, 'struggle to define themselves in a world that abandons the aged female'. Was it Moira's voice? The video jacket confirmed that it was. Despite their struggle to define themselves in terms of socioeconomic conditions, the old bags in the shelter were rather good at sneaking in bits of their own sly personalities. Moira had apparently not seen this happening and Lenny enjoyed those scenes in which the emotional tone of the voiceover ran counter to the women's knowing digs directed at the uptight manager of the shelter and the sexual appetites of the gay male attendants.

Moira's second year production was shot in a very untidy terrace house in Collingwood featuring incense, batik wall-hangings and four women, one of whom was Moira herself. It was a feminist share-house drama, except nothing happened. Fortunately it was only fifteen minutes long, a full five minutes of which were given to a sing-along as they worked together in the kitchen to produce a one-pot meal of garlic, lentils and pumpkin. Despite the loose, cinéma vérité handling of the camera, complete with clattering magazine, there was evidence that some moments had been staged, as if Moira had hoped to capture a mood that hadn't existed and was forced to fake it. There were a number of dodgy moments, including an argument (apparently captured as it happened) in which the levels of mulled wine in the women's glasses rose and fell suspiciously from shot to shot.

Lenny inserted the final student's work. So far Annabel seemed the girl most likely to succeed, with her commercially savvy advertisements for new Australian chic.

She was unprepared for the work of Gabrielle Danaher.

With little money spent on costumes or props, Gabrielle Danaher had made a real film, the story of an old man who, after the death of his wife, resurrected his lifelong dream of becoming a professional saxophonist. But the man was tone deaf and could produce only a flurry of freakish notes. There was little dialogue. Sympathy for the old man was developed in the narrative as his strange music started to make sense and grow on you. He eventually found his place as a soloist in a free jazz band, where his atonal approach reached the audience it deserved. The film didn't have Janus's editing flash or Annabel's hip sheen, but with twelve minutes of scratchy sound and vision Gabrielle had created a new universe of worn saxophone keys, nightclub dressing rooms and the lines on the face of an old actor.

The second video was longer, happier, in colours so bright they seemed freshly painted onto the film. It was a road movie: two women finding their way across a burnt Australian landscape. It contained all that Moira Middlemiss had tried to say in her ponderous women's documentary in a couple of short sequences, and breezed ahead of Annabel Lear in its satire; Danaher took risks, showed the ordinary in extraordinary ways. When she got her hands on the right tools, there would be no stopping her.

Lenny emerged from the library and went down to the first floor. She wandered along the corridor, glancing into open doors, getting a feel for this place she was so supposed to know. She pushed open one of the fire doors and looked down onto the car park. Students were beginning to arrive.

Further along the corridor, Graeme Pluckrose was inside the workshop examining a broken fresnel lens off a light.

'Hi,' Lenny said.

'Lypchik,' he said, without looking up.

'Did you do that?' she asked, bending over the benchtop to look at the lens.

Pluckrose smirked. 'I did not, thank you. Mr Tuyen broke it. He doesn't want to settle for a week of filming like everyone else, he has to start early. So I say fine, then he does this. Not the most responsible character, our Harry.'

'Why didn't you say no?'

Pluckrose opened his mouth, closed it, opened it again. He sniffed. The sniffing came before his pronouncements, as if Pluckrose's brain needed more oxygen than everyone else's to form sentences.

'I'm too lenient.'

'So, Harry's a bit of a worry, is he?' Lenny probed.

'He's doing what they're forcing him to do. Grabbing as much as he can. As you should know, this place is nothing more than a low budget production house. What we do here at Aquinas is churn out as much footage as we can, however we can. The law of averages says that sooner or later somebody's film is going to win a prize, a trophy at some national or international event. We don't care about the students per se; we care about having an entry in the Barcelona Film Festival or the Berlin Kino. Prizes lead to opportunities and attract private funding. People like to back winners. My job is to keep thirty-year-old equipment functioning to fuel all those dreams.'

'Ray told me some equipment has been deliberately damaged.'

'We live in troubled times,' Pluckrose admitted. 'Or perhaps it's someone who saw one of our films and decided the best thing was to stop us before we did any more damage, ha, ha.'

There was no suggestion in Pluckrose's manner that he actually believed this. Lenny had met his type before. Technicians, computer scientists and the like, all maintained a positive self-image by a process of daily confirming the ignorance of the general population. They did it by laying traps, such as the one Pluckrose had just set for her. Had she agreed with him on the second-rate nature of Aquinas's cinematic output, he would have snapped back that Aquinas's films were often technically superior to those produced at the VCA and AFTRS, and made for less money too.

'Yes,' Pluckrose continued, tweezers picking at slivers of glass from the shattered lens and placing them in an empty 100-foot film can, 'we all know that Aquinas is supposed to be the future of film. What was it: "The art of the film must produce an aesthetic response in the spectator?" Drage wrote that. Good old Kenneth. Ever seen *Hard Skies*? His one go at a feature back in '71.' He sniffed. 'Too earnest and arty for its own good. Apparently.'

Lenny Aaron – David O. Lincoln Academy of Film graduate – nodded wisely. Here was a chance to shine! 'Perhaps he should have taken the example of Roman Polanski. I believe the economic reality of film making had a beneficial effect on *his* work. Forced him to concentrate on fantasies that had a cultural as well as a personal significance.' She was hitting her mark with a vengeance. 'But it's very rare, the ability to blend artistic vision with commercial appeal.'

'Right ...' Pluckrose hesitated, perhaps sensing rote learning rather than knowledge. 'I'm not a huge fan of Polanski myself. Although I have read just about every book on him written in the last twenty years.' A threat.

Lenny ploughed on: 'A symbol of his times. His achievements as a film maker are overlooked due to his spectacular private life.' That would have to be enough. Her Polanski repertoire was dry. She glanced at her watch and backed away. 'I've got an appointment. But we have to get into this again another time.'

She left him staring after her with a piece of glass gripped tightly between his tweezers and continued along the corridor. Most of the small rooms on this floor were editing suites, cube-shaped and sterile, enlivened only by graffiti. The chunky Steenbeck editing machines took up all the space with just enough room for a stained plastic chair. The carpets smelled of spilled food, beer and vomit. It reminded Lenny of a Saturday night ride on the Lilydale train.

She spotted a calico bag suspended under a rectangular, metal frame. These were the trim bins. Hanging from a wooden rail were long pieces of 16 mm film, marked up with white chinagraph pencil waiting to be edited.

Lenny approached the edit suite where Emily Cunningham had died. The room was empty. Alana Zappone had told her the police removed the Steenbeck as evidence. The bloodied carpet had also been removed and someone had scrubbed the walls ready for repainting. Lenny tried to imagine the murder scene. Cut throats meant a lot of blood. Emily Cunningham would have been drenched in it within two minutes. And the murderer? Had he been bloodied too? How had he gotten away?

As in the other edit suites, there were no windows and the sliding door's deadlock was lockable from the inside with a knob and by key from the outside. But Emily hadn't locked it – or she had unlocked it because she knew the person outside, trusted them.

Lenny shook herself. This was not her investigation. She had to concentrate on theft and vandalism, not murder. Unless she found a connection between the two. Of course, it was her duty to pursue all avenues . . .

There was a woman's voice in the corridor: 'Harry, if you don't stop making remarks like that, I'll have to speak to Ray about it. I don't want to take it that far, but I will.'

Lenny poked her head out of the edit suite and was immediately spotted by the woman. It was Lucy Peel. There was no sign of Harry Tuyen.

'Can I help you?' A friendly voice. The third year supervisor was tall, almost as tall as Lenny, with her long hair in a loose plait, well-pressed ivory pants and a pale lavender blouse that matched her eyes. The eyes were outlined by the thickest, longest black lashes Lenny had ever seen. A double row of lashes, she thought.

'Hello,' Lenny said. It was time to offer her hand but she didn't. She never shook hands unless it was forced upon her. Germy fingers, thumbs and palms squeezed into hers. No thanks. 'I'm Lenny Lypchik. Trouble?' She gestured down the corridor in the direction she supposed Lucy's harasser must have gone.

'Not at all. Oh! You're the returnee.' The warm smile from her file photograph appeared. 'Well, we'll be seeing a lot of each other. I'm Lucy Peel, your supervisor this year.' This pronouncement trailed behind it a soft, short laugh. 'That was just Harry before. He's no trouble, just a kid with too many hormones. Ray told me you were here five years ago. We'll have to sit down together this week and have a chat about what you're planning for your final year production. Ray says you'll be shooting last, so we've got a few weeks before we need to start panicking, but we should talk about your ideas at least. You'll crew for the other students as part of your assessment, of course, and Ray told me your second year film is in the library, so I'll pop in and have a look, get a bit of an idea about you. Any time you need a chat my door is always open. It'll be a bit tough for you coming back mid-course like this. But you had some family problems and you couldn't get back at the start of the year?'

'Yes.'

Lucy waited for more information. Lenny didn't provide any.

'I see. Well, you'll soon feel back at home. We're finishing off Janus's shoot today. All the exteriors have been completed, so we're in the studio. If you want to come down and help us finish up, you're very welcome.' Lucy interjected her soft laugh throughout the conversation. The more she heard it, the more Lenny realised it was striking some false note in her. It was a strange, repetitive sound that would be interpreted (by someone without Lenny's stoic misanthropy) as the natural expression of a deeply happy woman.

She accepted the invitation to join the shoot in progress. They walked in the same direction down the hall, Lucy Peel's hands clasped behind her back.

'I read in the paper that a student died here recently,' Lenny observed.

'Emily,' Lucy nodded. 'We're all just coming to terms with it. It's very hard.' Her eyes became moist and there was a sad smile on her lips. 'I'm sorry, Lenny. I'm still emotional about it. The way she died was so *horrible*. If she'd been ill or it had been an accident, well . . . she'd still be dead, of course, but somehow it wouldn't seem so . . . so unfair.' She hesitated, perhaps realising she was saying too much, revealing too much. She made a conscious effort to pull herself together and even managed a smile. 'I've got some things to organise, Lenny, so I'll have to ask you to excuse me. It was good to meet you and I'll see you down in the studio in about half an hour.' She smiled again and tripped down the hallway like a twelve-year-old running through a field of buttercups.

Needless to say, the supervisor's show of emotion had an impact on Lenny. She despised emotional people. Consequently Lucy Peel went straight to the top of her list of suspects; it took little to imagine the gentle-faced supervisor quietly closing the storeroom door behind her, pocketing as much equipment as she could and then going fucking bananas with a baseball bat.

Lenny knocked on Ray's office door and pushed it open. A man was crouched next to the desk, wiping the carpet with paper towels. She recognised Kenneth Drage from the newspaper photo in the Aquinas files. His hair and beard were almost completely white now, and he squinted at her through tortoiseshell glasses.

'Who's that?'

'Lenny Lypchik.'

'Ah. Come on in.' She noticed a trace of something pink across the knuckles of his right hand. It looked like paint and she remembered that he was an oil painter. 'Nasty business down here. Runny cat poo. We've one that lives in the building – Sardines. Comes and goes as it pleases. We've more or less adopted it by default. Alana – Ray's PA – has had to take it to the veterinary clinic. We've decided it must have worms because it's forever licking its bottom. I believe you're rather an expert with cats.' He dropped the paper towel into the wastepaper bin and slid into the chair behind the desk.

'I've known a few.'

'That's what Ray said. She's not here, by the way. She's at the Melbourne Businesswomen's Symposium. But she left you your ID card.' He handed it to her. Her egg-face gazed out from under a layer of laminate stamped with the Aquinas emblem.

Kenneth patted the front of the desk, wanting her to sit opposite him. She slid into the low chair. Kenneth smiled. 'I'm not so sure I can see you down there.' They both smiled over Ray's executive feng shui.

'Now, on behalf of the board of directors I welcome you to Aquinas. I'll do what I can to assist you in your investigation although I have to admit the equipment problem has been overshadowed in the last month by Emily's death. Even when the police aren't here continuing their inquiries, I find myself thinking of little else.' He hesitated. 'I'm sorry to rattle on about it, Lenny. In your business I imagine you become inured to violent death, but for the lay person, well, if you see it through my eyes, I'm afraid it's a devastating experience. As the oldest member of staff, I've tried to be a comfort to the others, but I find myself wondering if I'm not the weakest link, the least able to cope.' He shook his head and moved to the tea-making facilities on a filing cabinet. 'OK. Milk and sugar?'

'No.' Three and a half years of drinking *bancha* and *mugicha* had turned her off dairy products in tea. She took the cup he held out to her. 'Do you mind if I smoke?'

'I do mind, but perhaps you'd better anyway.' He was teasing her. 'You sound like you need it.'

'Thank you.' She lit up. 'Do you have any ideas about this equipment theft?'

'No,' Kenneth said firmly. 'Not a clue. It's not as if we have much to take and it's mostly ancient. We still edit on four-plate Steenbecks, you know. The industry moved to digital editing ten years ago. It's hard to imagine anyone would want our stuff now. Amateurs perhaps. Some of the names – Zeiss, Arriflex, Nagra – have a certain nostalgic glamour, the heyday of portable film equipment, etcetera. The vandalism is something else. There seems no explanation – unless Steven Spielberg is getting jealous of us.' He chuckled to himself.

'Do you think the theft could be connected to Emily's murder?' Lenny asked.

Kenneth paused for a moment, considering. He was, thought Lenny, the sort of man who would pride himself on giving precise answers to every question. The type who made an excellent police witness.

'Anything is possible,' he said finally. 'Although the police have yet to discover a connection. But if there is, if Emily was killed because she discovered the identity of the thief, well, perhaps there's a motive for murder there. But so brutally? To take her eyes? I am not experienced in police work, of course, but it seems like more to me. As though it was supposed to mean something. Or am I over-dramatising? I suppose we amateur detectives are rather foolish in our speculations –'

Lenny agreed with him. Taking the eyes. Cutting them out of a living young woman and then letting her bleed to death. It was personal, all right. But she didn't comment. It was best to let the interviewees talk sometimes, let them speculate without interruption.

Kenneth reached for a notepad on the desk, tore off a sheet and balled it, rolled it back and forth between his palms. 'Emily was not popular with the other students. She had a need to wield power. Where that came from, your guess is as good as mine. The money perhaps. She was wealthy and her father was inclined to overcontrol . . .' He crushed the paper, tossed it into the bin and began on another. 'I'm unfair. Mr Cunningham loved his daughter, I'm sure of it. And I felt it was best to advise him that our insurance company had hired an investigator for the theft and vandalism since your investigation, Lenny, might at some point impact on the investigation into his daughter's murder. I may as well tell you now, in case you meet him, that he's a strong-willed gentleman with certain . . . let's say, old-fashioned notions. But what he – and Mrs Cunningham – want is for their daughter to be allowed to rest in peace. Absolutely understandable, I think. The police investigation and the media coverage have been shocking experiences for them. If you can avoid questioning them, Lenny, do try. But I digress slightly. As far as Emily's personality is concerned, it's best perhaps that you form your own opinion of her, if you find it necessary to do so. Cate gave me the impression that your part of this investigation was strictly in terms of the theft and vandalism?'

'Background,' Lenny said. She pulled out her notebook. 'What can you tell me about the other third year students?'

Kenneth Drage crossed his arms and smiled at her. His teeth were small and even except one upper tooth right in the centre which sloped across the other. 'I know Galaxy has asked you to focus your attention on the third years, but I find it hard to believe one of them is involved. Perhaps in a worst case scenario a student would steal, but there's the vandalism – why would they destroy equipment they need for their own projects?'

Spite, envy, rage, disappointment, despair – Lenny's list was a mile long.

'All right,' she said. 'Tell me about the school in general.'

'We're competitive here.' Kenneth took happily to the change of tack. 'Throw them in at the deep end and all that. But there's a spirit of camaraderie. The students have a lot of heart.'

'Why do you throw them in at the deep end?' Lenny asked.

Kenneth laughed. 'Well, we didn't have any money when we began and, as I mentioned, we've never really caught up with the industry in terms of equipment. I shouldn't be admitting this but the truth is, Bob Heywood and I developed the original curriculum around whatever we could scrape up: a couple of wind-up Bolexes, the odd Arri, a handful of lights. But over the years our no-equipment, on-a-shoe-string reputation started to work for us. The media picked up on it. You see, the idea appealed to a certain powerful class of critic brought up on the semi-improvised films of Godard and Truffaut. Did you know Godard wrote the script for *Breathless* on the back of a matchbox?'

Lenny didn't.

'Well, thanks to these critics – past and present – we now have "the Aquinas Method". We began to have some success at festivals, and that sort of thing leads to greater ambitions all round. In the last decade the pressure has increased on the students to get their third year productions a television or cinema release, which of course means producing longer films and an emphasis on commercial considerations. And of course we've been a public institution for some time now.' His lips compressed slightly. 'Which means we have the minister breathing down our neck, too.'

'Mr Drage –'

'Kenneth, please. It's all first names here. We're all artists, all in the same leaky boat.'

'Even Ray?'

'Ahh!' He beamed. 'Well, Ray is a special case.'

Kenneth picked up the photograph of himself, Ray, Hermione Arnfeldt and the state premier, and peered at it, tapping the glass with a fingertip.

'I hand-picked Ray for this position,' he said. 'She was a former student. Made lovely films that were never going to make any money. I had to talk her into the job, if you can believe that. She didn't like the administrative aspects then, but she soon took to it. Surprised me. Without her private fund raising capabilities, Aquinas wouldn't have survived this long. The kids tend to take out their frustrations on her. No doubt you've seen the student toilets.'

'Is the school in financial trouble?'

'The board is concerned, and it should be. We may yet be forced into an amalgamation with the VCA. They produce fine work, of course, but as a co-founder of Aquinas I have what you may call a sentimental attachment to the notion of it remaining a separate entity.'

'Who gets to choose the new board member now that Hermione Arnfeldt is dead?'

'The rest of the board. We have several candidates in mind. We'll make a formal approach when it's decided.' He sighed. 'The board will be a different animal without Hermione. She was very much the leader. Far more difficult to replace her at the Film Commission, of course.' He shook his head. 'She had a very strong vision for the future of Australian film.' He peered at Lenny. 'Are these questions relevant?'

'Everything's relevant at this stage of the investigation. Tell me, why do you give the students only seven days to shoot their films? It doesn't seem long enough.'

Kenneth nodded.

'Part of our history,' he said. 'When we began the school the third years made tiny films – no more than five minutes long. A week was more than adequate. Now they're producing twenty minute epics.' He shook his head. 'But we have the same limitations we've always had in terms of time restrictions. There are eight students in each year so even allowing seven days per student we take up two months of our school year in shooting. With the added syllabus requirements of script writing, preproduction, editing etcetera, there just isn't any more time available. And of course we're a learning establishment, Lenny. We must set limits – otherwise the wealthier students would privately fund greatly extended shoots and that's hardly fair, is it?'

She saw his eyes drift to a point behind her head. Someone must be looking through the glass door. The venetian blinds were open and they were exposed to anyone in reception.

'Someone's there –' Kenneth said.

Lenny turned and looked into narrow green eyes. It was Gabrielle Danaher. She looked older than twenty-eight, was pale almost to the point of anaemia, thinner than her file photo, and her hair was a thick ponytail of tangled dark red. She entered without knocking.

'Excuse me, Kenneth, we're shooting. Lucy sent me to fetch the returnee.'

'Well, you've found her. Gabrielle, this is Lenny Lypchik. Lenny, Gabrielle Danaher – our resident genius.'

'Please . . .' Gabrielle looked uncomfortable.

Kenneth laughed. 'And our only modest student. All right, I won't embarrass you any further. You two go down to the studio now. I'll see if I can pop in later.' He dismissed them with a smile and Lenny followed Gabrielle from the room. To her surprise they didn't go down the main stairs.

Both fire escape doors were open and Gabrielle headed for one of them.

'Is Kenneth right?' Lenny asked as they walked down the steps. 'Are you Aquinas's resident genius?'

Gabrielle didn't look at Lenny. For a moment it seemed she would not answer. When she spoke, her face betrayed no emotion, the expression as flat and blank as a Noh mask's.

'Yes,' she said.

CHAPTER 7

A Hard Day's Shoot

The door near the bottom of the fire escape was open. It led into the green room and from there into the studio, which was dark except for a light shining from what Lenny smugly identified as a blondie positioned to one side of a stainless steel table. There was a redhead too, she noticed, heavily scrimmed. David O. Lincoln would have been very proud.

The room was hot and rank with body odour. A young man, eyes closed, lay on the table's surface. To Lenny's unaccustomed vision, the Aquinas students were dark blurs around the perimeter of the studio.

Someone dipped into the blondie's light and out again. Lenny recognised Harry Tuyen. The person directly in front of her had a shaved head with a long strand of hair in the centre: Moira Middlemiss. Lenny began to see forms and even colours more clearly as her eyes grew accustomed to the dark.

'OK, we go for a take.' This was spoken with a marked Eastern European accent. Janus Onyszkiewicz's baseball-capped head leaned into the camera's view finder. 'Roll tape.'

'Rolling . . . Speed . . .'

'Frame,' said Janus. 'Mark it.'

'Scene four, shot seven, take one.' The slate cracked.

'Action.'

The actor opened his eyes, slowly sat up and gazed into the camera.

'Cut. Print it.' Janus stood back from the camera's viewfinder. 'Next one is shot twelve.'

'Do you want the other lens?' Gabrielle had moved away from Lenny when they entered. She reached down into a small box.

'Leave it,' Janus snapped. 'Nobody handles the Zeiss except myself.'

'Janus doesn't like the ladies touching his equipment,' Harry said from somewhere in the darkness. 'He's saving himself for his special woman.'

Janus said nothing, but Moira took the opportunity to moan gently and swoon to the floor. Lenny fully expected those close by to rush to the stricken girl's help. It was her experience that even in these callous times a woman who was prepared to faint could be reasonably sure of gaining attention. But no one made a move to help Ms Middlemiss.

'It's my last day of filming,' Janus complained. 'I'm too busy for this.'

'I have an *imbalance*,' rejoined Moira from the floor. 'I'm highly allergic to inorganic chemicals. Did someone open a bottle of nail varnish?' She peered into the darkness but it seemed that nobody had opened a bottle of nail varnish, nobody was smoking, and nobody was wearing hair gel. There appeared to be no reason for Moira's sudden collapse. She didn't let that bother her.

'It's only my force of will that allows me to be here at all,' she said emphatically. 'I'm seeing an acupuncturist.' She got to her feet, glanced suspiciously at a tiny bottle of lens-cleaning fluid and placed a hand to her temple.

Lenny stepped back, tripped over a sandbag and put her hand out to stop her fall. There was a tremendous crash of shattering glass and the room went black as something sliced into her face.

The studio lights came on almost immediately and Lenny saw Gabrielle standing by the door with her hand on the switch. The blondie lay on the floor, its lens smashed. Lenny touched her face. There was a cut near her nose where a barn door had caught her. Blood trickled down her cheek.

'What have you done? Who are you?' Janus demanded of Lenny. She started to explain. 'Stop,' Janus said contemptuously. 'I don't have time to hear your long-winded explanation. Leave my set.' He unlocked the camera from the tripod, resting it on his shoulder, and turned to Harry. 'Next, I want the high hat next to the table.'

He turned away with the camera still balanced on his shoulder. Moira stepped forward dramatically and put her hand on the lens to hold him. 'Janus, stop! Someone's been hurt.'

'Now, now, everyone . . .' Lucy Peel's hands flew out to embrace the room. 'Let's all take a long, calming breath. This –' she gestured at Lenny, still standing amongst the remains of her first smashed piece of film equipment, '– is Lenny Lypchik. Our returnee.' She came over to Lenny and examined her cut cheek with soft fingers.

'It's not deep, but we'd better get you to the clinic. I'll have someone go with you. I'm sorry this had to happen on your first day back.'

'Ouch!' Moira Middlemiss yelped, clutching a foot. 'Glass!'

'Where are your shoes, Moira?' Lucy asked.

'You know I don't wear shoes.' Moira glared at Lucy and bent down to her ankle bracelets and blue-glitter toenails. Her Nikon camera bounced against her breasts. 'I think it's only a sliver.'

'Let me see.' Lucy knelt down by her student's side.

Moira partly raised her foot for the examination. She rested a hand on the supervisor's shoulder to balance herself, pressing down hard as Lucy fussed over her foot. After allowing Lucy to examine her foot for a few moments she murmured, quite casually, 'You're hurting me,' and Lucy said she was sorry and stood up, her face flushed, her lavender eyes wide.

'I can't see any glass,' she mumbled. 'I think you're fine.'

Moira raised her camera and snapped off a photo of Lucy's face.

'For my collection,' she said. She didn't bother to thank the older woman.

'The film in that camera belongs to me,' Janus said. 'It is for the purpose of stills for publicity for my film. You owe me one photograph and equivalent developing costs.'

'Should I take Lenny to the clinic?' Harry stepped close into Lenny's personal space and held out a handkerchief. 'Press this onto it.'

Lenny glanced at the hankie. It looked clean but at the very least it had spent time in his pocket with lint and God knows what else. Never trust a stranger's handkerchief; besides, he chewed his nails and there was a blood blister on the tip of one thumb.

'Thank you, no.' She stepped back.

'Is this a break then?' A bored voice came from high up a ladder. Lenny spotted Annabel Lear, blonde hair shining, a tool belt hung stylishly low on her designer army-disposal hips, her blouse exposing just enough of a deliciously flat tummy. The perfect face pouted, the delicate shoulders lifted. Nothing here of either deformity or conformity, Lenny thought. Some people just got lucky at the gene pool party.

'The scheduled break is not for one hour,' Janus announced to the room in general. He seemed to avoid addressing people directly, opting for a less personal, noticeboard type delivery.

'Do I really have to be here for the whole day?' Annabel complained. 'I'm just so not interested in being the gaffer. I have a meeting with the executive vice manager for film development tomorrow and I could be preparing my application.'

'Annabel,' Lucy sighed, 'you know we rotate through the positions, including the less exciting ones. Each job has the same amount of importance. You're part of a team.'

Annabel slid down the ladder and sashayed over to Lenny. 'Well, I'm bored, aren't I? I'm not going to pretend.' She smirked. 'At least the newbie livened things up a bit.'

'It's not funny. The barn door caught her,' Harry Tuyen said. 'She could have lost an eye.' There was a silence as the full weight of Harry's observation sank in.

Harry was standing too close to her – those hormones again. Lenny reached for a muscled shoulder and moved him back.

'Thanks, but I can take care of myself,' she said.

Annabel took out a packet of bubble-gum balls and popped one between tiny, even teeth. She peered at Lenny's cheek. 'Anyway, she already has a scar she hasn't bothered to fix, so she can't be too worried about the way she looks.' Her mobile rang. 'Hello? Oh hi, Miranda! It's my publicist,' she said, quickly stepping away from the group.

Gabrielle Danaher said to Lenny: 'I'll show you to the clinic.'

They left the studio and crossed the quadrangle together, Lenny pressing a tissue against her cut. They went out of the campus through the main gate and Gabrielle steered them left down Moor Street.

'What's the deal with Moira and Lucy?' Lenny asked.

'What do you mean?' Gabrielle sounded cautious.

'There's something going on there.'

Gabrielle looked at Lenny curiously. 'That's pretty fast work.'

'Accurate?'

'Perhaps Moira likes games. I don't get involved.' This was said with the slow precision of someone who rarely offered opinions to anyone, let alone strangers. Gabrielle's manner would have been interpreted by Lenny's mother as snooty. They walked the rest of the way in silence. Lenny made a note to take more care when speaking with Gabrielle, fearful she had already given grounds for suspicion.

The Moor Street Medical Centre was small and busy. A TV blared in the kiddies' play corner and a teenage mother and her toddlers were snuffling together in a row. A young woman blew her nose hard as Lenny and Gabrielle entered. In one corner of the room a bearded man with pinprick pupils was lolling about, a yellow drizzle running from his nostrils.

Lenny began her germ-repelling eye-blink routine. She turned back to the door. 'I'll try somewhere else.'

Gabrielle surveyed the queue. 'They take emergencies first,' she said, misinterpreting Lenny's reluctance.

Lenny held her breath as she crossed the room. She knew she mustn't touch anything. She looked at her hand in horror. It had already fingered the door knob. She hadn't been thinking. How many creatures were already migrating from her fingertips under cover of her sleeves?

A nurse entered the hutch. 'Come right through,' she said, harbouring God knows what – her apron appeared to have been borrowed from a butcher's.

Gabrielle took a magazine and sat down. Lenny entered

the examination room and found a small, dumpy woman squeezed into a white medical coat fishing remnants of chocolate eclair from her mug of tea. She licked her fingers and gestured for Lenny to sit. 'Hello, I'm Jill. Let's take a look at you.'

'Not with those hands,' Lenny said.

'Good thought.' The doctor washed her hands with soap and water and towelled them dry.

She wiped the cut with an antiseptic that etched into Lenny's face like battery acid. 'Oh, this isn't too bad. Just a couple of stitches, I think. Very superficial. Mind you, a couple of centimetres north-east and it would have been your eye.'

'No stitches,' Lenny said. 'Just a Band-aid.' Dr Jill ignored her and threaded up. 'No point bothering with anaesthetic for something that small. What on earth made you dye your hair such a dramatic black?'

'Fashion,' Lenny answered as the needle pierced her skin.

Dr Jill was a good seamstress, and was soon standing back to admire her work.

'You'll need to come back in a couple of days so I can snip them out.'

'I'll do it myself.' Lenny's gaze passed over the prescription pad on the desk.

Outside the clinic, she pressed a couple of pills onto the back of her tongue, savoured the taste and swallowed. She caught Gabrielle staring at the foil packet as she returned it to her pocket.

Lenny's pager went off and she angled the screen display out of the sun. It was a message from her service: CAP1 – Cat Alert Priority One. Now that was more like it. She had been spruiked recently by two old ladies handing out fliers on the pavement. They had opened a paging service to supplement their pensions and promised personalised service and cheaper rates without compromising on performance. Lenny already had a mobile phone and had argued that she didn't need a pager but had found herself subjected to a slick sales campaign. Flexibility, they said, was the key to growing a successful business. Allowing prospective clients access via all avenues of technology. No limits. Reach for the stars. Go for gold. They had buttered up and bullied. And she had bought a three-month package deal. Since then she had received one message intended for a Footscray butcher (she assumed) and another to deliver a regular Hawaiian pizza to an address in Kensington. But Misses Attwood and Rendell seemed to have got it right this time, bless their perfumed hearts. She turned to say goodbye to Gabrielle, but the student had disappeared.

Lenny hurried back to her office. A British Blue named Fluffy, owned by Mr and Mrs David Worthing, was missing in Carlton. The Worthings promised two hundred dollars if the cat was recovered that day.

Lenny laid out her catching tools on the desk top: hessian bag, leather gloves, catnip and assorted temptations, a pheromone-impregnated mock-up of a female rear – all in order.

As she drove out of Footscray, a bus with Councillor Thomas Walstab's face on it drew alongside. The message under the image was reassuringly fascist: 'Stamping Out The People You Want Stamped Out!'. A Timberland boot had squashed the final word. Lenny wondered if it wasn't also hovering over her head.

As she drove, Lenny recalled what she knew of the British Blue: large head and body, blue-grey, short silky coat and a placid personality were the breeding standard, although she never put much store in temperamental evaluations such as 'placid'. Cats seldom enjoyed being stuffed into a hessian bag.

At Rathdowne Street she spotted her competition and pulled over. A tall, middle-aged man was foraging in a clump of bushes near a pizza restaurant. Tim McDiamond was the second-best cat catcher in Melbourne, and right now he was cursing himself for wasting bait on a moggie. The little feral was a blur of furious angles under his gloved hand. At least he had got the colour right, Lenny smirked.

McDiamond hurried over as she wound down her window. His smooth pink face leaned into hers. He had immense, springy black hair and a heavy wedge of moustache: the Saddam Hussein of cat catching.

'Thought I'd see you here, Aaron,' he sneered. 'Two hundred bucks brings everyone out of the woodwork. How about we work this one together and split the fee?'

'Piss off.' Lenny got out of the car.

'I heard about your dad on the grapevine. I'd like to express my condolences, because my mum died a couple of years back. Shocking thing when you lose a parent. I know just what you're going through and if there's anything I can do –'

'There is, actually: mind your own business.'

They glared at each other. Lenny stepped away from him, pulled miniature binoculars out of her bag and directed them towards drains, trees, recycle bins – anywhere small enough for a cat to hide.

'Owner's house is just up the road,' McDiamond offered sulkily. 'I spoke to them – well, the wife. Big terrace with a Mercedes outside. He's an MD, she's a CPA. No kids. I reckon we could push the money up if you want to work it together.'

Lenny strode away from him.

British Blues were grey and in a cement world it made

them difficult to spot. The first thing you learned in the cat catching line is that you can't expect to find the client immediately; it can take all day. You have to ask questions, make a proper search and be patient.

So it came as quite a surprise when Lenny glanced across the street to find a British Blue preening next to a letterbox. She crossed the road, moving in slow motion, hessian bag and mesh gloves at the ready.

Approach slowly, she reminded herself, look out for the jump. Cats could spring six times their own body length. She was almost there, almost had her hands on it, when two small boys came out of a house shrieking at each other with skateboards under their arms. The cat was history.

'Dickheads!' Lenny glared at the boys.

'Skank!' They clattered away.

Lenny scanned the area, but the British Blue was gone. Then Tim McDiamond appeared around the corner from a trattoria carrying a twitching, fully occupied bag. He was grinning even before he saw her.

'Straight into my arms,' he cackled. 'Good work, Aaron.' He shook the bag, making the cat inside scream. 'Pedigrees are always the nastiest, aren't they? Spoiled rotten. Anyhow, I'm off to collect two biggies. Ta-ta!'

Lenny headed back to the shopping mall in a dire mood. There was nothing more day-spoiling than being thwarted by a rival cat catcher. A few incidents like this and her reputation would be in tatters.

The *Herald Sun* had been shoved through the mail slot. She frowned: Councillor Walstab was on page two, saying that veterinarians, pet shops and the dog and cat *retrieval* industry should be placed under local government authority to prevent 'certain disreputable types from taking advantage of our pet owning community.' The nerve of this guy! She could really see herself in a green council uniform, doffing a cutesy council cap and pulling a pay cheque from City Hall.

Anastasia's accordion began bleating through the wall. If I Had a Hammer. At maximum volume. Over and over again.

'Hey!' Lenny hammered a fist against the dividing wall. 'Shut that shit up!' After a couple of Russian expletives, the tune resumed at a softer volume. It seemed business was slow all over.

Lenny sighed and settled down to her ritual of office cleaning. It was the only thing guaranteed to bring her out of a mood.

Two hours later, high (but not high enough) on disinfectant fumes, she reached down to her desk drawer and pulled out a ravaged box of Tylenol. When she ground them up in her mouth the taste was savagely bitter, but she liked it. She considered an aspirin chaser but knew that aspirin could increase the liver toxicity of Tylenol. It paid to practise responsible medicine.

CHAPTER 8

Bill Hunter Saves the Day

Lenny had a script tutorial with Kenneth Drage at Aquinas the next morning. The manila folder she carried marked 'Second Draft' held a rough story she had made up about a woman who murdered her grandmother, chopped her up with an axe, dissolved her in acid and took the lot to the tip. It had taken her ten minutes.

When she parked her car she realised she was early and filled in half an hour wandering down Brunswick Street. Which coffee shop to choose? Bar Open was a shrine to orange vinyl and featured pictures of various royal families and the Kennedys – imperial chic – but it was closed. Vertigo had enormous pieces of cake and dizzying, spiral-metal fixtures. It was also closed. Mario's was open, but full. Too many beautiful people crowding its tables both inside and on the pavement. Eyes which tried hard to disguise their curiosity lifted briefly as she walked by. Was she that actress from –? She was not. The eyes fell again.

Lenny decided on her old favourite, The Black Cat. She had a latte surrounded by posters of bullfights and jazz albums, then walked back to Aquinas.

She jogged up the stairs to the second floor library. The large windows opened out onto the quadrangle to let in fresh air. Both fire doors were open and students wandered in and out. Others sat at the desks examining texts or in front of video monitors wearing headsets.

Lenny opened the door at the far end of the library and entered the tower. Compared to the main library, the Robert Heywood Memorial Library was tiny and outdated. The oak table in the centre of the room was distressed with gouges and graffiti, and the mismatched wooden chairs were an afterthought, their surfaces dusty. The window – small and dirty – looked down onto the quadrangle. Lenny continued up a spiral staircase to the next floor. There was a small vestibule outside Kenneth's office where students waited their turn to enter.

As it happened, Kenneth was behind in his schedule, so although Lenny was five minutes late, she found Moira Middlemiss still waiting. Lucy Peel was sitting next to her and their heads were close together. Moira was smiling. Lucy was talking and she looked agitated. She sprang up at Lenny's approach and nodded before disappearing down the staircase.

'Lucy Peel,' Moira smirked after her. 'She's a sad case.'

'Really?' Lenny tried to sound disinterested. This close, Moira's body was an alarming mixture of incense and sweat.

'She's married – I mean just for a start that's a strike against her. It's so unnecessary to conform to society's expectations, isn't it? That piece of paper has no meaning. And she took his name, you know! *Mrs John Peel*. If I was her I'd at least go around calling him my partner, not my *husband*. My partner would never expect me to do that. We have a really open relationship. He's a musician. Have you heard of The Sebastian Mott Band?'

Lenny had not, but worked on an expression that registered enthusiastic uncertainty.

'They're in *Who's Who in Australian Rock*. Sebastian, my partner, has a separate listing under his own name.' Moira smiled and examined today's dark purple nail polish, fanning out her hand for Lenny's benefit. 'They're gigging this week, if you're interested.'

'Oh, well, I –'

'Lucy and Emily had a relationship, you know,' Moira confided. 'One-sided in terms of feeling, of course. Lucy handled it badly. I mean, she let herself become filled with dark energy when it ended. I could have told her from the start she was heading into a dragon's lair. Emily didn't know how to love. Her spirit was closed. She had an MBA, you know, that's what did it. The business world is completely aspiritual. Emily never stopped thinking about how to get what she wanted, no matter what she did to everyone else. Annabel is worse. Far worse, spiritually. I can't even repeat what people are saying about her.' Moira leaned into Lenny's personal space. Apparently she could repeat it. 'They say she's buying her career with the hairy purse.' She snapped erect. 'Hi, Annabel!'

Annabel Lear's cover-girl face was blank as she appeared at the top of the staircase. Had she heard, Lenny wondered. Annabel went to a slotted box near the office door and dropped an envelope into it, slender arms swinging, light as a feather in her fluorescent Fubu sneakers.

'Hi.' There was nothing in her voice to indicate she had heard Moira's slander.

'What are you up to?' Moira said, looking at the box.

'I'm too busy to see Kenneth today. He'll have to just jot a few comments on my latest draft. I'm having lunch with my agent at Southbank, then I've got a development meeting with the head of Cinemedia. Catch ya!'

Annabel's golden head turned down the stairs as Moira continued to run a New Age blowtorch over her character.

'She's trying to fuck her way into Cinemedia. I couldn't live like that. My partner and I are totally into each other. I mean sexually, philosophically, spiritually – you have to be, don't you?' Lenny nodded. 'Although sexually is the most important. We always say if the sex is gone then the relationship is over, right? My last partner was the poet Adam Brain. You've probably heard of him. He did performance art down in St Kilda and he was on ABC TV too. I don't see him much now, though. He's really jealous of my new relationship. Guys always are, aren't they? They can't let go. He's still in love with me even after all this time. When I read his interviews I can still see it. It's subtle, but it's there.'

'Kenneth is in, isn't he?' Lenny took advantage of the fact that Moira had to stop for air.

Turquoise rings wafted. 'Yes, but I'm next. He's way behind. His tutorials are compulsory. No one would attend them if they weren't. We can fail the whole course unless he OKs our attendance sheets. Talk about delusions of grandeur. And I'm starting my shoot tomorrow! I've got a great script and I'm a hundred percent locked into it. I won't be making any changes so why waste my time here? But he insisted I still come for my final session. He's still trying to influence me to go against my impulses. But he has nothing to offer. Believe me, I've got his number. Gauloise?' Moira held out a crushed packet.

Lenny shook her head.

'Who's in there now?' she persisted.

'Harry.' Moira held out her left hand to show a large silver ring in the shape of a mermaid, long hair winding back around the finger. 'Isn't this beautiful? I got it at a market in Daylesford last week. I spend a lot of time up there because I hate the city. My family live in Thornbury now, but I grew up near Geelong so I'm used to a more peaceful atmosphere. I'm a Libran, freedom-loving. It's a challenge with my imbalance, of course. When I was a child it was even more pronounced. There were all these wattle trees near my school. Well, I just loved them. The gorgeous soft yellow. The fragrance. I just had to press myself against them, drink them in. I'd end up in hospital, of course. Sensory overload, they said. But we Librans have to get our fix of mother earth every week or we go crazy.' Moira laughed at the wonder that was herself.

Lenny said: 'I was hoping to take out some equipment and do some tests at home this week, but Pluckrose says it's not on. There's an equipment shortage.'

'Yeah. Someone's nicking it. We lost a Bolex in June. Then a Nagra and a shotgun mic. Ray had a fit. And we've had heaps of stuff nicked off the trim bins and out of the lockers. Someone took a pile of film cans from Harry's locker just last month. He freaked! And someone trashed one of the film edit suites. I've got my theories about who. What you know at this school means everything. It's the power source. What you know, what you want and how to get it.'

'I suppose people tell you things all the time.'

'I'm accessible to everyone. I can adapt my personality to suit everyone's level. You probably don't even know, but I'm doing it with you, right now. It's a gift, but it's a blight too. People try to get close to me and I want to say "Stop! I don't have enough energy for you all!" I was reading this book about the Greek oracle at Delphi and I thought, I know exactly how that woman felt. But the thing is that no matter how many demands people put on me, I cope really well. I reach into myself and find exactly the amount of energy I need. It's from meditation. You should try meditation, Lenny. Someone like you would really benefit from it. I'm thinking of teaching. Just small groups. Sharing.

Listening to people's thoughts – you know what I mean?'

'I –'

'It's funny, but a lot of people think my documentary could start a new trend. Gabrielle's going to edit for me. She asked me if she could. I said fine. Editing's just not creative enough for me. It's too synthetic. I've got to be with people when it happens, making it happen. I've got some footage to show Kenneth today, although he's such an old luvvie, it'll be beyond him. Lots of hand-held. What are you into this year, Lenny?'

'–'

'Did I tell you my partner's in my documentary? He's been a joy to work with. So aware. I knew as soon as I met him that his soul was developed, like mine.' Moira chuckled, swathed in Gauloise rings. 'For me, people are transparent. I've always had a talent for reading people, seeing right into them.' She smiled, paused.

Sometimes people fish for compliments so hard that there is no human way to avoid supplying them. 'I wish I was like you,' Lenny said as sincerely as possible. Waves of nausea rushed through her body, but Moira's smile turned wistful at the corners. She took a deep breath and nodded.

'It's funny you should say that, because a lot of people do. I think the staff here finally appreciate what I'm trying to achieve. Lucy and Ray – even Kenneth is just starting to get me.' She paused to blow a sophisticated line of smoke across Lenny's face. 'And Lucy told me she's under my spell . . .' The cigarette halted between chest and mouth. 'That makes me sound like a witch!' Moira's delight at this new incarnation of herself was palpable. 'Well, I *am* really! I can always get people to do what I want.'

The door opened. Harry appeared in the frame. He said, facing back into the room: 'Yeah. All right, Kenneth, I'll consider it. But it's got to be as I see it. I've got my own instincts, OK? My own way of doing things.'

'He's such a typical male,' Moira said as Harry grinned at them and bounded down the stairs. 'It's all ego with men, isn't it? Me, me, me.'

Kenneth came to the doorway and peered at them. 'Lenny?' he smiled. 'I thought so. You may as well run along. I'll have to see you later in the week. I'm afraid I've let myself get behind and Moira always needs a lot of help.'

Moira gave him a frosty stare. 'Kenneth, I've got an appointment with my aromatherapist in an hour.' She stepped into the office and Kenneth followed.

Lenny prepared the first part of her plan to identify the Aquinas thief. She had been assigned a locker. Inside the locker, pushed right to the back, she placed a cardboard box, and inside that she carefully positioned one of her favourite mechanical devices: a giant rat trap. Someone in Aquinas had sticky fingers. If they tried to steal anything belonging to Lenny Lypchik, they'd have broken fingers. The padlock she used to seal the locker was an enticement to attempt theft. It was tiny and cheap, and looked like you could snap it off between thumb and finger.

She then spent half an hour sitting outside in the quadrangle reading the newspaper, smoking and thinking about Emily Cunningham's death. Could it possibly have anything to do with the thefts?

Harry Tuyen and Gabrielle Danaher came across the quadrangle. Harry smiled at her. 'We've got to get together and have a serious talk about the sort of films you're interested in making.' He put out a hand and touched Lenny's shoulder playfully. 'I want to know all about you. But not now. Got to go.' He raced towards the student canteen, shirt-tail flapping down under his loose sweater.

'He uses dashing off as a punctuation mark,' Gabrielle said.

'Does Moira always talk about her boyfriend in such depth?' Lenny chain-lit a Marlboro.

Gabrielle ignored the question. 'I got out your second year film,' she said. Lenny wondered if her cover was blown already. It was, by anyone's standards, a bad effort and someone with Gabrielle's talent must have found it excruciating.

'I had a disappointing year,' she hedged.

'This year is the only one that counts. They're showing some films now, in the screening room.' It was by way of an invitation. Lenny accepted, and the two made their way to the curtained room. They sat together in the front row.

Pluckrose was the projectionist. He went about the task with brisk competence in his white lab coat, twisting the heavy steel reels together, threading the film though its labyrinthine path. Aquinas's History of Cinema film sessions were non-compulsory and open to attendance by any of the students from first to third year. Gabrielle and Lenny were eventually joined by Janus Onyszkiewicz and four first years. The afternoon's program was Jane Campion's *Sweetie* and Maurice Murphy's *Exchange Lifeguards*. Lenny, who had seen neither before, found *Sweetie* well performed but depressing, an uncomfortably familiar story about how family life can imprison and control. *Exchange Lifeguards* was, on the other hand, not at all disturbing emotionally, but horrifying in terms of its art. It was a sex and surf romp with dog fart jokes, Julian McMahon and –

'Elliott Gould . . .' Lenny murmured in dismay at his appearance. She had noticed during her recent study of Australian films a peculiar tendency for the casting of overseas stars where Australian actors would have been more appropriate. Scripts were stretched and pummelled to

94

allow for the presence of the international drawcard or, much worse, the overseas performer tried an Australian accent. In Lenny's opinion it never worked. She didn't like Meryl Streep in *Evil Angels*, she didn't like Kirk Douglas in *The Man From Snowy River*, she didn't like Brian Dennehy in *The Man From Snowy River II* and she especially didn't like Tom Selleck and Laura San Giacomo in *Quigley Down Under*.

Kenneth arrived at the end of the double feature to comment on the two films and take questions. He answered the students' questions with wit and humour and had a few questions of his own for them, leading them away from specifics into a general discussion of the Australian film industry. He squinted at Lenny in her front row seat. She guessed his quandary: exclude her from questioning altogether and risk blowing her cover; ask her a question she wasn't ready for and also risk blowing her cover. He went as wide as possible.

'Lenny, in your view what has been the most important feature of Australian film in the last twenty-five years?'

She hesitated. A long-winded pontification? A succinct assessment quoted verbatim from the books she had read? She ran through titles, directors and settled finally on actors. One actor in particular stood out; the ubiquitous presence in Australian film that never failed to impress. She took a deep breath.

'Bill Hunter.'

Everyone turned to look at her appreciatively. Kenneth smiled and nodded. Even Gabrielle murmured 'interesting', and Lenny knew she had passed the first test.

CHAPTER 9

Director's Cut

At her flat early the next morning Lenny watched as Cleo Aaron sniffed around her basket at her large collection of toys. Disdaining them, she settled on a balled-up yellow post-it note and writhed on her blanket, rending the paper with her claws. Her slanted eye gleamed at Lenny. Was she happy, Lenny wondered. Could a cat be happy? She reached down a hand and stroked her pet. The cat purred deeply and arched its neck up into her hand, then turned swiftly and struck deep with her teeth. Lenny pulled free. Petting aggression: no one understood it. A cat appeared to want affection and then as quickly rejected it, attacked its owner, only to return again minutes later for more. She remembered Freud's conclusion: 'The neurotic repeats instead of remembering.' He should have been a vet.

The morning news was doing a piece on recent drink-driving fatalities in and around Melbourne. Hermione Arnfeldt, former NFC director and Aquinas school board member, featured prominently. Her death had galvanised the state government and the police. Apparently Melbourne's streets were going to face an increase in the number of booze buses.

She gazed out her window and saw Sally and Mel off to university with matching backpacks, pink helmets and happy smiles. Ah, young love. The phone rang.

'Lenny?' Why did her mother always make it a question? As though there was ever anyone else in Lenny's apartment.

'Yes.' Cleo brushed against her legs and she allowed the cat a small caress on the head. It mewed and pounced back onto its post-it. 'What is it?' Her mother could hold a pause for ten minutes.

'I dreamt about Daddy.'

'Will you not keep calling him that. I never called him Daddy in my life.'

'When you were little –'

'So little that I can't remember so it doesn't count.'

'It does.'

'It does bloody not.'

'Lenny, we're both grieving.'

'I'm not.' She tried to make a fist with her left hand. The damaged nerves refused. 'And the reason for this call?'

'I . . .' Another long pause. 'Nothing.'

'Then I'll hang up. Bye.'

'Why do you always turn on me?' Her mother wept. 'I have to tell you something important.'

'What?'

'Come over tonight for tea and I'll tell you.'

'No.'

'Please. Lenny, I need you. Please . . .' A smugness behind the wheedling. Perhaps there was something there.

'All right.' Lenny put the phone down. Cleo jumped up onto her lap and she stroked the cat gently then watched as a left upper feline incisor ground deep into her thumb. Cats adjust their grip on small prey until they find the tiny depression at the base of the neck. Cleo was using Lenny's thumb to practise the spine-severing bite. In agony, she didn't make a sound. Sometimes you had to show the little shits you could take it.

'Glide! Glide! Stay up on the balls of your feet!' Whack! Whack! Thunk! The *shinai* hit Lenny's *do* and she crashed to the floorboards. Her thumb was still throbbing, and it was only 7 am. Too early to be taking a beating.

Dr Sakuno pulled off his *men*, a heavy helmet with a metal grille to protect the face. The white bandanna tied around his brow had slipped and he pushed it up. His slender face was damp with sweat, cheeks flushed. He reached down to pull Lenny up. It was the third time this morning he had sent her sprawling.

'You are sloppy. You better stop thinking so much or I'll defeat you every time.'

He was tetchier than usual and there were shadows under his eyes. The sleepless nights of the new father, Lenny supposed. A month ago she had spotted him in traffic with his wife and family and been amazed to see a baby capsule in the back seat of his car. He hadn't mentioned it, of course.

Dr Sakuno had two children already – sixteen-year-old Kumiko and fourteen-year-old Yoshihiro. He had often gloated to her about how the Japanese rationed themselves to two. Two was affordable in the current economic climate; two meant the right amount of attention to be spent on 'family activities'; two was the same as everyone else in Japan. But it seemed Mrs Sakuno had gone against the pack. By accident or design, Lenny wondered. She had congratulated Dr Sakuno briefly at their next session. His icy 'thank you' curtailed further conversation on the subject.

They practised in the city gym whenever he could be bothered to book it, or when she was desperate for the contact. He said that after three years of treatment she should be ready to move on – but if she wanted to continue to throw good money after bad, who was he to stop her? Lenny had tried to imagine a time when she would end their sessions, a time when she would discuss her problems and feelings with a family member or friend. But they would give her sympathy and affection, and what could she do with that? Dr Sakuno gave her indifference and honesty. He was her lifeline.

'Raise your *shinai*. *Gambare!*'

Whack. Whack. Parry. Whack. Crack! The *bogu* covered her body in the four legal attack zones: head, wrist, torso and throat. Dr Sakuno hit her in all four areas before he declared them done for the day. Lenny bowed, defeated and angry. And aware that she shouldn't be. Part of her kendo training was to overcome her emotions, to control the situation.

The first time they'd met again after her father's death, she had said 'give me anything that will help'. She was after drugs and he gave her kendo – literally, 'the way of the sword'. Here was a sport where conscious thought was suppressed and winning was considered not as important as achieving a mental, spiritual and physical calm. Lenny suspected Dr Sakuno would prefer all his patients to go the kendo route. It was a very Zen solution: action rather than discussion.

She was still a beginner and still practising with the *shinai*, a long stick made of four pieces of bamboo fitted and held together by a leather handle. A string stretching from the handle to the tip of the stick represented the cutting edge of the sword. Strictly speaking, she was supposed to improve herself through the sword, not actually study swordplay itself. Zen was riddled with these tantalising paradoxes, cooked up by a sect that knew enough to bamboozle its wealthy patrons with esoteric mysticism: 'What is the sound of one hand clapping?' Hakuin the priest asked nearly three hundred years ago. The answer is irrelevant, the question itself so undeniably cool that the *koan* functions as an advertising jingle for Zen – once heard, never forgotten.

All very well, but Lenny was eager to advance to *ken-jutsu*. *Kenjutsu* students learned techniques of war and used a *bokken*, a kind of wooden sword, or even a *katana*, a steel sword, to reproduce the slicing effect of true blade-work. It was more the kind of thing she was after.

'You are too nervous with your left arm. The skin must be toughened by now, so forget about it,' Dr Sakuno commented. He had been with her in the hospital a year and a half ago when the nurse removed the stitches. Michael Dorling's original scar had been neat and surgical. The one left by Vivian Talbott's vicious and repeated stabbing was a ridged web of ugly red tissue that meant she would wear long-sleeved tops for the rest of her life. 'Revolting,' Dr Sakuno had said.

'You're not still afraid, are you?' he asked.

'No,' Lenny lied.

Dr Sakuno pulled off his *men* and tossed it onto the floor. Lenny did the same. The hall was air-conditioned but they were both sweating heavily. Lenny flopped onto a bench. There was always a post-practice analysis. Actually, a chance for him to criticise everything she had done during the practice and then draw parallels with the rest of her life. Depending on his assessment of her 'current weakness of character', the conversation part of their session ran any-where from five to thirty minutes.

'You're not going to get better in this frame of mind. You have no resolution, no endurance.'

'I'm trying.'

'Australians always say they are trying, as though trying and doing are the same.' Wipe on, wipe off, Lenny thought sourly. 'As with most foreigners, you're studying kendo with the wrong goal.' Lenny didn't respond. It was considered rude to interrupt your *sensei* and unthinkable to challenge him; although, occasionally, there was a kind of Zen idiot savant who could get away with it.

Lenny liked the story of one of Hakuin's first disciples, a fifteen-year-old girl named Satsu who asked him to elucidate a difficult point in the Lotus Sutra. As the sage's lips opened to speak, she said 'Thank you,' and left him with his mouth hanging open.

'You can never be Japanese.' Lenny's contemporary sage interrupted her reverie. 'Never! In Japan there are foreigners who try to become more Japanese than we Japanese ourselves. They learn how to wear a kimono, how to perform the *sado*, the tea ceremony, even how to write *kanji*. To them we say "Oh, how wonderful you are!" But in truth we think it is sad. Only the Japanese are Japanese.'

Dr Sakuno reached out and squeezed Lenny's upper arm muscle. 'Too slender.' His laser eyes burned through her. 'I cannot be responsible for a person who continues to fill her body with medication when she has sworn to stop. This is a sad psychological dependence! I inform you that you are going to kill yourself if you do not cease. What more do you expect me to do?'

It was not, Lenny thought, a good time to confess she had bumped up her drugs from OTC to prescription level.

'You think that because your father is dead you have an excuse for this behaviour?' He would not let her evade.

'No.' Lenny closed her eyes. She hadn't eaten breakfast and her head buzzed. 'Stop picking on me.'

'*Yumei sakai o koto ni shimashita ga,*' he said and she understood the meaning because he had said it to her many times in the last year. *Your father has crossed from this world into the next.*

'Kendo is not about self-defence. You're never going to be walking down a dangerous street with your *shinai* under your arm. Stop thinking about it as hitting out. Your father is six feet under. It must be faced: face it.'

'*Hai, sensei*,' Lenny sighed. Buddha said pain was caused by attachment to circumstances and things that were impermanent, and that to rid oneself of the attachment was to rid oneself of pain. But she *had* faced it. She had done everything she could to break the attachment. Ted Aaron was dead. She would never see him or hear from him again.

'Have you developed a friend?' Since her father's death Dr Sakuno had harped long and hard on the lack of friends in Lenny's life.

'No.'

'You run the risk of being *otaku*.' *Otaku*: an obsessive, a person who is alone in life because they want no friends – or because no one wants to be their friend. Computer *otaku*, TV *otaku*, video game *otaku*. A freak who prefers to stay in their room on the weekend absorbed in their sick hobby rather than go out with a group of thirty like-minded beings on a six-hour bus tour with pre-paid lunch stop. An *otaku* was a loner. A loser.

'I can't make friends.' This was as true now as it had been her entire life. She was *neko otaku*. Cat freak.

'Try. Shower.' Sakuno dismissed her. The session was over.

Lenny stayed under the water for a long time. As she dried herself, she realised Dr Sakuno had said nothing about her black hair.

On the way to Aquinas she popped in at the Victoria Parade pharmacy again. Margie's mouth dropped open.

'What?' Lenny asked.

'Your hair!'

Tawny Owl Aaron thought on her feet. 'Do you like it? All the girls went crazy for piercing and black hair. I think we were camped over an old witch's coven or something. I let them make me over. I'm too soft with those kids –'

'Oh . . .' Margie chewed her lip. 'I thought your blonde hair was nice. So did you have a good time?'

'Huh?' Lenny's eyes were roving over the shelves behind the girl. So many bottles, so little time. 'Oh! No, we had casualties, lots of casualties. One girl was abseiling and slid down the rope: lost all the skin on both hands. We had a broken arm – pony trampling – and the littlest girl of them all fell into a nettle patch. There's a board of review next week and I'll be lucky to keep my position.'

'That's terrible!' Margie gasped.

Lenny leaned across the counter and stared into Margie's eyes. 'That's right, it is. But thanks to you I had all the painkillers I needed. If I'd taken a capsule less, little Rowena would have suffered the agonies of hell after writhing in those damn nettles like she did. When I close my eyes I can still hear her screams.' Lenny placed a prescription for Valium on the counter, watching the girl's eyes. There was no reaction. She suspected Margie didn't have a clue about the family business. A few minutes passed and the script was filled without a word from Dad, who was turning out to be more of a misanthrope than Lenny. She couldn't believe her luck.

Ten minutes later, the Valium kicking in nicely, she was on the Aquinas campus. She went up to the first floor to check her locker. Everything was present and untampered with. The rat trap remained unsprung.

In the TV studio Moira Middlemiss was preparing for her major production shoot, laying out costumes in the green room. It was still early and, according to Lenny's copy of the shooting schedule, the crew weren't required for another hour, but she had wanted to come early, wanted a chance to question Moira rather than be an overwhelmed listener. Moira knew something, bragged about knowing something. Perhaps today she would tell what she knew.

'We're not starting until ten,' Moira told her impatiently. 'Didn't you read the call sheet?' She took a packet of photos from the make-up table. 'Look at these and tell me which is the most intimidating.'

Lenny accepted the photos and skimmed through them. She was perusing a series of breast cancers. Not the nicest thing she had ever seen, but very far from the worst.

'This one.' She handed them back. Moira seemed disappointed at Lenny's coolness. She foraged in her floppy shoulder bag for her cigarettes, pulled out a crushed packet and kicked open the door that led to the car park. A refreshing gust of air came into the stuffy room which smelled of old costumes and dust. 'I'm going to project the cancers on the wall behind the band. I could be more graphic, but with TV as a possible market I'm self-censoring.'

Lenny followed her into the studio. Moira looked contentedly around the set, which had been designed to resemble a seedy inner city pub. There was a pinball machine pushed up against a black curtain and a couple of drinking posts complete with glasses.

Aluminium equipment cases lay in a heap along with lights, cables, stands and reflector boards. Lenny opened the camera case and examined the contents. 'This Arri is pretty bashed up,' she said, picking up the German camera.

'The good one, the SR, got stolen. That's the bad one. It's too noisy no matter how many times Pluckrose looks at it. I mean, the good one was hopeless too, but not as bad. It's a challenge to rise above the equipment we're given, but that's my job as an artist, sweetie.'

'I suppose no one knows who's stealing the stuff,' Lenny observed. 'Not even you.'

Moira seemed about to say something, then turned away to place Victoria Bitter mats under the beer glasses. 'I'm doing a cameo in my film,' she reverted to her favourite topic. 'I do one in all my films. I could have been an actor. I auditioned for NIDA, but I turned them down.' Her eyes turned dreamy. 'Lucy said she can get my film shown on the ABC. Isn't that awesome?'

'I heard Emily was trying to get her work on at the ABC too,' Lenny lied.

'Fat chance,' Moira sneered. 'All right, she had money to shoot anything she wanted. Emily was loaded. She won the prize for best video in first year and best film in second year. Have you seen her films? They're passable. But how can you explain her winning two prizes in a row? The same way she got into the school in the first place: Daddy's money. You know he's that Cunningham Hardware guy? Equal opportunity access at Aquinas. Hah! She was pressuring Kenneth this year too, trying to get the Silver Shutter. Fortunately Kenneth isn't the sort who is persuaded by money. I think people will be surprised when the Shutter's announced this year.'

'Why? Who do you think he will choose?'

'At the moment, everyone thinks it'll be Gabrielle. You know, I'm tired of everybody going on about Gabrielle. Yeah, her work is creative. The talent's there. But there are other people in this course who are equally – if not more – talented.'

'Did anyone borrow money from Emily?' Someone desperate to pay back a loan might steal expensive equipment. She had to find out who needed the money most.

'Everyone borrowed from Emily, just about – Gabrielle, for sure.' Moira was coy. 'Look, just between you and me, you've probably guessed anyway – it's Gabrielle.'

'Sorry?'

'Stealing the equipment.'

'Why do you say that?'

'I told you, people are transparent to me. Like glass, really.'

'You saw her taking something?'

'I didn't need to. Believe me, Gabrielle is capable of anything. Do you know she's dealing?'

'Dealing what?'

'Speed, ecstasy, you name it. She even has her own pill called pink dolphins. She didn't tell you about that, I bet. Wouldn't want to ruin her chances as Kenneth's pet.'

'I see.' Lenny wondered if this was just one of Moira's psychic insights. 'Did you borrow money from Emily?'

Moira tensed. 'Three hundred. But she didn't want it back. It was a drop in the ocean to her. Has anyone mentioned that she had a phobia about her hand? She was always hiding it away as though no one would notice. It just drew attention to it.'

'Her hand?'

'Just the thumb really.' Moira held up her own thumb to demonstrate. 'It was deformed. All red and the skin was hard and wrinkled. It looked like a crab leg. I would have had it cut off if it was me.'

Moira picked up an envelope from a chair and removed an eight by ten glossy of a boy who resembled a handsome, starved rat. 'This is Sebastian, my partner,' she said, her eyes flickering over the image. 'Isn't he gorgeous? I'm so honoured he's doing this film. He's so busy. He's a theatre actor as well as a musician, you know. Did you see him in *Coriolanus* last year? He was totally transparent and incredibly complex at the same time. I could use you in my film,' Moira made a rectangular shape with her two hands and used it to frame Lenny's face. 'You have a ...' She hesitated. It was difficult to sum up Lenny's egg head and crooked teeth cinematically. '... a natural humanity.'

'You're too kind,' Lenny rejoined.

Moira shrugged. 'I just need ugly heads.'

Sebastian Mott gyrated across the mock stage, swung around in a wide arc, Gibson guitar swishing dangerously close to the camera lens. Music was cyclical and while techno, the frenetic disco of the nineties, was still boss, four-piece garage bands with thrashing guitars were making a comeback. Lots of screaming, sex, speed and sweat. Lenny had never really gotten into the music scene. Once, years ago, she and Danny Hoyle had gone to see a band after a late shift. She had caught a glimpse of the microphone post performance. It was encrusted with spit, lipstick and food particles, one of the most disgusting things she had ever seen.

Sebastian Mott and The Sebastian Mott Band were trendy of clothes and dreadlocked of hair. Every modish prop – pieces of bone and metal through nose and lip, tribal tattoos, enormous sneakers – had been enlisted to enfranchise a small amount of talent with a large amount of energy.

'I know I can't cook you, so I'll fuck you!' Sebastian screamed into the mic. Damien Walters, the first year monitoring sound levels, winced and shook his head over the mixing desk.

'Cut!' Moira stepped forward. She held a light meter in front of Sebastian's face. 'Janus, did you get the framing exactly how I told you?'

Janus's voice was thick with scorn. 'Exactly as you said.

It will not cut with the previous shot, but that is your choice.'

'We should probably go again for sound,' Damien Walters offered quietly. 'The levels were a bit high.'

Moira's raised hand silenced him as she turned to her partner. 'That was fantastic, Sebastian. Your face was so . . .' she paused as Sebastian moved forward to soak up the compliments. 'I saw Kundalini rising up your spine. Let's do the close-up and then we'll do scene fourteen. Where's continuity?'

'That's you,' said Kenneth Drage, materialising at Lenny's side. He and Ray had stopped by to watch the proceedings. Ray remained at the door, slightly distant from this, the creative side of the business.

Lenny stepped forward with her Polaroid camera. What to record, she wondered. She had been continuity for one day on the David O. Lincoln Academy shoot and knew that it meant wandering around with the camera, taking Polaroids and making notes to ensure everything looked the same from shot to shot. Her flash went off in Sebastian's face.

'I want a copy of that,' he said, without bothering to look at her. 'For my portfolio.'

'Have this.' Lenny handed the photo over.

'Don't you need it?'

'I could never forget how you look right now,' she buttered smoothly. From what she had seen so far, Moira's po-faced rockumentary about the ups and downs of a band on the edge of commercial success could do with some mis-matched continuity just to liven it up.

'Show me what I'm doing on the playback!' Sebastian commanded, and Moira complied. They stood before the monitor watching a mini Sebastian pout and wiggle like a maggot on a barbecue plate.

'The levels are just how we want them,' Moira said to Damien on the sound console. 'We're aiming for raw passion.'

'Yeah, I get that.' Damien was a nice boy, keen, eager to help, genuinely enthusiastic for the project. 'That's wicked. But I think if you –'

Sebastian was whispering something to Moira. 'Twenty-minute break, everyone,' she shouted. 'And clear the set. *Now!*' She turned to face the lecturers standing near the studio door. 'Everyone, please.'

Ray glared back at her, clearly irritated at being forced from a facility she technically controlled. Kenneth wore his usual bemused expression. Only Lucy Peel, who had watched the proceedings quietly up to this point, stepped from the shadows to protest.

'Is a break really necessary, Moira?' she asked in a quiet voice. 'You've got a lot of shots to cover.'

'Sebastian wants to go through the song again. He doesn't feel comfortable rehearsing with what he perceives as non-sympathetic elements standing around. I need *all* of you outside. That includes you, Lucy.'

There was an audible gasp from the rest of the crew. All eyes were on the third year supervisor. Now we'll see the real Lucy Peel, thought Lenny. The worm will surely turn. But to her surprise, Lucy turned quietly and left the studio.

'Well, Cate, I'm sure we both have things to do,' Kenneth said before the principal could explode. He put a diplomatic hand on her back and shepherded her out.

'Gabrielle!' Moira called, without looking to see if she was there. Gabrielle went to her side and they walked away from the others. Lenny heard Moira say 'Samantha' before they were out of earshot. Moira was smiling. She couldn't see Gabrielle's face.

Lenny joined the rest of the crew on the lawn outside,

watched as Gabrielle came out of the studio into the quadrangle, closed the door behind her and disappeared down the tunnel that led to the back gate and car park. The sound recordist, Damien, decided he needed a cup of coffee and headed for the canteen. Annabel Lear produced her mobile phone.

'No one is to talk to me,' she said, nibbling on a hot pink lower lip. 'I'm working. I don't get breaks.' She was performing herself brilliantly today, as always, and a revue of knowing laughs and screen culture gossip was soon falling into the phone's mouthpiece. Chatting, flirting and generally networking, Annabel wandered across the quadrangle and disappeared into the canteen.

'She has her second year film entered in a festival in San Francisco,' Janus said with genuine admiration. 'Her current lover is Marcus Grant. He won the best short film at the Australian Film Industry awards this year and has just received funding for his first feature, title to be announced.' He glanced at his watch. 'I will be in the library when we are required again. Someone will call for me.' He went into the main building.

Pluckrose came out of the storeroom in his lab coat, carrying a box of small lights. He studied them and sniffed. 'Hard at it, film students? Geniuses at rest, perhaps?'

'Must be tough being the janitor,' said Harry Tuyen lazily, eyes closed and lying on his back. Lenny waited for Pluckrose to rise to the bait, but he didn't. He stared at Harry for a long moment then shook his head and walked towards the main staircase.

Lenny jumped. Harry was caressing her arm. *Touching* her. It took all her self-control not to break his neck. Undercover, I'm undercover, she reminded herself.

Harry chuckled. 'What sort of person are you, Lenny?' He sucked his index finger in what she supposed he imagined was a sensual gesture, and stroked it across her wrist. Undercover be buggered.

'Piss off,' she said. Harry grinned at the encouragement.

Students from Design and Animation hurried across the quadrangle. Sardines, the school moggie, raced by with a limp mouse clamped in its jaws.

'I can't wait to graduate,' Harry said. 'I've got a few contacts already. People who recognise the sort of films I make, you know. High quality action. Kenneth's had a squiz at the stuff I've done so far this year and he says just the soundtrack is enough to let him know it's my usual stuff. Old Ken's always trying to get me to layer in the thematic shit,' he laughed. 'And lose my audience completely, right? Everyone knows it's all about how things look. No one gives a shit about what's underneath. Sometimes it's better if nothing's underneath – makes things easier.'

'What do you think of the staff?' Lenny probed.

'Losers teach. Ray is obsessed with her own career, Drage is obsessed with the fine print, can't see the big picture any more. Happens to 'em all when they get to his age. And Lucy is . . .' Harry pulled a face. 'Lucy and Emily were *off*. Two women is disgusting.' He licked his full lips, sat up a little and rested on one elbow. 'You've got beautiful eyes.' His hand brushed against her thigh. Be nice to him, she told herself. He's young and he's male.

'Harry,' she said smoothly, 'I've got a problem. I want to get some equipment from the storeroom. You know, get a head start on my film. I want it this weekend. Pluckrose told me there's no chance of taking out anything until my officially scheduled week . . .'

'Gotta be in the know.' His hand made small swirls on her thigh.

'You could help me convince him.' She tried to pout, lips

stuck out as far as they could. She felt like a puffer fish. 'I really need it.'

'I could help you.' Harry's hand encompassed hers.

'Do you two have a special relationship or something?' Lenny kept her voice light, breezy.

'Don't worry about him, he's a wanker.' Harry moved up and put an arm around Lenny's shoulders. 'There's something special about you, Lenny. You're not like the other women here. I saw your second year film and it's really out there. You have a lot of different voices in your head. Why don't we spend a bit of time together? You can help me edit, if you like. I need a second opinion. And I've got a lot of footage,' he smirked.

'Only if you tell me how you got Pluckrose wrapped around your little finger.' Lenny felt like she was having an out of body experience, watching herself flirting. She took his little finger in her hand and held it. This close she could plainly see a thin line of dirt under the nail. Did real flirts notice things like that? They surely must. Even sluts must have to draw the line somewhere.

'Let's just say it's what you know in this school that counts.' He smiled, tongue poking out between his teeth. There was a pinprick ulcer right on the end of it. Lenny's eyes widened – was he going to go oral on her?

Her grip on his finger tightened automatically and he glanced down, frowning.

'Pluckrose's pathetic,' he said. 'He couldn't even save Emily – hey!' She released the finger.

'Sorry.'

'By the time he got there Emily was dead as a doornail. Blood all over the place like a fucking horror movie. And her eye sockets cut open. He nearly wet his pants with fright. I suppose it did look pretty off, though.' He stopped, realising what he had just said.

'You were there too?'

'No, I was imagining.' Harry rolled away and inspected his finger. 'You bloody hurt me.'

Gabrielle appeared and looked down at them. 'Time to go back,' she said. Lenny thought she looked frightened. Her face under the dark red hair was whiter than usual.

'If you see Janus, tell him he's not needed for this scene,' she told Harry. 'I'm going to do camera. You're not required either. Sebastian says he wants to perform in front of a women-only crew.'

'Is Janus the best camera operator?' Lenny asked Gabrielle as they headed back to the studio.

'He has the baseball cap, the scuffed work boots, the flannel shirt, the Eastern European name, he's male ...' Gabrielle left the thought unfinished. Her conversation reminded Lenny of her films – she created a picture and then expected you to fill in the blanks.

They reached the studio door and Lenny reached out for the handle. At the same time, the door flew open smashing back against the brick wall and rebounding with a metallic smack. Lenny winced. The playback tape was on and the studio interior vibrated with guitar power chords. Sebastian Mott tumbled out almost into her arms. 'Moira's been killed –' he muttered and vomited over the steps.

Lenny ran inside.

The green room door was open and she could see Moira's pale legs with their lace-up boots sprawled on the floor inside. The band members were hovering in the door frame, their faces a sickly light green. The loud music and the coloured overhead lights gave the scene a seedy night-club-near-closing-time feel. Lenny stepped past them to look into the green room. There was blood, a lot of it.

Someone from the band screamed: 'She was working on the shot list! The door was shut!'

113

Lenny crossed to the mixing desk and pulled down the master fader. The music cut out. Everyone seemed to notice her for the first time. They waited for her to speak.

'My name is Lenny Aaron,' she said. 'I'm a private investigator. I want you all away from that door and I want someone to call the police. Now.' No one moved but they all stared at her, examining her in the light of this new information. Then they edged away from the green room door and Gabrielle nodded at her and turned to the exit.

Lenny knew that after the Homicide Squad arrived she would have no chance to examine the body, so with the Polaroid camera still hanging around her neck, she entered the green room.

Moira lay across the floor, filling its width almost exactly, her black and purple many-layered skirt riding up her hips to expose white panties with pink flowers. The panties were cotton, the cheap sort bought at supermarkets rather than department stores, Lenny noted. Death's little revelations; there were no secrets from the reaper, not even your brand of undies. She surveyed the rest of the body.

The upper half lay in a pool of darkening blood. There was a deep cut in the side of the throat and the eye sockets were filled with a red pulp the consistency of a soft-boiled egg. The single, long strand of her hair was a saturated, crimson rope. The room smelled of blood and theatrical make-up, and the musty costumes looked down from the racks like a mob from rent-a-crowd. The Nikon camera was, as ever, around Moira's neck. The scenario had the look of a deliberately perverse fashion shoot – one you might see in *Colours* or *The Face*: 'Serial Killer Chic: Fashion to Die For'.

Moira's hands still clutched at her throat where they had tried to stop life's awful exit. Lenny took a photo then leaned in close to get a look at the wounds. The eyes were gone as in Emily Cunningham's case, but the throat wound was different; not a clean slice across as it had been with Emily. This time it was just a deep stab between the collarbone and the larynx. The cut was about two centimetres wide. More than adequate for the job. Judging by the amount of blood lost, the knife had struck the jugular. Moira would have died within minutes, after collapsing from blood loss.

Lenny took another Polaroid and looked around the room. There was no sign of the murder weapon. The door between the green room and the studio had been closed and with the playback system at full volume, the boys in the band wouldn't have heard a thing.

'I've called them.' Gabrielle appeared in the green room doorway. She looked down at the body and raised a hand to her face. Lenny saw she was sweating.

'I'll wait with the others,' she said. 'If you're all right by yourself.'

'I'm all right by myself,' Lenny said, and Gabrielle left the room again. Lenny foraged in a wicker costume hamper, found a pair of leather gloves and pulled them on, then checked the door to the car park. It was unlocked. The killer must have entered and exited here. The school's back gate was a few metres to her left. It was open too, of course. And a quick glance upwards told her that the fire doors on both the first and second floors were wide open. The killer could have come from inside or outside the campus.

She turned back to the body and crouched beside it, as near as she could without getting blood on her shoes. In doing so, she almost stepped on the eyeball resting on the floor close to Moira's left ear.

There is something shocking about seeing an eyeball detached from the body. For a start, they are a lot bigger than you would expect. Many a police officer hit the floor when the forensic pathologist sliced into the slippery, resilient surface to release the inner fluid with a soft, pressure-driven hiss. Lenny forced herself to lean closer. There was no sign of the other eye, but it could have rolled into a corner, or been stepped on. Or taken.

If one eye had been taken, was there a reason why the other had been left behind, or had the killer just run out of time? The murder of Emily Cunningham in the middle of the night had been carefully planned, but this one had been a risk. The killer – if it was the same person – was decompensating. Not satisfied with the thrill the first kill provided, they had lost the ability to control their actions, becoming reckless, impatient and far more dangerous.

She turned her attention to Moira's shoulder bag and took a Polaroid of the interior. Already a siren's piercing scream could be heard across the campus, and she forced herself to concentrate on the things inside the bag: a cheap leather wallet, keys, Body Shop cosmetics, an Ampex half-inch sound tape. Why would Moira be carrying a tape around? Usually sound tapes were stored along with the film cans in the lockers. This tape had 'R & A' printed in purple on the label. 'R & A'? Lenny took a Polaroid of the tape from closer up.

Then she saw the photograph. The faces of both the women were clearly recognisable, their expressions somewhere between frenzied sexual pleasure and flashlit surprise. The edit suite made a natural frame which Moira had used to some effect. How unfortunate that the two participants had forgotten to lock the door. This was what Lenny called a quality clue, and she reached out to claim it.

'Don't touch that!' Ray, sheet white, walked across the room. She stared down at the body. 'Go and wait with the

116

others in the studio. I'll stay with Moira until the police come. She was a student at my school. This is my responsibility.'

Lenny's eyes narrowed suspiciously. Why would Ray volunteer to stand guard over a bloody corpse? But before she could speak, Lucy Peel appeared in the doorway.

'Oh God . . . Oh God!' The luminous lavender eyes rolled back in her head and Lenny sprang forward just in time to stop the third year supervisor from fainting head first into the body.

CHAPTER 10

The Homicide Squad

Lenny went through two packets of Polaroid film, shooting everyone in the studio: Sebastian red-faced and crying, the rest of his band quietly shocked; Gabrielle expressionless, Harry trying to look manly, Damien Walters, the first year student, quiet and concerned as he devoured his second muffin from the catering trolley. Annabel wide-eyed on her mobile phone. Janus sitting alone in the corner taking the camera apart, handling the Arriflex with a consideration he did not extend to people.

Lenny walked over to where Lucy Peel stood at the edge of the studio, sipping Coke from a plastic bottle, seemingly oblivious. Ray had gone, under police supervision, to break the news to Kenneth.

'What do you want?' Lucy glanced at her. She was still white with shock. After her collapse Lenny had carried her out of the green room to the sofa in the studio. She had come around quickly, but remained prone and shivering until the police arrived and began preliminary questioning. She was stunned – then angry – when told Lenny's true identity. 'Do the police want me again?' she asked bitterly.

'No. They're busy with the body.'

'Oh God!' Tears splurted and Lucy wiped at them. 'I'm

not being much help to anyone. I don't know why I continue.'

'Your husband still doesn't know, does he?' Lenny asked. It was obvious that Lucy was distraught and in no state to answer questions. All the better to ask, Lenny thought.

'What?' Lucy's eyes were huge.

'About you and Emily.'

'You had no right to pass yourself off as a student. I saw your so-called film in the library and – despite serious concerns about your ability – I have spent some time over the last couple of days considering how best to help you this year. And now I find out you're a lie.'

Lenny said: 'The police asked you about your relationship with Emily after she was killed, didn't they? They'll ask you about it again today.'

'Stop it!'

'They might see a connection between Emily's death and Moira's.'

'What do you mean?' Lucy trembled. 'I told them last time I don't have anything to do with all this. Why would I hurt Moira? She was . . . She was a hardworking student.' The tears trickled from lavender pools. 'I can't believe this has happened.'

'Moira liked to play games with people,' Lenny said.

The heaving shoulders were immediately still, as if Lucy's body had forgotten its distress.

'I don't know what you mean.' She straightened and gave a neat performance of confusion and surprise. It was not unlike the expression on her face in the photo from Moira's bag. Lucy Peel sitting on the edge of an editing machine, Emily Cunningham's blonde head turning to face the camera lens from between her supervisor's bare thighs. A photo now in police hands.

Lenny knew the procedure: they would try to catch Lucy

119

out in a series of lies first, softening her up for the blow. Her interrogators would be men and when they decided the moment was right they would slide the photo across the table to her to try to force a confession. But if Lucy had killed Moira, why hadn't she taken the photo from the bag herself?

'She wasn't manipulative,' Lucy lied badly. 'Why would you say such a thing?'

'She showed me the photo,' Lenny lied back. 'We had a laugh over it.'

Lucy froze. She looked to see if they were being overheard, her body rigid, then stared at the ground. 'If you tell my husband, I'll kill you,' she said. Her voice sounded empty, flat.

'Is that what you said to Moira? Or did you say if you tell my husband I'll cut out your eyes, like I cut out Emily's?'

Lucy was white-faced. She looked as if she was going to be sick 'How can you say something like that? Moira wanted me to get her documentary onto the ABC. I've a friend there and Moira knew it. She told me she'd show my husband the photo – I couldn't let that happen. For his sake, if you can believe that. Not for mine. I love him. Please – where's that photo? If the police find it they'll show John.' She began to cry again. 'They'll think I killed Moira. They'll think I did that horrible thing to her. Her eyes . . . God!'

'If you have something to offer the police, you should offer it now. They can be quite discreet when they want to be.'

Lucy hesitated.

'Cate,' she said finally. 'Cate Ray. Moira had some sort of deal with her this year. I don't know what. She was blackmailing me, so I wouldn't be surprised if she was blackmailing other staff too. She liked to find things out, Lenny. She used to sneak around with her radio mics making tapes of private conversations. That's why she liked photography too, of course. She had no real talent for it. If you've seen that awful photo you'll know she got the framing completely wrong.'

'But your face was in focus.'

Lucy gasped and headed for the catering trolley. Her hands trembled as she took a jar of instant coffee and poured a generous portion of it into a cup of hot water. She swirled it and took a greedy gulp. Lenny was impressed with this amateur's style in a field of experimentation so close to her own heart.

'Tell me more about Moira and Ray,' she prompted, her mind rapidly checking and cross-checking facts already gathered: an Ampex sound tape in Moira's bag – a recording of a private coversation? 'R & A.' R for Ray perhaps? That would fit in with Lucy's suggestion of 'a deal' between Moira and Ray. But who or what was A?

'I told you, I don't know anything concrete.' Lucy wiped a hand across her mouth. 'But Cate spoke to me about establishing a special prize for documentaries this year. The school's never had a documentary prize before and since Moira's was the only doco, it would go to her by default. When I think she might have shown John that photo . . . I have a son too, you know. He's only six.' Lucy's lips thinned and her voice shook. 'Moira was a nasty little bitch.'

Sebastian Mott's head appeared around the door. His face was red and swollen. Lucy hurried past him out of the studio.

Lenny surveyed the miserable figure of the quasi rock god. He did have a dreadlocked, pre-Raphaelite thing going, and she could see he looked to *Guitar Player* for that stance. Sebastian would have spent many a lonely night playing along to Stooges and MC5 CDs, rending the seat of his jeans till he got them just right. He was a hundred percent designer rebel; his teeth were straight and white, his breath mint fresh and his immaculate skin was the result of years of proper feeding and good breeding. Further examination would probably reveal that he lived with Mum and Dad in the basement of their Carlton bluestone and transported his equipment in the Land Rover they had given him for his twenty-first.

Sebastian cut in on her reverie:

'She knew who did it, that's why they killed her.' He shuddered. 'She knew who killed Emily. Moira was there, the night Emily died. We'd done some Super 8 and she wanted to edit it. Someone let her in. She said she knew who did it.'

'Moira was there?' Lenny moved a step closer. 'What did she see?'

'She wouldn't say. It was one of her secrets. She always liked to have secrets. She said what you knew was the source of all power, you know?'

'Ms Aaron?' A senior detective appeared. 'We'll interview you now.'

Lenny was taken out of the studio and up to the second floor Animation School office where the interviews were being conducted.

Inside sat Detective Senior Sergeant Danny Hoyle, in front of a wall covered with cartoons. Buzz Lightyear and Daffy Duck figurines had been pushed aside on the desk to make room for police files.

Lenny dropped into the chair across the desk from her old police partner. They had been at the academy together, been constables and senior constables together. He was the nearest thing she had had to a friend at any time in her life.

He had come to the hospital after Michael Dorling hurt her, had tried to help. Of course she had rebuffed him. As hard as she could because when she was down, at her lowest point, the very last thing she could tolerate was sympathy and kindness from someone she liked. He had sensed it and abandoned her to her therapeutic misery.

He looked much the same. Tangled brown curls over a handsome face with a perfect, straight-toothed smile. Probably had the same open, warm-hearted personality too. He had always played good cop to her bad cop.

'The boyfriend is talking motive to anyone who'll listen,' she offered. 'Apparently Moira was here the night Emily Cunningham was killed.' Danny said nothing. He just looked at her silently for a whole minute. She bristled. Did he think his sad police interrogation techniques were going to affect her? As though she didn't know the way things worked. The outward display of cold professionalism overlaying the inward rush which every detective had in the first moments of a wrongful death. Investigating murder was a cop's biggest buzz. Better than drugs, Lenny recalled – if you could deal with the moral downside that a person had to die to trigger the pleasure.

'You touched the body,' Danny said finally. Lenny glanced at her fingers but they were spotless. She had been very careful not to get any blood on her. 'I know you,' Danny continued, 'you couldn't resist it. We haven't located the murder weapon yet, but the bag contents are proving quite useful.' He pulled a list from under Daffy Duck. 'Wallet, incense sticks, Tiger Balm, house keys, eyeliner, lesbian oral sex photo –' He let the list fall to the desk.

Lenny kept her expression neutral while she scanned it upside down. There was a discrepancy between the listed contents and what she had seen in Moira's bag. The Ampex sound tape was not on the police list. It had been there when Lenny examined the body but apparently was not there when the police arrived. Lenny remembered how she had caught Lucy Peel when the supervisor fainted, had carried her out of the green room. Cate Ray had been left behind with the body. Not for long. The police had arrived thirty seconds later. But long enough. Definitely long enough for the principal to bend down and remove a piece of evidence from Moira's bag.

So 'R' was for Cate Ray after all. Should she tell Danny the school principal had nicked a piece of evidence from the crime scene? As if on cue he said:

'You want to tell me everything you know about this case?'

'I wasn't in the studio when it happened,' Lenny replied. Let him find out about the Ampex tape himself. A good private investigator played her cards close to her chest and never cuddled up to the police unless she had to. It was bad for the reputation.

He examined his notes. 'No, you were outside in the quadrangle with five students: Harry Tuyen, Damien Walters, Annabel Lear, Janus Onyszkiewicz and Gabrielle Danaher, right?'

'Yes, but we were only together for a few minutes. Harry is the only one I can vouch for. The others didn't stay with me. As for the staff, I don't know. They all left the studio before me.'

'Lucy Peel says she went to her office to get an aspirin for her headache. The secretary, Alana Zappone, met her in the corridor on the first floor. Kenneth Drage was viewing a second year film in one of the edit suites. Zappone says he asked her to call the Treasury Theatre about a booking, which she did. Cate Ray went to see Susan Hyslock, the head of the Animation Department, who was out. But the secretary there spoke to her briefly. The technician, Graeme Pluckrose, was in his workshop and alone for the entire period.'

Lenny nodded. It didn't surprise her that Pluckrose was the only person without an alibi. He would enjoy the singularity. She could imagine him lecturing the police on forensic technique.

'Annabel Lear says she was in the canteen having coffee with two friends from the Design School,' Danny continued, reading from his list. 'We're checking that. She says she saw Damien Walters having coffee across the room, and he says he saw her. However, there is an internal staircase from the canteen to the first floor and from there, as I see it, anyone could access the car park via the open fire escape doors and from there enter the green room.' Lenny nodded.

Danny went on: 'Janus Onyszkiewicz was in the library and was remembered by the librarian. I quote: "He was his usual obnoxious self. Goes out of his way to be remembered, pompous little git." Harry Tuyen says he was with you the whole time. Right?'

'Right.' Lenny agreed.

'Gabrielle Danaher says she was having a smoke in the car park, completely alone. She didn't see anyone and no one saw her. I asked her how, if she'd been in the car park for the entire period, she could have avoided seeing the killer enter the green room. She said,' he glanced at his notes again, '"I was sitting on my motorbike, facing the other way." Convenient.'

'There are the students and staff from the Animation and Design schools to check out before you jump to any conclusions,' Lenny pointed out. 'And the rest of the first year film students. You're right that the fire escape doors provide access to the car park, and therefore the green room. No one would think it was worth noticing if someone was on the fire stairs. But the killer could have come from outside the school. It could be a complete stranger, random.' Why was she bothering with this little lecture, Lenny wondered. Gabrielle Danaher had been in the right place at the right time.

The truth was that Lenny admired Gabrielle Danaher's work. Perhaps Kenneth Drage was right and Gabrielle was some kind of genius, the future of Australian film. Of all those she had seen, Gabrielle's films had been the only ones with an original intelligence. There had been moments when Lenny felt she was inside the film herself, rather than viewing it. They had forced her to make a brief but definite connection with the world she liked to keep out there, at arm's length. Gabrielle could stop the world and start it again like a child playing with a top. What more could you ask of any artist?

And there was another, more insidious reason. Gabrielle was an uncommunicative loner, a terminal misanthrope. She was also the possessor of a pale, pointy face, slim-hipped body and a tangle of wild red hair. Lenny Aaron was smitten.

'There's something else. Look at this.' Danny pushed a photograph across the table. It was a colour print of a little girl leaning against a large tree. Round smiling face, curly dark brown hair in bunches with woolly ties, projecting teeth, maybe eleven or twelve years old, soft, lemon yellow dress that perfectly matched the blooming silver wattle tree behind her.

'Samantha Burridge,' he said. 'Seventeen years ago there was a full scholarship program on offer to one of Melbourne's most prestigious private girls schools. Eight state school girls from across Victoria were short-listed from a preliminary examination. Two made it to the final inter-view stage, both from the same primary school outside

Geelong. Friends. This one,' he tapped the photo, 'fell into a canal on the way home from school. She suffered a blow to the head and drowned.' He pushed another photo across the table, a close-up of a small, bloated face, tongue bulging. A little girl's corpse on a stainless steel table, waiting for the Y-incision and the other indignities of unnatural death. Lenny had seen dead children before. She waited.

'The other girl got the scholarship,' Danny continued. 'She might have got it anyway. Any idea who she is?'

Lenny lit a cigarette. Perhaps Danny guessed at her reason for defending his prime suspect and he was doing this deliberately. 'Gabrielle Danaher,' she said casually, deliberately. 'Was anything proved?'

'There were rocks in the river bed but forensics could never be certain that the blow to the head was a result of the fall. Gabrielle and Samantha lived in the same area. They walked the same path home every day. There were shoe prints from a second pair of child-sized shoes on the canal bank. They didn't match any of the shoes later examined in the Danahers' home, perhaps because she was smart enough to get rid of them. Police interviewed her under strict supervision. She was – I quote the report –"a very calm child". She didn't cry. She wasn't frightened. Only answered yes and no to the questions, went home and got her scholarship. Twelve years old.'

'What about her parents?' Lenny could imagine twelve-year-old Gabrielle, surrounded by police, clever enough to realise she was suspected of murder, giving them as little of herself as she could. She also remembered Gabrielle and Moira standing together in the studio and Moira saying the dead girl's name: Samantha.

'British immigrants.' Danny read from a file. 'Came here when Gabrielle was eight. Father disappeared early in the picture. The social worker thought he used the wife and kids to get himself a place on the immigration list, then dumped them. The mother was variously employed but more often not. She drank.' Danny tapped the file with a well-manicured finger. 'Gabrielle dragged herself out of a crappy childhood and maybe killed someone to do it.

'Now we have two more deaths. Emily Cunningham and Moira Middlemiss. No connection; except Cunningham was using amphetamines and Danaher has a record in that area.' He glanced at the file. 'Counselled at age sixteen selling marijuana, convicted at age twenty for using ecstasy. Fined and warned. Three strikes and she's out, Lenny.'

So that was why he had all this information about Gabrielle. If out of all the suspects in the Aquinas murders hers had been the only name to come up with a prior conviction, she would automatically have gone to the top of the suspect list.

'So you're thinking a drug connection caused Emily's murder,' Lenny said. She agreed that it was possible. Drugs and alcohol were often at the root of violence and death. 'But what's the motive for Gabrielle killing Moira?'

'Still looking,' Danny admitted.

Lenny looked at the first photograph again. Yellow dress, yellow tree. A big one, maybe twenty metres tall. There were silver wattles all over Victoria. And then her first conversation with Moira downloaded from memory: *My family live in Thornbury now but I grew up near Geelong ... There were all these wattle trees near my school.* Samantha Burridge and Gabrielle had attended a primary school just outside Geelong. Ten to one Moira had been a pupil at the same school. She forced her face to register no emotion. The Aquinas records didn't go back that far into student histories. Danny didn't know yet. But he would find out.

'Are you going to arrest Gabrielle?' she asked.

'Not just yet. Waiting on forensics. But if she did it, she's got ice in her veins, taking a risk like that in broad daylight.'

This perplexed Lenny too. Finding Moira alone in the green room, the decision to kill and mutilate, exiting through the car park – Gabrielle had been leaving a lot to chance for someone who had such control over her films. A successful film required as much thought in pre-production as it did in the actual execution.

'Where are you with the theft investigation?' Danny asked her and she gave him a brief rundown, including the unsuccessful rat trap in the locker ploy.

'Very ingenious.' He paused. 'No doubt you've learned a lot with your cat business.'

She ignored him. Her pager went off: *Barber Shop*. Were the Misses Attwood and Rendell getting their wires crossed again?

'If you find a connection between the theft and vandalism and these murders, I'm the first to know, understand?'

The door opened and a smiling face popped around it, long thin strands of hair greasily combed across a bald head, nose pink and freckled, suit a crumpled, rayon nightmare. Detective Senior Sergeant Ron MacAvoy winked at them. 'Len, mate!' he grinned. 'The old threesome back together, hey? Quite a team we were.'

'Still are,' Danny said.

Except that they were trying to put the future of Australian film in jail.

MacAvoy's face lost its pleased-to-see-you glow and a dramatically subdued expression took its place. Lenny had seen it a lot in the last year. 'I was sorry to hear about your dad. Dan says he was the only person you ever cared about.'

Lenny glared at Danny who blushed, and so he should. This was why she hated sharing confidences: when they weren't kept, they reflected badly on the giver and the receiver.

As Lenny headed down the corridor to her Footscray office, Anastasia's voice accosted her from deep in the barber shop. 'You got my message!' She was excited about something, bobbing slightly on her platform heels.

So the pager message had been right after all. Just when Lenny'd been thinking she would have to get tough with those two old idiots, they had come through.

'I've really helped you, Lenny,' said Anastasia as Lenny reluctantly entered her salon. 'You owe me for this one, I'm thinking.' She preened, gesturing at the cage next to her cash register. 'I got it for you. The one you've been after for two weeks. The one in the photo on your wall – Brain.'

'Brian.' Lenny looked into the cage. 'Where did you find it?'

'Well, it's a good story – hey!' Anastasia smacked her customer's head. 'This shaver will go right through your skull if I slip, OK?' Her scowl re-formed its gleeful aspect as the heavily pierced teenage male slumped back into the chair.

'I spotted it around the block in the garden of that big white house when I was on lunch break. I had to sneak over the fence and trick it with the cat nap.'

'Nip.'

'Not even a scratch. It's very friendly.'

'This is the wrong cat,' said Lenny flatly.

The shaver dug into tender, teenage scalp. 'No!' Anastasia threw her utensil onto a trolley and strode to the cage. 'No! It's just like the photo on your wall! A red tabby with the curls. This is for sure Brian!'

130

'This is a red tabby,' Lenny agreed. 'But it's a Devon Rex. I'm looking for a red tabby La Perm.'

'This is La Perm! Isn't it?'

'No, you're a moron.'

'Lenny –' The fake blue eyes watered.

'It's obvious. Devon Rexes have wavy hair. La Perms have small curls.'

'Curls . . . waves . . .' Anastasia crumpled. Then the full horror dawned: 'I've stole a cat.'

'Stolen.'

'Don't rub me in, Lenny, it's embarrassment.'

'Embarrassing.'

'Please!'

'You'll have to return it.'

'OK. Help me?'

'Hey!' The boy in the swivel chair stood and stabbed a finger at his head. He was six feet tall with a black snake tattoo down his lower jaw and neck.

Anastasia turned on him. 'Can't you see we are discussing a crime here? What a rude!'

She marched over, pushed his head down and finished him off. 'There – bald! Ten bucks.' He paid up and slouched out, another satisfied customer.

Lenny looked at the preening feline. The Devon Rex was a much prized show cat, quite rare in fact. This was the only one in the neighbourhood. It was never allowed outdoors and its favourite snack was tuna sushi. Lenny knew a lot about this particular individual. Its name was Bertrand Russell and its pretty silver collar was custom made by a jeweller in Collins Street. Yes, she knew a lot about this cat because it had often featured in the local newspapers along with its doting owner, Councillor Thomas Walstab.

CHAPTER 11

Annabel's Script

Friday morning. Another chilly September day. Lenny stalled for some time then finally called the primary school outside Geelong. Her suspicion was soon confirmed: Moira Middlemiss had been a pupil there at the same time as Gabrielle Danaher and Samantha Burridge. Had she been a witness to the murder of one child by another and then chosen not to speak? Perhaps for some time she simply hadn't remembered. Lenny knew from her police force experience that children blocked out disturbing memories and made unreliable witnesses in court. But if Moira had remembered something later and then found herself unexpectedly in the same circle as Gabrielle again, she may have followed her usual pattern and tried to use the information to get what she wanted. Gabrielle – proud, aloof – would deeply resist any kind of hold over her independence.

But Gabrielle Danaher was not the only one without an alibi. Pluckrose didn't have one either; Cate Ray had only spoken to the animation school secretary for a minute. Of the others she was unsure: Lucy Peel, Kenneth Drage, Alana Zappone, Annabel Lear and Janus Onyszkiewicz all appeared to have alibis, at least for some of the time period during which Moira had been killed. But Harry Tuyen was definitely off the hook. He could not possibly have killed Moira since he had spent the entire period groping Lenny's leg.

Lenny dropped in at her office to give the caged Bertrand Russell a plate of Whiskas and a bowl of water.

Anastasia had become hysterical when she learned who Bertrand's owner was and insisted Lenny keep the cat in her office. Anastasia's extended family was gradually migrating southwards and the barber was terrified of getting on the wrong side of government at any level. Babushka's visa was at stake.

Lenny wasn't sure how to deal with this new development. If Thomas Walstab found out she had his pampered pet in her office, he was going to do her for cat-napping at the very least. She could just imagine how that was going to look on the side of a bus.

She was locking the office door again when Mike Bullock came out of the porn shop, his arm around the shoulder of a small man in a shit-coloured suit. The man blinked at Lenny uncertainly, held a rectangular brown-paper package closer to his chest.

'Don't mind Lenny,' Mike reassured him with a pat on the back. 'You just enjoy that, mate. Have yourself a private party. You've got a classic video there.' The man nodded and hurried away.

'*Bondage Babes at the Booberama*,' Mike confided to Lenny. 'Some men like to watch a few of the ladies going at it together. Not my kind of thing, of course.'

She strode away from him.

When she arrived at Aquinas, reporters were crowded around the Moor Street entrance. The media interest in Aquinas had renewed with a frenzy. Moira's death was page one.

Lenny pushed past the reporters and entered the tunnel

that led into the quadrangle. She checked her locker. The box was still there, the rat trap still primed to punish inquisitive fingers.

She opened the door of the Aquinas screening room. The 'Russ Myer: King of the Nudie' lecture had been scheduled to begin at 10 am. Despite the death of another student, the police presence all over the small campus and the press outside, Cate Ray was insisting that classes proceed as normal.

Lenny had seen the TV interview. Ray, in a black power suit and very pale make-up, had managed to convey business savvy and mourning in equal proportions: 'This is a tragedy. Emily Cunningham and Moira Middlemiss were potentially two of the best auteurs of their generation. They were very special human beings, very determined, with an extraordinary range. Like so many of our students thrown in here at the deep end, they were battlers. The words quit and fail were simply not in their lexicon. And they will not be in ours. We will go on in their honour.'

In the screening room there was a lectern in front of the seats for the speech that would precede the films. It was a tiny room and both the velour seats and the projection cubicle at the back looked as though they had been installed when the school opened more than thirty years ago. There was no one present, save for the blonde head nodding in the front row. Lenny recognised Annabel Lear's high-pitched, earnest voice talking on the phone.

'Absolutely! I know . . . One minute you're in school and the next minute you're at Florentino's chatting with Jane Campion.' She trilled happily. 'OK. I'll call you.' She folded the neat device into her Prada bag and noticed Lenny. Her blue eyes shuttered slightly and she edited her smile for the minor league.

'My Channel Nine connection,' she explained. 'I met him

at an industry party last week and he won't stop calling me. I mean, I'm practically *living* with someone now. I'm just not available. But you wouldn't believe how many men have told me they're in love with me. My publicist has to fight them off! It's not just my looks, although I am blessed in that area. But people are also attracted to my calm centre. I'm a scientologist, of course. It's helped me to achieve goals. You can't believe how many financially successful creative people are scientologists.'

She raised her perfect eyes to the ceiling. 'This lecture's been rescheduled for ten-thirty. The guest lecturer is running late. I'm surprised he's coming at all the way this place is at the moment. You know the press are like everywhere and I had to fight my way in here. I'm like, give us some space to grieve, you know?'

Lenny slid into the seat next to the school beauty. She saw that the pink lips were natural, not lipsticked, and the peach skin was without make-up. Lenny, always aware of her own physical imperfections, was painfully at one with them now. Mediocrity confronted with perfection must tremble a little, and Annabel had a built-in seismograph that could detect admiration at thirty paces. She beamed. Lenny pulled out her cigarettes and Annabel stopped her.

'Lenny, you can't smoke in here. Anyway, smoking is so bad for the skin. You'll get those lines around your mouth from sucking in your cheeks all the time.' She paused. Lenny already had them. 'It's probably put five years on your face and you can't afford that, can you?'

Lenny lit up and went straight into interrogation mode: 'Any idea who's stealing film equipment?'

Annabel gave her a cool look, considering. 'Your incarnation as investigator is so much more natural than film student. To be honest, I never bought you as a talent. You've become real for me now.'

'And that means so much to me.' Lenny, to match Anna-bel's huge blue eyes, stretched hers as wide as she could, which wasn't very wide at all.

Annabel sensed she was being mocked. Her mouth made a gorgeous little moue of distaste.

'I don't know about the stolen gear, Lenny. Although I can totally understand why someone would smash this place up. We've all experienced the stresses and strains of film making.' She smiled a quick, stress-free smile.

'It's such a trip, isn't it?' she continued, 'Moira getting killed in the green room of all places. And getting her eyes cut out too – like Emily. Wicked!'

'Were you ever involved with Emily Cunningham?' Lenny followed her lead. This was the real investigation – the theft of the equipment was uninteresting. At best, it was probably a smokescreen. Something was going on at this school, something evil amongst these potential little Oscar winners.

'Well, Emily was interested in getting together with me, of course. Everyone is. I'm straight by choice, but sometimes, you know, it pays to be open. Still, if I'm going to have a lesbian fling it won't be with a deformed accountant. Emily was a bean-counter. She should have got a job working in finance. She did an MBA before she bought her way in here. She was ambitious though, I had to admire that. And she knew how to make her dad's money work for her.'

Annabel toyed with a strand of hair. Pretty girls, in Lenny's experience, always played with their hair. Touched it, moved it to the front of their shoulders and then to the back, tucked it behind their ears, made faux ponytails of it in their hands and then let it drop. It seemed to reassure them.

'Did Emily have a relationship with any of the other students? Harry, for example?'

Annabel shook her head and leaned across so that her lovely mouth was closer to Lenny's ear. Warm breath caressed her lobe. 'Even if he was gorgeous, Emily wouldn't have touched him.'

'Really?'

'Mmm hmm.' Annabel reached into her bag for a hair clip, spent a minute searching for the right position for a loose bun, then changed her mind. 'Emily hated chongs.' Her voice became a whisper. 'She thought there were too many Asians in the country and we're not part of Asia, no matter what anyone says, we're a white country. But you can't say those things in our circle. If you want to be in the arts in this country, the last thing you can do is, like, deny the ethnic minorities. I mean, wow! Just cut my throat right now!'

'Did Harry know how she felt?'

Annabel sighed. 'It wouldn't have stopped him. Some men are sex maniacs. Like, first year he asks me to have a look at his video in the edit suite and the door is shut, and before I know it Harry's lifted me up into the air. His hands were under my armpits! And he's holding me way up and saying if I kiss him he'll let me down.'

'Did you kiss him?'

'As if! I told him I'd lay harassment charges and he gave up. He tries the same routine with every woman in the school. He tried it with Emily and she freaked out and called him a slant. I know because I was editing down the corridor. He came out of there looking . . .' She paused, a thrill passing over the exquisite face. 'Murderous! But just between you and me,' Annabel continued thoughtfully, 'she shouldn't have been so choosy. The sex angle came out a lot in her films. I think it was related to body dysfunction, personally. Men are so image conscious these days and she had the thing with her thumb, the giblet. She probably never felt attractive, you know? Poor thing.'

'Who do you think killed Emily and Moira?' Lenny asked.

'Don't know. But your main suspect should be Lucy Peel. That whole relationship was just business for Emily, getting better grades. But Lucy was a sap about it. She's been freaked out all year and it's only a matter of time before word gets back to her husband. I wouldn't be surprised if Mr Cunningham told him. He's not a man I'd like to cross and he fucking hates dykes! You should hear him go on about them. He was obsessed with Emily being his little princess. I bet he had a meltdown when he found out about her and Lucy. And then there's Mrs –'

Annabel stopped short. Lenny was surprised she had revealed so much. 'Of course he's a wonderful man in many, many ways,' Annabel continued sweetly. 'He's considering funding a short film for me after graduation. A big fan of my work.' She glanced at Lenny's jeans. 'You should stay away from denim, Lenny. When I was a kid I *lived* in 501s, like everyone. But now! That whole Hard Rock Café look makes me cringe.'

'Did Emily lend or give you money?' Lenny ignored the fashion tip.

Annabel shrugged. She pulled a bottle of Evian from her bag and drank from it delicately. 'I'm dehydrated. When I was younger I never felt this way. Since I turned nineteen I just soak up the water like a sponge. Once you hit twenty-three they say your skin turns to pastry.' She took in Lenny's piecrust.

'Just answer my question. Did you take money from Emily?' Lenny gazed directly at her target and Annabel went completely still. Her face blanked, like someone had used a remote off-switch. Small fingers moved minutely on the Evian bottle. The pink lips folded inwards. Her eyes went out. Annabel was shutting down.

'No,' she said in a small voice. She pulled a laptop out of her bag and said, as if to cheer herself up: 'I just have no time today!'

The door opened and Harry and Janus entered. It seemed no one was upset enough about Moira's death to miss a day at school.

'This is going to be fucking great!' Harry sat down right next to Annabel. 'I've seen all these films. Russ Myer is a fucking genius.'

'You cannot describe the work of a pornographer who is obsessed with large breasts as genius,' Janus replied.

The remainder of the students filtered in and took their seats. Kenneth Drage entered, the guest lecturer behind him. Lenny glanced around the room. Gabrielle was absent. Kenneth stepped forward.

'Our lecture today focuses on late twentieth century erotica in film, with special emphasis on Russ Myer, and it will be given by our special guest, Professor Geoffrey Tynan. Over to you, Professor Tynan.'

'I thank you.' Professor Tynan wore a severe grey suit, white shirt, darker grey tie. His hair was cut short and carefully combed, his glasses conservatively rectangular. Lenny supposed when you were lecturing in smut you had to work harder at your credibility. 'Let me begin with a challenge to the notion that erotic film making is anything less than art. Close investigation of the work of Russ Myer provides evidence that this director was arguably the greatest auteur Hollywood has produced.' A ripple of amused interest passed through the room.

Professor Tynan held up a poster of *Motor Psycho*: 'From writing to editing to cinematography, this man had ultimate control of his chosen form. He was the master of what those in the erotic film industry categorise as sheer naughtiness. His work was provocative visual entertainment at its peak. From sensual lingerie through PVC and latex wear, Myer was a man who specialised in making an audience feel randy. Obviously, with our time constraints I cannot hope to cover in detail the full breadth of Myer's achievements. However, I will give you a brief history and overview of the man and his dyno-breasted muses. It began, if I can go back in time, with his training as an industrial photographer . . .'

He was good, but Lenny had heard better. Professor Tynan needed to have a chat with Mike Bullock. She slipped out before the end and Kenneth Drage joined her in the chilly quadrangle.

'Not my idea of an appropriate lecture topic,' he said. 'But Cate seems to think we need to broaden our perspective.'

He had a Pentax camera in his hand and pointed it up at the tower. He zoomed in and frowned.

'I'm trying to get a good visual record of the school as it stands,' he said. 'I'm planning a retirement project, a history of Australian film, but I was considering a second book based simply on Aquinas. I'm painting the cover images myself. I'm undecided on a title though. What do you think of *Rebels with a Cause?*'

Lenny shook her head. 'Clichéd,' she said. 'The police report on Moira's death said you were in an edit suite upstairs and spoke to Alana Zappone.'

'Yes, I asked Alana to call the Treasury Theatre to see if they were free for our graduation screenings this year, and they were.'

He smiled and handed her the Pentax. 'It's a bit cloudy today but would you take my photograph? Tilt the lens up so the tower's behind me.'

Lenny peered through the camera at Kenneth's face. Either his face or the tower would be sharp: she was unsure how to get both in focus. There had been something about that in the David O. Lincoln Academy textbook, but she couldn't remember what it was. She snapped off a shot anyway.

'Thank you very much.'

He wouldn't be so grateful when he saw the result.

She glanced around the Victoria Parade pharmacy. There were no other customers. She strode up to the counter and placed her latest forgery in front of Margie.

'Hi, Margie. How are you today?'

'Good, thanks, Helena. Back so soon?'

'I woke up today with this horrible cough. You know how it is when the seasons change. One thing after another. The doctor's given me a script for something a bit stronger than usual. I suppose he knows best.' She barked out a cough and pressed a hand to her throat.

Margie picked up the prescription.

'You poor thing!' she sympathised. 'My mum's got a bad cold too. It's going around, I think. Just a sec. Dad! Prescription!' She handed it back across the shoulder-high counter behind her and a large, hairy hand scooped it up. 'Do you want any aspirin or Codral or stuff today for your troop?'

Lenny shook her head and cast down her eyes. 'Rowena –'

'The girl with the nettles?'

'That's her. Last night she pulled her leg out bungee jumping, so we've disbanded for a while.'

Margie gasped. 'No!'

'Yes, it pulled right out of the socket and it was only the connective tissue that stopped it from –'

To Lenny's horror, a door opened in the side of the dispensary and a giant in a huge blue lab coat stalked towards her. He had extremely thick, horn-rimmed spectacles and fierce, curly red hair all over his head, face and arms. He was over six foot and towered over Lenny, who had to resist an urge to bolt.

'Do you know what this is?' He was holding the prescription in one orangutan paw. 'This medicine is what they give patients in hospital after they've had a lung removed, to immobilise the respiratory tract. It contains a high percentage of methadone. Why would you need something that strong?'

'It's just cough medicine. I've got a bad cough.' She tried to hack without success. 'Not right this moment but I coughed before. Margie heard me.' Margie nodded, but she wasn't smiling any more. 'I have a horrible tightness in my chest – almost suffocating. The doctor wants me to take this while I wait to see a specialist.'

She was trying, but she had pushed too far this time. Methadone, synthesised by German chemists during World War II when the Allies cut off their opium supply, was until recently the prescribed detox aid for heroin addicts. It had taken her some time with her bible, *The Essential Guide to Prescription Drugs*, to find this particular cough medication. It was available on prescription. It was not an illegal drug. What was his problem?

The giant chemist turned to his daughter. 'How often is this lady in here?'

'Pretty often.' Margie gave Lenny an apologetic glance. 'She was in yesterday. Her name's Helena. She's a Tawny Owl, she goes camping a lot . . .' Margie ran down, looking Lenny over closely now, perhaps noticing for the first time that she looked nothing like a Tawny Owl. 'She always buys Tylenol and Panadol because the Brownies are always having accidents. And there was some other stuff on prescription before . . . valum . . . valerum . . .'

'Valium?' prompted the red giant.

'That's it.' Margie bit her lip. 'Did I do something wrong, Dad?'

'No, it's all right.' The pharmacist folded up Lenny's prescription and put it in his pocket. 'Take your break now, Margie.'

He waited until the teenager had left them alone, then leaned in close to Lenny. She could smell the antiseptic on his burly arms. He was probably a union player, front row. She realised her black hair, earrings and bony white face were weighing against her.

'Listen, you,' he smiled, nasty but controlled nasty, 'if I see your ugly face again, I'll call the cops. Now piss off back to Swanston Street.'

'But I have a cough!' Lenny protested. 'That is a prescription from a bona fide doctor and you have an obligation to fill it.'

'You come in here one more time asking my daughter to sell you narcotics and I'll call the police. Do you understand?'

'I wouldn't dream of coming back. I'll take my business elsewhere.' She sounded like her mother, self-righteous, powerless.

'You do that, sweetheart.' He folded his arms.

Lenny walked out of the shop and down the street, her head held high. There were plenty more pharmacists in the world. She was so busy reliving the indignity she had suffered, all the things she should have said, that she forgot all about the prescription still in the pharmacist's pocket.

CHAPTER 12

The Girl From Wangaratta

At 7 pm Lenny was back on the Aquinas campus, checking the logbook. Janus and Harry were on the list of students permitted to use the editing suites that evening.

She headed for the stairs. After her awkward moment at the pharmacy she had stopped off at the Victoria Parade MacDonald's and wolfed down a cheeseburger with a handful of Nō-Dōz and Sudafed. The Haldol she had taken earlier to ease her irritation had worked a little too well, making her drowsy. It was always the way. Anti-anxiety and anti-depression drugs brought on lethargy which she was forced to combat with caffeine and stimulants. Why the hell didn't the drug company just manufacture something with all the best ingredients combined? The Lenny Pill, that would make her feel anything but Lenny.

As she walked down the corridor, Janus, coffee mug in hand, came out of the student common room.

'I am not interested in answering any of your questions, investigator,' he said. 'To summarise for you, I have stolen nothing. I have destroyed nothing. I watched your so-called "second year" film in the library. It's shit.' He stepped past her.

'You can thank the David O. Lincoln Academy for that,' Lenny quipped.

'I spit on the David O. Lincoln Academy and all its former students,' said Janus, going into an edit suite and closing the door.

Lenny spotted a light under the door of edit suite three. She knocked and it slid open.

'Hello, Harry.'

A photo of himself from yesterday evening's paper was taped onto the wall beside him. All of the students, except Gabrielle, had been interviewed about Moira's death. Annabel had even worked in the title of her third year film.

He grinned and reached a hand past Lenny's hip to slide the door closed. 'Thought you might show up. My turn to be grilled? Want to make sure I don't have the other eyeball in my pocket?' She ignored him and he shrugged. 'Have a look at this for me while you're here. You girls have a different way with images. Men are thinkers. Women have the big feelings. You can watch how I cut.' He grinned and patted a plastic chair next to him. Lenny stared at the wet mark on the seat. Water or the remains of a sugary drink? She took out a tissue, wiped the seat, then slid into it, dropping the tissue into the bin.

Harry began to scroll images across the Steenbeck's screen. Technically he shouldn't have anything to edit yet, but Lenny remembered he was working on the sly, using the equipment Pluckrose had permitted him to take out.

She watched in silence. There was a very bloody hospital sequence after a bloody road accident scene. Like his first and second year efforts, it was thrilling stuff. The images were pockmarked with chinagraph hieroglyphs, the hastily done splices blistered with trapped air bubbles. The sound quality, however, was remarkable. If she closed her eyes she could imagine she was right there at the scene. She said as much and Harry nodded.

'That's Kenneth. He used to be a sound man himself before he started this place and even if we have to skimp on cameras, he insists we always have good sound equipment. These are some of the best speakers you can get.'

He grinned and produced a bottle of grey liquid from beneath the desk. 'I make this myself. Let's have some together.' He swigged from the bottle and held it out to her. Lenny shook her head. The risk of mixing alcohol and the amount of pills in her body was one thing; the germ culture from Harry's lips now raving on the sugary bottle-neck was quite another.

'I'm depicting the violence of urban life against the serenity of the Australian vista. This country is a perfect backdrop for film. We're lucky. Shouldn't let too many outsiders in, I reckon. Foreigners cheating their way in and getting industry jobs here, taking positions in our best schools while Australians dip out.' He shook his head. 'People'll do anything to get into this country and take our opportunities.'

Lenny thought, if they want my life, let them have it. Still, Harry had just opened a door. Not a pleasant one but, as Lenny knew, the investigator has to jump over many dodgy doorsteps.

'That's ironic coming from you, isn't it?'

'Huh?' Harry dribbled Vietnamese moonshine.

'Some people might not want *you* here taking opportunities.'

'What are you talking about? I was born in Melbourne.' He was smiling still. Only the slight tension in his neck betrayed that he had understood her sly, racist remark. She was testing the waters, seeing how thick-skinned Tuyen really was.

He said: 'You're really beautiful.'

When his mouth swooped towards hers she used the side of her hand to give him a sharp clip to the throat. He sat back, startled.

'Is that how you tried to get Emily to kiss you?' Lenny lit a cigarette.

'What are you being rough for? Get out of here if you're going to be like that.' He reached for the door, but Lenny's boot held it shut.

'You said you like having women close by, well it's just us two in here, cosy together. I'm in the mood for conversation too. Tell me why you were here the night Emily was killed and how you got in.'

'I didn't touch her. I knew she'd be working back late and I just wanted to speak to her.'

'To ask her for money?' If so, join the queue.

'She wouldn't speak to me again after the time she kissed me.' He shrugged at Lenny's glance. '*I* kissed *her* – whatever. I was going to apologise.'

'And ask for money.'

'I didn't get to ask for anything, did I?' He swigged on the bottle again. 'She was dead when I got here. The door to the edit suite was open. I saw Pluckrose run down the corridor to the phone, then I looked in the door to the edit suite and Em was sitting in the chair. She was covered with blood. I've never seen that much real blood before. I was sick later.' He paused, remembering. 'I figured the cops would come for sure and I got out of there.'

'How did you get in?' Lenny repeated her earlier question. 'Did you have a key or did someone let you in?'

'The back gate was open – I can't remember why. Someone dropping gear off, maybe.' Harry lied badly. 'I didn't hurt anyone, but I won't say I liked Emily. Nobody did really.' He rubbed his neck. 'There's a rumour her dad's cash got her in here. I mean, her work was OK but there's no way she was the top student. She loved this place though. Most of us can't wait to graduate and get out into the real world, but she really loved being here. I reckon her dad would have bought her the whole fucking school eventually. I kissed her because she was all over me!'

'Yeah, you're so gorgeous.' Lenny yawned in his face. 'Where was your father born anyway? Not Melbourne. The way I hear it, Emily called you a fucking chong –'

This time she got the reaction she was looking for: he lunged. They were both in the mood for a fight, so it went well. She dropped her cigarette and they grappled together, mangling, slapping and gasping. The room was too small for the chairs to tip over and they swung back and forth between the desk and the door, banging their arms, heads and legs as they short-punched and head-butted. Harry was stronger but Lenny was far more experienced, and she finished him with a hard uppercut that rocked his head back.

'Stop it, stupid.' She pushed him more gently as he tried to come at her again. 'Or I'll really hurt you.' Her dropped cigarette was beginning to burn the carpet and she stamped it out.

'Moll!' He started crying and buried his face in his hands. The crying was more disturbing than the violence. His muscular shoulders heaved up and down as he sobbed. 'What did he have to cut their eyes out for anyway? That's so fucking sick.' If this was the cunning crybaby routine of the cold killer it was a good one, Lenny mused.

Feeling better, she lit another cigarette and waited.

'My mum and dad don't want to be naturalised.' Harry's eyes were pink and moist. 'They're saving enough money to go home and settle down when they retire. As if they can ever fit in Vietnam again! They've been here too long. They're Australian. I'm Australian! Just because I don't look like fucking Emily Cunningham! I'm sorry about her eyes – but she was racist. It's no wonder she got herself killed.

'I tried twice before I was accepted into this place,' he continued. 'The way they interview you here, asking what are your favourite films like that means anything. I had two really great films to show them. No go. It took me till the third time to wise up to what they were really after. The first two times I wore a suit.' He laughed bitterly. 'Third time I came in with a shaved head, smelly clothes, no shoes. I showed the same films, but I talked up a storm about my Vietnamese ethnicity. Wham! I was in.'

'Did you like Moira?' Lenny asked him. She had known he was present on the night of Emily's death. She had provoked him, to see if Emily's racism had been the cause of her death. But even if it was, she couldn't figure his connection to Moira Middlemiss's murder.

'I didn't do anything to her either.' He began rewinding his film. 'You know I didn't because I was with you the whole time. I didn't even fancy her. Did you see her head, for God's sake? I don't go for women who shave their heads. She had more hair under her armpits than on her scalp. Horrible, you know?'

'Hmm,' Lenny said. Her neck ached where he had gotten a nasty pinch in.

'Tell me about Pluckrose, Harry.'

'I don't know what you're talking about.'

'Yes, you do. You know exactly what I mean. But what I want to know is *how much* do you know? Is he involved in the murders?'

'No! He –' Harry stopped, as though considering the question anew. He shook his head. 'No way. Pluckrose wouldn't have the nerve for that kind of thing. He's small-time.'

'Just the theft and vandalism then?' For this had always seemed obvious to her – and she assumed to the police. Graeme Pluckrose often worked late and he had his own key. He had plenty of opportunity to remove equipment and to destroy equipment. She had only to discover the motive. And to discover whether or not his animosity extended to murder.

'You're not much of a detective, are you?' Harry taunted, feathers still ruffled. 'We've all seen you sneaking those pills. What kind of fucked-up junkie are you?'

Lenny, who had planned to end by apologising about the racist Asian stuff, bristled instead.

'I have legitimate prescriptions for my medication.'

'Bullshit.'

'Thank you for your cooperation tonight. I may have more questions for you at a later date.' Offended, she became deadly formal. Harry saw through it and laughed in her face.

'You're not the police,' he sneered. 'I don't have to tell you a fucking thing.'

She left him winding his gore-fest back and forth, searching for any frame that didn't contain guns, or men reaching for guns, and snipping it out.

The Aaron house in Box Hill was a fawn-brick bungalow set back on a flat lawn with no trees or bushes; the grass was whipper-snippered to a soily stubble. The rarely opened windows were small and there was a chimney, although the fire had never been lit even on the coldest of winter days.

It was Lenny's mother's house. This was the first time she had not thought of it as her parents' house, and it was enough to get her running up the drive and smacking hard on the door, keen to get the visit over with.

'C'mon, I'm here!' she yelled.

Her mother appeared wearing her tracksuit and slippers and a hairnet over plastic curlers. They were the old sort, with hard plastic spines that bit into your head like needles, but she persisted in coiling her hair around them every third night and sleeping with her head held in one torturous position.

'Lenny, I am glad to see you. Why didn't you use your key?'

'I lost it.'

She had thrown it away.

'What on earth have you done to your hair? It's horrible.'

'It's no worse than yours. I need some aspirin.' Lenny stepped in. She felt her skin prickle, the horror of family contact providing, as it always did, a certain macabre thrill. The house smelled of cabbage and onions, and there was only twenty watts worth of light anywhere, because Veronica Aaron liked to save power.

'What is it? Are you sick?' Her mother was an eager nurse. Lenny remembered that from her childhood. Emotional despair merited no reaction, but a skinned knee had found her swamped with attention and treats. 'Oh my lord, and your face! You've cut yourself!'

'God, I hate coming here –'

'Lenny! What a nasty thing to say.' She didn't have to look to know the small hands were being wrung against the floral apron tied around the floppy stomach. 'If you have one of your moods, you needn't think you can take it out on me.'

'I don't have one of my moods. I've got a headache.'

She followed her mother into the kitchen at the back of the house and pressed herself into the chair that had been officially hers her whole life. It was part of a set of four matching chairs around a laminated table: one for Mum, one for Dad, one for Lenny and one for that school chum she never brought home for afternoon tea. She closed her eyes and breathed deeply.

She could hear footsteps, cabinets opening and closing, the sound of running water. A cool glass was placed in her hand.

'Take these.' Two pills were placed in her other hand and she took them, recognising Tylenol. It would have little effect in such a small dosage, but psychologically it was a fixer. Meanwhile her mother babbled on:

'I know I'm only an old fool. You don't listen to me. You want me to be something different ... I don't know what.'

Lenny had prepared for this evening, determined not to let it get out of hand. Dr Sakuno had gone through acceptable familial behaviour patterns and she was ready to begin his drill. She must open with what he referred to as a 'false courtesy'. Some comment about the neatness of the house, beauty of a particular plastic flower arrangement, any reference at all to an attractive article of clothing. It would be accepted as an overt sign of affection where none at all was felt. It was against every fibre of her being but, through clenched teeth, Lenny uttered the words: 'Is that a new lipstick you're wearing?' She was rewarded by a happy nod.

'Two for ten dollars. Wash your hands before tea,' her mother ordered and Lenny, who never needed a second invitation to clean up, went into the bathroom. It was tiny with a yellow duck motif in the tiles around the bath, a bright yellow shower curtain and a reassuring bleach smell. She scrubbed like a surgeon, up and down each finger, gouging her fingers into the soap to make sure the active antibacterial agent got any sneaky germs hiding under the nails.

She became aware of a metallic squeak in the garden, a familiar sound from her so-called childhood. She looked out. Ugg boots dipped into the frame of the narrow, lead-paned window above the basin and then disappeared. And again. Swung in from the left, paused in the air for a moment, then fell out of view. Lenny strained to widen her field of vision, but the window's slender confines frustrated her curiosity. The velocity increased. Small legs came into the picture, swung out again, fell away. Someone in the garden was using her swing, someone she couldn't see properly, no matter how she twisted in the foot-wide frame of the tiny window. Half a face came into frame: small, fattish. Hard to tell if it was male or female.

Lenny went back into the kitchen. 'What's that on my swing?'

'Mmm?' Her mother didn't look up from her potato-peeling.

'On the swing. In the garden. At the back of the house, where it's always been.'

'Oh, yes.' The peeler was placed against a stripped potato as her mother rose and went to the kitchen door. 'Come in now, dear!' she called.

'Is dinner ready?' a child's voice replied.

'Not quite. But it's too late to be out now – and Lenny's here.'

A small bloated face of Asian origin appeared in the back doorway. Its owner was probably twelve years old. Above a broad forehead the short black hair terminated in a high, pudding bowl fringe, as if the creature were auditioning for the part of a Vulcan dwarf in Star Trek. The nose was a twist of beige putty, the mouth a sloppy little hole that hung open with indolence or stupidity – it was hard to tell. This bizarre child-thing was wearing an old blue jumper which Lenny vaguely remembered, and shorts so tight her thighs strained threateningly against the fabric, splurting out at the hems. It was the ugliest child Lenny had ever seen and it stared at her from behind thick brown-framed lenses.

'Lenny, this is Kylie, Kylie Wong.' Her mother tied an apron around her waist and went to the stove, laying out sausages on a chopping board. She didn't meet Lenny's eyes. 'I've got a pie for dessert. Pecan. Coles had them reduced but they always put the expiry date earlier than it should be, to be on the safe side. And there's Delicious Dollop cream for on top. Kylie, I told you about Lenny. Lenny's got a headache tonight, so we have to be careful with her.'

'How d'ya get that cut?' The child's black eyes didn't waver from Lenny's red-rimmed sockets. It bit a piece off its thumbnail and spat it on the floor.

'What is this?' Lenny asked her mother.

'Kylie Wong,' her mother said casually, as if she were explaining the presence of a new vase. She hummed to herself, a high, nervous sound.

'What's she doing here?'

'Kylie, could you lay the dining table, please?' Something was about to blow and Lenny sensed she was being fitted up for the boiler suit.

Kylie remained at the kitchen table, opened the tub of Delicious Dollop and spooned a big mound of thickened cream into her mouth. Veronica Aaron pricked the sausages. 'I hate it when they pop their skins, don't you, Lenny?'

'Never mind the bloody sausages,' Lenny snapped. 'What's going on?'

Her mother put down her fork and said rapidly: 'Your father and I talked about this before he passed away. You know I've never lived alone and I need a bit of chitchat. I'm not like you, I'm sociable. You know I always go to the church fete and I've got my little knitting group but –'

'I'm fostered,' Kylie Wong cut in, oozing whiteness from the corners of her mouth. 'I sleep in your old bedroom.'

'What?'

Veronica Aaron picked up the fork and drilled the sausages. 'Your father and I saw a documentary on TV about the Chinese plight and those poor little mites and it just looked awful. You know they're only allowed to have one child. And they all want boys, you know. Sometimes if a girl is born they just put her in an orphanage or in the street where ninety percent of them die and – oh Lenny! Our hearts went out to them and we thought, we'll take a little Chinese girl. Well, it was so easy too. You just dial an 1800 number and have a talk. There's a fair bit of paperwork too, of course. And a police check. I passed that with flying colours.' She chuckled. 'Except they wouldn't let us adopt because of your father's condition and then we're getting on a bit. But they said even at our age we could foster. Of course when I became a widow I wondered about continuing but Daddy and I planned it so I thought why not? And they said it was still OK if I wanted to as long as I was providing a safe and secure environment so –'

'Wait!' Lenny held up a hand and turned to the child. 'Where were you born?'

'Wangaratta.' The cream had been abandoned and the child had moved on to trying to touch its nose with its tongue.

'That would be Wangaratta, Victoria, I suppose? Not Wangaratta, Szechuan?'

'It's only fostering . . .' Her mother slid the sausages into the frying pan. They spattered excitedly. 'It's different from adoption.'

'That's right. It means she can go straight back.'

'Lenny!'

'You must be crazy. What on earth do you know about bringing up a child?'

'I'm your mother.'

155

'I'm waiting.'

'Lenny!'

'She goes back.'

'You oughtn't let yourself be jealous of a little girl.' There was a gleam of triumph in her mother's eyes. So this had been the reason for the dinner invitation. It was her mother's way of showing her she wasn't needed any more. This, from someone who had spent the last sixteen months begging for attention. Such a slick turnaround was not to be tolerated.

Lenny walked out of the kitchen towards the living room. Her chest felt tight. Every time she returned to this house she was swamped by memories of her childhood, a childhood dominated by her father's illness. She loved him. She *had* loved him, she corrected herself immediately. But he hadn't taken a healthy breath her entire life. She hated his lungs. She hated his constant gasping. Most of all she hated his long-suffering niceness, his determination to be pleasant even in the face of the most god-awful death on the planet. Why couldn't he at least be angry even then? He'd gone to his fucking grave grateful for his meagre lot.

'Did you vacuum thoroughly in here?' she called out as she scanned the living room.

'Yes, fussy pants.'

'In the sofa?'

'Yes –'

'You better have.' She pulled a big cushion off the sofa to check. Veronica allowed lint and food crumbs to build up for months at a time. If there were any particles of any kind back here that was it, she was going. If there was a snotty tissue stuffed behind a cushion, she was going. If there was –

There was nothing. She *had* vacuumed. Lenny folded herself into the cushions.

The girl from Wangaratta had followed her and they sat amidst the orange and olive 'modern' wallpaper and the brown carpet in her mother's living room.

'I always spew when I've got a headache.' Kylie Wong was sitting on a pouf next to the sofa. The little gargoyle was fishing for a connection. Lenny wondered if her mother had been training it.

'I can spew one metre and forty centimetres.' Comparisons! Lenny remembered the game well. 'If I really tilt my head back and pump it from my gut. I used to be the second best at the home except for Mitchell Watson and he could do one metre and forty-five so I'm going to be better soon because he's fourteen and I'm only ten.'

'You're a bit big for ten, aren't you?' Lenny was drawn against her will. Freaks always intrigued her.

'I'm fat. I wasn't the fattest kid in the home though. Guts Raynor was twice as big.'

'Did Mrs Aaron get you from a children's home?'

'No. That was last year when Ma went to Tassie. She put me in the home for six months.' She paused, eyes glued to the TV. 'Ma said I didn't have to go in the home this time, but. She said I was gonna be fostered. Your mum's not the first to foster me, but.'

'Don't say *but*. It's "though".'

'What is?' The creature blinked at her.

'Never mind.'

'I've been fostered heaps before. Sometimes Ma can't cope by herself. She says she can't see her way around dealing with me as well as everything else she has to do. So she fosters me out. Ma's gonna have me back ... but.'

'Why don't you go and help Mrs Aaron.'

'I don't like cooking. I like eating, but.' In the half light of the lounge room the child's eyes seemed almost closed with fat. Lenny studied it. The head was squared to match

157

the frames of its glasses and it had a double chin.

As usual, the TV was on like background music and it was news time. Aquinas was the second story in. Lenny watched as her police file photo loomed on the screen. The private investigator involved in last year's Talbott family murder investigation, Helena Aaron of Footscray's H. Aaron Investigations, was currently employed by the Galaxy Insurance Corporation investigating a series of thefts at the Aquinas School of Film and Television. Police were unwilling to speculate on whether the thefts were connected to the recent gruesome murders. There was a shot of Lenny's office in Footscray, followed by a cat with scabies lurking behind a Safeway dumpster. It stumbled past the rotten vegetables spilling from the dumpster and slipped in a patch of oil. Lenny's file photo appeared again. The message was clear – she was a dirty bitch who worked the gutters. Walstab would be delighted.

'Isn't that you?' The child's finger fudged over Lenny's fuzzy TV face.

'Don't put your fingers on the screen.'

'Did you get to see the bloody eyeballs and everything?'

Lenny leaned close to the ugly little face.

'Yes,' she whispered. 'I saw the eyeballs, hanging by a thread, dripping blood from great empty sockets.' To her disappointment Kylie Wong's mouth was hanging open with excitement.

'Everything's cooking nicely now!' Her mother appeared in the door, backlit by the feeble kitchen light. 'Why don't you show Kylie some of your old toys?'

'Because this isn't a pyjama party,' Lenny rejoined. Dr Sakuno said that she and her mother were caught in a ritual of abuse. He pointed out that her mother thrived on opposition and therefore it would be more of a victory for

Lenny if she countered with kindness to spite her. Lenny was all at sea: what if he were wrong?

Her mother placed the pecan pie on the mountain-ash coffee table and arranged plates and teaspoons around it.

'I'm not staying for dinner.' Lenny made a snap decision. She rose to her feet. 'You've sprung your big drama. Congratulations. I'm off.'

'Oh, Lenny, dinner's nearly ready and I got the pie especially!' Veronica whined.

Lenny paused at the front door, her hand on the knob. The scene was somehow familiar, cinematic – the pecan pie, the girl, the rotten mother.

'Kylie can eat it,' she said. 'After all, it is Kylie's pie, isn't it?'

She drove home in a blur of temper, so grumpy that she almost missed it. Heading along Canterbury Road towards the city, something caught her eye in Surrey Park, a blur of arms and legs on the very edge of her vision. Her eyes were alert to peripheral distraction – a legacy of cat catching – but this movement was human and the shriek was a woman's.

Lenny pulled up in a no-parking zone, considered her options, then smiled as a thought came to her. She twisted round and surveyed the kendo body armour, helmet and *shinai* still on the back seat.

In under two minutes she was ready to roll. It was difficult running in full armour and she began to breathe heavily in the cool night air as she ran across the grass. She could hear them now, laughter and short screams. Two men and a woman.

She launched through a clump of bushes with a terrible cry. All three people before her howled in fright. Two men crouched over a woman who lay stretched out on the grass. Lenny raised the *shinai*. She brought it down on the crouched assailant's shoulder, knocking him forwards onto the woman whose clothes he had been tearing then reached out with her foot and pushed him to the side.

'What the fu –' The second man, pants down around his ankles, tried to run backwards and dropped to his knees. Lenny pulled the blunt end of the *shinai* back and rammed it into his testicles. He doubled over, vomited and began to moan. The first man was getting back to his feet. She twirled and, with a centred shriek, let him have it in the face. He dropped like sparrow shit.

'Don't kill me ... don't ...' His nose streamed blood. Lenny grinned beneath the helmet's bars. Of course she wouldn't *kill* him. Even as a police officer she had never *killed* anyone. But she had seen a lot of death. Road accidents, domestic violence victims, bar brawls, knife attacks and shootings. It had washed over her, a steady, background static of hate. She never even wondered what was happening to those things zipped into body bags. Out of nowhere, she remembered her father's fear, once when he hadn't been expecting her visit and turned a death mask to her a split second before it disguised itself, morphed into a smile of welcome, became Dad again.

Her biter-bitten was trying to crawl into an azalea bush. He froze as Lenny called him out, then came, cowering in the grass at her feet. He grovelled well.

'Who are you?' he whispered.

Lenny reached down a glove and helped the woman up. She was older in the moonlight, at least fifty, with a large boil on her chin and a tooth missing. She spat at the man. 'Bastard!' she screeched.

'I'm sorry,' he sobbed.

'Are you really?' said the woman. She removed a vinyl stiletto, swung back her gnarled forearm and drove its spike into her attacker's cheek. He screamed and put his hand to his face. His thumb accidentally slipped through the puncture left by the stiletto and he found himself touching his tongue. He screamed some more. The woman swung the weapon back again. 'I'll fuckin' do ya –'

Lenny restrained her. Something was wrong, upsetting her rescue scenario. 'Excuse me. You're safe now,' she said pleasantly. 'Just call the police.'

The woman wrenched free. 'Get fucked!'

Lenny squinted. 'What did you say?'

'I'm *working*, moron! They'll say I asked for it.'

Lenny turned to the man who was helping his friend up, one hand over the hole in his face. He was still waiting for an answer: who was she? She raised both her arms in the air.

'I am watching you. Beware! I am ... I am ... Beware!'

The unhappy punters staggered deeper into the park. Lenny could see a group of skinheads heading towards them. She tried not to think about what would happen when the parties met. It was proving to be a big night for the two chums. The prostitute saw the skinheads too, and tugged at Lenny's arm. She allowed herself to be led back to the road.

'Give us a lift?' the woman wheedled coyly. Close-up she smelled of gin and roast beef, and she needed a shave. Lenny shook her head. A taxi appeared further down the road and she pointed to it. 'What kind of a rat-arsed superhero are you?' the woman sneered.

Lenny slipped into the front seat of her car. The prostitute checked her lippie in the wing mirror. 'Yeah, go on – piss off, Sir Galahad,' she said, casting a speculative eye over the male driver showcased in the window of the approaching taxi.

Lenny waved a fat blue superhero's glove as she drove away. She waited until she was out of sight before removing the helmet and tossing it onto the back seat. Her face was coated with sweat. But Dr Sakuno had been wrong: there had been an occasion to use her equipment, right here in the real world.

CHAPTER 13

Lunch Date

Lenny spent the weekend studying the profiles of the third year students and Aquinas staff members. The murders of Emily and Moira now dominated her thoughts. Who really cared about the stolen equipment any more? Young women were having their eyeballs cut out of their skulls. And anyway, there had to be a connection, didn't there? What about the sound tape Ray had stolen from the green room? 'R & A'? Ray – most likely – and A? Annabel Lear was Lenny's prime suspect. It seemed unlikely to her that cuddly, exuberant Alana Zappone was involved in a secret scandal with Cate Ray.

Saturday and Sunday night she popped into her office to feed Bertrand Russell. She took him out of the cage to let him run around for half an hour but he sat quietly, refusing to cooperate. He pursed his pink lips and smiled at her, as if he knew what a hot potato he was, a hot potato smothered in the sour cream of scandal. She hoped to God he didn't die of some perfectly natural illness before she figured out what to do with him.

She was still furious with her mother over the Kylie Wong fiasco, but in retrospect she supposed she should have expected something like this. For one thing it was the kind of over-the-top gesture her mother thrived on. And having spent most of her adult life as a vigilant and devoted nurse to Ted Aaron, Veronica Aaron had a chronic need to care for someone; Granny Sanderman would never provide much in the way of a substitute. That one let you get close all right, just close enough to give you a pinch or a bite. Lenny knew she was to blame for the situation. There was a gap that had to be filled in Veronica's life and Kylie Wong was filling it in her stead.

Late Sunday night she needed to unwind and decided to go to see a film. She went to the Lumiere in Lonsdale Street, which was showing *Touch of Evil*. The print had been restored to Welles' original vision. 'Magnificent! Classic!' screamed the posters.

Lenny bought a packet of Fantales and sat down on the black vinyl couch underneath a wall of posters promoting European art films, John Cassavetes and Stanley Kubrick. A man and a woman sat beside her clutching *Touch of Evil* handbills.

'Welles had to fight every inch of the way for this one,' the man said. He wore black jeans, a black leather coat, a dark grey shirt and black slip-on boots. 'The opening shot is a masterpiece.'

The woman nodded. From the way she kept staring at the walls, the people around her and even the ceiling – anywhere but her partner's face – Lenny guessed she was a blind date in full regret.

They filed into the cinema, the curtain opened and the film began. The first shot was indeed an interesting piece of work. After that, to Lenny's mind, it was all downhill. Marlene Dietrich was great – this was the perfect vehicle to showcase her mastery of cheesy camp – but Charlton Heston's Mexican cop was just plain silly and she sniggered to herself at the extremely unscary evil bikers frightening Janet Leigh in her motel room.

The next morning she spring-cleaned. It was an inaccurate expression for someone who did most people's idea of spring-cleaning once every three weeks. She scoured the interior of the oven with brillo pads, defrosted the fridge and dusted the top of the wardrobe. Then she called Gabrielle Danaher.

Gabrielle answered the phone sounding tired, then surprised to hear Lenny's voice. She agreed, since they had no shoot scheduled that day, that she was available to be interviewed and so around noon Lenny parked outside her house in North Fitzroy. It was a former workers' cottage, built in the twenties but fallen into disrepair. Someone had thrown a groundsheet over part of the roof and weighed it down with sandbags. It was garbage day and the wheelie bin was overflowing, the black plastic recycling crates stuffed with milk cartons, wine bottles, unopened bills and a handful of local streetpapers: *Melbourne Star Observer*, *BrotherSister*, *The Yarra Leader*. A motorbike, Gabrielle's she supposed, was propped against an iron fence which had every other railing missing.

The grass in the garden was waist high, except where it had been squashed with two broken rows of bricks to form a pathway to the front steps. There was a stack of cardboard boxes piled up on the verandah, half covering the windows. Those bits of the windows that were visible near the top were cracked and crisscrossed with gaff tape. Lenny knocked on the front door. No one answered.

She pushed gently and the door swung back. A long corridor ran from the front door through to the back of the house where there was another open door. The atmosphere was ripe with the friendly smell of marijuana, which seemed to have stained the prim, mint-green walls a funkier hue in places.

Off the corridor to the left were four doors – presumably

bedrooms – each padlocked: perhaps the household already knew that one of them was a thief and possibly a serial killer. Lenny went past the bedrooms and found herself in the room with the open door at the back.

It was a living room. At least, it was struggling to be a living room. It had neither curtains, blinds nor carpet for assistance. There was a yellow vinyl sofa with a cushion missing against one wall facing a single kitchen chair with a portable TV on it. One side of the TV had been got at with a blowtorch – or perhaps had fallen onto a heater – and looked like a dripping candle.

The *Herald Sun* was scattered about on the floor. Lenny picked it up automatically to place it on the sofa and a headline caught her eye:

'KOMODO MAN' ATTACKS JOGGERS'

Box Hill workmates Matt Alabakis and Philip Johnson sustained serious injuries last Friday after a vicious attack in Surrey Park. The two friends were jogging when they were set upon by a large reptile-like creature. According to Mr Alabakis, their assailant had the appearance of a giant lizard. 'Like the Komodo Dragon, that big lizard in Bali,' said a shaken Mr Alabakis after receiving stitches for a facial injury. The two men claimed they had not been drinking and that the 'Komodo Man' was covered with scales, had hard, bony shoulder blades and some kind of facial deformity. The Komodo Dragon is found exclusively on Komodo Island, 450 km east of Bali. A spokesperson for Melbourne Zoo denied reports that one of their three Komodo Dragons had escaped and was currently at large in the Box Hill area.

The story was accompanied by an artist's impression of 'Komodo Man'. To her horror, Lenny recognised the vague outline of her kendo outfit. She folded the paper and put it in her shoulder bag. Going out through the back door, she stood at the top of a rickety flight of stairs and looked down.

Janus Onyszkiewicz, Gabrielle and another boy were standing in the back garden staring at something. Looking up, Janus saw Lenny but made no attempt to alert Gabrielle or the other boy. She knew he would have thought it a weakness to do so – an unnecessary communication, a frivolous waste of his energy.

Eventually Gabrielle glanced up and waved. The other boy, pointy-jawed with shaggy grey hair and a bad complexion, peered up too. As Gabrielle stepped away towards the stairs, Lenny saw what they were looking at. A tubby teenager lay on a blow-up mattress, nude except for scarlet panties and sunglasses, sunbaking despite the cool air. Her large breasts rolled down near her armpits and her stomach was a pearly ball. She spoke with a thick German accent:

'If you are strong you can have the tan all year round with willpower. And it is spring now – not so cold. So am I having this great body, or what, Gabrielle?'

Gabrielle ignored her and came up the stairs. 'You're early.'

'I'm exactly on time.'

Gabrielle shrugged. 'You win.' Lenny followed her into the kitchen. Gabrielle opened the fridge, which was held shut with a strip of gaff tape, and pulled out sliced white bread, margarine and plastic cheese. It was the only time Lenny had seen ants running *out* of a fridge.

'Lunch?' Gabrielle asked.

'Thank you, no.' There was no way she would be ingesting anything in this shithole.

Gabrielle shrugged, went over to the sink and selected a knife from the pile waiting to be washed up.

'How long have you lived here?' Lenny asked, eyes never leaving the knife as it gouged into the margarine and began to butter its filthy way across the bread.

'Ah! The investigator's first question. Two years.' Gabrielle didn't cut the bread and didn't use a plate. As Lenny watched, she took a mouthful, chewed and swallowed. Lenny forced herself to speak:

'Janus doesn't seem the type to –'

'– live in a dump like this?' Gabrielle finished. 'Who else would have him? Emily was here too. Before she died she rented a bedroom and slept here two or three nights a week. She wanted to get away from her parents sometimes. Not that it worked. Abel, her dad, called to check on her every night. But it was good when she was here. She bought a lot of food. We got Saskia – you saw her out the back – after Emily.'

'Is Saskia your girlfriend?'

The remains of the sandwich vanished into Gabrielle's mouth. She licked a buttery finger then examined the nail, picked out some dirt beneath it and flicked it away.

'Pointless question. Also leading,' she said.

Lenny wanted to wash her hands but the towel hanging over the sink was encrusted with food barnacles.

Gabrielle went to the sink and filled a rusty kettle with water then put it on the gas. From a milk crate in the corner she took two cups from a filthy pile.

'None for me,' Lenny said quickly. 'Tell me what you know about the equipment theft at Aquinas this year.'

'I don't know anything about it.' Gabrielle replied. 'Do the police think it's connected to Em's death? Or Moira's?'

'I'll ask the questions, thanks.'

Gabrielle smiled slightly. 'Fuck!' She dropped a cup and it smashed onto the floor. A large cockroach ran out of the shattered pieces. Lenny's hand moved instinctively to her mouth.

Gabrielle used her boot to push the broken cup to one side.

'This house is riddled with roaches,' she said. 'I had one on my pillow last night. I was asleep and there was this soft twitching against my cheek. I opened my eyes and a huge bastard was looking right at me. Its feelers were brushing against me. I was eating chocolate last night.' She touched a fingertip to her teeth reflectively. 'It probably wanted a taste.'

'You didn't come to the Russ Myer lecture,' Lenny said.

'I've been busy. The police still seem to think I can help them with their investigation. They think I *am* their investigation. They think I cut Emily's throat, then cut out her eyes. Then I stabbed Moira in the throat and made off with one of her eyes as well. I suppose you do too? Or maybe you just think I'm the thief? Selling off Aquinas equipment to fuel my drug habit, and smashing things in a rage when I lose control.'

'Tell me about your drug habit,' Lenny suggested. Gabrielle's mouth compressed. It had been a slip caused by anger and she regretted it. She shook her head.

Janus appeared at the door. 'Saskia is mooning the neighbours.' He glared at Lenny. 'I have no information to offer you, Investigator.'

'I came to see Gabrielle.'

'Good.' He stalked out.

'Does he have a girlfriend?' Lenny asked.

'There's a woman who calls. He's never happy about it.'

'Why are the police focusing on you?'

Gabrielle poured boiling water into her cup and dangled a tea bag in it. There was a purple sludge-line of lipstick on the rim of the cup.

'They have elephant memories.' Gabrielle sipped the tea without removing the bag. She finally noticed the lipstick.

'Jesus, Saskia is a dirty bitch.' But it didn't stop her taking another sip.

Lenny cracked. She took out a bottle and poured a pile of pills into her palm. She selected a pale lavender one. Haldol 0.5 mg. *Sayonara* misery and spleen.

'What are you taking?'

Lenny swallowed. 'It's none of your business. But I forget – you're speaking as a professional, aren't you?'

'You can't prove I'm dealing,' Gabrielle replied. 'You can't prove it or you wouldn't be able to resist telling me. If I was, it would be to fund my films. It wouldn't have anything to do with these murders. Or the thefts.'

'Did Emily ever give you money?'

'Sure.'

'How much?'

'Five thousand. I was with her in the bank when she withdrew it.' Gabrielle smiled. 'She filled out a slip and they slid the whole lot across the counter. I've never held that much money before.'

'Drug money?'

'I helped her in a few different ways, Lenny. But the five thousand was for assisting her with her second year film. She hired some equipment privately to do pick-ups. I was DOP for her this year too. And I used to advise her on editing. Since you're asking for the truth today, it didn't help much. Emily's work was never very good.'

'You have a history with Moira.'

Gabrielle became very still. Her eyes narrowed for a long moment and then she smiled again.

'Congratulations. I was wondering when someone would dig that up. You are referring, of course, to her attending the same primary school as me?'

'At the time Samantha Burridge died.'

'Quite the bizarre coincidence, don't you think?'

'The police will naturally assume she knew something about Samantha's death. Something that implicated you.'

'Naturally.'

'And you were in the car park when Moira was killed. You must have seen someone go into the green room.'

'I was facing the other way.'

'Bullshit.'

'Prove it.'

'If they put it together with your drug record and the fact that Emily was using amphetamines, you're very high on the suspect list, Gabrielle.'

'They know about the drugs already, of course. It's on my file. But they haven't figured out Moira went to the same school yet. You're one step ahead of them, Lenny.'

'Was Moira blackmailing you?'

Gabrielle only shook her head. 'You know, this is my fourth experience with the police,' she said. 'And I have to say they're very intimidating when they think you've done something.'

'Have you done something?' They locked eyes. Gabrielle tilted her head slightly, considering, ran her eyes down Lenny's long, thin body.

'Why? Fancy me as a killer, do you?'

This annoyed Lenny. She didn't like to think she could be found out so easily. Although Gabrielle lived in a pigsty, Lenny was already prepared to attribute most of the rotten hygiene to the influence of Saskia and the other flatmate. Janus probably wasn't the sort of person to wash up after himself either. Lenny imagined herself showing Gabrielle the pleasures of cleanliness, the two of them spending long afternoons together in a sterile environment sipping *macha* from clean bowls. She forced herself to concentrate.

'If you're guilty, Gabrielle, I'm going to find out.'

Gabrielle smiled. 'I am guilty, Lenny.'

CHAPTER 14

Twirling the Spools

It was Tuesday morning. Kylie Wong, spinning for the twentieth time in the office chair, laughed like a lunatic. Lenny looked away. Her mother had asked her to 'have' Kylie for the morning while she went to visit a friend. Lenny, remembering Dr Sakuno's theory that she could create more anguish by thwarting her mother's need for opposition, had agreed. It seemed to work – her mother had been very suspicious and told Kylie the number of the emergency service 'in case anything goes wrong'. Lenny smiled as she avoided holding Kylie's grubby hand. She would show her mother how to win this game.

'Can I play with the cat?' Kylie pointed at Bertrand Russell, the furry stick of dynamite set to blow Lenny's livelihood to smithereens.

'No.' Lenny thrust five dollars at the child. 'Go and buy an ice-cream.'

'You're just trying to get rid of me.' Kylie Wong pocketed the money. Lenny opened the door and waited until Kylie passed through it, then closed it with a sharp click.

She tidied up, locked her office door and glanced around the corridor. She waited for a few minutes. How long did it take to buy one ice-cream? Perhaps Kylie Wong had become lost amongst the crowd and wasn't able to find her way back to the office? That wouldn't be abandonment, it would be an unfortunate oversight, an accident.

Lenny raced out to the car park. The key turned easily in her car door. She slipped into the driver's seat and shut the door. Just as she turned the key in the ignition, Kylie materialised at her window, sticky ice-cream in hand.

'You were trying to dump me!' She squinted through her glasses.

Lenny wound the window down. 'No I wasn't,' she muttered. 'Let's go. It's time I dropped you off.'

'Wanna suck of my ice-cream?' Lenny shook her head. Half of it was already running down the child's wrist. Kylie got into the passenger seat and turned up the radio. Lenny turned it down. They glared at each other.

'You're mean.' Kylie kicked her feet rhythmically. 'Mum said you're a nutcase 'cos you're seeing a doctor for mental patients.'

'How's school?' Lenny changed the subject.

'I was off sick yesterday.' Spoken with the cunning smile of the healthy shirker. 'I had a temperature so Mum said I didn't have to go. Excellent, eh? I'm in grade five at Box Hill Primary.' Kylie wound down her window and flung out the remains of her cone.

'I hate it, but,' she continued. She opened the glove box.
'Shut that.'

'Nobody likes me 'cos I'm new.' Kylie shut the glove box and wound the window up and down. 'And who wants to be friends with the fat Chinese kid?'

A better person than Lenny Aaron would have embarked on a speech at this point, something about believing in ourselves, because we're all special. Lenny murmured: 'You're breaking my heart.'

She had already telephoned the Victorian child welfare

service and checked out this whole foster parent scam. To her relief she discovered it was unlikely to be long term. The emphasis these days was on returning the child to its real family *as soon as possible*.

'How often do you see your parents? Do they live in Melbourne?' They must. The welfare people had told her they matched children with foster parents living in the same area as their real parents.

'We used to live in Nunawading but Ma's gone off again.'

'Gone off?'

'She phoned me last night and said she was off up to Sydney for a few months. I wish she'd take me.'

'Me too.'

'She's got a new boyfriend in Sydney, she says. Ace, hey?'

'What about your father?'

'Dunno.'

'Dunno where he is?'

'Dunno who he is.'

'Charming.'

'Well your mum says you're a lezzo.'

Lenny pulled over to the side of the road, switched off the engine and used all her energy to control herself. She turned a perfectly blank face to the child.

'I'm sorry?' The voice that several years of police work had honed to serration.

'Not me! She did!' Kylie protested. 'She said you never have any boyfriends and you're never going to get married and you're either an old maid or a lezzo.'

Lenny leaned in close. She could smell the ice-cream on the child's breath. Kylie tried to wriggle back into the door. 'You're a very annoying little girl and I don't like annoying little girls. Especially nasty, rude ones who can't keep their mouths shut. So you'd better watch out around me. My mother is right. I'm a nutcase. You don't know what I might do.'

Liquid raced down the chubby cheeks, a hiccuping sob came from the soft lips.

Lenny stared out of the window. She waited. She glanced back. Now the pudgy shoulders were heaving. She heard the word 'meanie' spoken in a half defiant, half frightened voice.

She reached into her jacket, took out a handkerchief bleached to within an inch of its life and thrust it at Kylie.

'Here.'

'Don't want it.'

'Wipe your eyes and here –' she handed over a mini pack of tissues. 'Blow your nose on those.'

'But I can use the hankie.'

Lenny snatched it back. 'Use the tissues,' she said. Kylie blew hard. 'Right.' Lenny started the car again. 'Let's get you home.' To Mrs Aaron's house, she amended mentally. After all, it was a short-term arrangement.

'What do you wanna catch cats for anyway?' Kylie flicked the radio from station to station until Lenny's glance made her stop, sigh and sit back. 'I like dogs better. So does Mum.'

'Veronica isn't your mum.'

'She said I could call her Mum. She said she was like my mum now. She's an oldie though, hey? Ma's only fourteen years older than me! She's good-looking too. All the guys go after her. She has a new boyfriend every year! I'm gonna be like that when I'm grown up. I saw you on TV again. Your mum says you're a private detective. Like in the movies, except you haven't got a gun or anything. Have you ever been shot or stabbed or anything?'

'Yes.'

'Excellent!' Kylie bounced in her seat, her plump chest making premature breasts. 'Show us your scars!'

'Show *me*,' Lenny corrected. Her mobile rang and she answered it.

'Lenny Aaron?' It was Ray and she sounded venomous.

'Yes?'

'Cate Ray here. I think we'd better discuss whether or not your presence in the school has any chance of preventing the death of any more of my students. Be in my office at eleven.' The line went dead. It was twenty to eleven. Lenny wondered whether she was supposed to feel intimidated, but she was ready for the school principal. The previous day's lunch with Gabrielle had been disturbing in more ways than one. But every interrogation yielded something useful, and Gabrielle Danaher had inadvertently provided the final piece of a small puzzle.

'Where are we going?' Kylie Wong asked. 'Are we having lunch soon?' Lenny pressed on the accelerator.

She left the kid in the car park behind Aquinas.

'You're not supposed to leave children in the car,' Kylie protested. 'What if someone crashes their car into me? What if someone kidnaps me?'

'Who would want you?' Lenny shot back. 'Keep the doors locked and don't touch the radio.'

She arrived at the principal's office after first letting herself into the storeroom to pick up a couple of things. She had slipped a Nagra into her shoulder bag along with a fresh sound tape and a tiny lapel mic.

'You're relieved of your duties,' Ray said the instant Lenny stepped through the door. 'I consider Moira's death to be entirely due to your incompetence. I can't allow you to put further lives at risk.'

Lenny stubbed out her cigarette and lit another. Her shoulder bag containing the equipment from the storeroom rested on her lap.

'I was hired by Galaxy, not you,' she said. 'And I'm not a security guard. Frankly I'd advise you to sack your security. They're not working as a deterrent. It seems to me that anyone can walk in and out whenever they feel like it. Half the school was apparently sneaking around the campus the night Emily Cunningham was killed. It's not my job to protect anyone. It's not my job to solve your murders either.' As she said this, she realised that every inch of her was straining to do so. 'I was hired to investigate theft, which I am doing.'

'With zero success. If you wish to save face, I'll let you resign but I want you off the campus.'

'Since I came here,' Lenny mused, 'I've had a bit of time to observe the way things work. And I've come to the conclusion that Aquinas is a learning institution in name only. It's much more about competition with the focus on winning an overseas festival or getting your third year film a TV release. The Silver Shutter and the prizes you award personally are very important in that regard. They create interest – professional interest – in upcoming students' work.'

Ray seemed puzzled by Lenny's change of tack.

'Now, say I was, just for example's sake, Emily's dad and I wanted Emily to have a better chance than the others even though she didn't deserve it. I wonder if there wouldn't be some way I could persuade the person who controlled the prizes to cast more than a casual eye over my little precious's opus?'

'Aaron, you've overplayed a sad hand. Forget about resigning – you're fired. I want your locker cleaned out and your key returned to the office by tomorrow morning.'

Lenny waggled a finger in Ray's face. 'Now, imagine that Moira knew someone was accepting donations of a personal nature to influence her prize-giving judgement. But how did Moira know about this? Well, she fancied herself as a bit of a prophetess, and a prophetess has to know everything that's going on. So she got herself the equipment to do it right – cameras, recorders, microphones. Even tiny mics that fit anywhere.'

Lenny took a Nagra tape recorder out of the shoulder bag and placed it on the edge of the desk. Then she unwrapped a fresh tape, threaded it onto the Nagra and positioned a lapel mic about the size of a fingernail on top of a pile of books. She smiled. 'This bit's important. See? I'm labelling the tape, which is one of the things the David O. Lincoln Academy taught me.' She drew out a purple pen and wrote 'R & L' on the tape.

'R for Ray, L for Lenny,' she explained.

Ray looked from the tape to Lenny's face. A stray hair was pushed back into the severe line of her bob.

Lenny switched the Nagra on to record and the spools twirled. 'Moira might – Wait! Let's make sure we've got a good level . . .' She played the tape back: *Moira might – Wait!*

'That's fine.' She beamed and switched the machine back into record mode. 'Now, as I see it, Moira might have bugged an office – even this office. She might have taped a private conversation with one of her radio mics – say, Mr Cunningham talking about the Aquinas prizes for first and second year, and how his daughter came to get both of them. When she heard this conversation, Moira might have decided she was in a position of power, a position where she could make a few demands. I'm talking about black-mailing a staff member, of course. Perhaps she asked for a new prize, a documentary prize for something like the one she was making. Perhaps Moira carried the tape around in that bag of hers to threaten the relevant party on a day-to-day basis, to make sure they didn't change their mind. I'm talking about an Ampex half-inch sound tape, like this one, that had 'R & A' written on it in purple pen. R for Ray, I mean. And A for Abel. Abel Cunningham, Emily's father. The police might see a motive for murder there. In fact they didn't find a tape in her bag, did they? But I saw it in her bag next to her dead body, just before I left you alone in the room. So I might be able to help the police find out who has that tape now.'

Ray pursed her lips and a sneer furrowed the top of her nose. 'Even if that tape existed, you'll never find it now.'

She was right, Lenny thought. It would take little effort to run it through the bulk eraser, that powerful magnetic machine that nuked any sound and video tapes passed into its humming interior. Moira's evidence would have turned into background hiss in seconds.

Lenny took a Polaroid out of her bag. It was the Polaroid of the Ampex tape in Moira's bag. She held it up for a moment, let Ray get a good look at it, then dropped it back into her bag. 'Trust me,' she said. 'Even if they can't prove what was on the tape, they'll arrest you for removing evidence from a crime scene. And if it goes to a jury, that won't look good, Ray. Juries think the person who steals evidence from the murder scene is the murderer.'

Ray was silent for a minute, weighing her options.

'Ms Aaron . . . Lenny.' She smiled shyly. 'As you know, there are stresses associated with being a professional woman. My husband – you must have heard of him. Richard Gyopar of Gyopar and Robson Design. Well, he's threatened by me. We've adopted a boy, you know. I'm not interested in pregnancy but Richard wanted a child. In the end I gave in. I find it's still the woman's role to compromise, don't you?'

'This is going to become relevant, isn't it?' Lenny interjected.

'I'm trying to explain how the . . . the fictional scenario you spoke about may have happened.'

'OK.' Lenny blew a couple of smoke rings towards Ray's poster of *The Maltese Falcon*.

'Richard wanted a boy. So we adopted Wayne, who is fourteen years old. Richard also thought we should take one unlikely to be chosen by other prospective parents, an older one. You could say Wayne was a cast-off. Wayne! Richard won't even let me change the name. I wanted Xavier or Theodore.' She laughed.

Lenny thought of the pudgy little troublemaker in her car. Was she flattening the battery by mucking about with the radio?

'Shortly after Wayne came into our lives, Richard made a disastrous investment. It was in a Docklands project that never got up. My husband isn't a political animal, Lenny. He was, for want of a better word, a chump. A chump for the same developers who are now building the world's tallest building.'

'The one on Norfolk Island?'

Ray nodded. 'Those bastards.'

'So you needed money . . .'

'Boarding school fees are exorbitant too.' Ray spread her hands wide. 'And there was his clothing. I couldn't have him wearing the Kmart crap he came with. On top of that he still goes to a psychiatrist for behavioural problems he picked up playing league. And a speech therapist, of course. Once we get the western suburbs out of his accent he'll have a better chance at school. These things take time and money. I hope that helps explain things for you.' She looked up at Lenny, seemed to make a decision. She drummed her fingertips on the desk top, her Rolex scattering sunlight.

'Look, I was hasty in regard to your position. You're doing valuable work for the school. Extremely valuable. I couldn't be happier with your efforts to date. I certainly anticipate us enjoying a long, successful partnership as we work together to end the theft and vandalism Aquinas has suffered recently.' She smiled again, leaning into the lapel mic. 'And I can assure you that any suggestions of administrative impropriety here at Aquinas are fantasy.'

'So you're saying you didn't accept money from Emily's father to allow her into this school? Or elevate her grades? Or award her your personal prize two years in a row, even though her work was universally panned as crap?'

Ray wrenched the Nagra off and rewound the tape. She untwirled the locking nuts, removed the reel of tape, slammed it into her desk drawer and gestured to the door. 'Good luck with your investigation, Lenny. I'm busy.'

Lenny took her time slouching out of the office. She felt marvellous.

Kylie Wong scowled at her when she got back into the Celica.

'You were ages and I'm bored.'

Lenny reached for a bottle of cough medicine from the glove box.

'What's that stuff?'

'It's medicine. I've got a cough.'

'I haven't heard you cough.'

Lenny had a list of vicious barbs ready to silence the child but the memory of Ray's unfortunate Wayne silenced her. She looked at the child: obese and never likely to be pretty.

'If I say I've got a cough, then I've got a cough,' she said.

'One of the nurses at the home loved that stuff.' Kylie Wong sucked the corner of her thumb. 'Because it's mostly alcohol.'

Mostly codeine, Lenny corrected mentally.

'She stole it from the medicine cupboard,' Kylie continued. 'I tried some but it's terrible.'

'Not if you've got a cough.' Lenny started the car. 'And I've got a cough.'

CHAPTER 15

Mr Cunningham in the Living Room with Pincers

Kylie Wong forgot all about the cough medicine and the orphanage nurse in the excitement of the couple of hundred dollars Lenny ran up at a boutique in Brunswick Street. The clothes were a small improvement. Lenny dropped her off at her mother's house and said she couldn't come in, she had an appointment to keep. For once it was true.

Misses Attwood and Rendell's latest communication was that the Cunninghams had finally returned her call and would see her at their Hawthorn East home. She had wanted to see them for some time now, especially Abel Cunningham. *He's not a man I'd like to cross and he fucking hates dykes*, Annabel had said. Perhaps Mr Cunningham hated Lucy Peel, then. But what had her relationship with Emily done to his feelings for his daughter? Turned them to hate, to revulsion? And Moira, who had taped his private conversation with Cate Ray – did he know about that?

The Cunninghams' landscaped garden was hidden behind a three-metre-tall stone fence. The iron gate was open and Lenny drove in. It was a ritzy mansion for Australia's hardware royalty, she thought. Must be selling a lot of hammers and nails.

The hardware king opened the front door, rosy cheeks glowing and both hands firmly tucked (as they were in billboards across the state) into the oversized pockets of his jacket. Only the smile, familiar to all who had passed his green and white bannered chain stores, was missing. The blue business suit looked as though it had seen a few too many days and his TV toupee was missing. He was completely bald. His eyes were narrow and sharp and Lenny saw obsession in their red-rimmed stare.

'I'm Lenny Aaron.' She held out her hand. He reached out and gripped it hard. Lenny looked down and discovered the genetic origin of Emily Cunningham's thumb. Her father's right arm stopped at the wrist and became three hard, unnaturally red nodules. They curved around her hand.

The other hand was amputated, or perhaps had never existed at all. It had been replaced by a large metal creation. Not a hook. More like mental pincers that she supposed could reach out for a book or even accept coins. Certainly he never gave either limb a showing on national TV.

He read her mind. 'Congenital,' he said. 'Call me Abel.'

She nodded. As with any human being confronted by another bearing witness to life's cruelty, a thought slipped into Lenny's mind: thank God it's not me.

There was a long pause during which he examined every part of her appearance and made it clear he didn't like what he saw.

'Through here.'

She followed him down the long corridor. He opened a door and they entered a formal living room. A large oval table covered with a thick linen cloth held photos of Emily at all stages of her life. She had been spotty during her teenage years and had taken to wearing power suits during her early twenties. Through French windows a carpenter could be seen at work assembling a pagoda out of prefabricated pieces of pine.

Daphne Cunningham was in a reclining rocking chair, a tartan blanket pulled up almost to her neck. She made a move as though to rise from the chair and then, at the last moment, placed a hand to her temple and slipped down again.

'Ms Aaron, help us –' She held out hands that reminded Lenny of plump white fish. Halibut. Around one of them was looped a pearly set of rosary beads.

All the furniture was undersized. And the room reminded Lenny of a doll's house whose dolls had been bought separately and were too big for it. Abel Cunningham rang a bell while Lenny wedged herself into a tiny armchair.

'No, no! Not there!' Abel yelled. Lenny was struggling to her feet when she realised he was yelling at the man outside, building the pagoda.

A young woman in a checked blue tunic appeared at the door.

'Tea, thanks, Jenny,' Abel said. He opened the windows. 'Gently, now. This thing is designed to fit together as smooth as butter. Each piece of wood slots into the next. That's the beauty of the design.'

'The good china, Jenny,' Daphne ordered. She looked anxiously at Lenny. 'You do like tea? I find coffee gives me a headache, although young people today seem to exist on it.' She shrugged helplessly, a victim of her inability to understand so many things. She was only in her mid-fifties, but certain women have an early grandmotherhood; called, as it were, to the doily before their time.

'Tea is fine, Mrs Cunningham.' Lenny said.

'Daphne and Abel. I saw you on TV.' Daphne smiled gently. 'Last year, too, when your arm was cut open by that dreadful Vivian Talbott in Brighton. I met her at a

184

charity function once, you know. I could have told you she'd end badly.'

The TV news was on. An elderly man walking home from the Pump House Hotel in Fitzroy reported that he had been pushed into the fountain outside the Royal Exhibition Building by Komodo Man. Police had issued a general warning to inner city Melburnians to avoid night-time park walks. Lenny examined the revised artist's sketch, which was becoming more detailed, more fanciful. Needle-like teeth sprouted from a nascent kendo mask. It was a powerful image, like something out of an advertisement for a science fiction film. The staff hack had obviously enjoyed the break from court sketches.

Komodo Man had captured the city's imagination, and he would become more glamorous, more ferocious, with each successive 'attack'. Even if Lenny explained to the police and press what had really happened, there would be a percentage of the population who would continue to believe in Komodo Man. Truth was irrelevant once the seed of fantasy was sown. There was a wild beast out there because Melburnians wanted a wild beast out there.

'What a frightening story.' Daphne shivered. 'Other people to be preyed on, murdered . . .' She pressed a piece of starched lace to her eyes.

'It's the medication,' Abel offered. 'The doctor's got her on some powerful stuff for her nerves.'

'Don't make excuses for me, Abel.' Daphne's temper showed through her sweetness. 'I'm sure Lenny doesn't need it explained to her that a woman suffering the loss of the only person she's ever loved would be in distress. And if that person takes one or two pills to cope – to *survive* – well, I'm sure Lenny wouldn't judge harshly, would you dear?'

Lenny's mouth opened and closed like a fish sucking the

edge of the tank. The pill bottle in her pocket felt like a lead weight. How awful to be accurately summed up by someone so ... pathetic.

The tea came. They both waited for Lenny to drink. She leaned forward and took a cup that was so small she had to hold the handle between her index finger and thumb and grip hard. Perhaps this was Abel's psychological gambit, to make drinking as difficult for those with commonplace appendages as it was for him. She drank the contents in a gulp.

'Delicious.' She opened her notebook. 'Right, then. Did Emily ever talk to you about the thefts at Aquinas this year?'

'No.' Daphne sat forward slightly. 'Do you think she knew? Do you think that's why she was killed?' The mother reminded Lenny of the daughter. The same plump jawline, pink lips, cold stare. 'I've told the police that it's all wrong. I think they mistook her for someone else. No one would want to hurt my Emily. It's unthinkable, isn't it, Abel?'

Abel's eyes bored into Lenny's for a long moment, then he glanced out the window.

'Chisel!' he yelled. 'Don't force it!' He turned back to Lenny. 'Em never spoke about any thefts. The first thing we knew about that was when we read about it in the paper. Em wouldn't be involved in that sort of thing. She could have bought every piece of equipment in that school twice over. I always got her everything she wanted.'

'Our girl didn't steal,' Daphne agreed.

'OK.' Lenny hesitated. How much did the wife know? 'Did she ever talk about her relationships with the other students or with the staff?'

Abel nodded. 'Me and Em were mates,' he said. 'She was a smart young woman. Worked hard and knew what she wanted. Already had one degree under her belt. She had a keen mind for business and she got into that film school first try too, didn't she? First try. That's not easy from what I gather.' He looked Lenny in the eye. He would be wondering how much she knew, how far he could push the fiction that Emily had achieved what she had in her short life without his financial intervention. 'There are some students apply four, five – six times to get in.'

'She was special.' Daphne rattled her doll's cup in its saucer. 'I brought her up to be refined. Not one of these hard, modern ...' She paused, taking in Lenny's appearance, reached into a crocheted pouch at her side and pulled out what Lenny recognised as a bottle of Prozac. She slipped one onto her tongue, swallowed a mouthful of doll tea and smiled. 'I find certain combinations of pills provide more relief than others. I wonder why? I suppose you've met Annabel? She's been to see me. She was Emily's best friend, you know. She was a great support to me at the funeral. Often visits me now.'

'Emily lived in a share house, didn't she?'

'No.' Daphne was startled. 'No! She might have stayed over with friends sometimes. But she lived here. With us. She had everything she needed here. She would have lived with us until she married.' Daphne trembled. 'Ms Aaron will you ... will you avenge my little girl? Will you do that for me? Will you?'

'I'll do my best to find out how your daughter died as far as it relates to the thefts at the school, if in fact it does at all,' Lenny said. 'That's my job. The Galaxy Insurance Corporation is paying me.'

'Oh, not for money! No!' Daphne's hands flew up to her neck. 'For love! For love of Emily. You must fight for her because she was special. You do know what it is to lose someone you love, don't you?'

It was time to get out of there. But for some reason Lenny's bum was glued to her seat. 'Well –'

187

'They say death is final.' Daphne's hands moved on her rosary beads. Her fingernail dug hard into Jesus's neck. The body of Christ was about to be decapitated. 'But if God exists then death can't be the end, can it? I have the love of Him in my soul.'

Lenny glanced at Abel but he was staring out the window at the semi-erect pagoda. It looked cheap and flimsy, the sort of thing a third-rate wedding photographer might use as a studio backdrop. Abel would have been the target of Daphne's questions many times. What did he offer in reply? That Christ should have stayed a carpenter? That he should have served his apprenticeship, got a job and kept himself out of local politics?

'Do you believe in God, Lenny?' Daphne was staring at her, waiting for an answer. The hands were holding the rosary beads tautly.

'No screws, no hinges and no nails,' Abel murmured. 'A bloody marvel. Once we get this into the stores, it'll sell like ice in Cairns. Ever been up north, Lenny?'

She shook her head.

'My father was born in Gordonvale, not far from Cairns. Nice little town.'

The rosary beads snapped, the Messiah hit the coffee table with a metallic thwack and tiny spheres rolled across the floor.

'My God!' Daphne shot out of her rocker and lunged across the floor. She began gathering up the rosary, holding the bits tight in her fist. She glanced up at Lenny. 'Help me, Lenny. Find out who hurt my little girl.'

Abel's metal hand pecked at the cloth of Lenny's shoulder and she jumped. He had risen from his seat without her noticing. He gestured for her to leave the room and joined her at the front door a minute later.

'It's just the medication,' he reiterated. 'She's not normally this far gone. I knew about that student place of Em's, of course. Very poor structurally. Termites, rising damp – the stumps were rotted through at the back. A disaster area. But she needed her own place sometimes. She lived here full-time during her first degree and Daph tended to baby her. Nothing wrong with that, but she wanted to be like the other young people this time. Bit of freedom. I told her it was silly to be in a dirty hovel playing eighteen when you're twenty-nine going on thirty. We could have put her in one of those new apartments, one of those Nondas or whatever they're calling them, down in St Kilda. But she told me to mind my own –' He pulled the door open. 'Emily was the most important thing in my life. She and I were close.'

'Listen,' Lenny cut him off. 'Annabel Lear is probably not the best help your wife could have right now.'

'No kidding?' Abel smiled. 'I know she's after my money for a film or something. Not hard to spot, though she's pretty good with the charm. She makes Daph happy so I'll let her string me along for a while. But I'm a businessman, not a fool. I know what money's worth.'

'Something you share with Cate Ray.'

Abel Cunningham let his eyes wander over hers for a moment. Their optic nerves communicated the nuances. He nodded. 'Ray's a businesswoman. We've had a few conversations about this and that. Lovely English oak desk. We did do some business, actually.'

'Really?'

'That's right. I polyfilled a leak in her window. The frame had rotted almost all the way through. You can't be too careful with the Melbourne damp.'

'Absolutely.' Lenny agreed. 'By the way, how did you feel about your daughter's lesbian relationship with her supervisor?'

A cord snapped inside Abel Cunningham's spine. He

seemed to pitch towards her and for one moment she thought he was going to hit her. Even with her training and experience she would have trouble warding off a metal prosthesis. But it didn't come to that. He managed to keep it all together, but the hate flickered in his salesman's eyes.

'My daughter was a normal girl, Ms Aaron,' he said in a small, choked voice. He looked up and down the garden as if someone might be hiding behind a rose bush, listening. 'I'm warning you, I don't want to read anything else in the newspapers. We brought her up to be normal. She knew better than anyone that it doesn't work out in this life to be different. It's up to the individual to choose.'

'Bullshit,' said Lenny Aaron. 'How did you find out about Emily's relationship with Lucy?'

'I got a filthy email at work which I traced back to Aquinas. I wanted to have a few words with the sender. Unfortunately there's at least a hundred people have access to the same computer.'

'So you didn't find out who it was?'

Another pause. 'No, not in the end. It didn't really matter, though, because all that filth was finished. The Peel woman just wouldn't accept it. Kept calling here asking for Em. I met with her once to set her straight. She was in a real state. She sits across the table saying how she and my Em *love* each other.' He spat out the words, his eyes narrow with hate. 'And I tell her to stay away. I tell her if she goes near my kid again I'll kill her. Then she starts crying and asking for money. Demanding it! Never seen anything like it. She was like a demon.'

'Why do you think she wanted money?'

'She was a blackmailer, wasn't she? Cool as a cucumber.'

'You just said she was crying.'

Abel thought about this. 'Must have been from the shame. I made it clear to her that she wouldn't be getting my money and that I expected an end to the matter. I made it very clear. Emily was killed the next day.' Tears welled up in his eyes. 'Goodbye, Ms Aaron.'

He closed the door in her face and Lenny heard him shouting at the carpenter.

She went back to her office and listened to her messages. Someone had found a dead cat in a gutter around the corner. Could she come and pick it up, dispose of it? No offer of reimbursement. What did people think she was, a bloody charity?

She stood at her window, gazing out onto the car park. She watched a royal blue Volvo pull up and its occupant get out. It was Walstab. He was wearing Ray Bans and a Country Road polo shirt which matched the colour of the car. Lenny watched as he headed towards the video store.

She grabbed Bertrand Russell and dropped him into her shoulder bag. He didn't seem the least surprised. She slapped on her Cutler and Gross sunglasses and stole into the car park.

The Volvo was locked. She tried the back and that was locked too. Through the huge panes of the video store front, she watched Walstab handing in his video at the counter. He proceeded into the body of the store and disappeared amongst the racks. Lenny hurried after him, the cat in the bag thumping against her hip.

The video store was almost empty, no doubt the reason Walstab had chosen this time to come. It was one of those American chain stores, over-designed just because it could be. There were game machines along one wall with a bank of computers labelled Free Internet Site beside them. A serve-yourself coffee bar offering cappuccinos and lattes was set into an alcove nearby. Ahead of her, row after row of laminated shelving the same stars and stripes blue as the carpet. Each row was categorised by genre and about a mile long. A chrome-plated barrier swung back to let Lenny in.

She avoided Romance and took a left down Comedy. Walstab was strolling along, hands in pockets, towards Family Drama. He stopped briefly at Adult. He glanced round to make sure no one could see him before he picked up one of the titles. Reaching the end of Comedy, Lenny squatted and unzipped her bag. The counter was an ocean away, across waves of plastic cases. Bertrand Russell, who was proving to be the most docile cat Lenny had ever known, stared up placidly from her bag.

Her plan was to send the cat down the same aisle as Walstab and have them meet by chance. Then, while he was discussing his good fortune with the staff, she would make her getaway. Even if he saw her, he would not recognise her with her present black-haired student look, not if she was quick.

She watched him dawdle in Family Drama. He still had one eye on Adult, but he had noticed the security cameras. Lenny released Bertrand Russell at the other end of the aisle and gave him a shove. He didn't move. She nudged him. He sat there like a brick of diazepam.

Walstab was moving into Cartoons. She picked up the cat and ran parallel to him up Action. When she got to the end, she peeked round the corner. He was about a quarter way down the aisle in front of Disney Classics. Lenny reached round and dumped Bertrand Russell.

It was done. She was starting towards the exit counter when she saw Walstab strolling into Golden Years Of Hollywood without a cat. She looked over the top of Action. Bertrand Russell was still sitting where she'd left him. Panting, she ran back up Action and collected him.

She was planning to drop him over the top of Australian Movies and let him fend for himself, but at that moment the door from the car park burst open and a group of primary school girls chattered their way towards her, and Teen Romance in the row behind.

Lenny zipped Bertrand Russell back into the bag and headed for the exit. She would have to think of another way to return her famous guest. Could she post him? A courier service, perhaps? As long as there were air holes, she could probably squeeze him into something not much bigger than a shoe box.

'Hi. Could you open the bag, please?'

Her thighs were pushing at the barrier beside the counter, but for some reason it wasn't swinging back. A boy, very tall and spotty, My Name Is Paul, was facing her over the counter.

'Could I check your bag, please?'

She stared at him, caught off guard.

'No, I don't think so,' she said eventually. What sort of world did they live in that needed this level of security to protect rows of empty boxes? 'I'm in a hurry. I have an appointment. Open the barrier.'

'Open your bag, please,' he repeated. He glanced across to the far side of the store towards a door marked SECURITY, his eyes bright. She saw that he had already labelled her a thief. The social glue that binds a community together in empathy dissolves the moment you put an eighteen-year-old in charge of a shop the size of a football field.

'I'm not a customer,' Lenny said. 'I don't even have a card.'

'I'm not concerned with that information, madam. Now I must request that you open your bag, please. I have asked you three times and this gentleman is waiting.'

She saw him on the farthest edge of her peripheral vision. Walstab, right behind her, holding a copy of *Aladdin*. She turned back to the cashier and whispered: 'Open the barrier. Now.'

He leaned into her face and smiled until the yellow-red pimples at the corners of his mouth rose to his cheekbones. His pale, chewed finger stretched towards a button labelled ALARM.

Lenny said: 'Don't do it, pizza face.'

He stopped smiling and pressed the button.

The door marked SECURITY flew open and a boy who looked about thirteen emerged with an electric cattle prod, his mouth full of food.

'Talk to me, buddy!'

'Over here, mate!' screamed his colleague into Lenny's ear. 'She's got something, I can sense it.'

Lenny slammed the heel of her Dr Martens once, then twice, against the chrome barrier. It twisted back with a creak. The cashier lunged over the counter, missed and thudded onto the bright blue carpet.

'Hold her!' yelled the cattle-prod kid, running through Horror. 'I'm charging.' The machine whined in his hand.

From the floor, the cashier tried to ankle-tap Lenny. She kicked him gently in the face like a goodnight kiss and he groaned and lay still. She looked around for Walstab.

Believing that he was the centre of the universe and therefore the focus of every event, including assassination attempts, the councillor had assumed standard hostage position, face down on the floor with his hands behind his head.

'Thomas Walstab!' she cried.

'I'm not him,' whined the would-be mayor.

'Don't lie to me.'

'Don't kill me,' he begged.

'I have a message, Walstab. You stay away from those pet people. Stop persecuting 'em, d'ya follah?'

He nodded his forehead against the carpet.

She was out of time. Security Boy was only a couple of

rows away and she didn't fancy being on the end of the Ozzie Zapper. She slipped out of the video store into the car park. The last thing she saw as she disappeared into the shopping centre was the kid zapping a life-sized figure of Darth Vader and giving her the finger.

CHAPTER 16

Nil by Mouth

That night's TV viewing was a red-letter one: the Test Match had started in England. Lenny loved cricket. It was the slowest, dullest sport in the world. Men standing around holding pieces of wood, examining the grass, occasionally trotting from one end of the pitch to the other and statistics, endless statistics. She spent a pleasant night snoozing to silly mid-offs, ons and the like. At 3 am she was woken by a noisy commercial break. The cricket was rained out and replaced by a film, *Hard Skies*: Kenneth Drage's only feature. She plumped her pillow, rubbed her eyes and watched with interest.

Hard Skies was the story of a young immigrant family struggling in the outback in the 1930s. Not much happened plot-wise, but it had a sensitive, painterly structure. Lenny recalled from her research that *Hard Skies* had been a mild art-house success which disappeared within a month or two of its first screening. Further films had not been forthcoming. Kenneth's careful aesthetic hadn't gone down too well with the Maoist anti-intellectualism dominating Australian campuses and culture at the time.

The next morning she drank *mugicha* at her flat's kitchen table and listened to Mel and Sally's laughter downstairs.

They were dividing their recycling into paper, plastic and glass. What a merry time they were having! Lenny thought of the tossed-together jumble she stuffed into the wheelie bins at the last minute. How did some people make even recycling fun? It seemed suddenly to be the secret of all happiness.

She read an article about Sydney's Fox Studios in the *Age*. Apparently key members of Australia's film community were concerned that the industry was in crisis. Not least because of the number of big films being produced at Fox. Insiders claimed that the studio was providing work for Australian technicians but leaving producers, actors and directors out in the cold. She wondered if Kenneth would agree.

Like her mother, Lenny left the TV on for background noise and her attention was drawn from the newspaper when Annabel Lear's face filled the screen. Lenny turned up the sound. Annabel was, as always, gorgeous in a snug pink sweater with three bunnies dancing across her perky breasts. Cartoon chic. Brunswick Street's Mario's gleamed behind her, its boutique window of young and interesting faces looking up from their electronic diaries and laptops to watch, with envy and admiration, someone younger and more interesting getting all the attention. It appeared Annabel was doing some location shooting, but Lenny suspected the camera tripod and blondie set up on the pavement were window dressing.

'Of course we may never find out who murdered Emily and Moira,' Annabel was saying. 'I'm not even sure I should be discussing their deaths with you. Do I have the right to speak for them? Is it my story to tell? All I can say is we're scared and we want it to stop.' Her eyelashes fluttered moistly. Lenny wished they'd go closer. She wanted to see if those glycerine tears could handle a close-up.

The interviewer asked her if she planned to leave the

school. Annabel pressed a hand to her chest and allowed it to tremble.

'We're all sensitive to that pressure. But we try to go on as before for the sake of the school and the arts community. Is there fear? Danger? Well, of course. But film has always been about taking risks.' She sighed and Australia sighed right back over its Corn Flakes. 'I'm working on a film proposal now, as it happens. I haven't got a production deal because they say I'm too young.'

'How old are you?' the reporter asked.

'John, I'm nineteen.'

'Well, you've got your entire career ahead of you. Thanks for talking to us today.'

'Thank you.'

As the camera pulled reluctantly away, Lenny marvelled at Annabel Lear's poise. She had just occupied the most important position for a young film maker – right in front of the camera lens – and introduced herself to any members of the film industry who didn't already know her. It was marketing genius.

Lenny's pager beeped. *Call your mother* urged Misses Attwood and Rendell. Veronica Aaron certainly had access to Lenny via all avenues of technology. She was already a constant presence on the mobile phone. And she had thrilled at the news of the pager service although she had sworn she would only use it for genuine emergencies.

'What do you want?' Lenny snapped the instant her call connected.

'Oh, Lenny! Lenny, darling –'

'Spit it out.' Lenny was balancing the phone against her shoulder while she turned the pages of the *Age*. Her mother was making less sense than usual, and then she thought she heard the words 'lump' and 'surgery'. She repositioned the phone.

'Say that again.'

'I should have told you before, but I didn't know how you'd take it. I saw this nice specialist a week ago and had an ultrasound and a mammogram. He said he doesn't think it's . . . you know. But he wants to be a hundred percent sure, so I'm going into hospital today. I'm to check into the Royal Women's at lunchtime and I can't have anything to eat. Nil by mouth, as they say. They'll be operating this afternoon. It's a day procedure so I'll be out by this evening. A full anaesthetic, of course. You know how that always makes me a bit sick after.' A pause. 'Lenny?'

'I'm still here.'

'Will you come with me to the hospital?' Silence. Lenny's teeth gouged her inner cheek ferociously. 'They said I have to go home in the company of an adult.'

'You know I'm in the middle of a case.' Moira Middle-miss's breast cancer photos floated across her vision and she shivered.

'There's no one else. I need you.'

'Oh, for Christ's sake –'

'And would you . . . could you bring Mum?'

Lenny gasped. 'Not a chance!'

'Lenny, she'd want to be with me at a time like this.'

'Yeah, to gloat.'

'Please, Lenny –'

'I'll think about it.'

She hung up quickly. She didn't want to hear tears and thank yous, didn't want to be the wretched person her wretched mother depended on. But above all else she didn't want to be confined in a car with her grandmother. She dialled another number, had a very short conversation, and was soon driving towards the only help she accepted in her life.

Dr Sakuno, waiting in his kendo gear, was annoyed. He thought emergency sessions were indicative of backsliding, a sign of weakness. Plus they had agreed on a time and she was ten minutes late. She blathered about traffic. He cut her off with a raised glove. He was not interested in excuses. In life, he said, there was only on time. Early was inconsiderate and late unforgivable. He stalked away, swishing his *shinai*. Lenny hurried into the women's changing rooms and tugged on her kendo gear.

Someone had left a mid-week copy of the *Herald Sun* on a bench in the corridor. It was open to an article on Komodo Man. Packs of men were staking out parks close to schools and pubs to prevent attacks. A couple of gay men had been bashed on the weekend and their attackers had pleaded the Komodo defence. Things were getting crazy. Everyone wanted him captured and no one wanted him captured. He was a ratings winner, Melbourne's Loch Ness monster.

'My mother is ill,' Lenny told Dr Sakuno when she entered the practice hall. 'She's having a biopsy for a lump in her breast. What do you know about that kind of thing? I mean, what are the statistics?' He was a doctor. Well, he had a PhD in psychology.

Dr Sakuno looked at her for a minute, gauging her mood before replying.

'If she has the breast fully removed there'll be a scar. In Japan they sometimes remove the breast and take it to the husband so that he can check the cancer for himself. Otherwise how can he know for sure? We like to be sure.' He pulled down his mask.

Lenny swung at him. They fought in silence for some time but she was too tired to do well. Kendo's aspired-to mental and physical calm was an impossibility. The Sudafed wasn't giving her the usual kick. She was going to have to take something stronger; except that she couldn't help wondering, ever since she'd met Mrs Cunningham, whether she shouldn't try to cut down on her pill intake.

She could if she wanted to, of course. It was entirely her choice. Anytime she wanted to she could just stop. She faltered and took a mean blow to the shoulder. Dr Sakuno pushed up his mask.

'My grandmother had breast cancer,' he said flatly. 'It metastasised. She was dead ten days after the mastectomy. These things happen.'

'Dad asked me to take care of her and be nice to her. It's difficult for me. I don't like her.' Lenny's *shinai* moved back and forth restlessly. She hated confiding emotions; it meant she must be experiencing them.

'Speech is unnecessary,' Dr Sakuno said. 'The Japanese have developed the art of communicating strong feelings with the fewest number of words.'

'Yes, yes, I know.' Lenny sighed. 'But I just feel so –' Her *shinai* swished up and down, back and forth.

Dr Sakuno stared her down. 'You are a long-term patient. *Kao ni doro o nuru na*. Don't make me lose face.'

'But –' Her hands clenched hard around the *shinai* as she struggled for the words. 'Just for once I want to feel ... unburdened. Do you understand?'

'End of session,' he said, moving back. They still had half an hour.

'Wait a minute –'

'Enough.' He was turning away when she struck him, her *shinai* catching him on the side of the temple, sending him to the floorboards.

He stared at her. Then, decision made in an instant, he leapt to his feet and came at her. His *shinai* whacked into her arms and hands, jabbed hard into her chest, smacked her shoulders. She made no attempt to protect herself and he knocked her to the floor with a wide, illegal slash to the side of her head.

'Kendo is about courtesy!' He hit her shoulder. 'About

respect for others!' A stab to her stomach. 'You will!' Whack! 'Develop!' Whack! 'Your character!'

She followed him towards the changing rooms like a beaten puppy. They walked past the newspaper lying open on the bench and the kendo-like outline of Komodo Man attracted Dr Sakuno's attention. His eyes darted back and forth between the sketch and Lenny's armour.

'It's *you!*' he gasped. 'You are Komodo Man. *Tokagenohito!*'

'*Sensei*, it's a misunderstanding –'

'You lunatic!' The doctor fled. She didn't give chase. But he had come through for her again, she realised. There she was, floundering, trying to make sense of her father's emphysemic demise and her mother's defective breast. Anyone else would have put an arm around her shoulder and given her a few gentle words of encouragement. Dr Sakuno had given her a solid thrashing. The man was a psychological genius. Her entire body felt swollen and bruised. A genius with a big stick.

She collected Granny Sanderman from the hospice. The old woman was unhappy to be disturbed. She was watching a video, *Misery* rewinding over and over the part where Kathy Bates uses a big mallet to break James Caan's ankles. She fought hard, just for the fun of it, when Lenny loaded her into the front passenger seat.

'Why do I want to go to the hospital?' she asked, her breath like sweaty mustard filling the Toyota. 'Let 'em cut both her tits off. What's it to me?'

A couple of times she grabbed for the steering wheel with her right arm and tried to kill them both. Lenny slapped her hand hard the second time.

'No need to get vicious,' Granny Sanderman grunted.

Veronica Aaron smiled from beneath the crisp white sheet of the hospital bed. In half an hour she would be prepped and 'under the knife'. She fondled a pink plastic band around her wrist with her name on it. She had a *Women's Weekly* and a Catherine Cookson paperback on the bedside cabinet to read later when she was in recovery. Everything was as it should be in a medical crisis. Kylie Wong, Lenny and Granny Sanderman were all crowded into her room.

'Look at this!' Veronica held up a small white card. 'They already tested my blood. They told me to keep it in my purse at all times. Laminated. Very nice. Apparently the blood bank's a bit low at the moment, though.' She shook her head. 'If I need a transfusion I can't imagine what I'll do! I'm A positive. What blood type are you, Lenny?'

'B miserable,' Lenny replied.

'Well, Mum's the same as me, I think. Aren't you Mum?'

Granny Sanderman looked across from her wheelchair, parked on the farthest side of the room. She was ravaging her daughter's collection of chocolates.

'You're not getting any of my blood. Who gave you these cheap things?' She spat a lime truffle onto the floor. 'I suppose the little chong brought 'em. No idea of our tastes, have they? Get 'em from the Vietnamese grocery, did you, missy?'

Kylie Wong was sitting on a chair at the side of the bed, chewing gum. She continued swinging her legs and reading a comic, having already decided that the best way to piss off the old woman was to ignore her.

Lenny stood at the side of the bed, arms folded, as she had done for the half hour since they'd arrived. The anaesthetist was coming for a chat soon. The procedure itself would not take long, but Veronica would have to spend some time recovering from the anaesthetic. If all went well, Lenny would be able to take her home later that afternoon.

'Do you have any idea what this kind of operation costs?' her mother said. 'Thank goodness I always keep top cover. I'll hardly have to pay a thing. It's the surgeon – Of course, he's the best in Melbourne. Then there's the anaesthetist and the theatre nurses. Lovely, they are. All very well trained, very expensive. Look, Lenny, this is the latest model bed.' Veronica Aaron proudly exhibited the control pad. 'This one to go up, this one to go down, and three levels of reclining.' She demonstrated. 'Now you won't get that on Medicare.'

'All the flavour's gone out of my chewie.' Kylie Wong took the gum out to look at it then popped it with her finger and stuffed it back into her mouth. 'And I'm thirsty.' The child had managed to get a great big tomato sauce stain down one of her new Quiksilver sweatshirts.

'Go and get some water,' Lenny said. Her arms and shoulders hurt from Dr Sakuno's therapy. She wasn't in the mood to play big sister.

'Oh, Lenny!' Her mother reached for her purse, smiling fondly at Kylie. Something about hospitals brought out an extra sprinkle of saccharine in her mother, Lenny thought. Especially when she was the star performer. 'Here's a dollar, Kylie. There's a drink machine in the corridor.'

'What am I gonna get for a buck?' Kylie Wong took the purse and fished out another dollar coin. 'Can I get salt and vinegar chips as well?'

'No.' Lenny took the purse and put it into the drawer. Kylie Wong waddled off. 'You shouldn't let her get sugary drinks. She's already too big. She'll become obese.'

'Lenny, all children go through a puppy fat stage.' Her mother smiled.

'Do you have everything you need?' Lenny had promised her father to take care of his wife, to be nice to her. It had been a promise made in weakness, a tie she did not want.

'Oh yes, I'm very prepared, thank you. In good hands.' Veronica's pale blue eyes were scared despite the cheerful blandness of her manner. It was somehow disturbing, seeing this woman in genuine fear. Lenny looked away.

'Do you know, Lenny,' Veronica continued, 'if the worst comes to the worst, you can get a rubber breast with a nipple attached for a bra-less look. As if I'd be going bra-less at my age! Here, do you want to have a look at where they think it is?' Her mother fumbled at her hospital gown.

Lenny reeled back.

'Put it away!' She had never had a close relationship with her mother's breasts and didn't intend to start now.

'Well, there's nothing to see, really. You can feel it, though. It's not like the way your breasts normally feel lumpy. It's quite different.'

'I wouldn't know.' Lenny didn't feel her breasts. Didn't ever think about feeling them. Neither did she know the clinical names for the various parts of her vagina, nor had she ever felt the need for self-examination with her fingers and a hand mirror. Some things were best left to the horrors of the imagination.

'Ooh, Lenny! You should do a monthly check. You'll end up in my position.' Lenny doubted she would ever be sitting in a hospital bed reading *Maryann and Bill*.

'Perhaps I should see if Father Harrigan could pop in and see me today,' Veronica Aaron said, spying a new vision of herself: the Dying Catholic. 'I need to confess my sins.'

'I'm sure you do. Go on then, I'm listening.' Lenny edged her hip against the bed. It was as close as she could get to sitting at her mother's bedside.

'Well, I don't know . . .' her mother prevaricated.

'Come on.' Lenny cracked her knuckles. 'I've been keeping score of all the things you've done wrong in your life. Let's see if our lists tally.' She picked up a knitting pattern and held it up between them like a confessional grille. 'Pretend I'm not here. It's just you and God.'

Kylie Wong came back in alternately blowing and sucking on a straw bobbing in a Fanta.

'You'll be struck down for blasphemy if you're not careful, Lenny.' Veronica Aaron snatched the knitting pattern. 'You want to set a better example for Kylie.'

'We're going,' Lenny gave up. Her mother half reached for her hand. It was a performance Lenny had witnessed many times. Her mother could summon theatrical emotion quicker than Lillian Gish. Yet surely this was genuine fear, deserving of a genuine response?

'You're coming back to take me home, though?' The tremulous voice.

'I'm going to take what's-her-name back to the hospice first.'

'She wants to stay with me.'

'No, I don't.' Granny Sanderman choked, her mouth filled with chocolate.

'What if I wake up and they've cut it off?' Tears ran down pink and white striated cheeks.

'You never had nice boobies anyway,' Granny Sanderman commiserated. 'Saggy even before you had that one.' She threw a Savoy Truffle at Lenny. 'And your nipples were always too big and brown as well.'

Lenny shook her head. 'It's just a biopsy. They won't cut it off without discussing it with you first.' Lenny wiped a smear of chocolate off her arm. 'You're losing your aim,' she said to her grandmother.

'Better than loosing my tit,' replied the wheelchair demon.

They left. Granny Sanderman gave a running commentary on everyone they passed from the ward all the way out to the car park. She didn't want to sit in the back so that

Kylie Wong could sit in the front. Lenny insisted. They scrapped. Lenny won. She belted the old woman into the back. Tightly. Then she tied her hands together with an octopus strap.

Kylie Wong sat in the passenger seat playing with a battered Barbie and Ken. Barbie's eyes had been redrawn with texta to resemble Kylie's almond-shaped ones. The famed Barbie blonde hairdo was a mess, having been dipped in some black substance, possibly ink. Ken, however, was still as blonde as an Aryan storm trooper.

'Ma went after white men,' Kylie explained.

'Was your father white?' Lenny tried not to look as Ken ripped off Barbie's blouse and pressed his handsome plastic face against her pneumatic breasts.

'I dunno. There was one last year, before Ma put me in the home, he had yellow hair and green eyes. He was a truckie. He let me ride in the front cab with him. Ace, hey? He punched Ma in the face and she dropped him. He wasn't my dad, but.' Kylie looked at herself briefly in the wing mirror then turned her face to Lenny. 'There was this guy when I was a kid. He was whiter than anything! He was a wino, spent the rent money. Ma said she'd never go with another boozer. She did, but. It might have been him. She never said. Do you reckon my dad could've been white?'

Lenny surveyed the round face carefully. 'I can't tell,' she said.

'I reckon he had glasses ... though,' Kylie said and smiled at Lenny.

'Must have been an ugly bugger,' Granny Sanderman offered from the back seat.

Kylie Wong probed Ken's beige muscles with a chewed digit. 'I'm gonna marry a man who looks just like this.'

When they dropped off Granny Sanderman the old

woman told the nurse that Lenny had threatened to suffocate her in her sleep. The woman's lips twisted in a severely suppressed smirk. Lenny understood: the hospice staff were long past caring about their vicious guest. They had suffered without complaint her pinches, spitting and verbal abuse; but this year she had stabbed Matron's chest above the heart with a pencil leaving a bluish stain under the skin like a bad tattoo. Matron, a strong woman who had served in Vietnam, was rumoured to have purchased a can of capsicum gas which she kept in her pocket whenever she went, trembling, into the Sanderman pit.

CHAPTER 17

Bullies & Teacher's Pets

Veronica Aaron was released after a trouble-free recovery period. She had sat in a comfy chair in the hospital, was given hot tea and biscuits, her vitals were checked and found to be adequate. She was sent home with the knowledge that she would have to wait a couple of days for the results of the biopsy. Consequently, Lenny's night was taken up fending off bosom-related telephone calls. Finally, she unplugged the phone.

At Aquinas the next morning she checked her locker. Still no sign of a break-in. She wondered if she should bait the trap. A fresh, unopened 400 feet of colour stock would probably do the trick.

Alana Zappone bounced along the corridor towards her with her isn't-life-gorgeous smile.

'How's it all going?' she asked, her African bangles clunking at her wrists as she sipped her tea. Lenny was glad of the opportunity to question her least likely suspect.

'Good thanks, Alana,' she lied. She had to keep it all light and friendly with this one. Zappone's type didn't react well to the heavy hand. 'By the way, if you don't mind my asking, you were up here the day Moira died, is that right?'

'I keep forgetting you're an investigator and not a

209

student.' Zappone smiled her Tosca-sized smile. 'Yes, I was here. I'm in the clear, though.' She waggled her finger in Lenny's face. She counted off her two alibis with theatrical poise: 'I saw Lucy and gave her a tablet for her headache, and I called the Treasury Theatre for Kenneth and told him it was clear for the screenings, which he was very happy about. What a terrible day. I didn't sleep at all that night or the next.'

'Was Kenneth in an edit suite?'

Zappone nodded. 'He shuts himself in like the rest of them. You can't see clearly on those screens unless it's dark.'

'Which edit suite?'

The secretary sipped her tea thoughtfully. 'Number three, I think. Let me check.'

She placed her cup on the reception desk and went out into the corridor. Lenny followed. Zappone glanced up and down the row of doors, calculating.

'Yes, it was three. I remember because I had a run-in with Janus about the same room.'

'Janus? Why?'

'The students are supposed to clean up the edit suites and remove any extra equipment they've been using when they leave. The evening Moira died I went into suite three to switch off the light and I stepped on a . . . a thingy. Graeme Pluckrose was very annoyed when I took it to the work-shop, I can tell you. It hadn't been signed out of the store-room for starters, and I'd broken it. He gave me quite a lecture about the cost of repairs. Well, you've met Graeme.'

'A "thingy"?'

Zappone laughed. 'I'm useless on technology, Lenny. Film equipment all looks the same to me, black and silver thingies in various sizes. Anyway I took it down to Graeme to fix. I remember! It was a transmitter.'

'A transmitter? What did Janus want with it? He wasn't shooting.'

'He was booked in to use the room that day. I thought it was a bit silly and selfish of him considering he was supposed to be working on Moira's shoot. But he wanted to come in and out during the breaks and he said other people could use it when he wasn't there. That's what Kenneth did. But Kenneth was only in there for about fifteen minutes while he watched that film.'

'What did Janus say about the transmitter?'

She folded her arms, remembering. 'I gave him a lecture about leaving things lying around. He said he didn't discuss equipment with secretaries.'

The phone rang in the office and Zappone excused herself. Lenny had someone else to grill that day. She walked back along the corridor to a small room tucked into a corner at the back of the first floor.

Lucy Peel looked up as Lenny entered her office. She looked exhausted, purple shadows like eggplant slices underscoring her lavender eyes.

'What do you want?' she sighed.

'I want to talk about the thefts happening in this school.'

'I can't tell you anything, Lenny. I don't know why anyone here would steal anything – or destroy anything. I can't help you.'

'Is that what you told the police?'

'Told the police?' She laughed harshly. 'They weren't interested in that. They wouldn't have cared if I'd stolen half the gear in the storeroom.' There was a long pause. Lenny had been involved in enough interrogations in her time to know when someone was desperate to talk – despite their protests to the contrary.

'They were much cleverer than I'd have thought,' Lucy said finally. 'They treated me like I was in shock. Cup of sweet tea, pat on the shoulder. Take my time. But then just like the last time, after Em was killed, they began this bloody game over my private life. I told them what I told them last time: I'm not involved in all this. I told them I didn't hurt Emily. I would never have hurt her! But they have the photo Moira took, so I suppose in their eyes I'm the enraged lesbian. Do you think I'm going to be arrested?' She laughed a little wildly and slid back into her chair, picking up a large crystal from the desk and caressing it.

'Emily gave me this when we first got together, when she was pretending to like me. She got it at Camberwell markets. The energy from it is exponential.' She saw Lenny's face. 'It is, don't smirk. Moira touched it once and she got an energy surge so powerful, it jolted her neck.'

'I bet it did.' Lenny took the crystal in her own hand, held it, rotated it. She handed it back, eyebrows raised.

'Ah! But you don't believe in the spiritual,' Lucy observed. 'Don't you believe there's a purpose to all this? Why we're alive? I've been thinking about it since Emily died.' She held the crystal close to her heart. 'There is a beauty to life, a purity. When you believe in something, Lenny, when you see it clearly and cleanly, when you have a vision, an ideal ...' She wound down, embarrassed. 'It's a beautiful thing worth fighting for.'

'What did you do when Emily broke up with you?'

Lucy's eyes watered. 'Nothing. I was upset. I was her supervisor, for God's sake. This has all been ridiculous!'

'Why did she take up with you?'

There was a long pause. Lucy held the crystal between both hands on her desk. 'This is very difficult to discuss with someone who is for all intents and purposes a stranger,' she said. 'You – as much as the police – care little for me. I understand that, you've been hardened by your occupation. Everyone thinks it was her good business sense:

screw your teacher for better grades. There was some of that in it, I'm sure. Of course there was. But I believe that Emily began a relationship with me partly because it amused her and to anger her father. She was afraid of him, I think. He was very possessive. I don't know, really. Emily was secretive about the details of her family life. They babied her, I know that much. She was thirty, for God's sake, and they treated her like she was eighteen. She was a funny mixture, really. Partly the spoilt child they wanted her to be and partly . . . tough, I suppose. Hard-headed. Or determined to be so. She could be an adult with me and I think she liked that. It wasn't all bullshit, what she had with me. And whatever you may think you know about me, Lenny, I want you to believe that I was the one who entered the relationship with no ulterior motive whatsoever. I was – I am – innocent.'

'Abel Cunningham said you demanded money.'

'I said that, yes,' she whispered, pushing the crystal away, eyes fixed on a spot halfway across the desk. 'Emily had broken with me very brutally. I was humiliated and I said what I said to get back at her in some way. John and I struggle to make mortgage repayments. I didn't mean it so much as . . .' She shook her head. 'I was *angry*. Mr Cunningham would never have given me money anyway. There was some talk about discount flooring. He knew John and I were planning an extension to the sunroom. Baltic pine. I doubt he truly meant it.'

'And he said he'd kill you if you didn't stay away from Emily?'

Lucy shook her head, surprised.

'No. Is that what he told you? Well, I suppose he prefers to remember it differently under the circumstances.' She smiled, a sick grimace. 'He said he'd never let his daughter be with someone like me. He said he'd rather see her dead.'

The supervisor's eyes were no longer on her but looking over her head to the door. Lenny turned. Gabrielle was staring at them through the glass panel. She opened the door.

'Lucy, Kenneth's ready to start his lecture. He said you might find this week's topic interesting.'

'Thank you, Gabrielle.' Lucy shuffled a bundle of papers together and got to her feet. 'Lenny, we'll have to end our chat for now, I'm sorry. Anyway, I have nothing further to add to what I've told you. If you'll excuse me . . .'

Lucy hurried ahead of them down the corridor. Lenny and Gabrielle walked side by side. The student had a spring in her step, seemed happier than usual. She caught Lenny's look and laughed.

'I submitted a short film to the London Film Festival this year and I've been accepted.'

'Congratulations.'

'If I win they might fly me over.'

'Let's hope you're not in jail, then.'

'Fuck you, Lenny.'

They glared at each other and entered the screening room together.

'The Hollywood film,' Kenneth was saying as they found their seats, 'is finely honed at both the marketing and the promotional stage to ensure maximum demographic success.' A murmur of agreement from his audience. 'It therefore disqualifies itself as a genuine work of art, which cannot be sold, like margarine, on the merits of its ease of spreading.' Confusion set in amongst the audience. 'Does a film that is guaranteed to appeal to ninety percent of the population have a right to be called art, or is it simply the science of marketing in action producing iconic blurs – hero, nemesis, lover – as a by-product? Should we limit ourselves to considering film in terms of the bottom line? I put to you today that the basis of a successful film industry is not money. It is creativity, ideas and passion.'

A few yawned. Conversations broke out amongst the first year students who turned sideways in their seats. Apart from Gabrielle and to a lesser extent Janus, Kenneth had lost them.

Harry Tuyen was one of the yawners. He represented the majority of the students who had been accepted to Aquinas since the current third years. They regarded aesthetics – if at all – as the domain of the VCA and the AFTRS. Film, for the new generation of Aquinas students, meant action. It was car chases, gunfights and clever camera angles. If an 'old' director was praised at all, it was for a technical achievement, like the opening shot of *Touch of Evil* or Hitchcock's set-building *tour de force*, *Rear Window*.

Kenneth was an articulate speaker with a sincere passion for his topic, but this audience could not care less that the purpose of film was to heighten awareness, to create an art form with its own set of codes, its own language. To this new breed of Aquinas students, film was not a method of communication. It was a career path promising fame, prestige and the chance to meet Tom and Nicole.

After the lecture Kenneth handed out extra material with references to Caravaggio, Picasso and even Andy Warhol. Lenny saw most of the students assign it to the bin on their way out.

'We have to consider the funding bodies when evaluating our script ideas,' Annabel protested in the corridor afterwards. 'They want movies with a wide appeal.'

'Kenneth's senile.' Harry Tuyen summed it up for the first years, where he seemed to have a big following of nodding male heads. 'Who cares about evaluating aesthetics? Kenneth likes *films*, right? Well, I like movies. I make *movies*. The Russ Myer lecture was better than that shit.

What do you reckon, Gabrielle?' He stepped close to her, closer than usual. To Lenny's surprise, she tolerated it and smiled at him.

Lenny flushed with confusion. Her feelings for Gabrielle were complicated by her own fear of intimate contact, but also by Gabrielle's status as a suspect. Harry touched Gabrielle's shoulder and whispered something into her ear. Lenny turned quickly and hurried down the corridor.

The next day Lenny was supping a mug of *bancha* at her window when she spotted it – a car parked opposite her block of flats. Not just parked. Lurking. The figure inside pretending to read a newspaper was Abel Cunningham.

She ran downstairs and was almost at the car when he saw her. His eyes were cold as he turned the key in the ignition. Lenny's hand was wrenched from the door handle as he hit the accelerator. Was Cunningham playing amateur sleuth, following her because he wanted to know who'd killed his daughter? Or did he want to make sure Lenny didn't find out what had really happened? Lucy Peel had said he'd rather see Emily dead than a dyke. The initial reaction of homophobic parents everywhere, Lenny thought. Or was this one homophobe who went that extra mile?

At 1 pm that day, Annabel Lear's shoot began. In the Aquinas television studio, the young director stood on a box surveying the group of students and actors before her. The blonde hair hung loose and shimmered under the work lights. A red and white polka-dot blouse matched enormous red sneakers and the black pants hung fashionably low around slender hips, exposing a good three inches of flat stomach. Her belly button was pierced, her hands speckled with adorable plastic jewellery and her face glowed. She was the happiest Lenny had ever seen her.

'I want everyone to understand that I'm going to be busy directing. That's what I do. It's not something I'll want to be discussing with any of you. I don't want to hear, "Annabel, where do you want the blondie?" or, "Annabel, what time is the break?" I won't be on that wavelength. Sorry.' She pressed a small fist to her polka-dot heart. 'I'm the director, and I'm incommunicado. Basically I don't want any one of you talking to me or even approaching me. Think of the space around me as a no-parking zone. If you have anything to say to me, any questions, you relay them through Hayley.' She gestured at a tall girl wearing black Levis and a blue tank top. 'My 1st AD.'

Hayley didn't bother to smile. Like most of Annabel's crew, she was a professional. It was, Lenny knew, against Aquinas policy to allow anyone other than Aquinas students to fill the major crewing positions. Despite this, Annabel had employed a professional gaffer, line producer, set designer, costumer and cinematographer. Even Janus Onyszkiewicz – deemed too amateur for this shoot – was relegated to a minor role.

Gabrielle, Lenny discovered, had been allotted the double role of sound assistant and caterer, which meant holding the boom pole and minding the tea trolley. And damned fine tea it was, too. There was a tin of Lapsang Souchong, another of Darjeeling, a warm, milky thermos of Chai, a carton of soy milk and a range of carob and yogurt biscuits and fruit muffins. Nothing like the Lipton's and Family Assorteds of Moira's rockumentary. Lenny wondered where the money was coming from to fund Annabel's extravaganza.

Angry voices flashed from the centre of the studio. The gaffer was going ballistic. He and the DOP had been pondering how to get the actor's face to reflect the data she was looking at in a computer monitor. Apparently Janus had suggested using a redhead with a half blue gel, then projecting a page of statistics onto her face. It was a cheap, ingenious suggestion. Unfortunately, the gaffer hadn't thought of it first.

Roughly fifty, this gaffer was lean and weathered. He wore a blue singlet, torn jeans and rubber-soled work boots. There was a leather toolbelt around his waist from which dangled gaff tape, screwdrivers and pliers.

'Don't tell me how to do my job, *mate*!' he thundered. Hayley stalked over.

'What's up?' she said. Her voice was neither sympathetic nor conciliatory. Hayley was a professional and interested only in the process. Individual crew members' feelings were so low on her list of priorities as to be irrelevant. Perhaps it was necessary, Lenny pondered. Perhaps the production of small, human films, the sort that win raves at noble, international festivals, relied on proven, fascist techniques.

'You kids think you know the lot!' the gaffer bellowed. 'It's not all out of books, you know! Not here in the real world!'

The wail of the mastodon scenting extinction. It was inevitable, Lenny thought, that old-school gaffers would be replaced by university graduates, people who carried in their heads the equations necessary to determine current flow as a function of cable diameter and composition, people who knew not only that the red wire was good and the brown wire bad, but why.

The DOP, Fyodor Iramenkov, approached the tea trolley and pointed at the Darjeeling. He had badly styled hair, a pronounced belly and wore glasses with huge, hexagonal frames of clear plastic. Gabrielle was across the room talking with Harry, their heads close together. His hand moved up and down her arm.

Lenny supposed she would have to do the honours.

Fyodor's gesture grew impatient as she hesitated. She wanted to be amiable and agreeable, she did, but she just didn't like the look of those glasses.

'Get it yourself,' she said.

'Do you have any idea of the positions on a film set?' He leaned across the trolley. 'I am the person who controls the camera.'

Lenny walked outside for a smoke. Gabrielle followed. They sat side by side on the grass in the quadrangle. It was chilly and Gabrielle wrapped her bony arms around her body. For a long time neither of them spoke. Lenny was first to break the silence.

'What's with you and Harry Tuyen? Why was he stroking your arm in there?' And more to the point, why were you letting him?

Gabrielle said nothing loudly.

'How much money did Annabel borrow from Emily?' Lenny tried again.

Gabrielle accepted the direction change at once. She smiled.

'Annabel Lear doesn't have to kill anyone to get ahead in this business, Lenny. She already has it in the palm of her hand. In a closed circuit film culture like Australia's, there are only a certain number of vacant positions: Greek comedy film maker, Anglo doco maker, avant-garde animator, white female director, Aboriginal female director – that's the way it works. The status of each position changes with fashion, but at any given time there has to be someone in each spot. This is all decided by funding body managers – bureaucrats – the only people who make a decent living from film in Australia. The most likely candidate for each position is someone who *looks* right. Annabel will be the next young, white female auteur because the current one's film just bombed and the critics

219

are distancing themselves and Annabel knows everyone by name at all the financing bodies. The boys will have to wait for a while because we have quite a few male directors.'

It was a long speech from someone who rarely made them. Gabrielle had become almost impassioned, became aware of it and paused for a moment to recover herself. 'Unless you're blind, Lenny, you already know all this. In our society it's how things are perceived, how they are seen to be, that matters. Not how things *are*.'

Lenny knew it was true, but hearing it depressed her and she felt in her pocket for an aspirin, had the foil packet half ripped open before she realised what she was doing. Well, she did have a headache. She was a bit under the weather. She popped a couple in her mouth and pulled out her cigarettes.

'Emily told me Annabel borrowed twenty thousand from her,' Gabrielle said. 'She's obviously going to be the big commercial success from our year and I suppose Em thought it was a worthwhile investment.'

'Do you have any idea who's stealing from the school or who killed Emily or Moira? If you do, you must tell the police.'

Gabrielle shook her head:

'Who am I to point the finger and say, this person is a thief, this person is a murderer? Do you know what it's like to be accused of something like that? Do you understand anything about guilt? Real guilt? There are times when things should be left to take their course.'

They were sitting close together. Lenny could smell the light lemon soap Gabrielle used, see how unusually short her black eyelashes were. She cursed herself for noticing. For one thing, Dr Sakuno had recommended a friendship, not a relationship. And the last time she'd fancied someone, that person had cut her arm open and fired two bullets into her.

'What are you two doing out here?' Hayley appeared clutching her clipboard. 'We have professionals in there waiting for a cup of tea! That's your job, Gabrielle. If you choose not to participate, it'll go in my report and you won't get your points for crewing. You've got thirty seconds.' She turned on her heel.

Kenneth had joined Lucy at the side of the set. He smiled at Lenny as she closed the heavy, soundproofed door behind her. Adhering to the Aquinas Method, neither supervisor showed any sign of interfering in the consultation around the Arriflex BL camera.

Janus's suggestion had apparently been adopted and an overhead projector shone onto the actor's face, creating the computer screen effect. A column of luminous green digits rippled over her nose when she moved.

Carefree and oblivious to the process that she was – officially, at least – presiding over, Annabel chatted to a Film Victoria executive on her mobile while she ate a length of celery.

She slipped the phone back into its pink holder. 'I've got that zinging in my teeth again,' she announced to the room, forgetting she was incommunicado. 'My doctor says it's the amount of tension in my body. My stress levels are enormous!' She skipped over to the tea trolley and examined some wholegrain bread and dips. 'Is that tahini?'

'All right, everyone. Quiet on the set! This is a take.' Hayley positioned herself just behind the camera to the left. Annabel hurried to her side, licking her fingers. 'Roll sound,' Hayley said in her flat, executioner's tone.

'Rolling,' said Sound.

'We'll tail slate this one,' Hayley said. 'Roll camera.'

'Speed,' from Sound.

'Frame,' from Camera.

Annabel looked at Hayley, who nodded. 'Action!' Annabel shouted, eyes shining.

'Cut!' The middle-aged sound recordist called it and shook his head, the weight of the world on his shoulders. A veteran of hundreds of professional shoots, including many recent Australian successes, he was silver-haired and lugubrious. Even his small moustache drooped. 'Air-conditioner started up. You could mask it with atmos in post, but if you want good, hard sound it should be dealt with now.'

Gabrielle started to lower the boom which hovered two feet above the actor's head as she sat at the computer terminal.

'Wait!' Fyodor stopped her. 'Tail slate.'

A terrified first year in a long willow-print dress ran onto the set. She clacked the slate at the camera like she was trying to drive it away.

'Scene eight –'

'Upside down!' Fyodor yelled. 'Upside down!'

The slate girl was blinded by the lights. She stood alone in the bright circle and put her hand to her eyes.

'Come on, people! We're wasting time!' Hayley yelled.

The girl was trembling. 'Scene ei –'

'No!' Fyodor screamed. 'Upside down!'

With a glazed expression, the girl began to bend her thin body sideways. Then she realised what he meant. She turned the slate upside down and said: 'Scene eight, shot eleven, take one, tail slate,' in a small voice. Fyodor made her crack the jaw of the board three times before he let her scurry to the darkest corner of the studio.

The air-conditioner hitch hung in the air, threatening to become a full-blown dilemma. All eyes were on Annabel.

'I didn't hear anything . . . Hayley?' Annabel was scared – she was being asked to make an artistic decision.

222

'I'm on it.' Hayley's toolbelt swung towards the hapless machine.

'Just shoot the fucking thing,' yawned Harry Tuyen, leaning over a reflector board. 'We've got this covered in the wide anyway.' He grinned at Gabrielle, who managed a small smile.

Throughout these proceedings, including the bullying of the slate girl, neither Kenneth nor Lucy Peel moved to intervene. The girl was weeping now in her corner, clutching the slate to her chest. The Aquinas Method wasn't working its magic there and Lenny predicted an early drop-out. Annabel Lear's set resembled a primary school playground, complete with bullies and teacher's pets. She made herself a cup of tea, wondering, not for the last time, why they included film under the banner of humanities.

CHAPTER 18

The Graeme and Harry Show

The next week passed slowly ending with a well-attended wrap party for Annabel's shoot in an expensive café in Brunswick Street.

Veronica Aaron had received her biopsy result, was not dying of breast cancer and was not happy about it.

'All that worry and fuss! You'd think they could have told me it was *nothing* from an X-ray! It's like I always say, these doctors can't wait to get the knife out.' Such hypocrisy from someone who couldn't wait to get her leg up on the operating table was breathtaking.

Lenny still had Bertrand Russell in her office. The smart thing to do was to drive round to Walstab's house in the middle of the night and dump the cat over the fence. But she was still fired up after the incident at the video store and was looking for a way to make the situation work for her. Until she figured out what that was, Bertrand Russell would remain in his cage.

The Aquinas murders were temporarily knocked off the front pages. A Bendigo father of three primary school children and a toddler drove them out into the country in a Kombi van for a day trip and gassed the lot of them with exhaust fumes. Motive unknown. Grandma's tears were page one, Aquinas pushed to page three.

The police, as far as Lenny could figure, were no closer to solving the murders. She avoided Danny's cautious smiles and MacAvoy's eager waves whenever she saw them across the quadrangle. She had pinned the Polaroids of Moira's bloody death across her living room wall and stared at her close-up of the eyeball for inspiration. None came.

It was now the first day of Harry Tuyen's shoot. Lenny had to admit that, unlike Annabel and her crew of hired professionals, Harry was at least throwing a bone to his fellow students. Gabrielle was his designated 1st AD and Janus his DOP. Lenny also planned to be there for Harry's shoot. Harry *knew* something. It was time she found out what.

Alana Zappone was in the common room stirring a cup of coffee. She nodded at Lenny but for once her round diva face was without its happy smile.

'I hate disappointing people,' she said.

'Me too,' Lenny lied. 'What's wrong?'

'This.' Zappone took an envelope out of her pocket. 'We're always getting them from people who want to become film students. And this man has sent us a lovely little 8 mm film too. And a really funny script he's developing.'

'So what's the problem?'

'He's forty-two.' Zappone said it like it was the end of the world. 'We only take students between seventeen and thirty-nine. I mean, I understand it. We have to give the younger people a chance. And maybe this gentleman should have made more of his opportunities when he was younger. But still, it's a shame, isn't it? I'll send him a nice personal note, I think, rather than the form letter.'

'That's very considerate of you,' Lenny's mouth said

while her mind wandered down another path. Here, at last, was a clue. It had seemed obvious to her from the start that one person in particular had plenty of opportunity to steal and vandalise Aquinas film equipment. Only motive – lack of it – had stopped her from making an outright accusation. But now she had an idea.

'I need to see the school records,' she told Zappone. 'For previous applicants to Aquinas.'

'Ooh.' Zappone was intrigued. 'Well, they're probably on microfiche somewhere about the place. Come with me and we'll have a squiz. I don't know how far back they'd go, though.'

They went back just far enough. Her suspect had applied to Aquinas for eight consecutive years and been rejected each time. The last rejection letter had been ten years ago but the person had waited until this year for their revenge. And the reason was in the Aquinas files: *Lives in North Brunswick, aged forty, single.* Officially too old to apply. Whatever dreams Pluckrose had had of becoming an Aquinas student were at an end. It must have tipped him over the edge.

Lenny smiled at the information in front of her. She had him now. If she could just push him hard enough, he'd tell her everything. How hard to push was always the question. But he was slight and she could probably give as good as she got if it came to a fist fight.

The quadrangle was empty. She headed for the equipment storeroom and knocked. No answer. She turned the handle but the door was locked so she opened it with her master key. She'd wait right here, give him a nice little surprise when he returned. He wouldn't like it that she had crossed his line again. It would get them off to a good start.

The storeroom hummed with the reassuring aroma of

Ajax. Pluckrose was obsessively tidy and clean – factors that went in his favour. No need to forage through mounds of cables and light stands and Nagras and cameras. Everything in its place and a labelled place at that. The floor was so clean you could see a fuzzy reflection of yourself in it, if you were the type of person who looked for that sort of thing.

A cockroach walked across her duplicate's face. Lenny squashed it under her boot. Still alive, it scuttled under a cabinet. Lenny never allowed herself to be thwarted by insects. She tugged at the cabinet until it came away from the wall.

There it was! Even with half its legs missing and a goob of something white squirting from under its shell, the roach crawled on. They said these things could survive an atomic blast. She pulled off her boot. Survive this, sucker! Slammed down the boot in rapid succession until all that remained was a sludgy roach remnant, then used a wad of tissues to wipe it up.

As she bent she saw something else: thick strips of gaff tape across the back of the cabinet near the bottom. Lumpy in the middle. She raked at the edge of the tape with her fingernails until it came free. Under the gaff tape was a bundle of newspaper clippings sealed in a plastic bag.

Lenny stepped outside the storeroom and closed the door behind her. There were a few students in the quadrangle now but still no sign of Pluckrose, so she hurried up the main stairs into the toilets, locked herself into a cubicle and slid the clippings out of their protective bag. She found herself looking at newspaper items on the deaths of Emily Cunningham and Moira Middlemiss. A photo of each student had been ringed with a red marker pen and a number written across the face – one, two – in order of their deaths. Eight rejection letters. Eight students enrolled in Aquinas each year and two were dead already. Not getting enough satisfaction in destroying property, had Pluckrose moved on to destroying people too?

She went out into the corridor and placed the bundle in her locker then lit a cigarette, sucked all the life out of it in four monumental puffs and started on a second. Was it really going to be this easy, she wondered. She had always felt that Pluckrose must be the thief. She had had an instinct and been proved right. But thief, vandal and killer all rolled into one?

She pushed a window open to let in some fresh air and looked down into the quadrangle. Kenneth Drage was standing with his weathered briefcase, his face tilted to the sun. She left the window and went down to join him. He didn't register her presence at first, lost in his thoughts.

'Kenneth,' she said and he jumped.

'Lenny. Good to feel the sun on your face, isn't it? I know we've been through shocking times here recently but I have to say I feel the school is going to survive, Lenny, and be better than ever.'

Before she could respond to what, given the circumstances, was a rather naive sentiment, Pluckrose burst out of the storeroom. He had something in his hands and he was furious and breathing hard as though he had been running. He knew she had found his little stash, that much was clear. Lenny had never seen him so worked up.

'Who's been in there without permission? Someone has crossed the line.' He saw Lenny and pointed at her.

'It was you!'

'It was me,' she confirmed warmly.

'What is it, Graeme?' asked Kenneth. Pluckrose hesitated. He didn't want to confront Lenny in front of a third party.

Lenny's eyes were on the device in his hands. It was a radio transmitter. The police used them. A lapel mic was taped onto the chest and attached to a transmitter which sent the signal back to the police recording machine.

'Alana Zappone brought a radio transmitter to you the day Moira died, didn't she?'

Pluckrose blinked at the change of tack. He hesitated.

'Well, if you can't remember –'

'Alana brought me a Lectro Sonics transmitter she'd stepped on. It wasn't that badly damaged as it turned out.'

'What do you use them for here?'

'Communication between production assistant and director over two locations. Instructions to actors when the director has to be distant from the action, in a very wide shot, say. We have good sound equipment here. People shouldn't be taking it out without my say-so – and they should be watching where they put their big feet.'

'They're making remarkably compact sound gear these days,' Kenneth commented. 'Not like when I started out and everything was the size of a suitcase.'

'Yes,' Pluckrose agreed, eyes on Lenny, willing her to hand over his newspaper clippings. She shook her head at him.

'I remember when we did the wild sound for *Hard Skies*,' Kenneth laughed. 'My word, the trouble we had. It was a windy day and I was trying to get atmos for a quiet alley. Then, if you can believe it, a tram went by . . .'

Lenny left them discussing developments in sound technology. She wanted to find Harry before the day's filming began. She had the motive now. She was sure Pluckrose was the vandal. She wanted Harry to tell her if he was also the murderer. She strode back up to the first floor, wrenched open doors to edit suites, marched down the corridor, burst into Ray's office and generally spent all her energy in five minutes without finding him. She was about to give up when she heard a voice coming from around the corner in the common room. Someone was groaning. Nothing comprehensible. An odd sound. Almost a gurgle.

When she got there she discovered it was Harry, but by this time he wasn't even gurgling any more. He had passed out and Ray was kneeling at his side. Her fingers oozed scarlet as she tried to stop the blood running from his cranium. Lucy Peel held his hand and gazed down at him, her lavender eyes enormous and frightened. Her own hands were also crimson. Harry was sprawled on the carpet, arms and legs spread wide, with a Nagra at his side, its lid shattered. There was a nasty cut under his right eye. Blood from the head wound ran onto the floor and the school moggie lapped it up like a gourmand.

Ray looked up at Lenny, eyes darting. 'Lucy was here before me!'

'Cate!' Lucy protested. 'Lenny, it looks like someone tried to cut out his eyes. But they must have heard me coming. Thank God!'

Lenny checked for a pulse then pushed Ray out of the common room. 'He's alive,' she said. 'Get an ambulance.' The principal hesitated for a moment then turned and ran down the corridor. Lucy stood up and backed away.

'I didn't do anything, Lenny,' she insisted. 'I found him just like this.'

'Get a blanket,' Lenny said. Lucy Peel picked up the cat. Its lips were shiny with bright red gravy.

'Come on, Sardines. Come away with me.'

Lenny moved the bloodied hair with her fingers cautiously. The skull was cracked open. Best not try to roll him over or move him at all. She wasn't up to having pieces of brain matter spill out into her hand. He moaned.

'Harry?' She bent close to his ear. 'The ambulance is coming. Hold on.' What did he know? And what if he should die now without a friend nearby, without any kindness. She should squeeze his hand, make an attempt at comforting him. She didn't.

'Who did this to you?' she asked. 'Did you see them?'

'Gabrielle . . .' His voice was a hoarse whisper. '. . . killed Moira. She had the knife . . . blood . . . in the tower . . .'

He passed out again. Lenny reached for his neck. Still a pulse. Still a witness, then.

The police took over the same rooms they had last time to conduct their interviews. Lenny was in the quadrangle, waiting for her turn. She had waited two hours. The ambulance men came, went up, brought Harry out on a stretcher. The Nagra was wrapped in plastic. Harry's words looped through her brain and she wondered if she was going to repeat them to Danny.

The Aquinas School of Film and Television was officially closed pending further investigation. Ray's strident protests had fallen on deaf ears. The board had already made an announcement to the press.

It was Gabrielle who had told Lenny about the school's closure. She had plopped down on the grass beside her, smoking hard.

'They won't reopen this year with this kind of publicity,' she said. 'We may all get a pass credit without finishing the course. I won't get to edit my film now, I bet.' She studied Lenny's grim face. 'They've got Pluckrose in there now. I'm next. I've got nothing to tell them, though.'

'Well, I've got a few things to say,' Lenny said. 'For starters I'm going to tell them what Harry told me.'

'I thought he was unconscious.' Gabrielle stared at her.

'Not right away. He hung on for a few minutes. And while he was hanging on he told me he saw *you* with the knife that killed Moira.' She kept her voice low. 'That's why you've been letting him be your new best friend, right?

But why persist with it when it's far easier to smash his brains out with a Nagra? He's lucky Lucy Peel came along when she did or you'd have had his eyes to add to your sick little collection. Want to explain that bit to me? Why you have to disfigure them as well as kill them?'

Gabrielle's face assumed a preternatural blankness.

'He told me he saw you in the tower with a bloody knife,' Lenny persisted.

'I didn't attack him, Lenny.'

Shiny black shoes appeared.

'We're ready for you now, Ms Danaher.'

Gabrielle followed the young detective up into the interview room.

Pluckrose came out into the quadrangle. He stared at her. Confrontation time. Lenny pushed herself to her feet and followed him into the storeroom. He was waiting with his arms folded.

'OK,' she said drily. 'Kenneth's not here now, so you can drop the act.'

'I want my things back,' Pluckrose said. 'You had no right to take them.' He looked tired and defeated now. A middle-aged repairman who had once dreamt of being a film maker.

Lenny recalled how, when she'd first seen Pluckrose this morning, he'd been out of breath. Running away from Harry's body? Trying to cut out the eyes the way he had with Emily and Moira? What was this obsession the killer had with vision, she wondered.

'You've been stealing and destroying Aquinas property,' she said. 'Harry knew it. I think he caught you at it once and that's why you gave him so much leeway. But it was getting too scary, wasn't it? All these police around. Asking questions. Harry was starting to think he should tell the police the truth. So you tried to kill him. Like you killed the others.' She wanted it to be him. If it was him then it couldn't be Gabrielle and Harry was just raving.

'I didn't kill anyone.'

'Harry got whatever he wanted from you. You probably gave him a master key so he could come and go whenever he wanted. Is that how he got in here so easily the night Emily was killed? The night you killed her?'

'I'm innocent of murder. It's too –'

'Chaotic?' Lenny offered. 'Let me pitch you a story. It's a thriller, medium budget. A lowly technician with artistic pretensions is jealous of a rich woman who bought her way into a prestigious film school when he couldn't. That's the butterfly wings. He decides to get rid of all the students, one by one. Now here's where it turns into a black satire on meritocracy: even after he's killed all the film students, he still doesn't get in! Because he's forty years old. He's passed the age limit. Deranged, he realises the killing has to go on forever, with no hope of him ever getting a place. What do you think about Robert Downey Jr as you?'

Pluckrose hesitated then shrugged. 'I let Moira in the night Emily died,' he said. 'She was willing to pay for the privilege. Extra money for me. I deserve it, the amount of work I put in here. But I wouldn't have let Moira in if I'd been planning to kill Emily, would I? I wouldn't have wanted a witness.'

'You planned to kill them both and it went wrong,' Lenny said. 'Let's see what the police think.'

'Give me those papers.'

Lenny shook her head gently and sighed. 'Finders keepers. Anyway, the police will be turning over every inch of this place and since I put the papers in my locker with a sign saying "big, juicy piece of evidence", even they must have found them by now.'

'You interfering bitch!' Pluckrose hurled himself

forward, fingers fastening around her throat. She fell back against the door.

'Going to cut my eyes out too?'

He squeezed harder. She was beginning to wonder if she'd gone a bit far with the suspect-baiting when the handle turned from the outside and she fell back into the quadrangle. She looked up into Danny's face. He held the incriminating newspaper clippings in a clear plastic evidence bag. Pluckrose backed deeper into the storeroom, flanked by cans of film.

'We'll need to talk to you again, Mr Pluckrose,' Danny said. 'We now have reason to suspect you may be involved in the unlawful deaths of Emily Cunningham and Moira Middlemiss and the attempted murder of Harry Tuyen. And you, Ms Aaron –' He watched her scramble to her feet, rubbing her neck. 'You don't leave town.'

'I suppose you're over the moon?' Ray snapped at Lenny, who had gone to give the principal an update on the situation. 'You've finally shut us down.'

They were in the principal's office. Ray was seated at her desk while Kenneth stood examining a book on film aesthetics from her collection. He turned to Lenny, trying to deflect some of Ray's bitterness, forever the peacemaker although he was trembling with fatigue.

'How are you holding up, Lenny? Are they finished downstairs?'

'They've taken Harry to the hospital,' Lenny said.

'He's alive then? That's something isn't it, Cate?'

'Wonderful!' the principal agreed. 'That's one less funeral I have to attend this year.'

'We could all do with a cup of tea, I think,' Kenneth suggested. 'I for one am deeply shocked by this morning's events.'

'Nothing for me,' Lenny said.

Ray muttered: 'I'll have coffee. Bitter and black, like my future.'

'Steady on, Cate! Perhaps this time the police will have some luck.' Kenneth fumbled with the teaspoon and it fell to the floor. He foraged on the carpet for a moment, picked it up and – to Lenny's relief – put it aside and picked up a fresh one. 'Harry will perhaps be able to identify his attacker and the whole nightmare will end.'

He turned to Lenny.

'What can I do to help?'

Ray snorted. 'Nothing! You can do nothing, Kenneth, *savvy*? We are closed for business.' Ray bit her biscuit in half. Crumbs scattered over her suit but she didn't bother to brush them off. There had been a change in Ray since the closure was announced, as if under the stress of recent events an unexpectedly emotional incarnation was unburdening itself after years of smooth repression.

'Do you know how much work I've put in here?' she continued, rapping a harsh tattoo on the desk with her palms. 'I thought I'd done well to survive the bloody board's efforts to chuck me out. Wrong! Hello? Earth to Ray? This time the bastards have won.'

'Cate! When this has all died down ...' Kenneth countered.

Ray shook her head. 'How do you expect me to attract funding for Aquinas now? Where you send your children for a film education and we remove their eyeballs. That'll get the parents interested in us, won't it? Face it, Kenneth, we're fucked.' She ravaged another Toffee Pop.

The phone rang. Kenneth answered it. It was Danny. Ms Aaron was required upstairs. Lenny left them to their own devices and headed for the second floor. Annabel Lear was floating down the stairs with a Sony headset gilding her hair. She saw Lenny and shut off her music.

'Isn't it horrible?!' Her eyes gleamed. 'Poor Harry.'

'You hated him.' Lenny wasn't in the mood for bull-shitters, even the beautifully turned-out variety. Annabel tasted her lipstick for a moment.

'Lenny, you're right. But I feel just terrible about that now.' A helpless shrug. 'I've been such a child in my relationships, don't you think?'

'I think the way you ripped off Emily for twenty thousand dollars was pretty adult.'

Annabel's pretty lip curled, but her light, tinkling voice never altered pitch as she poked a finger into Lenny's chest. 'I've done a little investigating myself, H. Aaron. I know all about your cat catching thing in Footscray. It's quite pathetic, a woman of your age having to make a living out of lost animals. Don't get in my way, Aaron. I'm so out of your league, you'll still be wiping cats' arses when I'm at Cannes.'

'Maybe.' Lenny stepped back so the finger lost contact with her chest. 'But I won't be licking them.'

'Take me off your suspect list. Anyone will tell you that none of the victims was a threat to me, so why would I bother to kill them?'

'So who did it?'

'Who cares? Miranda, my publicist, thinks maybe someone didn't like their films.' Annabel sniggered. 'I know I didn't.'

CHAPTER 19

Dr Sakuno Turns the Screws

Lenny wanted to explore the school after the others had gone but it proved to be impossible. The police were taking no more chances. Pluckrose was under arrest and the Aquinas School of Film, Animation and Design had been sealed off and the students sent home.

Danny was annoyed when Lenny informed him about Pluckrose's series of rejections as an Aquinas student and her subsequent discovery of his newspaper clippings. He said she had a responsibility to come forward with evidence as soon as it was discovered.

'I only just discovered it!' she protested.

'I want to know everything you know. Now.'

And so she told him that Pluckrose was forty, that from this year on he was too old to become an Aquinas student, that it had pushed him over the edge, that she believed Harry had somehow known about the vandalism and theft and had been blackmailing Pluckrose to get his hands on equipment.

'But that's the bit that throws me,' she admitted. 'Let's say Harry knew about the theft, knew it was Pluckrose. He pressures Pluckrose to give him equipment, access to the school, whatever. If Pluckrose is also the killer, why does he wait so long to attack Harry?'

'Do you think Pluckrose is the killer?' Danny pushed his chair back to escape Lenny's cigarette fumes.

'I don't know,' she replied cautiously. 'This assault on Harry looks like a copycat, doesn't it? The assailant thinks he's killed him with the blow to the head then attempts to cut the eyes to make it look like the other murders. But he doesn't go through with it, he just nicks the skin open and runs off. Too gutless. Now that sounds like Pluckrose to me.'

It was time to bring up the other information, the statement of a witness currently undergoing an MRI to determine brain injury. It was time to tell him what Harry had told her about Gabrielle Danaher.

She hesitated and tried to understand why. Partly it was the films. She remembered Gabrielle's story of the old man and the saxophone, the pity in the images, the care taken in the details. It *was* the films, she thought, they were special. Kenneth was right about Gabrielle, she was some kind of genius. But if she was guilty? Should her ability be protected? Did it deserve a special consideration?

'We're searching Pluckrose's flat,' Danny told her. 'We're hoping to find the murder weapon used to kill Emily Cunningham and Moira Middlemiss.'

'I see,' Lenny said.

'Looks like it wasn't Lucy Peel.' He paused, knew she was holding back. 'Or Gabrielle Danaher.' He watched her, waiting.

She let him wait.

He pushed a file across the table and said: 'Did you know about this?' Lenny opened it. Details of a young man, an immigrant. Entrance into Australia. Residence. Part-time job. There was also a picture of a young woman, maybe twenty-five years old, hair in plaits, overweight, bad skin. The name on the back of the photo said Jennifer Grigg.

The same name was on a photocopy of a wedding certificate. The groom's name was Janus Onyszkiewicz. The marriage had taken place three years ago.

'Visa groom,' she observed, recalling what Harry had said about foreigners cheating their way in to Australia and getting film industry jobs. He had known about this.

'Looks like it.' Danny pulled out a copy of Janus's passport. 'He came here on a holiday and got married. There's no evidence he's ever lived with Ms Grigg. We interviewed her and her story is they've broken up.'

'Harry sometimes taunted Janus about a woman,' Lenny agreed. 'But it's weak if you're thinking of it as a motive for murder. This country is full of visa frauds. Hardly anyone's ever deported.'

'Maybe Onyszkiewicz didn't know that and Harry pushed his luck too far, threatened to tell the authorities.'

But if the attacks were connected, what reason did Janus have to kill Emily and Moira?

'From now on if you find anything, it comes straight to me. Got it?' Danny was her old colleague, but he was still a cop and she wasn't. Don't get too smoochie with the cops, she reminded herself. It was bad for business.

She pushed back her chair. 'Are we finished?'

'For now,' Danny said without looking up.

Lenny walked into the car park. Gabrielle, swamped in her motorbike helmet and leather jacket, caught up with her at her car, placed a hand on her arm for a moment as she slid her key into the lock.

'Lenny.' No urgency or fear in the voice. They stared at each other through the dark helmet visor.

Lenny opened her door but didn't get in. Gabrielle took off her helmet and pulled at her moth-holed t-shirt.

'I didn't hurt Emily or Moira or Harry –'

'Graeme Pluckrose has been arrested,' Lenny told her

flatly. 'The police have evidence pointing to his guilt. I think they're wrong. I think he stole and destroyed equipment and I think he attacked Harry. But I don't think he killed Emily or Moira.'

Gabrielle's eyes widened. 'I see,' she said finally. She glanced back over her shoulder toward the school. She didn't want anyone to overhear them.

'In fact, I'm sure Harry didn't touch them,' Lenny persisted.

'Look, it's not up to me to help him.' Gabrielle's hands were shaking now. She seemed very small, young and defenceless. 'You think it's me, don't you? You really think I go around cutting out people's eyes? Lenny, if that's what you think, don't do me any more favours, OK? Just tell the police what Harry said. Get Pluckrose off the hook. I fit their profile. They're just looking for a chance to arrest me. Give it to them.'

The green eyes were teary. It was almost irresistible.

'They'll go easier on you if you tell them what you know,' Lenny managed.

Gabrielle jammed her helmet onto her head. 'Thanks for the advice, Investigator.'

Back at her office, Lenny was wound-up and tetchy. She needed help. She grabbed her phone and dialled.

'This is Dr Sakuno's office. Mariko Oyama speaking. How may I assist you?' Mariko. Lenny had met her several times. A rake-thin, ice in her veins, fashion plate Dr Sakuno had imported from Tokyo a year ago. His Australian PA's insistence on keeping family photos, flowers and small toys on her desk had driven him to the end of his tether. Mariko's desk was devoid of personality.

'It's Lenny Aaron. I want to speak to Dr Sakuno.'

'Dr Sakuno is in Tokyo, I'm afraid, Ms Aaron.' Mariko

liked to say 'I'm afraid'. She had studied the Queen's English at a conversation school in Oxford for two years and British touches – hardly, terribly, precisely, gracious, goodness me, I dare say – littered her speech. She gave Lenny the shits.

'This is an emergency,' Lenny said.

A tinkling, ice-cream van laugh. 'Come now, Ms Aaron.'

'Give me the Tokyo number, Oyama san.'

'Excuse me for saying so, but Sakuno *Sensei* instructed me not to contact him in regard to certain patients. I can without a doubt put you in touch with a very good psychologist who could act as an interim adviser.'

'Give me the number.'

'Ms Aaron –'

'Don't make me come in and force it out of you, Mariko.'

Once before they had had a face-to-face confrontation across Mariko's immaculate desk. Lenny's mastery of Japanese included a choice range of expletives, which, mild as they sound when translated into English, have a devastating effect on a Japanese. The PA was unwilling to go another round. She snitted out the number.

'You are a bully,' she said and hung up.

Japan was an hour ahead of Melbourne.

'*Donata desu ka?*' The voice on the other end of the line belonged to an older woman.

'I want to speak to Dr Koichi Sakuno,' Lenny said. '*Sakuno sensei wa irrashaimasuka? Renny Aaron desu,*' she said, substituting the katakana R for her name's L.

There was a sharp cry of fear at the other end of the phone. Her reputation had preceded her. The handset crashed down. Lenny imagined crisp white *tabi* whisking over wheat-coloured tatami.

'Ms Aaron?' Dr Sakuno's voice was different – thicker, as though he had had an injection at the dentist and couldn't get his tongue to move correctly. He was drunk. Strictly teetotal in Australia, in Japan he had reverted to stereotype: the hard-drinking, middle-class male. Collective drinking is a ritualised obligation for the Japanese male, a social requirement. Sanctioned by alcohol, things can be said which would be out of place at the office. Dr Sakuno was letting his hair down because he was required to.

'How did you get this number? How dare you disturb me during a social gathering. I'm hanging up!' There was silence but she heard him breathing.

'*Sensei*, I need your help.'

'Forget it, Komodo Man.' She heard the clink of beer bottles and loud chatter in the background. Voices yelled in unison: '*Kampai!*' He was talking to someone else. '*Chigau, chigau ... Taishita koto nai.*'

'Please. My investigation –'

'What?' To someone in the room with him. '*Hai, hai!*' A hearty chuckle.

'Remember how you advised me to get a friend?'

'Mmm?'

'I haven't. It's all wrong. For me, I mean.'

'Naturally.' She had his attention now. 'You are innately unlikable. Who would wish to be your friend? I have thought it over and I am cancelling my advice.'

'You can't cancel advice.'

'I've just done it. Forget friends, Helena san. You have none and you will never have any.' A pause. A discreet belch and then: 'This conversation is really about your father.'

'No, no.'

'Yes, yes. You were a bad daughter to your father and now you are repenting.'

'That's a terrible thing to say!'

'*Ryoyaku wa kuchi ni nigashi.*' Good medicine has a

bitter taste. 'If you face the truth you will feel better about yourself.'

There was a rustle of activity and amongst merry protestations Dr Sakuno allowed himself to be led away from the phone. She heard the melancholy tune of '*Hotaru no Hikari*', 'The Firefly's Light', a drinking song about the shining brevity of life.

'Lenny, is that you?' A young female voice, unaccented English.

'Yes.' She pulled herself together. 'Who is this?'

'It's Mickey.' Kumiko Sakuno, sixteen years old. Sakuno's Australian-born daughter. They had met once.

'Tokyo's a real shithole,' Mickey said. 'Get lost, will you!' to someone else. 'Jesus! There's about twenty of Dad's uni mates here, a reunion. They're tragic. The beer's excellent, though.' She paused. 'Are you all right? Dad's pissed, but if you want I'll get him to call you back when he sobers up.'

'No, no.' Asahi-assisted, Dr Sakuno had given her a swift and accurate diagnosis. A bad daughter to her father. 'It's not important, Mickey. Hang in there. Bye.' She hung up. Bertrand Russell watched her smugly from his cage. Cats see all, hear all and gloat over all.

The next morning's investigative agenda included paying a call on Janus Onyszkiewicz and meeting with Kenneth Drage. Kenneth had been surprised by her request but she was beginning to feel that the answer to the murders was right in front of her. Kenneth had been longest at Aquinas and she wanted to hear what he thought about everything, the nature of the school, its staff and students. If you understood the people, she thought, you understood why they died.

Technically her job was over. Pluckrose was the thief. She

had succeeded. But she had gone too far into this murder investigation now to drop it and move on. She needed to finish it.

She had no appetite and tried to stimulate one by laying out her best *sara kobachi*, blue and white ceramic cups and bowls purchased via Dr Sakuno's Japanese mail-order catalogue last year. They did look lovely. Peaceful. But she didn't have the energy to cook rice and fish, and she had no Japanese pickles left. So she slopped milk and orange juice into two of the cups and ate a small apple while she stared at the TV. Morning breakfast shows were all covering the arrest of Aquinas's alleged serial killer and failed applicant, Graeme Pluckrose.

After breakfast she stood at her medicine cabinet and ran a finger along the white labels of the various stacks of bottles. There was a minute wisp of lint in the corner behind the Bex powders. She removed all the bottles from the cabinet, went to the kitchen and brought scalding water, disinfectant and a cloth back into the bathroom. It was unthinkable that containers with contents for her mouth should be held in a dirty cupboard. She scrubbed. Her mind buzzed lightly from the fumes. As always she used the disinfectant in too great a concentration and felt slightly faint. Nice.

Later in her office she heard a fight break out in the parking lot. A Chinese voice screaming. *Yang guizi!* Foreign devil. Lenny had looked it up on an Internet Chinese–English dictionary because she heard it so frequently.

A rap on the door made her jump. She threw a blanket over Bertrand Russell's cage.

'Come in.'

'Excuse me? Is this H. Aaron Investigations?' A portly white male hovered in the office doorway. He wore a press-studded red and green western shirt, stone-washed blue jeans with rhinestone trim, and what she supposed he imagined were cool cowboy boots. He held a black vinyl handbag with a gold clasp. His hair was thick and grey and seemed to grow all over his head and face. It was what happened when you didn't trim your beard and moustache regularly, Lenny thought. His hands were dreadful too. Covered with low-grade dermatitis. She would have to take care not to touch him. Further scrutiny revealed soft orange hairs adhering to the shirt: a cat owner.

'I'm Lenny Aaron. How can I help you?'

'Saw you on the box. G'day.' He squeezed his bottom into the visitor's chair. 'Jeez, you look crook.'

The handbag popped open and a hand pulled out a plastic pack of photographs. 'What do you reckon to that then?'

The cat in the photo had salmon toned markings on a warm, pinkish cream background. The coat was short, the eyes deep gold and almond shaped, slightly tilted. The head was a rounded wedge, the body medium sized with only moderate muscling. Lenny glanced up.

'Spotted Mist,' she said casually. 'Appeared in 1975. The first breed developed entirely in Australia. Gentle, playful, home-loving. The standard penalises any show of aggression on the bench.'

The man nodded. He scratched at his thumb.

'Name?' Lenny pulled out a form.

'Jim. Jim Ryback. That's Big Jim to friends.'

'Mr Ryback, then.' Lenny printed. 'And the cat's name?'

'Jim Ryback Junior.'

'Little Jim to his friends?'

'Are you taking the piss?' He blinked at her.

'Not really. Missing how long?'

He glanced at his watch. 'Two hours.'

Lenny flicked through his photos. Jim Junior appeared

to have his own room with a deluxe basket trimmed with red ribbons around a denim cushion. The room was dominated by a cat climbing frame in the shape of two giant mushrooms.

'Where did you last see him?'

'I was working at the shop this morning and it was quiet so I took him out for a walk, you know? Picked up a cappuccino and a doughnut.' He paused.

Lenny forced a smile. 'I'm with you.'

'Then we're off to the park for a bit. I've got the ghetto blaster with me and we have a bit of a nap. Bit of music. Not that radio stuff they play now. I like my music to get me going, you know. Country, you know. A man and a woman and –'

'Mr Ryback –'

'Jim.'

'Mr Ryback –'

'Big Jim to m'mates.'

'Mr Ryback, what happened to the cat?'

It transpired that Little Jim had gone missing while Big Jim was taking a nap. After searching the neighbourhood, Big Jim had called his vet for help. The vet, as all good Melbourne vets must, recommended H. Aaron Investigations. Big Jim lived in Spotswood, not too far from Lenny's office. Easy money, she thought. But then:

'I know where she's got him,' Big Jim growled. 'Brunswick.'

'Sorry?'

'She'll have taken him to Brunswick.'

'She?'

'My ex-wife, the scrag.'

'You think your ex-wife took your cat?'

'I know she did.'

Big Jim explained. His recent ex had apparently fought

long and hard for custody of the Spotted Mist. But since Big Jim had purchased the cat a year before his wedding, Esme Ryback didn't have a leg to stand on. Big Jim couldn't retrieve the cat himself. Esme had slapped him with a restraining order after – *she said!* – he cut the toes off all her shoes.

'She's determined to have him, but I tell you what: when I get him back, if she tries anything like this again she's going to be met in force.'

Lenny wrote the address on the application form. 'I'll need a two hundred dollar retainer.' He couldn't wait to get the yellow notes out of his wallet.

'That's m'girl!' He slapped his thigh. 'I'll be waiting back at the salon.'

'Salon?'

'I'm a hairdresser.'

'That explains those hands.' It was out before she could stop it. They both glanced down at the inflamed hands and then up at each other. Big Jim flushed.

'Sorry. It's from putting me hands in chemicals all day.' Big Jim's feelings were hurt, but he bluffed it out manfully. 'It's not that bad, is it?'

'I'll have your cat back to you tomorrow at the latest,' Lenny promised. It was as close as she could get to an apology.

CHAPTER 20

Target and the Art Gallery

Janus didn't know she was coming. Danny had told her he had a part-time job in a rundown suburb on the outskirts of the city. Lenny suspected he had chosen this area because no students or staff from Aquinas were likely to wander through. He must have thought he was safe, protected by suburbia from his arty friends.

When she walked into the Sunshine Target he was working at the register. He didn't look like a haughty European cinematographer today. His red and white striped uniform was pinned with a tag that said 'Hello My Name's Janus'. He looked tired, and his face flushed crimson when he saw her.

'What are you doing here?'

Lenny held a lemon cardigan in front of herself. 'Think this is me?'

'I have nothing to say to you, Investigator. Pluckrose has been arrested. He is a thief and probably a killer. What else is there to say?' He glanced around and, as if on cue, a balding man in a smelly polyester shirt appeared beside him.

'Trolleys, Anus.'

'Janus. My name is Janus.'

248

'Just get your arse outside.'

Lenny watched him round up the shopping trolleys. There was no point offering to help; he would refuse. She held out her cigarette pack after he had finished and he took one. They sat next to the St Vincent de Paul clothing bins.

'I've seen some of your work in the school library. You're a talented editor.' Lenny approximated a warm smile.

'I know. Do you have a tic or something?'

Her lips sagged into their usual flat line. 'Look, I know about Mrs Onyszkiewicz and so do the police.'

'Harry! He can't keep his mouth shut.' Janus wiped his hands over the top of his head. 'Will you inform Immigration?'

'No. Not if you tell me what I want to know.'

'I married her in good faith. I loved her. I still love her, only she won't have anything to do with me. She just wants money. She says she'll tell people that I married her for a visa, but I didn't. I love her! I will swear it on the bible. Listen, I have a future in the industry here. I must stay in Australia. This is a real chance for me –'

Lenny cut him off: 'Did Harry make things tough for you?'

'He's a boy,' Janus snorted. 'Joking around. Betraying trust.'

'Did you attack him with the Nagra? Did you try to cut his eye out?'

Janus jumped to his feet and flicked the cigarette onto the tarmac. 'The police say it is Pluckrose, so it is Pluckrose. Who am I to question the police? It is nothing to do with me. I am guilty of nothing. I love this country.' He was red-faced. 'I studied English night and day. I worked two years to save the money to come here. Australia . . .' He said the word like it was magic. Lenny envied him. 'I love it. But I would not kill anyone just to stay.'

249

'Did you borrow money from Emily?'

'No.' He stared at her, angry rather than afraid. 'And I did not kill her. I would not kill a woman.'

'What about Moira?' What indeed? She couldn't see any connection between them.

Janus shrugged. 'An idiot. She told me she was going to get the Silver Shutter award from Kenneth. He is interested in beauty, you know. Artistic achievement. I don't think she had any chance in the world, but she was obscenely confident about her small talent.'

'If Pluckrose is innocent –'

'He is guilty –'

'– if he's innocent, then who killed Emily and Moira? Who attacked Harry?'

He hesitated, smoked hard.

'Bad luck,' he said. 'They were in the wrong place at the wrong time. Life is like that, you know? Random. They would never have succeeded anyway. They didn't look right. It's important here, for success, the way you look. Maybe the most important thing of all. I'm thinking of having an image make-over when I graduate.'

Lenny sniggered. She just couldn't help it.

Janus glared at her. 'Insensitive cow.' He marched back towards Target.

She called out to him: 'Why did you have a sound transmitter in the edit suite the day Moira died?'

'What?'

'There was a transmitter. Alana Zappone stepped on it.'

He shrugged. 'I know nothing about that. Nothing. I must go back now.'

She watched him return to the store.

Kenneth was late. She stood outside the temporary art gallery in Russell Street where he had asked her to meet him. This was one of the locations where the Victorian Art Gallery was storing its pieces while the St Kilda Road renovations were under way.

She watched the traffic go by. Children persuaded their mothers to buy them ice-creams. A minibus brightly painted with the logo 'Off The Beaten Track' loaded up with British teenagers for a round-Australia tour. Their movements were slowed by Gore-Tex backpacks as large as bar fridges.

Kenneth appeared, breathing hard as he hurried towards the entrance. He noticed her at the last minute and stopped short, smiling.

'Lenny? There you are. I'm so sorry to be late. Taxi caught in traffic. I hope you don't mind meeting here. I'm coordinating a photographic history of Australian film for them next month. I've got a meeting later with the curator.' He gestured to the gallery doors. 'Not as good as the real gallery, but they promise the renovations will be worth waiting for. And I promise you we'll do the good stuff. I don't know about you, but I don't like installations. We used to have beauty and vision in our works of art, now we have bits of cows in formaldehyde.' Lenny had no idea whether she agreed with him or not. She was not the cultured cop of detective fiction, and there was no point pretending.

'Let's have a wander, shall we?' Kenneth led the way.

They entered the Australian exhibit. Lenny hired a two-dollar CD player at the entrance and fiddled with the controls. Something blared in her ear.

They stopped in front of Robert Dowling's *Early Effort – Art in Australia*. In the painting, a settler was painting Aborigines in front of a cottage in the bush. The Aborigines were wrapped in kangaroo skins and carried spears. The settlers, grouped around a baby, looked like they were ready to run back into the cottage and start shooting at the drop of a hat. The Aborigines looked hungry and fierce.

'This is an interesting picture, isn't it?' Kenneth continued. 'He painted it in London, you know. Perhaps the distance exaggerated the Aborigines' menace in his memory. A lot of tension, I think, between the two groups.' He smiled. 'Tell me if I go on too much. I've been around these particular paintings more times than I can remember.'

Lenny stared at the painting before them and admired the pre-genocidal feel. 'The baby playing with the cut-throat razor is an interesting touch.'

'What? What do you mean?' Kenneth stared hard at the painting, puzzled. He stepped closer to it, eyes almost touching the canvas. A security guard took a step towards him. 'No, that's not a knife, Lenny. It's a paintbrush.'

'Is it?' Lenny looked again. So it was.

'Now, perhaps you'll tell me why we're here, you and I? You said something about a talk?'

'About the murders at Aquinas.'

'I see. Well, the police seem fairly certain that Pluckrose attacked Harry and that he's the murderer too ...' He seemed to be searching for a way to help her.

'But you're not sure?' Lenny prompted. A large group of Japanese tourists with their guide came to join them in front of Frederick McCubbin's *The Pioneer*. There was a sudden frenzy of activity as everyone wanted their picture taken standing slightly to the left of it.

'This is from the Kit-Kat advertisement,' Lenny murmured, gazing at the three-panelled painting.

Kenneth sighed. 'Yes, that's the only reason most Australians know it. Still, I suppose any kind of exposure helps create a national image, even if it's only flogging chocolate.' He looked at her for a long time. 'To be honest, I am very far from convinced Graeme murdered those girls. I've known him five years as a staff member and he's not very sociable, not a friendly person, but he's excellent at his job. He keeps our clapped-out old stuff in perfect order. He works long hours and he's dedicated. These days that's something special.'

'You've been at Aquinas since it opened. You must have known he applied to the school eight times and was refused?'

He nodded. 'But I didn't allow his failure as an applicant to prejudice my feelings towards him as a member of staff.' His hands trembled again and he closed them. 'I felt it would be unfair to him to assume a connection between his personal history and our recent troubles. Even now ... I could bring myself to believe that he was involved in the theft and vandalism. That kind of behaviour is motivated by greed, envy or spite. The sort of dark emotions we all fall victim to to one extent or another. Degrading and foolish, yes – but it's not murder. We are talking about atrocity. That takes another kind of mind altogether, don't you agree? Frankly I don't believe Graeme has it in him.'

He sighed. 'I've been through all this with the police. All about the staff and students, all about the school. And there's so little I can really tell them. As I'm sure you know, my role over the last couple of years has lessened considerably. I told the police about the school as a whole, as I see it. I don't think they found it at all useful.'

'I might.'

He took a deep breath. 'There are, of course, the usual jealousies and factions. The school is supposed to be purely a learning institute, but I'm afraid ambition has overridden our original aims and it has become very competitive.'

'You mean the students hate each other?'

'Well, yes,' Kenneth laughed. 'Sometimes that's not a bad

thing as far as individual determination goes, but it can cause problems in a team situation.'

'If you're right and Pluckrose is not a killer, then it's possibly one of the third year students,' Lenny pointed out.

Kenneth stared at her. 'Yes. I helped choose them, you know. It was actually my last time on the selection panel. The current second and first years were chosen by Ray, Lucy, Greg and Flip. I remember I was particularly excited by Gabrielle and Brad Glenn.'

'Brad Glenn is the one who went to the AFTRS?' Lenny said.

Kenneth nodded. 'I chose him because he reminded me of myself at that age – the passion for art. Perhaps he was doing it deliberately, flattering me with mere imitation. I'm aware of the affection that damn Silver Shutter inspires. But I'm glad he went. The AFTRS has the sort of funding and resources we can only dream about.'

They paused to take in Robert Prenzel's *The Mathias Suite*. Lenny's headset described it as a gumnut art nouveau bedroom set. Cassowaries, brolgas, possums and waratahs peered out of the Queensland blackbean wood. It was horrifying. Lenny couldn't imagine sleeping in it without experiencing nightmares. 'What about Gabrielle?' she prompted.

'Gabrielle?' Kenneth didn't meet her eyes. 'Gabrielle is a brilliant film maker, a genius. I'm afraid I've been a little indiscreet in making my feelings known. It's caused some resentment amongst the other students. There's some darkness in Gabrielle. She'll never tell me, of course. I've pulled dribs and drabs out of her. She and I had a talk after Moira was –' He stopped abruptly. 'I'm not prepared to go further with this. It was a private conversation.'

'Why? Because she's a genius? Because even if she's guilty of murder, you'll let her get away with it?'

'She is *not* guilty of murder.' Their eyes locked.

'All right. Let's move on then. Emily Cunningham,' Lenny continued. 'She was rich and by all accounts not very talented. She lent money to other students to gain favour and she had a failed sexual relationship with your supervisor, Lucy Peel.'

'I don't know what to say.' Kenneth was embarrassed. He narrowed his eyes and stared hard at Sidney Nolan's *First Class Marksman*. Ned Kelly as a couple of black squares against the landscape. Boogly eyes, clumsy hands clenched around the gun, firing into nothing. The painting was owned by a former TV comic turned producer. Kenneth looked at it for a long time, squinting slightly, head to one side.

'Lucy is a very fine young woman,' he went on finally. 'And a good teacher. The students have always been fond of her. I think her weakness has been that she's too kind. She's a very gentle person. As for her relationship with Emily, it was a terrible slip. The only one she's made as a staff member at this school. My instinct is that Emily instigated the relationship. She certainly ended it. Lucy was her supervisor and should have been more careful. I would never countenance a relationship with a student. It's overstepping a boundary.'

They paused at James Wigley's *Dividing the Fishes*. A mucky, dark painting with Aborigines rendered as gargoyles. Kenneth gestured towards the top right hand of the picture and Lenny noticed a cat.

'I've often wondered, is that a native Australian?' Kenneth asked.

'There are no original native Australian cats,' she said.

'Really?'

'Australia, Papua New Guinea and New Zealand separated from Asia eighty-five million years ago, long before

255

cats evolved. The only cats in this country are those descended from cats brought here in the nineteenth century. They were imported to control the European rabbit.'

'Well!' He was impressed, but laughing at her at the same time.

Lenny stopped in front of Russell Drysdale's *The Rabbiters*. Two twig-like men were dwarfed by a dead gum grinning like a skull from the ochre cliff behind them. 'What about the other students?' she continued.

'Moira Middlemiss got into the school for two reasons, neither having anything to do with her potential as a film maker.' Kenneth looked pained. 'She's a young woman and we are still looking for a balance in the industry. We began, against my wishes, a conscious policy to increase the numbers of women in the film world. I'm not sure it's fair to favour gender over talent, but that could be my inability to recognise my own sexism.' He delivered this with a wry smile.

'And the second reason?'

'Lucy and Ray were rather taken with her personal style.'

'What do you mean?'

'I'm embarrassed to explain it.'

'Force yourself.'

'Well ...' Kenneth folded his arms across his chest. 'There's rather an unpleasant aspect to our business and to the arts in general. I call it the groovy factor. That's how out of touch with the vernacular I am, but I think groovy still works. Put simply, Moira looked the part.'

'You don't think she had talent?'

'Oh, of course she had *some*. We would never admit any student who didn't show any promise at all. Moira was adequate. Besides, she made documentaries. We always like to have one documentary maker in each intake.'

'And Harry?'

'He was accepted on his third attempt. I wasn't on the panel for his interview, I was ill at the time. Ray and Lucy chose him. I would say he's a fair cinematographer and a good film maker within the limitations of specific genres.' Kenneth shook his head. 'I did get a listen to his soundtrack for this year's graduation project and I must say it showed the usual commercial promise. He's very skilful with his use of modern music and effects. He's likely to be fully employed upon graduation.'

'Janus?'

'We chose Janus for his technical skill,' Kenneth said. 'He's a good lad. Too serious. He'll make a fine editor or cinematographer. As a writer and director he's not up to scratch. I've told him that.'

'And Annabel?'

'Will be the biggest success to come out of the school in years. After graduation she'll wet her feet in television, get funding from the NFC for a feature, have an enormous commercial success, then move to Los Angeles, make the right connections and Bob's your uncle.' His eyes were lowered.

'Why her?'

'She understands how the system works.'

'She's self-absorbed,' Lenny subtitled.

'Unceasing attention to self-interest secures success,' he amended. 'You become good at performing yourself. It impresses the people who are impressed by such things.'

'Did you tell her that?'

'You think it's unfair?'

Kenneth took her silence for assent. 'Society in the past placed value on social rank. It was loathsome and discriminatory. Our society lusts after money and fame. Equally loathsome, but I can hardly blame Annabel for it. And film, as I'm continually told, is a complex business these days.

257

Where once we had free-form and innovation, now we have commercialism. It's the new experiment. All I can hope for is that Aquinas staff guide the students as best they can. The kids should know there's more to film than box office returns.'

A Brett Whiteley hung near the exit: *Evening Coming in on Sydney Harbour*. It caught Lenny's eye and she activated the CD player.

'A man with a very special vision. He called his work optical ecstasy,' Kenneth told her at the same moment as the CD. Lenny listened on, admiring the white strokes of pleasure boats against the nightmare-blue of the harbour water.

'He was a junkie,' she said when the CD finished. 'He died of an overdose in a motel on the New South Wales coast.'

'No one ever said dope fiends can't be great artists. They just don't last very long. I'm sorry if I haven't been much help to you.' He rubbed his eyes and wiped his glasses. He looked tired.

'Tell me about Gabrielle.'

'That I cannot do.'

'You know she's guilty, don't you? You know she killed them and you're protecting her. Because you like her and respect her. I'm right, aren't I?'

Kenneth stared at her. For a moment she was certain he was going to nod, to tell her she was right.

'I have an appointment with the curator,' he said finally.

'Fine.' Lenny watched him walk away. He paused at the bottom of the stairs and groped for the handrail before he moved on. An old man and a nice one. But if he knew something, he was going to have to talk. She would make him talk.

CHAPTER 21

A Junkie Finally Gets What's Coming to Her

In the car on the way to Brunswick, Lenny considered her plan of attack. She had dealt with this kind of thing before. Divorce brought out the worst in pet owners. Still, Big Jim had given her a photocopy of the divorce settlement – divorce also brings out the petty bureaucrat in the combatants. She read the clause on Little Jim and he belonged to Big Jim all right, so it was your basic snatch and grab operation.

Parked across from the house, she opened her boot and pulled out a few cat retrieval items: the cat box, thick gloves and a packet of processed catnip. If only she had some human nip.

The house was a small red-brick one with a nicely kept garden. Two housewives with plastic shopping bags and purple hair nattered at the gate.

'Yes, he said she'll be on the antihistamines on and off for years.'

'My Bruce had to have his whole nostril cavity burned out under a general.'

'Oh, Teresa's had that! And a series of injections after they identified what she was allergic to. Turned out to be cat hair and couch grass and household dust mites. She had an injection once a week for twenty-six weeks. Shocking expense!'

'Bruce was overnight in hospital to have his nose surgically widened at the bridge.'

'Teresa's got a polyp in her left cheek.'

'Bruce still can't lie flat in his bed. He has to sleep with his head raised on three pillows.'

'Well, I must get home.' The purple hair with the tortoiseshell glasses gave Lenny a look. 'Wendy –' She waddled away.

'Pamela –'

From inside the house came the off-key wail of 'Blue Moon of Kentucky'. The vocals stopped when Lenny pressed the bell. Esme Ryback opened the door with a smile that zippered her lips all the way across her cheeks. The lips formed a small O of annoyance as she saw Lenny.

'I don't want anything.' She began to shut the door. Lenny's boot stopped her.

'I'm not offering anything.'

'How dare you!'

Lenny raised the cat box. She dared plenty.

'I've come for Little Jim,' she said. She noted that Mrs Ryback was also a fan of country and western fashion. The hair was pure Dolly Parton, an enormous cloud of white blonde. Was it Jim's handiwork, Lenny wondered. Unfortunately, the breasts didn't match the hair's ambition. Her chest was flat under pink denim and lace.

'Little –' Mrs Ryback took a breath and her hands flew up. 'He's mine! He's mine!'

Lenny took out the court order. 'Apparently not.'

'That fucking bastard isn't having my baby!' The door slammed hard on Lenny's steel cap. Doc Martens ground against wood. The Spotted Mist, curious, hovered around Mrs Ryback's feet and Lenny swooped on it. She had it stuffed into the cat box and was running down the street when she heard the banshee scream behind her. Mrs Ryback, carving knife held high, was coming for her. Lenny swung the cat box in an arc that hit the older woman on the shoulder and knocked her to the ground. Inside the box Little Jim mewed in terror.

Lenny stepped on the arm holding the knife, bent down, took the knife and tossed it away from them before allowing Mrs Ryback to stand.

'That fucking bastard is having your baby,' she said. The usual tears made their appearance and Lenny sighed. 'Get a grip on yourself. It's an animal. And it's not even your animal.'

'I love him.' Mrs Ryback's sobs shook her whole body. She held out her hands. 'Please. I love him so much. He's my whole life. Don't take him from me. Can't you see I'm the one who loves him the most?'

'Mrs Ryback, don't ask me to make judgements about love. I'm a cat catcher.'

In her car she lifted up the cat box and looked in at the Spotted Mist. Little Jim, true to his breed, mewed sweetly. He tried to lick her. Lenny gave him a chicken biscuit. At least *he* wouldn't be bothered, she thought. Little Jim would wonder about Esme Ryback for two minutes, then happily commit himself to Big Jim's fridge. She dialled the hairdresser's number on her mobile and said she'd have him back at the salon in half an hour. He sobbed quietly. Another satisfied customer.

Later, back in her office, she finally dealt with a small but dreaded crisis. For safety's sake she wore two pairs of elbow-length pink gloves anchored to her upper arms with layer upon layer of Glad Wrap. Nothing could get through. And yet, with her arm pushed as far as it would go down her office toilet, Lenny felt uneasy.

It had been flushing slowly for a week. Today it had refused to flush, the water rising slowly to the top of the seat. The plunger did not unblock it. There were two choices. The first – pay professional rates for a plumber – was unthinkable. This was the second.

She felt around. No one else could have dropped anything in here. She was the only one who used the toilet and, thanks to many lectures on the topic by her mother, Lenny never – ever – flushed panty pads.

Her glove tips brushed something and she grabbed it and tugged. It was a long yellow object with a green nodule on top and many wads of soggy toilet roll wrapped round it. A banana toy. Cleo Aaron, watching at the doorway, gave a delighted chirrup and bounded over for a sniff.

'You!'

She taped the banana up in a plastic shopping bag and poked it into the bin.

Anastasia burst into the room.

'He's here! In the car park.'

'Who's here?'

'Walstab.'

Lenny flung her rubber gloves into the wastebin, picked up Bertrand's cage and handed it to Anastasia. She wrenched open the toilet door.

'Get in there.'

Anastasia stepped into the small room and sat on the toilet, the cage on her lap.

'Oh Lenny, I'm afraid! Maybe –'

She closed the door in the barber's face.

A moment later Thomas Walstab was standing in front of her desk with a face like granite.

'You are Helena Aaron?'

'What can I do for you, Councillor Walstab?'

'Yes, I should think you'd know my name by now.'

'I take a keen interest in the local community. Especially people I may be suing for libel. Is this a business visit or are you just canvassing? I should tell you I vote Labor.'

'You surprise me. But I won't try to set you straight; this is a business visit. It's about my wife's cat.'

'I see.'

'It's missing. Been missing more than a week now. I believe it's an act of malice, that someone may be holding it for their own nefarious purpose.'

'I see.'

'I want you to know something, Aaron.'

'Yes?' Here it comes.

'My wife worships that animal.'

'I see.'

'And like a lot of other people in this neighbourhood, she's been taken in by your reputation. She happens to believe that you are the best chance for recovering Bertrand.'

'I *see*.'

'Seventy-five dollars a day, then?' He reached for his chequebook.

'Yes. But if I return the cat within a week, I get a three hundred dollar bonus,' she said, experiencing a strange elation. Perhaps this was a dream?

He paused, pen nib on paper.

'Is it likely you'll find him that fast? I went to one of your competitors a few days ago. He had no luck.'

'All modesty aside, Councillor, I'm the best feline investigator in Melbourne.' She slid him an application form.

After Walstab had refused to fill out half the questions on the form, calling them intrusive and unconstitutional, he left. Lenny let Anastasia out of the toilet. The barber had heard everything and wanted a cut of the booty since she was the one who had taken the cat in the first place. They haggled furiously for five minutes before Anastasia settled for a hundred bucks and went back to an interrupted tongue-piercing.

On a high for the first time in a week, Lenny settled down to a serious analysis of the Aquinas situation. Everyone seemed to be lying. In her career as a police officer she had come to the conclusion that most people lied and that they did it for one of four reasons: to evade trouble, to create trouble for others, to increase their own importance and, lastly, because they liked it.

She opened her desk drawer and foraged. Her fingers brushed against something at the back and she removed an old pill bottle with a missing label. She unscrewed the cap and poured a handful of cream-coloured pills into her palm. There was something stamped on each pill: SKF J10.

What the hell did that mean? She had so many prescription and non-prescription pills, powders and syrups floating around, it was getting hard to keep track of them. Oxycodone, she thought suddenly. Yes. Oxycodone with acetaminophen. It was a mild pain reliever she had tried a few months ago. No adverse effects. But she had found other drugs that gave more dramatic results and given up on it. She thought she had thrown that bottle away, but apparently not.

She hesitated. On principle she didn't like to take pills from unmarked bottles. Oxycodone *was* a cream-coloured pill about this size, wasn't it? Or was it a white pill about this size? No, it was cream. She was sure it was cream. She popped a few into her mouth and swallowed.

The phone rang at four o'clock that afternoon. Dr Sakuno was back from Tokyo. He was doing hospital rounds today but would be available to see her in his hospital office from four-thirty to five. He worked there two days a week doing general counselling duties.

'I'll be there.'

'Splendid.' Mariko reminded her to be prompt since the doctor's time was valuable.

Lenny, oddly tired, slurped some cough medicine as she drove. She had been thirsty all afternoon, going through a carton of orange juice and several cups of nasty-tasting tap water. She looked at her face in the rear view mirror: big eyes, red-rimmed in a gaunt egg-shaped head. Her vision went blurry for a moment and she braked. A car squealed and honked behind. She ploughed past a tram just as its passengers stepped down onto the road. The driver went berserk on his bell. Cleo meowed nastily from her box on the back seat.

The hospital car park was close to casualty. As she pulled in she saw a child running, a peripheral blur. That's dangerous, she thought, letting a child play unsupervised. Then a cat jumped in front of the car, and she swerved, and there was the child now following the cat. Lenny was aware of pulling hard on the wheel and a wall coming into focus and making a crunching noise, which she thought a strange noise for a wall to make.

Her eyes blurred again and she felt sick. She was out of the car now and the cat was sitting beside her grinning as though it had performed a good trick. It was the only thing in focus, so she lunged at it. It hissed like a tyre going down slowly and at the same time she noticed her car tyre going down slowly. She felt the familiar tug and rip of a scratch, then the cat was gone. A child's face looked into hers and said, 'She's dead', and she closed her eyes.

When she opened her eyes again she was somewhere else with lights that buzzed. It was a bed, surrounded by a pleated, mint-green curtain that extended to the floor. The ceiling had a smoke alarm. The fluorescent tubes and

265

general atmosphere of grimness completed the picture.

A hospital.

She looked down at herself, saw a blue smock and a plastic tag on her left wrist marked H. Aaron in biro. There was an IV catheter taped to the back of her hand. She tried to get up and found she couldn't. There were fabric restraints around her lower arms. Her legs were similarly bound. She couldn't move.

'Hey!' She put all her power into it and was surprised by the little croak that issued forth, but not by the response it met. At her sick bed throughout her life there had been one constant, niggling factor.

Veronica Aaron drew back the curtains and made her entrance downstage right. Kylie Wong ambled in two seconds behind her, chewing gum and grinning. In her arms she carried a familiar cat box. Cleo Aaron's one eye peered out.

'Oh, Lenny!' her mother howled, raising her eyes to an imaginary gallery. The audience exploded and she smiled graciously through her tears.

'The lady in the next bed is talking to herself,' Kylie announced, jumping up onto Lenny's bed. 'And the girl near the door keeps taking her top off and muttering.'

'Kylie! A bit of shush!' her mother said, maintaining the too concerned, too frightened smile. She looked very red in the face for someone standing in an air-conditioned room.

Lenny said suspiciously: 'Is this the psychiatric ward?'

'Oh, Lenny! Don't *say* that word. No one in our family's ever been committed before. I don't know what your father would think.'

Kylie Wong fingered the rough texture of a wrist restraint. 'These are excellent.'

'Free me!' Lenny commanded. She wondered if her mother was behind her incarceration, perhaps in league with Walstab. Perhaps they were lovers? She mustn't struggle, it would only confirm the misdiagnosis. But she couldn't help it. A burst of frenzied wriggling came over her and she put everything she had into pulling against the restraints.

'You've got Buckley's,' Kylie Wong commented on her struggles.

'Lenny, I can't free you, darling.' Her mother put out a hand to pet her hair, saw Lenny's look, and withdrew it to stroke her own mouse-grey frizz. 'The nurse said you had to wait until the doctor came and he's still on rounds. They said you might hurt yourself again.' In the theatre of her mind, Veronica's suffering was greater than her daughter's, fighting as she was against her natural instinct as a mother to free her child.

'What?' Lenny squirmed. 'Get me out of here! Untie these fucking things, *Mother*. I mean it!'

'Oh, Lenny. Please . . .' Her mother held fists against her wet cheeks while Kylie Wong enjoyed the show. A nurse opened the curtains with a flourish.

'Hello, how are you?' the nurse said, apparently to the oxygen cylinder beside the bed.

'We're fine thank you, nurse,' said Lenny's mother, welcoming her supporting cast. 'And how are you?'

The nurse didn't respond. She held out a thermometer. 'Mouth.' Lenny stared at her, lips compressed.

'Mouth or we'll go rectal. You choose.' The woman was overweight and bored. She probably had a two-hour trip every morning from her half acre in Reservoir.

'Rectal?' Kylie Wong's eyes widened with anticipation. 'Does that mean –'

Lenny opened her mouth. The thermometer went in and the nurse picked up her wrist and looked at her fob watch. They all waited for a minute.

'You're slow.'

She tried to say, 'I'm always slow. Why am I in restraints?', but with the thermometer under her tongue it came out as 'Umawasso. Wamaunrustuns?'

'Hmm.' The thermometer was examined and a notation made on her chart.

'Listen to me –' Lenny began, but the nurse was already swishing through the curtains, massive hips rolling like a couple of bear cubs wrestling under a white sheet.

Lenny pushed back into the pillow. When she got out of restraints she would have her revenge and it would be physical. Whether to start on Veronica Aaron, Kylie Wong or the world in general was the only question.

CHAPTER 22

Cold Turkey and Chicken Skin

She lay in the hospital bed for an hour. During this time her mother read aloud to her from a tattered copy of *Vanity Fair*. Lenny didn't recognise the names of any of the Italian aristocracy, Parisian interior designers or New York social-ites, but it seemed that they had had quite a laugh at the coming out of a debutante from an old family. Veronica explained to Kylie that 'old family' was American for a family like the Packers or the Murdochs, but a couple of hundred years from now, after the direct connections with business had dropped away and they all lived off their super.

The nurse came back and said 'Movie!' and like magic the TVs over each bed were showing *The Name of the Rose*. Sean Connery pontificated amongst a group of Italian character actors with ugly haircuts. Lenny, her mother and Kylie Wong watched the monastery library burn at the top of the hill, the corrupt inquisitor die and the young monk leave his life's one love behind. The credits brought them back to reality.

'Daddy and I love Sean Connery,' Veronica Aaron smiled.

'So they licked that poisoned book and then they died?'

Kylie Wong rolled her eyes at the film's plot. 'Stupid. What if they didn't lick their finger to turn the page? Anyhow, it was easy. You could tell it was going to be the old guy with the white eyes. Mum, what did he do it for?'

'Because he didn't have any friends.' Her mother didn't know either.

'To protect his own little universe,' Lenny snapped, wishing she was safely in hers.

'You have shamed me, Aaron *san*!' Dr Sakuno stood at the end of the bed in a white lab coat. As a consulting psychologist he didn't really need the white coat, but he took any opportunity to get into a uniform. A uniform meant power. He held a clipboard and swung it at her while he addressed her mother.

'This is what I have to deal with! Your miserable wretch of a daughter.'

Upstaged, Veronica Aaron made herself small in her chair.

'Untie me,' Lenny demanded.

'You could have killed the child. You are lucky the police were not called.' And then it came back to her. The car park. The child running in front after the cat. She had swerved to miss them and driven into a wall.

'I missed by miles,' she said, relieved. It was an accident. 'Didn't they tell you about the cat?'

'You staggered out of the car,' Dr Sakuno said, ignoring her. 'You began screaming at the young woman and her daughter. You stood over them, you threatened them. You brandished a fist. Your words were slurred and the mother describes you as' – he glanced at the clipboard – '"insane". She said you were also drunk. You collapsed and were brought into casualty, where it was found you were not drunk.'

'Of course not!' Lenny's relief grew. 'I'm never drunk.' Why couldn't she remember shouting? She was sure she hadn't threatened anyone. And what did 'brandish' mean? Had she punched someone?

'*Lithium.*' Sakuno tapped the board with a fingernail. He paused and when she didn't speak, said, 'Lithium was found in your blood work.'

'Oh? Oh! Well that was a mistake,' Lenny said. 'I can explain that. It was an old bottle in my desk and the label was gone. I thought it was Oxycodone.' She laughed boldly. 'Just a mistake, then. That's all. No problem. I should go home and rest.'

She understood it all now. In combination with the other drugs built up in her system, the lithium had caused an accidental overdose. It had to happen sometime, she knew. Combining pills the way she did was risky. Her toxicity level was always high. And lithium was always dodgy unless it was strictly supervised. She had tried it a couple of times and then decided the benefits weren't worth the danger. If only all this hadn't happened when Dr Sakuno was around.

'So, I'm fine!' she quipped brightly.

Dr Sakuno ignored her and from his coat pocket retrieved a piece of paper that Lenny recognised as one of Dr Henderson's prescription forms. So he had gone through her things.

'You may be relieved to know I have intervened to prevent the prosecution of this old fool, Dr Henderson.'

'I am relieved.' Her voice sounded small.

'He has retired as from this afternoon.' Dr Sakuno began to untie her restraints. Lenny remained flat against the mattress.

'What's the matter?' Kylie Wong skipped into the cubicle, a surgical mask tied around her head like a Jane Austen bonnet.

'Nothing.' Veronica Aaron pulled her close.

'Fortunately I have a connection here. They have agreed to discharge you under my supervision,' Dr Sakuno told Lenny. 'Since you cannot be trusted.'

'I can!' Lenny swung her legs over the edge of the bed. She glared at them, peeled the sticky tape off her hand and yanked out the IV needle. 'I can be trusted!'

'You're a drug addict,' Dr Sakuno said flatly. Veronica Aaron began to cry again and Kylie Wong struggled free of her grip to approach Lenny and say: 'A druggie! That's so cool!'

Lenny sat in the passenger seat of Dr Sakuno's Toyota Crown Majesta, Cleo's cat box on her lap. Her car would be towed back to her flat. Dr Sakuno would take her home. He had said he had a few things to discuss with her, but he was apparently in no hurry to begin. He stared ahead at the empty road.

He had found the bottle of cough medicine in her bag and the other bits and pieces of OTC pills she always had to hand, and he had dropped them all into a bin on the way to the car. He was angry, Lenny thought, and he didn't show anger, he radiated it. She could feel it bristling from him like porcupine quills. But overlaying his anger was the more familiar aura of cold discipline. He would not give in to rage. He would, however, be as brutal as he had to be to get his way.

She examined her face in the wing mirror. The cat scratch was nasty, running from the left side corner of her nostril down past her mouth to the edge of her chin. Beneath the hospital swipe of iodine, it was raised and weeping. It made her face look dragged down, like a stroke victim, and reminded her of Granny Sanderman. She shuddered.

'Thanks for having me discharged,' she said. She fiddled

with the switches on his miniature TV.

'Don't touch that, Komodo Man.'

'Drop it, OK?'

'You could have had convulsions, gone into a coma. You may have already caused irreparable damage to your heart and other internal organs. Next time I will permit them to pump your stomach. Do you know what that is like?'

'Yes.' Lenny remembered hauling overdose cases from the police paddy wagon into casualty. The tube down the throat. The horrible retching. The black stains under the fingernails.

'Give me a reason.'

'All right. I get headaches. That's normal, isn't it? And I've had a bad cough recently. So I took a bit of cough medicine. How was I to know there was codeine in it? Anyway, codeine is often used in combination with aspirin to enhance the pain relief.' She realised as she said it that it was wrong, that it sounded like someone who knew exactly what she was doing. She was supposed to be the victim of circumstance.

'The lithium?' he pressed.

'I told you that was a mistake! Look, I'm ill. I am. Maybe it's something serious.'

Dr Sakuno's lips thinned. 'Symptoms?'

'Well . . . I've lost weight, as you know. And I'm tired. I'm dizzy sometimes. I . . . I have to urinate quite a bit. My period has stopped.' He looked horrified at this and she rushed on: 'And my mouth is dry. Sometimes there's a metallic taste.'

'Not illness.'

'It must be something!' He was revolted by her, she thought. Like her mother before her, she shrank into her seat.

'You know what it is,' he said. He wanted her to admit it, she realised. He expected her to say, I'm Lenny Aaron and I'm a drug addict. But she wasn't saying anything of the sort.

At her block of flats she hurried out of the car with a quick 'thanks'. Dr Sakuno got out too. He ran his eyes over the unadorned brick rectangle that was her home. Mel and Sally were having a long goodbye kiss at their front door.

'Don't worry,' Lenny reassured her psychologist. 'They're engaged. Well, thanks again.' She opened her door.

He was still at her side.

'I'll make an appointment with Mariko, shall I?' Lenny said, waiting for him to take the hint and piss off.

To her amazement, he shouldered past her into her living room, took his shoes off and put them in the wooden shoe hutch by the front door. What was going on? Traditionally, Japanese people never entered another person's house without elaborate arrangements beforehand. It was considered rude and invasive.

'Look, I have a very busy schedule today,' she tried. Bertrand Russell sprang to mind. 'I have a client to see actually. So, if you don't mind –'

'If you are referring to the one feline currently residing in your office, your mother has already arranged for a Russian barber to supervise its care and maintenance. You are going to be otherwise engaged.'

Dr Sakuno closed the door behind them. He strode into the bedroom and Lenny heard the bathroom door open. She ran after him, because she knew what he was up to now.

He was standing in front of her medicine cabinet examining the rows of bottles.

'Haldol! Only a moron would take lithium unsupervised in conjunction with Haloperidol. Look here, where it says in bold letters for any idiot to see, TAKE STRICTLY AS DIRECTED OR CONSULT YOUR DOCTOR. Did you imagine, perhaps, that *you* were a doctor?' He unscrewed the lid and poured the contents into the toilet. Lenny went cold.

'That's just Tylenol,' she said as he opened another bottle and continued pouring her little mates into the dunny. 'What if I get a headache?' He looked at her. 'A genuine headache!' He continued to pour until all the bottles were empty. Then he went through her house. He opened every drawer, every cupboard, went through her clothes, unrolled sock balls, ran his fingers under every floor-level cabinet to check. He stood on a chair and peered inside the ceiling and on top of the wardrobe.

'Where are they?'

'There aren't any more.' She was grumpy now. This was going beyond psychological counselling. He had a real nerve. He had even checked her neat pile of panties.

'Where are they?'

'There aren't any more!'

'The public display of unhappiness is at best an incon-venience, at worst a pitiful embarrassment.' He was going over old ground.

'I know.'

'There is nothing more futile and energy-sapping than internal struggle.'

'Check.'

'How dare you do this to me.'

'Sorry.'

'You will not take another pill.'

'No,' she lied.

Dr Sakuno pointed at the big chair in front of the TV. 'Sit,' he said. 'We shall see.' She didn't like the tone of his voice, the way he sat determinedly on a large floor cushion opposite her.

She realised then what he was planning, and there was no way she was doing it. Not at her level of toxicity. 'You can't stop taking Haldol just like that,' she protested. 'You know you can't. Especially with all the other things I take. I have to come off it slowly, otherwise the pain –' She gulped. 'Look, what about one of those clinics?' Where everyone would be sympathetic and helpful. Gone were the days when the government, the police and the public at large were tough on drugs. People thronged to help the addicted these days. Safe injecting rooms, free needles, needle disposal units, detox programs. It had never been a better time to be a junkie. Yes, that was the best plan: she could spend a few days in a nice cosy clinic. A rest cure, really. Take her time about it. Get up and leave if the going got too tough . . .

Dr Sakuno smiled, a smile that made her feel sick to the stomach. There would be no clinic. She drew her knees up to her chin.

'I can't do it,' she said, controlling the urge to cry. 'I won't do it.'

There was no reply.

Fourteen hours later she no longer cared whether or not Dr Koichi Sakuno saw her cry. She wept solidly and hotly. She berated him, begged him, threw things at him. She paced from room to room. She vomited both in and out of the toilet like an animal marking its territory. She became feverish. She told him how much she hated him and what she thought of his stupid samurai ancestors. She mumbled and muttered and drooled horribly out of both sides of her mouth and nose. He sat on the *kotatsu* which he had placed by the door to block her escape, expressionless.

Once – after what seemed like a couple of hours of just staring at each other – she sprang at him, clawing for the door handle. He let her have a sharp right to the jaw. As she lay stunned on the floor, Cleo Aaron bit her ankle in a display of tag-team torture.

It was worse when he began to lecture her. He was almost chanting, so flat and rhythmical was his tone. Humans, especially westerners, have a tendency to believe that they are *here* and the world is *out there*, he said. Even the body is perceived as *out there*, as 'it'. And so the body is easy to abuse. It is not recognised as part of us. You must go past these limitations, change perspective to a state where both *here* and *out there* are happening at once. A state where 'I' and 'it' have a unity.

Lenny's eyes bulged and she tried to cover her ears with her hands. Her snivelling competed with his voice.

'Your father is dead.' Somewhere *out there* his voice found the worst part of it. 'And you wonder where he is. If, in fact, he is anywhere. You are afraid of and angered by your doubts.'

Shut the fuck up, she thought, but she couldn't speak.

'Accept your doubts, Helena san.' Her teary eyes were too blurred to see and she had no strength to raise her head off the carpet to look at him. 'There must be doubt. If you doubt yourself, you open yourself.' For a moment she imagined his voice was quite gentle, almost kindly; he had pushed past his distaste for her weakness and found a moment of tenderness.

'Open yourself to reality. You cannot survive if you are not like everyone else. Society will hammer you like a bent nail until you straighten.'

Lenny's whole body was drenched in sweat. She had seen this many times before in the remand cells. Addicts trembling on the floor, arms wrapped around their bodies, screaming for mercy. They never got any.

'I will tell you a story,' Dr Sakuno announced from far away. She snuffled carpet. 'A story of a great *yurei*, a ghost.'

'Orange juice ...'

'This is the *Yotsu-ya* Ghost Story. It centres on the frail beauty, Oiwa. Her husband, Iyemon, betrays her with a neighbour's granddaughter who wishes to marry him. The grandfather encourages the match and convinces Iyemon to poison Oiwa.'

'Give me juice ...'

'But the poison only disfigures Oiwa, leaving one eye bulging from a bald head. Iyemon torments his helpless wife ...' He paused to shiver dramatically. He held out an arm. 'There. Chicken skin. Every time.'

'It's *goosebumps*,' Lenny mumbled. 'What happens to them? Does he kill Oiwa?'

'Finally Iyemon impales Oiwa and her servant on a door and hurls them into a river. Thinking his troubles are over, he marries again. But!' A theatrical flourish of his arm. 'When he lifts his bride's wedding veil, he is terrified to see the vengeful face of Oiwa's ghost. Drawing his sword he mistakenly beheads ... his new bride.' He paused and took in a long, quiet breath.

'Is that it?'

It was.

Lenny lapsed into unconsciousness.

She woke to find herself propped against her chair. It was daytime, but what day? Dr Sakuno had moved from his door-guard position. Apparently he felt the escape-frenzy period of her withdrawal had peaked. He still sat on the cushion, legs neatly crossed, in front of the TV. Cleo Aaron lay next to him, head against his thigh. Purring too.

They were watching the news. The Aquinas drama flashed across the screen with photos of Emily and Moira, and of Harry, who was said to be conscious but unable to be interviewed. Pluckrose was still in custody. Ray's worst fears were realised in the slugline: The School of Death.

'That's my case ...' her voice was husky. 'I'm investigating at the school of death. You know, the eyeballs?'

'Who killed the women? I think that Pluckrose, the one with the mole on his cheek, is guilty. Never trust a mole.'

'It's not that simple.' Was it madness or drug withdrawal that made her argue criminology with a man who suspected large freckles? Although from a Zen point of view, his opinion was no less valid than hers. A central tenet of Zen was the importance of intuitive understanding: why not go after the mole?

'There are a lot of factors to consider,' she argued. 'I have to evaluate all the suspects. There's background research, interviews, crosschecking.'

'Is that so?'

'You don't understand investigative work.' She had reached the verbally combative stage of her withdrawal. 'What do you know about crime at all? You think there isn't any in Japan except what foreigners bring in.'

Dr Sakuno and Cleo gave her long, superior looks.

'Reconsider the mole.' He held Cleo up to his chest and she patted a soft paw at his chin.

'That's my cat.'

'Take a shower, Komodo Man. You stink.'

She did, then slept, awoke and repeated the cycle. It was dawn. But of which day?

Her ribs and hip bones reflected in her bathroom mirror reminded her how little she ate these days. The cat scratch on her face was still livid. Her stomach made a horrible noise and she huddled over the toilet. Nothing much left inside her, but it was all anxious to get out.

She spent ten minutes cleaning her lips, gums, teeth and tongue. God knows how many hours she'd spent spewing and drooling, but they needed a lot of work. The toothbrush raked back and forth across the flesh. Her gums were bleeding before she was satisfied. She used a spoon to

279

scrape yellow slime off her tongue. Listerine bit into any remaining germs.

She pulled on a fresh bra and panties, a white t-shirt and her loosest black jeans. It seemed to take forever to fasten them. Her fingers felt two sizes too big for her hands and her body like Play-Doh after a toddler-mauling. Cleo Aaron was fast asleep right where it was forbidden, dead centre on Lenny's non-allergenic Astro Boy pillow.

Dr Sakuno was in the living room. He glanced up as she entered. Around him on the floor was a large pile of old magazines and newspapers. He was sewing something, she realised. Sewing paper together. His eyes were red-rimmed and he was pale. 'We will discuss your situation.' He pointed at a chair and she sat.

'You punched me in the jaw,' Lenny accused. 'And you squeezed my arm really hard.'

'Please accept this as a token of my regret.' Dr Sakuno bit off a thread and held out his paper creation. It was origami, Lenny saw, hundreds of paper birds sewn together.

'*Senba zuru*,' Dr Sakuno said. 'One thousand cranes. It will help in your recovery, if you wish to recover. I have done five hundred. You must finish it.' He got to his feet. She saw him wince with cramp.

'Are you all right?' She held the five hundred Melbourne *Age* cranes against her chest.

'We Japanese can sit for hours without feeling the strain.'

'Uh huh.'

'Westerners' legs are too long, you see. I am returning to my home.' He picked up his briefcase. 'Finish the *senba zuru* before you leave the apartment.'

'If I get round to it.' He was at the door before it occurred to her to ask: 'What day is it?'

'Friday. I have been with you for two days.' He closed the door after himself.

CHAPTER 23

Gabrielle Shows and Tells

Lenny stayed in her flat the rest of the day, listened to several messages from her mother on her answering machine. No matter how little she did to deserve it (in fact she did nothing to deserve it), Veronica Aaron loved her. There was a message from Gabrielle too. *Hi, it's Gabrielle, I want to speak to you.*

She sat in front of the TV cutting newspaper squares and folding them into cranes before sewing them together. She paused only to drink water, eat small portions of fruit and steamed vegetables, go to the toilet and feed Cleo.

For the first hundred cranes she had assured herself that Dr Sakuno was a pig who had smacked her in the head, locked her up and tortured her. She was done with him and his Zen bullshit. She would find a psychologist with whom she could have a normal 'talk-based' relationship. She would lie on a couch and this new psychologist would say 'hmm' very gently from time to time as she got in touch with her feelings.

The next couple of hundred cranes brought doubt and guilt. She had disappointed Dr Sakuno again. She had failed herself. There followed a long and morbidly enjoyable period of dwelling on all the disappointments of their doctor–patient relationship.

Late in the afternoon she called his office. Mariko put her through after ascertaining whether the doctor was in to his most notorious patient.

'Yes?' His voice was the way it always was – *tsumetai*. Cold.

'Dr Sakuno, it's Lenny Aaron.'

'Yes?'

'Well, I'm sorry.'

'Yes?'

'You know. About the pills. The whole thing. And you started the cranes for me, which by the way I'm almost finished now ...' She waited in vain for encouragement. 'Anyway, I thought I'd let you know that I haven't taken anything.'

'Good. Excuse me.'

He handed her back to Mariko who arranged a weekly appointment, which was to continue until Dr Sakuno decided she was drug free.

'I understand from Sakuno *sensei* that we'll be doing a urine test every time,' Mariko said. '*Sensei* feels it's for the best. It's a matter of trust at this stage, I'm afraid. There's also the matter of payment for the forty-eight hours *Sensei* supervised the detoxification process. It's rather a large sum, as you can imagine.'

'He's billing me for that?' But of course he was. Lenny sighed. 'Stick it on my account.' She hung up, folded a page of the Green Guide into her thousandth crane and sewed it into place.

Cleo Aaron sat on a windowsill sunning herself while Lenny got into her full kendo outfit and practised the basic movements. In her weakened state it was painful just to raise her arms, but she forced herself to continue until she had completed a full cycle.

Then she slept. A long dreamless sleep. She woke up

because Cleo was pouncing on her arm and the telephone was ringing.

'Who is it?'

'It's Gabrielle. You didn't return my call.'

'That's right.'

'Come out to my place.'

'Forget it.' She peered at her G-Shock. Midnight. No time to be having secret rendezvous with spooky geniuses. She had gone down this path before and it had ended in blood, mostly hers.

'Lenny, I'll tell the police everything. But I want to tell you first. I want you to understand.' There was a slight tremor in the voice.

'All right.'

She dressed and prepared to go out. Put a torch and a flick knife into her shoulder bag. If Gabrielle Danaher was the killer and had any ideas about adding to her hit list, she would meet with opposition.

Cleo Aaron flopped on her back, four paws in the air at the kitchen cupboard, mewing hopefully. Lenny pulled out a salmon biscuit and handed it over.

'Go back to sleep now.' She stroked the one-eyed head gently.

She checked her mailbox on the way out. Three items. The first a cheque from Galaxy. As far as they were concerned, the Aquinas thief had been caught and therefore her employment was officially terminated. The second item was a stiff card envelope with purple calligraphy. Inside there was an invitation to the wedding of Ms Mel Stanwick to Ms Sally Vincent. The sweethearts below. They had registered their gift list at Daimaru. Finally there was a bill from the towing company that had brought her slightly dented car back from the hospital.

The roads were empty and it took less than ten minutes

to get to North Fitzroy. Gabrielle, fully dressed, stood outside her gate, smoking. She looked exhausted. She stared at Lenny, who was dressed in heavy steel-capped boots, army surplus pants and light bomber jacket.

'Harry's conscious,' Gabrielle began, her voice a bit higher than usual and faster. She was nervous. 'They'll be able to interview him soon. If he saw who attacked him, then maybe all this will be over.'

Lenny said nothing.

'Your eyes are clear,' Gabrielle said. 'You went cold turkey, didn't you?'

Lenny's voice was cool. 'You said you wanted to tell me everything.'

'Come on then ...' Gabrielle walked down the street away from her house and Lenny followed. At a large tree-filled park she paused. Two teenage boys lounged against a tree, shabby overcoats wrapped around them, one of their noses deeply pressed into a bag of glue, the other's eyeballs bulging. But they were not what made her hesitate. Gabrielle looked back, smiled wryly.

'Don't worry. This is show and tell, not trap and kill.'

Lenny reassured herself that she had the flick knife. But she had never stabbed anyone in her life. Did it take a special kind of character to push the blade through the skin into the muscles and internal organs?

They walked in what seemed to Lenny pitch darkness for a minute, then Gabrielle stopped by a large tree.

'Here,' she said and knelt down. She reached into a possum hole in the bark of the tree and pulled out a small package. She held it out to Lenny. 'Take it.'

'What is it?'

'A souvenir.'

Lenny took out her torch and flicked it on. The package was a small bin-liner. Inside was a soft cloth. And inside that a short but very sharp knife, brown with old blood.

'Moira's blood,' Gabrielle confirmed and waited, looking nervous rather than threatening.

'Where did you get this?' Lenny asked.

'I pulled it out of Moira's neck after I stabbed her,' Gabrielle deadpanned. When Lenny failed to respond, she continued: 'Moira was an unpleasant woman. She made it her life's work to get something on everyone. In my case she didn't even have to try. We grew up, as you know, in the same town near Geelong, went to the same primary school. She knew about Samantha Burridge. It was the highlight of the school year. There was gossip that I was "the child killer". What a surprise, then, when we found ourselves here at Aquinas together. Moira didn't really know anything. She wasn't a witness or anything like that. But she knew I'd been the main suspect. She knew everyone thought I was guilty but that the police just didn't have the evidence to take it to court. She couldn't wait to tell me I'd be helping her edit every year. It's not usual, you know. We can comment and advise, but in practical terms we're supposed to do all our own stuff. But Moira hated editing and she found out I was good at it.'

'If you were innocent of Samantha Burridge's death, why did you go along with it?'

'Who on this planet cares whether or not you're innocent?' Gabrielle laughed. 'The only thing that matters to anyone is how things look. And things looked bad for me. Poor white trash who got herself a decent education after her rival drowned under suspicious circumstances. Well, I'd had enough of that. Enough of Samantha Burridge to last me a lifetime. I wanted a clean start here. So I helped Moira with her editing. That was it.'

'But then she wanted more from you –'

'I had nothing else to give her.'

'– and you refused and she pushed and you killed her.'

'That's not what happened, Lenny. Anyway, if I'd wanted to kill Moira I would have done it when she told me her editing plan. I wouldn't have waited all this time.'

They stared at each other in the moonlight.

'All right,' Lenny said finally. 'What about Harry?'

'Harry saw me in the tower with the knife the day after Moira was murdered,' Gabrielle said. 'I was doing some research in the Robert Heywood library and I found it tucked behind some books on the bottom shelf. Harry arrived just as I pulled the knife out and he jumped to the obvious conclusion. He's ... let's say susceptible to female charms, so I snogged him a bit to keep him quiet. But that's *all* I did to him. Stupid, I know – but the police are going after me, Lenny. I'm scared. I didn't kill them –'

'But you were in the car park and you saw the person who killed Moira go in and out of the green room.'

There was a long pause and then: 'Yes.'

'Tell me.'

'I want to tell you about Sam Burridge first.' Gabrielle twisted her fingers together. Young. Frightened. Beautiful. 'Lenny, have you ever killed anyone?'

'We're not talking about me.'

'No. Well then ... Sam Burridge sat behind me in class. She was smarter than me. Enough to beat me for the scholarship. I suppose you know all about that?'

Lenny nodded.

'Well then, you'll see the police had motive but that's all they ever had.'

Lenny rewrapped the knife and put it back into the plastic bag.

'I'm useless at sports,' Gabrielle continued, 'but I can swim. Samantha couldn't.'

'You pushed her in the creek?'

Gabrielle smiled at the idea. 'I *did* think about lots of

ways to be rid of her. I was twelve, you see. But it was pure chance that she slipped into the creek that day. There was no one else around.'

'Slipped?'

'She saw something in the water. She leaned out to catch it and fell in. It had been raining for weeks and the creeks were all up. For a child it was deep enough to drown in.'

'Did she call to you for help?'

'Yes.'

'And you watched her drown?'

'Yes. It would have been easy to save her. But I wanted a better life, so I didn't.'

'Who killed the Aquinas students?'

'I'm going overseas, to London. I'm out of all this.' Gabrielle tried to move away but Lenny clamped a hand onto her shoulder.

'Tell me.'

'You and me . . .' Gabrielle lowered her cheek and let it touch Lenny's hand for a skin-scorching second. 'We're the same. We're never going to be with anyone. It's lonely sometimes, isn't it?'

'Tell me!'

Gabrielle hesitated, nodded, opened her mouth to speak then snapped it shut again.

'I like being alone,' she said. She turned on her heel and ran towards the light at the edge of the park. Lenny watched until she was gone, holding the bagged knife tightly.

At the edge of the park she spotted Abel Cunningham's car. He wasn't even trying to hide himself anymore. He stared at her and she stared back. His eyes were on the bag. If he stepped out of his car she was going to knock him down.

He didn't move. His eyes followed her as she walked past his car towards her own. When she started her engine, he started his.

CHAPTER 24

Guts and Gaff

She parked in Smith Street and walked down Moor, hearing Abel Cunningham do the same somewhere in the dark behind her. When she crossed the road towards the Aquinas entrance, she glanced back. He slipped behind a ghost gum and peered past its silver smoothness. The moon hung over the Aquinas tower, gleaming feebly, half covered with cloud.

Lenny crouched at the back of a parked Toyota HiAce and looked towards the main gate. It was sealed off with tape and two young officers stood guard. She touched the master key in her pocket.

There was a man chatting to one of the police officers. It was the second year film supervisor, Greg Waterman. Lenny listened as he harangued the police. The location shoot was having a much needed two-day hiatus. Waterman and one of his students had driven back from Horsham to return some props and equipment. The police didn't want to let him in, had instructions not to let anyone in. Waterman spat the dummy. He wasn't leaving twenty thousand dollars worth of equipment parked on the street in the middle of the night. He wanted to drop it off and then get home and see his wife. And kids.

Brilliant working of the family angle, Lenny thought. And it paid off. The older of the police constables mouthed 'five minutes' and held up five fingers for emphasis. Waterman turned in the van's direction and waved.

'Come on in!' he yelled.

The HiAce shook under Lenny's hand. The engine guttered, then took hold and she was doused in a foggy effluent. The tail lights lit the street red.

Lenny tried the handle of the HiAce's back door. It turned and the door swung open slightly. As the van lurched forward she put one foot on the step mount, slipped inside and pulled the door shut behind her. She stepped over lights, boompoles, tracks and rails then stopped short, eyes widening.

She was up against a face, a hard, cold face with an unearthly tan. She drew back to find she was surrounded by inquisitive eyes. Mannequins lay everywhere, their limbs stiffly entwined like socialites who had just met. They were stacked three high – a mass grave of fashion victims. What were the second years filming anyway? Lenny lay back and tried to look plastic.

The van paused. Waterman got in and she heard him talking to the driver, their voices muffled. Then they were moving, past the bright security lights over the gate, into darkness as they passed through the entrance tunnel, and out into orangey light as they turned onto the narrow drive around the quadrangle.

She watched the buildings flick by the window, calculating the van's speed. When she was ready, she pushed the door open and rolled.

She found herself under a line of wattles outside the canteen. The van continued to circle the quadrangle and stopped outside the storeroom. They had been given five minutes, Lenny remembered.

Keeping low behind a row of azaleas, she reached the film school entrance. The master key turned briefly in the lock and she was in. She waited just inside the door, letting her eyes get used to the darkness, then went up to the first floor. She was here to dump the knife. Let the police find it. Let them find Gabrielle's fingerprints and decide whether or not she was guilty. The future of Australian film would be out of her hands.

She was about to empty the plastic bag with the knife onto the top of the lockers in the corridor when she saw a figure move at the far end, near Ray's office. The figure had its back to her and was moving away. Who else shouldn't be here in the middle of the night?

Lenny placed the knife back in her bag and edged closer along the worn carpet, keeping near the dark line of the lockers. She was five metres away when the figure sensed her and turned. They were too far apart to see each other clearly: just two shadows moving closer in the darkness.

A familiar voice said: 'I knew you'd come. Now listen. My position from now on is to be fully guaranteed. I want the board behind me one hundred percent. If we're agreed then you can take this back and –'

'Hello, Ray,' Lenny said. 'Cleaning up?' Then she saw it, glistening against a bed of crisp, white handerkerchief in Ray's outstretched hand. A single eyeball, viscous and pale in the moonlight.

'You!' the principal snarled. She turned on her heel and ran into the inky blackness at the end of the corridor. Lenny followed.

Ray's footsteps pattered loud near the edit suites, then stopped. Silence. Lenny slowed down, not certain what the principal's next move might be.

Out of the darkness came a new sound, a sound out of place in the middle of the night. It was birds. Birds calling to each other, and behind their calls, a breeze and also children playing, crying out to each other.

Lenny crept up to the edit suites. She tried the door of the first one. It was locked. The second slid open and she pounced in, striking right and left, catching her hand on the edge of a shelved film can. The room was empty, the bulky Steenbeck grey and silent. Coiled soundtracks lay threaded across the playback heads where a student had left them.

The sound was coming from the next edit suite: birds, a breeze and children. As she edged her fingers towards the handle, Lenny anticipated the image on the screen behind the door. It would be a park, she decided. Images of children playing in a park on a summer's day. She clasped the handle and pulled the door open.

The Steenbeck was playing itself. There was no one at the controls and no image on the screen. Three atmos tracks were spooling from left to right, creating her park out of sound, out of thin air. The image had existed only in her mind.

There was a noise in the corridor behind her and she half turned. A knife shot out but Lenny's kendo training had given her an increased ability to move without thinking, to counter instantaneously. Even so, she couldn't avoid the blade. She felt it slice across the front of her t-shirt.

Someone was running down the stairs. Lenny held a hand to her burning abdomen and gave pursuit. If her intestines spilled out into her hand that was it, she would sit down and cry until she bled to death. Her legs had disconnected from the rest of her body and she felt sick, but somehow she kept moving along the corridor. In the darkness ahead of her there was a crash. She kept moving and then suddenly her legs banged hard into metal. She tripped forward and went flying through black space.

Her hand came away from her abdomen when she hit the bottom of the stairs. She was dead for sure now, she thought. Her insides would be tumbling down the stairs after her like red jellyfish. Perhaps it was best that it was dark. There was a delicious spasm in her skull. Her head would be split open. And to think it was Cate Ray all along.

'You're safe now, mate. Just lie there. You fell over a cabinet on the stairs, but you're OK.' The voice was familiar. Lenny opened her eyes. Ron MacAvoy was sitting on a chair next to her. She was lying on the common room's sofa with a smelly cushion under her head and her feet elevated. Her head felt as though it had been battered with a brick. MacAvoy grinned.

'Dan'll be up in a mo. He's down at the gate giving those two dozy constables a piece of his mind. Seems like they let half of Melbourne sneak past.'

'You shouldn't have moved me, idiot. I might have broken my neck or spine. I could be permanently damaged because of you.' She was so relieved to be alive she wanted to hug him.

'Nah,' he laughed. 'You were wriggling all over the place when we found you. You even sat up by yourself. You just don't remember it. You've got a nasty cut on your tummy, though.'

She lifted her torn t-shirt and stared at three strips of gaff tape stuck across her abdomen.

'You taped my guts back in with gaff tape?'

'It's just a flesh wound. A deep scratch really. You won't even need stitches, I don't reckon.'

'Gaff tape?'

'It's all I could find. I put one of my hankies on it first then gaffed over that.' He saw her horrified face. 'A *clean* hankie, Lenny.'

She was angry with herself. Angry that she had let herself be tricked by that sound, when anyone with half a brain would have known it was a distraction, a trap.

'Did you get her?' Cate Ray had tried to kill her. Something else too. Something foggy in her memory. She fought to drag it back. Cate had said something, something about the board. *I want the board behind me one hundred percent.* Ray had been expecting someone else tonight. Lenny remembered the eyeball glistening in the moonlight.

She tried to sit up but Ron's nail-nibbled fingers pressed her back. He had been smoking a cigar recently, judging by his smell, and she saw that his cheeks were lined with broken capillaries. One finger pushed the remains of a jam doughnut between sugary lips. It occurred to her that he was the generic flabby sidekick who had popped up in all the crime novels she had ever read.

'MacAvoy, you're going to have a heart attack if you don't control your eating.'

'It's happy fat.' MacAvoy patted his belly fondly.

'You must be ecstatic.' She wriggled upright and realised her bag was missing. MacAvoy eased her back to the sofa's grimy fabric. She glanced at the floor. There was her bag. And inside it the knife that had killed Emily and Moira. Cate Ray had evidently found a new one for tonight's attack.

She reached down to the bag. Ron MacAvoy picked it up first.

'Lie still. You may have concussion. You want something in here?'

She snatched it out of his hand.

'Cate Ray tried to kill me. We should –'

'We've got her.'

MacAvoy let her sit up this time. The pain in her forehead made her wince as she searched the place with her fingers.

'We grabbed her as she came out of the building making a run for it. She sees us, goes into a major panic, whacks her hankie over her mouth, starts crying and shaking and carrying on. Gagging. I thought she was going to hurl actually. What were you doing in here anyway?' MacAvoy asked the million dollar question.

Lenny fought fire with fire: 'What are *you* doing here? You and Danny?'

'Both on late shift,' MacAvoy explained. 'We were in the area and Dan wanted to pop in. You know how he is – likes to walk through the scene time after time, get a feeling for the atmospherics, like that can tell you anything about anything.' He shook his head, smiling.

Danny Hoyle stepped into the common room. He wasn't smiling.

'Len says Cate Ray assaulted her,' MacAvoy said.

'Ray says she didn't,' Danny replied

'Suspect denies the charge. I'm shocked.' Lenny was bruised and bad-tempered.

'We're looking for a motive,' Danny continued.

'Rumour has it Ray took money to allow Emily Cunningham into the school and then to boost her grades. Moira knew about it and blackmailed her,' Lenny said. 'I don't know why Ray would have killed Emily or why she attacked Harry. Maybe he found out something.'

But she remembered that when he woke up Harry was going to say he saw Gabrielle with the knife that had killed Moira.

'I spoke to Harry Tuyen today,' Danny said. 'He doesn't even remember being hit, so it looks like you'll be our star witness against Ms Ray.'

An hour later she was alone in a city centre police interview room. No windows. One table. Two chairs. Industrial grey. She had been provided with a styrofoam cup of something that called itself coffee, and had made a written statement. Danny had one big question for her. Why had she been in the Aquinas grounds that night? Answer: she had decided to collect her rat trap. That was her story and she was sticking to it. Her abdomen had been professionally attended to by a doctor who agreed with MacAvoy's assessment that stitches were unnecessary. She had cleansed the long thin cut and taped a dressing over it, then made Lenny sit with a large cold compress to the purpling bruise on her brow.

MacAvoy's balding head peeked around the door. He was troubled, puffed his plump cheeks, let out a windy breath.

'Cate Ray's asking for you,' he said. 'She's an odd one, isn't she? Sick as a dog when she got here. One of the female constables had her in the ladies room. She vomits for ten minutes solid, then sits there like a block of ice. The husband's on the way with a solicitor. You can have five minutes. We'll be watching and listening.'

Lenny followed him down the corridor to the next interview room. It was identical to the room Lenny had occupied. Ray was seated at the table. MacAvoy nodded at her.

'I've brought Ms Aaron for you, Mrs Ray.'

Ray ignored him.

MacAvoy left them alone and Lenny took a seat at the table. They stared at each other silently.

'Say something!' Ray broke first. 'You're as bad as the bloody cops. I got a couple of phone calls and something they said was coffee but I say was Mortein. That's it there.' She jerked her bob at a large stain on one wall. She held out her hands. 'I broke a fingernail. Constable Unferdorben broke my fingernail, in fact. He snapped it back when he pushed me into the car. I'm going to sue him for that. He reeks of Old Spice. That alone should be enough to convict him.' She glanced at the mirrored wall. 'Listening out there, smelly? I'm going to sue this whole department for false arrest.' She paused and looked long and hard at Lenny, who appeared to be dozing. 'I want you to tell them I didn't stab you.'

'You did.'

'I did not.'

'You did.'

'I did bloody not!' Cate slapped a palm on the table. 'Look, there may be a few minor financial discrepancies in the school records, but that's perfectly normal in an organisation of our size. Get me out of here, Aaron. They're your mates, aren't they? What about the one with the striped tie and the lard arse? He likes you. Tell him I'm innocent and get me out.'

'If you didn't stab me, who did?' Lenny argued. 'I'm not going to help you, Ray, unless you help me. I can just as easily tell the police I did see you stab me. You could spend a week in the lock-up before I realise it was a false memory caused by all the shock.'

There was another pause as Ray considered her options. Then she leaned closer, her voice soft. 'Aquinas needs me, Lenny,' she said. 'The board lost a four million dollar donation because of Emily's death, and the school needs solid management skills to survive. I'm the only one around who can do it. You have to get me out of here. I'm the only chance that school has.'

'What four million?' Lenny leaned closer herself.

'The board,' it was a whisper now, 'led by Hermione Arnfeldt, gave me notice earlier this year. And you know why? Emily Cunningham. Abel promised Hermione four million for a new studio if they gave his daughter my job next year. *My* job! She has a degree in business management, Hermione said. Expedience, Hermione said. A necessary accommodation for the financial security of the school. The ambitious little bitch. Hermione knew I couldn't say anything publicly – how would I ever get another position? The film world is so small.'

My position from now on is to be fully guaranteed. I want the board behind me one hundred percent. And quite suddenly it all made perfect sense. She knew who the murderer was. She just didn't know how they had done it.

'You were meeting the murderer tonight, weren't you?' Lenny laughed. 'And instead the police showed up and you were forced to make a meal of the evidence. I don't know how you managed to keep it down until you got to the station. What did it taste like?'

'Fuck you, Aaron.'

The door opened and two men entered, accompanied by MacAvoy.

'Richard!' Ray ran into her husband's arms. The lawyer hovered near the door in a crisp Collins Street pinstripe. Lenny winked at Ray over her husband's shoulder and left them.

'What was she whispering about?' MacAvoy asked in the corridor.

'Just tell her you'll be keeping an eye on her, MacAvoy. I think you'll find her ready to talk.'

'OK.' MacAvoy patted her arm. 'Good on you, Len.'

Opposite the police centre was a twenty-four hour coffee shop. It was three years since Lenny had been a police officer, but she still knew the menu by heart. She went in, ordered a latte at the counter and sat down in the booth opposite a man in a black beanie and mirrored sunglasses. The collar of his trench coat was up, there were lamington crumbs on his lips and he nursed a cappuccino in the claw of his prosthesis.

'Nice disguise, Abel,' she said.

Mr Cunningham pulled off the glasses. 'Was it her? Was it Ray?'

'No. But Emily's murderer will be arrested tomorrow. I guarantee it. It's all over. Maybe you should go home.'

He didn't move. He looked as close as Ray to a nervous breakdown. Lenny had no time for him now. Her mind was full of all the clues scattered throughout this case. The truth had been before her almost from the start.

She could have caught the killer herself tonight. If she hadn't been tricked by that damned soundtrack and got herself cut up and clobbered.

She glanced up at the TV on the counter where, as if on cue, the scheduled program had been interrupted by a news flash. The Aquinas School of Film, stamping ground of the serial killer – The School of Death – was burning. The tower came on screen. Flames leapt from the ground floor windows of the screening room, its heavy black curtains flapping crazily in the hot air. The blaze was spreading up the tower, the reporter said, where a collection of books and films was stored. The Robert Heywood Memorial Library was in danger of being destroyed. The news flash jumped back and forth between the reporter on the scene and the anchorwoman back in the studio. Back and forth. Vision and sound. Lenny's eyes opened wide as she watched. She had been so fucking stupid!

She was out of her seat and running for her car before Abel Cunningham could put his cup down.

CHAPTER 25

In Which the Killer Explains the Whole Thing

Lenny listened to the car radio's Aquinas update as she drove. Goddamn it! She should have known this would happen. Cate Ray was bound to tell all to the police eventually. The killer knew that. Destroying Aquinas was the only remaining option.

How, why and who, she thought. How, why and who.

How was easy. *Tricked by that damned sound.* Like a film sequence, nothing had ever been what it really seemed.

Why was more complex. But a phrase stood out from amongst the many conversations of the last three weeks: *to protect his own little universe.* She had thought the murders were about conflicts in the present, but they weren't: they were about the future. A vision of the future. A *vision* ...
Another thought suddenly occurred to her and she cursed herself.

At Aquinas she squeezed around the fire trucks and the men running about in silver suits. Greedy flames licked the top of the tower which held the library. The clock had stopped. She stared up at it. The sky was crimson and orange, crossed with coils of blue smoke. She headed for the stairs. A fireman called out but she wanted to know for sure, before it was too late.

When she reached the first floor she was overwhelmed by smoke pouring down the staircase. The fire had not yet reached this part of the building but she could feel the heat and the noise of the flames below. She saw a figure move in the shadows, further up the stairs.

'Wait!' she called.

The figure disappeared up the stairs to the second floor. Lenny followed. The main library was burning. The fire from the screening room below had come up through the air-conditioning ducts, which streamed purple smoke. Rows of video tapes were melting into each other; Sylvester Stallone movies blending indiscriminately with masterpieces of German Expressionism. A window exploded. Ahead of her the killer danced across burning carpet, opened the door to the tower and went inside.

Lenny hesitated. It was almost too hot to breathe. She pulled off her jacket and held it over her head, pressed her shoulder bag up to her face. Not much protection, but it was all she had. She sprinted across the floor and into the tower, closed the door behind her. Her boots were smoking.

Robert Heywood Memorial Library floor was warm from the blaze below. As Lenny watched, a fiery crater appeared at the base of one wall and a shelf filled with film cans collapsed, dislodging its contents. Coils of celluloid unravelled into the open pit, their glossy images consumed in blue flashes as the fire leapt up to meet them.

Lenny ran across the room to the spiral staircase. She couldn't breathe anymore but there was no way she could go back to the main library. She struggled up the staircase to Kenneth's office and shut the door behind her.

The office was supernaturally calm. Untouched by the fire below, it was not even warm yet. Kenneth's desk lay as he had last left it, making notes from a book called *The Celluloid Muse*.

The tiny door at the top of the stairs leading to the roof was open. Running up the stairs, she spilled out into the night air and filled her lungs. She pushed the door shut and collapsed against it.

She was on top of the tower. The moon had torn free of the clouds and sat directly overhead like a searchlight. Fire hoses created puddles of water at her feet and snaked in the air around the tower. The flagpole was wreathed in smoke, cut though by the occasional lashing of spray. The Australian flag billowed in the heat.

The killer was grey with smoke. One sleeve was burned away and she saw that a doctor would be needed for the left arm.

'What did you do with Emily's eyeballs?' she began, step-ping closer.

'I minced them and fed them to Sardines. I would have given him Moira's too, eventually. I had it hidden in my office. I cut a hole in the middle of my Pauline Kael book and popped it in there. How was I to know it was the one book Cate Ray would borrow? I didn't even know she liked Kael. She's going to tell them everything, of course. It'll mean the end of Aquinas as it should be. So I chose to end it now, with the fire that purifies.'

'It was about film, wasn't it?' Lenny coughed. Her voice was choked and roughened by smoke. 'The future of film. They were about to hand Emily the school on a plate and you couldn't let that happen.'

Kenneth Drage blinked through the smoke that poured up over the edge of the tower. He had no weapon, but as he backed towards the edge of the building Lenny realised he didn't plan to use one.

'The idea of Emily Cunningham as principal of Aquinas was and still is ridiculous,' he sneered. 'She might have managed the business side of it, but as a teacher? As a person responsible for the growth of film in this country? I thought they were joking. I told the board it was unthinkable, but I was outvoted. Hermione Arnfeldt pushed them into it. "Necessity," she said. Four million dollars worth. Money is the death of art, Lenny. Ray was bad enough, a good initial choice gone off the rails. I was happy enough when the board gave her notice. But Emily Cunningham was no alternative.'

'And the eyes?' But she knew already, from the very first meeting when Kenneth had peered up at her from the floor in Cate Ray's office. And later he had squinted, leaned in to examine things, exhibited signs of clumsiness, rubbed his eyes, commented on sound effects in student films. He had even failed to recognise her until she was right on top of him on at least two occasions. And at the art gallery he had chosen to guide her round a tour he knew like the back of his hand. 'You're going blind, aren't you?' she yelled.

'The ophthalmologist tells me I can expect an eighty percent reduction within the next year. Nothing he can do about it. At the moment I can still see to paint if I'm up close, but cinema is already beyond me. Still, the services for the blind are wonderful these days, I'm told.' Kenneth smiled bleakly. 'She could see, Lenny. Emily Cunningham could see and she still produced rubbish, would have encouraged my students to make rubbish too. She had her vision when all I had ahead of me were memories. She didn't deserve the eyes God gave her.'

You barmy old fucker, Lenny thought. 'I understand,' she shouted above the roar of the blaze growing beneath them. 'But why did you kill Moira?'

'She was there. She was there the night Emily died! Someone had allowed her onto the campus. Graeme, I suppose. She was there in the corridor when I came out of the edit suite. Standing right next to the door. She ran off and I thought she would go straight to the police the next day.'

'But she didn't. Because she wanted something from you, something only you could give her.'

'The Silver Shutter. And I could never do that. I told her no, but she kept at me. Remember that morning she came to me for a script tutorial? You were there waiting with her. She came in and began her demands again. I placated her, of course, told her I couldn't make any announcement until all the third year films were completed. But I already knew that she'd have to die. The Shutter is an award for artistic achievement. It must and will go to Gabrielle.'

'I know how you killed Moira. When Alana Zappone thought she was speaking to you, she was really speaking to your voice transmitted through the speaker system in the edit suite, wasn't she? You had a transmitter/receiver in both rooms. You were wired for sound while you were killing Moira.'

'I had a few rehearsals before the main event.' Kenneth smiled. 'I had to be ready. I never knew when the right moment would come. She had to die when there were other people around and when it would appear that I was else-where. That day in the studio, when I went down, I thought it would be another dry run. But there she was, alone in the green room, right in front of me. Loud music. It was the perfect opportunity.' He smiled. 'I had a scare when you started asking Pluckrose about that transmitter, I must admit.'

'Gabrielle knew you killed Moira, didn't she? She was in the car park and she saw you come out of the fire door and go down into the green room?'

He nodded.

'Gabrielle knew everything from the start. Even about Emily. We were having a chat about her films a week after

Emily died and she was looking at me. And then suddenly she said she understood how I felt. I knew she knew.' Kenneth's gentle voice was roughened by the smoke. His expression was kind, wistful. 'After I killed Moira, she came to the tower and took the knife from me. She was afraid for me. Not *of* me, *for* me. She's a genius. Unique. I would never ever have harmed *her*, you know.'

'And Harry?'

'That was Pluckrose. Harry's films are not to my taste but he was neither trying to take over my school nor the Silver Shutter. I had no reason to kill him. I hope you believe that.'

'I do.'

'Bob and I set this place up to *reinvent* the film industry, to produce innovators, leaders – not followers of fashion. I'm not an evil person, Lenny. I want you to understand that.'

'You stabbed me in the guts, Kenneth, so don't expect too much sympathy. Did you kill Hermione Arnfeldt too?'

'No, not Hermione, though her accident started me thinking. She was a number-cruncher, pure and simple. The NFC had just taken another budget cut and she had her sights set on rejecting any funding application she thought noncommercial. She intended to carry that philosophy over into Aquinas.

'I was at home cooking myself dinner and thinking how the school had all gone wrong and wishing that I could change things. And then the news came on and I heard she'd been run over. Gone! My main adversary on the board, gone like magic. I realised how easy it would be if they all disappeared.'

'They?'

'People who stand in the way of excellence. They think all they have to do now is reuse someone else's idea. It's all remakes.' He spat it out. 'Where's the art in that?' He was close to the edge of the building now, but she wasn't going to let him do it. She hadn't come this far to have the murderer splatter himself across the ground below before he could make a full confession to the police.

She played for time: 'If it's a perfect copy, perhaps it has as much value as the original.'

'Perfect copy?' He shook his head at her. 'No. No, I can't accept that. Perfect copies are not art. Part of the achievement of an artist is the originality.'

'All rightee . . . What about this then?' She stepped closer. She would be close enough to touch him in another second. 'Real art has no purpose, right? It's an end in itself.' He moved another step backwards. She held up a finger: 'But you could consider films – even slasher films – as a kind of entertainment art. A subsection whose role is specifically to entertain, to provoke a particular emotion.'

He stared at her, considering. Below them the window of Kenneth's office exploded. Small pieces of film floated upwards and danced in the hot air behind him. Lenny imagined how really unpleasant it would be if the roof collapsed.

'No.' Kenneth said. 'Slasher films are not art.'

'Who decides what's art anyway?' Lenny demanded. 'Gallery owners? Producers? Publishers? You? Conferring status on one type of product so we go out and admire it. If we didn't have government-sponsored cultural institutions, none of us would know what art is or what we like.'

'Art has a significant form.' Kenneth was warming to his theme as she psyched herself to grab him. 'Significant form is an indefinable quality that is recognised intuitively by the sensitive critic. And it has quality. We all recognise quality, even though we may settle for less at times. We know what it is, it's in our nature.'

'Kenneth –' A jet of water from a fire hose came over the top of the roof. He seemed unaware of it.

'I'm not sorry for what I've done.' He took another shuffling step backwards towards the edge.

'Kenneth, please. Let's talk more about your notion of the aesthetic. Didn't Hitchcock embrace the possibility of combining the commercial with the artistic elements of film?'

He paused and smiled, the smile of a man who has just seen through a David O. Lincoln Academy bluffer.

'Hitchcock,' he said thoughtfully. 'I never liked Hitchcock.' He stepped back and dropped over the edge of the tower. Lenny heard the firemen yelling below.

CHAPTER 26

It's a Wrap

Lenny waited on the roof of the tower in the breaking dawn. She used a tissue to take Kenneth's knife from her bag and place it on the rooftop. Here was the perfect place for the police to discover it. Smoke wandered around her but the flames and the heat were gone. After claiming Kenneth's office, the fire had lost momentum and come under the control of the fire hoses. A crane appeared and carried her to safety.

As she dried herself on a blanket, she watched Kenneth disappear into the neon blue interior of an ambulance. Before he lost consciousness, as he lay broken in the quadrangle, the ultimate critic and lover of film had confessed his crimes to Ron MacAvoy and Danny Hoyle.

Lenny gave a brief outline to Danny and promised to come in later that day to make a full statement. She made her way home against the tide of cleaners and other early starters trickling into the city. She was in bed asleep when the Aquinas story broke over the morning news.

A week later, she was still making news. There she was on the front page of the local rag along with Walstab, his wife and Bertrand Russell. Councillor Walstab described her tracking of the cat as a brilliant piece of detective work. In the light of Ms Lenny Aaron's proven skills, he said he would revise his harsh stand on the pet retrieval industry. 'I would have willingly paid twice as much to get Bertie back. You can't put a price on love, can you?'

Lenny dropped the paper on the barber shop counter and tugged at the dirty apron around her neck. Anastasia slapped her hand. The earrings were already gone. Now the black hair was being polarised to its original blonde. Lenny picked up the *Herald Sun*, found the entertainment news and flicked through it.

Annabel Lear – recent graduate from the Aquinas School of Film and Television – had been contracted by channel nine to develop a weekly drama entitled 'Her Majesty's Discretion'. It was to be a legal drama with a lot of the action centred around the personal life of the young female barrister and the cosy seaside suburb in which she lived.

All the Aquinas film students had graduated early. The minister had announced that Aquinas would not reopen. Instead, it would be amalgamated with the VCA the following year. Oddly enough, Kenneth Drage's 'art murders' had already inspired a flood of private funding that would be used for a new building on the VCA campus. It seemed that there was no such thing as bad publicity after all.

Kenneth himself languished in a psychiatric ward awaiting trial, both legs and his pelvis broken in several places. His film *Hard Skies* was enjoying a revival in art house cinemas and both a video and DVD release (with documentary footage of the killer at work) were planned. Re-evaluated as the master work of the Art Martyr, *Hard Skies* was film of the moment for Melbourne's cognoscenti.

In a small side bar on page five, she read that Pluckrose had been released on bail for the attempted murder of

Harry Tuyen and for the theft and destruction of Aquinas property.

'Done!' exclaimed the Barber of Footscray.

Lenny looked up from the paper. Lenny Lypchik was officially retired. The smudgy mirror welcomed back Lenny Aaron in all her blonde buzz-cut scariness.

'You have the sort of head only God could improve,' Anastasia murmured. She unpegged Lenny's apron and shook black hair tips onto the linoleum.

'Hey, they caught Komodo Man!' She gestured at the portable TV. An unshaven, beefy man in his late forties had the words Komodo Man superimposed across his chest. 'Komodo Idiot. My cousin detoured round the park for weeks because of him. They should throw a book at him.'

'Throw the book at him.'

'Exactly.'

Lenny turned up the volume. Mr Daryl Rowley, of 212 Ratherton Street, Richmond, had confessed to all the park attacks. He had even handed over his costume: travel blanket, tinfoil-covered cardboard box helmet, American football shoulder pads and broom handle *shinai*. His motive was unclear at this stage but he was undergoing psychiatric evaluation.

It would be pointless to get Rowley off the hook, Lenny thought. Firstly, because she would only entangle herself in a situation that had gotten way out of hand already, and secondly, because he obviously enjoyed the attention. Why piss on his fifteen minutes?

In her office she tidied and retidied her desk. She had a new client. A Maine Coon, a ten-kilogram cat, had jumped from the cab of a semi-trailer. Its owner, six feet four in stubbies and a work singlet, had arrived at her office that morning in tears, thrusting money at her. Maine Coons were like giant shaggy tabbies, easy to identify. But not yet.

She had something else she had to do first.

She drove to Gabrielle's house.

The garden was still a mess, the noticeable change being the absence of Gabrielle's motorbike. No one answered the door. But just as Lenny put her hand on the knob it was yanked open and Saskia pouted at her. The spring sun-bathing was not apparently a great success. Her face was still pale. She held a suitcase and wore a heavy backpack. Her breasts swung loose under her jumper.

'Film students,' she said. 'Pah! They have no fucking honour!'

A cosy-looking Holden pulled up at the curb. A small bald man beeped the horn.

'I have to go back home because one of those pricks is stealing my rent and food money,' Saskia explained. 'I'm waiting for my dole then I'm gone. That is my father.'

'Saskia, do you want a hand with your things?' Her father looked happy to see his little lamb coming back to the fold. Saskia trudged towards the car and wrenched the door open.

'Just drive,' she said.

Inside the house Janus was carefully folding clothes into a suitcase.

'If you are looking for Gabrielle, forget it,' he said. 'She pissed off.'

'What will you do now?'

'I have work at Open Channel as an assembly editor. It will be enough while I look for something else.'

'Good luck.'

'Luck has nothing to do with it. But thank you.' He handed her an A4-sized envelope. 'From Gabrielle, I think.'

Lenny opened the envelope in Gabrielle's room. Inside she found a letter.

Lenny,

I know the details will be important to you. When Emily died I knew Kenneth had killed her. I knew because I'd killed someone myself and I recognised the look in his eyes when he spoke about her. The funny little mixture of guilt and joy. He could have denied it to me, of course. I had no proof. But he didn't. I told him I knew how he felt. And he trusted me.

When Moira died, I was in the car park when he came out of the green room. He looked right at me, but he didn't see me. He didn't see anything. I remember that feeling, too, from watching Samantha die. Death makes you lose focus for a little while.

I went to his office the next day and told him to give me the knife and confess, that it was out of his control now. He would have killed all of them in the end. Perhaps even me. But I couldn't help thinking about Samantha. I didn't have the right to criticise him. I was no better. He gave me the knife and said it was up to me. I know you'll think I should have gone straight to the police. But Kenneth cared about something, Lenny. Not many people will fight to protect their vision any more.

I know Kenneth thinks I'm a genius. That's something, isn't it? I don't want to let him down. I'm in London by the time you read this, probably trying to borrow camera equipment.

Gabrielle.

So there it was. A neat little explanation and not a romantic word in sight. Had she really expected one? Lenny took out her cigarettes and lit up. Then she held the lighter to the corner of the letter and watched it burn.

CHAPTER 27

She Could Solve Crime

Veronica Aaron, Granny Sanderman and Kylie Wong were already at the grave when Lenny came up the hill that afternoon. She had made an agreement with Veronica. Today they would come here together but from now on Lenny would visit by herself, if and when she felt like it. She hadn't been much of a daughter to him anyway. After she stopped living at home she had hardly visited him. Why bother now? A bad daughter to her father. Dr Sakuno was right about that. She had faced it. And she *did* feel better.

Kylie Wong was tugging dandelions from the grass. She bared her dirty teeth at Lenny: 'Geez, you look rough!'

'Thanks.'

Her mother's leg was strapped at the knee. 'Yes!' she responded to the inquiry Lenny had not made. 'I fell in the kitchen. Putting away tea towels, if you can believe it! I tripped on one of Kylie's colouring pencils. Doctor said I was very lucky not to break my leg. Honestly, Lenny, that child is a holy terror when it comes to putting her things away.'

Kylie had probably received extra favour for services rendered. Lenny's eyes drifted to her mother's handbag.

'What are you taking for the pain?' She wanted to sound concerned.

'I'm not to talk about medicine with you.' Her mother's lips pursed. 'Dr Sakuno called me and we had a nice long chat and we decided it's for the best.'

Lenny's eyes moved to the vinyl bag swinging off the handles of her grandmother's wheelchair. Probably a little something in there. The old woman must take something for her Alzheimer's. A mild tranquilliser? Anti-depressants?

'Urrghhh . . .' Granny Sanderman's tongue lolled out of the left side of her mouth as far as she could stretch it – for certainly it was a deliberate act. Lenny and Veronica Aaron tensed themselves automatically for confrontation and were unexpectedly saved.

'Mine's bigger!' Kylie Wong's tongue was indeed longer, and she was waggling it in the old woman's confused face.

'Chink,' Granny Sanderman observed wildly.

'I'm gonna push her around the gravestones,' Kylie Wong told them. 'She can pick one out.' The ten-year-old stepped behind the wheelchair and set off with her surrogate grandmother.

Lenny focused on her father's grave. She was already having trouble bringing his face clearly to mind. She noticed the start of a weed poking through near the edge of the gravestone, and very faintly in the surrounding earth she saw the print of a cat's paw.

'I had a dream last night,' Veronica said, eyes darting occasionally after her mother and foster child. 'Your dad told me everything was all right. He said –'

'Everyone has that dream,' Lenny cut in. 'It's called regret.'

She had had a dream too. It had started with her happy imaginings before bed of what her life would have been as a samurai. The warriors' code, the brilliant fighting techniques, the prestigious retainer to a feudal lord. A lovely life.

313

But when she fell asleep she found herself in the crow-black rags of a second-rate Ninja. A strictly for cash assassin lurking in ceilings for hours on end, nibbling tiny portions of special food and excreting correspondingly tiny Ninja shits for days until she could drop soundlessly to the *tatami* below and slit her victims' throats.

Lenny didn't want that. She wanted to rise and see the morning star as though for the first time. Like Siddhartha, she wanted to be the star and be the space around it, be the Buddha. Instead, she was *sashimi no tsuma*: a fragment of sashimi garnish. Inconsequential.

But she could solve crime. It would have to be enough for one lifetime.

And what was the other thing she was supposed to attend to, that point that came up without fail in her dealings with the world? She looked over the cemetery gates and racked her brains. The thought shook itself free from wherever memory sticks, and she remembered: she had to be nicer to people. She turned back to her mother's hopeful face.

'All right,' she sighed. 'Tell us about your dream then.'